The Guardians
Path of Ascension

By
Bruce, R.F.

The Guardians: Path of Ascension

ISBNs:
Paperback: 978-1-7331318-0-3
Hardcover: 978-1-7331318-1-0
eBook: 978-1-7331318-2-7
Audio Book: 978-1-7331318-3-4

Front cover by Bruce, R.F.

Printed by Lightning Source, Ingram Spark, and Amazon, in the United States of America.

First Printed Edition, 2019

Edited by Amanda West, 7/25/2019

Bruce, R.F. revision date, 3/10/2026
www.BruceBooks.com

Special Thanks

I would like to say thanks to all those who contributed to this project through support, interest, or criticism. You have helped to make this possible.

Bonnie Capen
Michael Cartier
Nadia Justice
Daniel Kmic
Anthony Bui
Connor Moore
Tom Tijerina
Tom Woltz
Collin Barnes
Mate Govo
Arriana Spokes

Chapter 1

"Youthful Beginnings"

The blue shimmer of his buddy's eyes tells Simon volumes about his adversary. Even without the fancy eyewear adorned like goggles around his head, he can feel the shift in the air, the way it bends unnaturally around Seldin as he pulls the aether into his core. Between that and the calculations projected onto his lenses, he knows something is coming.

"You're not using the conduit," Simon comments knowingly, eyeing the whirling vortex of energy beside them—invisible to anyone except those in tune, despite its brilliance in the night.

Seldin's brow arcs slightly as a smirk stretches across his lips. "You can tell that?" he questions, and Simon casually taps at the elastic strap around his head. Seldin's smirk then grows into a smile at the very notion he's been found out. Although his secret might be blown, his heart flutters nonetheless with the sheer excitement of trying a new technique.

This mid-suburban park, not far from Simon's home, has been the christening to quite a few bouts in their time, for the two of them have always been competitive and friends from the beginning; they'd often meet here in this clearing for the sake of sport. The natural abundance of energy here has been a staple in their evolution, feeding them and their friends since they discovered their gifts.

With the moon to his back, Seldin gets ready while sinking low into a stance. The light dances reflectively off his pale skin while the wind whips around him, violently tugging at his black canvas robes and short brown hair. The cool air is soothing to the heat of his sweaty body, but this is no time to be calm.

Whoosh! A foot comes flying quickly across Simon's face. With an abrupt turn left, he rolls with the motion, allowing only the wind to graze him as he comes about, eyeing the weak point of an exposed back as his buddy's kick finishes the follow-though—bam!

In less than an instant, two palms clap Seldin's shoulders, forcing him to lurch, stumbling forward, and with intent, he slaps a hand to the ground before bouncing off then landing into a crouching stance. Immediately, he turns about, kicking a front sweep to Simon's forward foot as the two engage forearm to forearm, wrist to wrist. Each blow comes blindingly fast, strobing afterimages in the moonlight with delayed cracks of sound to their movement.

Although Seldin is the younger of the two at age fifteen and only half a year behind his friend, he is certainly not the weaker—a fact that Simon is well aware of as he carefully calculates every scrap of data spilling into his optics. He can hardly fathom how precisely his foe can channel the aether without assistance, augmenting the flow like a finely tuned throttle for actions that require strength and others that rely on speed.

Simon, however, is no pushover. His ability to interface directly with his devices grants him a level of thought unthinkable to most humans and limited solely by the hardware. It's a skill he's honed over the years and one that's kept his best friend on his toes for some time. Even so, the balance of power often shifts between them as competition keeps them sharp.

Back and forth the two of them go, circling around the conduit, neither able to seize the advantage nor willing to sample from the column of luminescent energy spiraling into the sky.

Swoosh—swoosh—crack! Their knuckles collide with a thunderous pop.

"Grrmmph," Simon grunts at a sudden sharp pain in his right hand. A yellow warning flashes in his giggles with a diagram of a fracture across his fourth and fifth metacarpals. He remains stoic, resting back in a stance, while staring his buddy down as he subtly clenches his fist to set the bones with a soft yet audible cli-click.

Pap! Seldin's left jab cracks a lens, rocking Simon's face and casting beads of sweat from his buzzed, spikey hair. He teeters back, flailing his arms out front to regain his balance—slap—bap— he blocks and counters with a right punch of his own to the left side of Seldin's jaw—crraacck!

"Grrnmh!" Simon grunts again, abruptly pulling away as Seldin pushes through his attack with a lunging knee aimed for his sternum. In that moment, Simon's eyes lock to the scan of highlighted targets in his view. Immediately, he slaps aside his friend's knee before strafing outside his guard and kicking out his back leg.

Suddenly, Seldin's world slows down as his mind races to catch up. His body turns horizontally in the air and before he can manage a counterplay, Simon's elbow crashes down into his sternum, delivering him to the ground with a breathtaking thud.

"Damn it!" Seldin exclaims, embedding a fist into the grass as he rights himself into a crouch. Simon chuckles loudly as his friend's energy drops down to a nonthreatening level.

"Whoa, that was some move you almost— no wait, you didn't even come close! What now, you throwin in the towel?" he taunts.

Seldin shakes his head, slyly cupping a hand behind his right knee. "Hardly," he pants, "I've got something new for ya."

"No, you don't," Simon says gloatingly, "because I'm gonna finish this." He steps into the pool of aether with outstretched arms as he welcomes the surge of energy.

Having little time, Seldin concentrates, focusing his breathing. The air around them swirls fiercely, casting gusts of dirt and throwing leaves every which way. Seldin can feel the pressure in his core increasing. A rush comes over him like goosebumps with the hair on his arms standing on end as the aether flows into the palm of his hand. At first there's heat as the energy builds to a smell of ozone and then a faint glimmer of light. Glancing down briefly before retaking sight of his target, Seldin then darts toward his opponent—his hand cocked into position, ready.

"Ha-a-an-ih!" Seldin's chanting voice echoes in the night.

Simon's eyes open wide, hearing a voice and the warning alarm blaring into his ear. Overwhelmed by the alerts, he panics just as his friend's attack closes in and then—

"Spi-i-i-h-a!" Seldin releases as he thrusts his palm against Simon's unguarded chest. The energy crackles and flickers with a loud burst of bluish-white light.

"Whaaat?" Simon shouts in surprise as he's thrown backward through the air, landing some distance away. Seldin immediately bursts into tear-filled laughter as his buddy slams into the ground.

"Holy-shh—did you see that? You flew like ten feet, dude!" he exclaims, rushing to catch up while shaking the sting from his hand.

Simon attempts to kip up then falls back onto his rear, still slightly dazed. "No," he huffs, "I was too busy falling—and it was three feet at best," he rebuts, saving face.

"Did you get any readings?" Seldin asks before plopping down in the soft dew-covered grass, and Simon looks over with a half-smile as he pulls off his goggles to inspect the damage.

"Your core was over 1,300 joules before you hit me," he replies.

"That's fantastic! So, our calculations were correct—that little thing can actually measure aether," Seldin expresses excitedly.

"And see it clear as crystal, but I had to suppress my own ability to be sure it was working at first. Once I was certain, it was a definite enhancement," he replies, testing the integrity of the lens with a press of his thumb before passing the device to his buddy.

Seldin waves off with a gesture of his hand and a shake of his head. "No thanks. I prefer to rely on my own senses, Simy. But 1,300 joules?" he asks with a breath.

"Yeah, that's higher than last week's bench test. Once I get back to the lab, I'll dump the data and run a comparative analysis," Simon says.

"I think it's right; me and Leon have been training a lot. We're hoping to fly by the end of the summer," Seldin states.

"That's a cool thought," Simon says as he rolls back in the cool grass, staring up at the large moon in the night's sky. "If I could fly, I know where I'd go." He points.

"To the moon?" Seldin asks with a half-smile.

"Mm-hm, if I knew I'd survive, I'd visit all the planets—but…" Simon sits up with a sigh. "I don't think it's possible," he says.

"Seriously, that's impossible—with all we've seen—all we can do? The math checks out, Simon," Seldin argues.

"You're the physics guy." Simon shrugs. "But you can't pick yourself up with a rope, Sei. I don't see how it would work," he rebuts.

Seldin just looks off with a sigh as he thinks about it. His eyes then trail back to his friend and his casual regalia: a tank top, shorts, and sandals. But it's the grey blotches and dark streaks on his right hand that draws his attention.

"What's with the veins?" Seldin asks.

Simon turns his hand about. "Oh, that's right, I didn't tell you." He grins. "Nanites," he replies.

Seldin cocks his head in surprise. "You never said they were ready—when the hell did you test them?" he exclaims.

"In the lab before coming out. Guess you weren't the only one with a secret." Simon smirks. "Version one was a success—how do you think I was keeping up with you? Last I checked, I topped out at eight hundred joules. The spider veins are just them pooling to heal my injuries. I broke my hand twice against you." He casually clenches his fist. "As for the color—well, a negative side effect is that I seem to be losing pigment, but I'll fix it in version two. So, *'hanid spire,'* huh? Whatever happened to no spells?" Simon asks.

"It's not a spell, Simy, it's a power thought. I got the idea from Dean. You pick a word or a short phrase to help bring your mind, body, and energy into focus. You know how I feel about sorcery. Besides, spells rhyme," he retorts.

"And you decided to chant in the Language of the Gods—what's that, uh… light gun?" Simon chuckles.

"Han ih spiha, is cannon of light; it… just came to me," he says.

"Whatever it was, you were fast, and your hair was all static-mo-fied," Simon comments.

"Well, that's something else I learned while training. I can raise and lower my power quickly, but it gives me goosebumps; it's such a rush," Seldin says.

Simon looks to him somewhat dismissively, while picking at blades of grass. "Oh, I've done that before. I wouldn't rely on it though. I liken it to overpowering a wire—eventually it burns out," he tells him, but Seldin disagrees as he thinks about it.

"Are you coming by tonight? I'd like to run some more scans," Simon asks.

Seldin looks his way. "No, I can't. You forget, I have school in the morning," he says.

"Oh, that's right! Tomorrow's your last day. Come Saturday, you'll be a free man," Simon says.

"Yeah, we can't all get out early. Leon has another year," he laughs. "We're all meeting up at the beach tomorrow night to celebrate."

Simon nods. "Jasra told me: she said Dean, Arius, and a few others should be there. Personally, I can't wait to test this out on the sorcerers," he says, gesturing with his goggles.

"It would be nice to finally get some good data on them; they always read deceptively low," Seldin comments.

"When do you ship out for college?" Simon asks, kinetically plucking a small rock from the ground for amusement.

"Eh, I'm not going," Seldin replies.

Simon snaps his gaze to him. "What? But I thought you were doing physics?"

"College is my dad's idea, Simon, not mine," he says with a harsh tone, then sighs. "I want to study aether. Besides, you didn't go."

"True, but I built Sim-Antics," he says.

"Exactly! You're doing what you want to do," Seldin rebuts.

Simon concedes with a nod. "What'd you tell your dad?"

"I..." Seldin hesitates, "...told him my plane leaves Sunday morning for Shemberg University, Ireland—"

"Sei—"

"With your computer skills, it'll be a quick fix, and I can always do college later," he says.

"Eh... why not just tell him?" Simon asks.

"I don't think he'd understand—you know how he is… there's no money in it." Seldin sighs.

"At least he gives enough of a shit to care," Simon comments with a sour face, while tossing the rock in his hand sharply to the ground.

"Yeah…" Seldin looks down. "I just think it'll be easier if he thinks I'm there," he says.

Simon looks to him. "Easier on him or you?" he asks.

Seldin thinks on that for a second, then shakes his head. "Can you do it?"

"Yeah, I can do it." Simon sighs. "But then what's the plan, hide out at the lab for the next few years?" he asks.

"And stay with you and Jassie?" Seldin lets out a chuckle.

Simon shrugs. "You practically live there now," he says.

"No." Seldin shakes his head. "It's north for me, Simy. I don't know how to explain it; it's like… something's calling me," he says, and Simon's eyes trail down.

"To be a… guardian," he mumbles, and Seldin looks to him immediately.

"Yes—you feel it, too?" he asks.

Simon shakes his head. "N-no, I don't know, but it's been in my head for a while."

"In your head? Simy, this is huge—you don't see the connection? Ooh, I wonder if the others are feeling this?" Seldin stands, turning away with his eyes to the sky.

"Maybe—well ok, say you're right: there hasn't been a guardian in centuries. I mean, a guardian of what?" Simon asks.

"Of life." Seldin looks inward; his eyes meander as he turns back toward him.

"That's a little much," Simon rebuts.

"No, Simon, that's what I feel," Seldin says, tapping at his chest. He then pauses for a second, gathering his thoughts. "Tomorrow, we'll ask the others."

Chapter 2

"Oil and Water"

There's a soft knowing smile on Jasra's face when Simon steps into their apartment.

"Sei win?" she asks, glancing to him from her seat on the living room couch, while fiddling with one of a couple watches at the coffee table.

Simon pauses at the door with a furrowed gaze to her before moving past her toward his workroom down the hall.

Jasra's eyes follow him for a second then fall back to the watch in her hand.

"Your father called; left a message."

Simon sighs. "What, he's got his hand out again?"

"He didn't say. Maybe he genuinely wants to talk; you haven't spoken since—"

"Pleaassee," there's obvious disdain in Simon's voice, "the man wouldn't be caught at my funeral without a check and free beer," he says, stepping into his workroom.

At his worktable, Simon peels back a flesh-colored flap on the top of his left wrist and attaches an intravenous line to a small circular port.

With the press of a button on the computer, a semi-clear metallic solution starts to flow down the IV as nanite data populates onto one of three screens in front of him. It shows a diagram of the microscopic robots and a detailed illustration of the work done on his body during the fight.

"Good," Simon says to himself, while smiling at the results. He takes a seat and inspects his broken goggles more thoroughly, holding them up to the light, before letting out a disgruntled sigh.

"Asshole." He shakes his head, and then connects them to the computer. An analysis of their comparable energies pops up, showing human-shaped diagrams, each surrounded by a set of concentric circles. The inner-most circle marks their cores with the outer representing their auras.

According to the data, Simon's core reached 970 joules of aether per second—up 155 from last week but still within the green, while Seldin's jumped from 465 to 1,315 and well into the red—highlighted by a warning flag.

Simon sighs at the readings. "Damn… we need another test," he says before turning to the third screen where he brings up the Shemberg University housing information page.

Jasra steps into the doorway, standing behind him. "Sei's not going, huh?" she asks, startling Simon, who looks over his shoulder at her.

"Uh, no," he answers, then turns back to his computer and starts hacking into the website.

That knowing smile returns to Jasra's face as she plays with the ponytail of her reddish-brown hair. "Did he say anything?" She pauses. "Anything important?" she asks.

Simon turns back and stares as if to answer with his eyes.

Jasra looks down with a soft nod.

…

The lights are still on at the Gardane residence when Seldin steps into the driveway. He takes note of the open garage door and the unfamiliar rusty bucket his dad is working on as he tries to slip by into the house.

"Hey!" Morgan Gardane yells. "Was hollerin for ya. Where've you been?"

Seldin stops at the front door. "Hangin with Simon," he answers.

"Oh…" Morgan grows quiet. "Tell him I said hey. There's pizza on the counter." He gestures with a tilt of his head, while toweling grease from his hands.

Seldin nods before stepping inside to a house that is about as well-kept as one could expect from a single father and his son. He stands in the middle of the living room, eyeing the path to his bedroom door, while debating whether he really wants pizza or not.

A sense of wanting fills him as he wanders around the emptiness of the place, and he pauses in front of a single-family portrait of himself from the first grade, his dad, and his older half-sister, who has long since moved out. Sighing, Seldin casts a silent gaze toward the sounds coming from the garage before heading to his room.

His bedroom is less orderly than the rest of the house with martial arts magazines and training equipment strewn about. Theres a mini-fridge and a desktop computer in the corner as well as some odd trinkets—sewing needles suspended on strings inside jars—and half-melted candles here and there.

Seldin mixes a protein shake, grabs an apple, and then flips through a magazine, while mimicking the various fighting techniques in the illustrations. A sudden ding on his computer gets his attention.

It's a message from Simon: "Your welcome," it reads with poor grammar and is attached to a screenshot of Shemberg University's housing record for Seldin Gardane.

He smiles, holding the apple in his mouth as he types back. "You're the best."

Seldin then turns with a hand toward one of the jars. He takes a breath, feeling an inner pressure moving throughout his body from his center below his navel to the palm of his hand. The needle in the jar points his way.

. . .

It's late. The murmuring sounds of chanting voices echo throughout the small cathedral hall of Watcher's Keep, which is filled with patrons in prayer.

"Khy-hy-rah! Khy-hy-rah!" they chant again and again as the high priestess, Lamryl motions for Theresa to approach the altar encircled by robed monks kneeling with hands pressed together and held up as they pray.

Lamryl gestures, moving her hands to signal silence.

"Tonight, we honor our fellow sorceress, Theresa, whose loyalty and long-standing support of this sanctuary has earned her the right to deepen her studies. The vote of this council has been unanimous. From this night forth, Theresa with serve as my second and carry the title of priestess."

The hall cheers.

Lamryl turns, picks up a chalice and passes it amongst the kneeling members, who each prick a finger to offer their blood. Once it comes back around, Lamryl pricks hers, then offers the chalice to Theresa.

"Drink of your brothers and sisters and take your place at my side," she says.

Theresa accepts the chalice with a nod, and then holds it up to toast the sanctuary and the council before drinking to the last drop.

...

Seldin watches through his mind's eye, moving his energy from a swirling mass below his navel throughout his meridians—the body's natural pathways. It's a warm, almost tingling sensation with notable pressure that flows from his center down through his perineum, up his spine, over his head, and down his chest, completing a cycle again and again.

"Sseellldiinn…" a gravelly voice calls to him and he opens his eyes with a sharp gasp at the mental image of a large insect-like eye staring into him, overlaid by a green and purple world.

With his heart shaking, he takes in a calming breath. "Y-you again… who are you?"

"We are dying… Life Guardian."

Beeep! Beeep! Beeep! His alarm sounds with the crack of morning, and he turns a sudden startled gaze to it from across the room. He rubs his eyes and shakes his head before feeling for the clock in his mind. With a simple gesture, he waves a hand to shut it off.

"Who are you?" he calls out to the voice again, scanning the room with his eyes, but the vision he saw mere seconds ago has faded, and there is no answer.

After a shower and a quick bite, Seldin steps out of the house and heads down the driveway.

"You runnin on your last day?" Morgan shouts from the garage. "Why not take the car for a change?" he asks.

Seldin continues walking, offering only a shrugging nod.

Morgan waves him over. "Come here a minute," he says, and Seldin groans with a hesitant turn toward his father.

"Come here a minute, jeez..." Morgan leads him into the garage and motions toward his car before lifting the hood to reveal a clean engine. He then leans into the driver's side window and turns the ignition. The car starts with a rumbling roar. Morgan then steps up beside his son and stares with a gaping smile at the car.

"You won't find any of these in Ireland," he says.

Seldin makes a face. "How would you know?" he asks with a somewhat cocky smirk.

Morgan sighs. "Weelll, if they do, it won't be like this one." He turns to face him. "You'll be the first Gardane to ever set foot into a college."

"I know..." Seldin averts his eyes. "I'm gonna be late," he says, and turns away, cringing at the very mention of the C-word, but that voice... whatever that was... fills him with nervous excitement. "Who are you?" he asks under his breath as he reaches the edge of the driveway.

"Don't forget! Graduation ceremony tomorrow morning!" his father shouts as Seldin breaks into a jog.

"Not too fast," he says to himself, while easing his energy just enough to maintain a reasonable pace.

...

A sudden bout of nausea kickstarts Theresa's morning with a rush to the bathroom as she dives face-first into the toilet.

"Huuurrrlll!" She heaves—her stomach wrenching and twisting in discomfort. After a few minutes, she sits back from the toilet and takes in a few well-needed gulps of air before turning to check the clock by her bed; she's late.

It's a quarter to seven by the time she makes it to the main hall where Lamryl is waiting.

"I'm so sorry, High Priestess. Please forgive my tardiness. I… woke up a little queasy," she says.

"Nothing too serious, I hope?" Lamryl smiles, and then gestures for Theresa to accompany her down the adjacent corridor before continuing.

"Have you given any thought to the members of your circle?"

Theresa shakes her head.

"As a head sorceress, you have the right to do so—and it is expected as a member of the council."

Theresa nods. "Yes, High Priestess."

"What about Seldin, the boy who—"

"No." Theresa shakes her head. "He'd never… he's an aether practitioner; the two are like oil and water," she says.

Lamryl smiles. "What a strange thing to say considering what you had to learn to get this far." She motions with an upturned hand, and then stops at a large set of double doors, which open before them.

"The sacred library?" Theresa asks with uncertainty as Lamryl steps inside, and then turns to see the young sorceress staring with an uneasy gaze.

"Come along, child," Lamryl gestures with a hand. A subtle smile stretches across Theresa's lips as she tries to maintain her composure.

"Only the most powerful sorcerers have such a privilege," she says.

"One of the many perks," Lamryl replies.

Theresa lowers her eyes out of respect before entering. Excitement fills her; she looks around at the voluptuous assortment of books.

"Your studies shall begin immediately," Lamryl says as she steps behind a desk located centrally in the rear of the library. There, she slides an old oil painting aside to uncover a small safe. The face of which bears a debossed hexagram-like circle with runes along the design and a thumb-shaped depression in the middle where a tiny pin protrudes. She then glances over her shoulder to Theresa, who promptly turns her back.

Lamryl presses her right thumb to the safe. "Vii sa lifo," she whispers a chant as it takes her blood offering. The symbol glows red and the door opens. She then withdraws a brown leather-bound book inscribed with ancient symbols.

"Come forth, my child," she says.

Theresa does as requested, and Lamryl offers her the book. She reaches out with a hesitant hand. The symbols on the thick leather cover glow, meld, and reshape as she takes it. The glow fades. Lamryl smiles.

"The Book of Roe…" Theresa says, reading the symbols with astonishment in her voice. They appear so foreign to her, and yet…

"Only one is ever given to a world. It has been passed down from high priestess to high priestess for centuries. And now, I'm passing it on to you," Lamryl says.

"What is this?" Theresa asks.

"A gift from the Guardian of Knowledge."

. . .

7:05 a.m. marks the beginning of the last day of school for Seldin. With exams well behind him, he heads to the senior recreation center. Rapid, excited footsteps approach from behind.

"Hey Sei!" Leon shouts as he catches up.

"Sup Lee."

"Check this out! I've been practicing with the needle in the jar like you said." Leon moves to an empty bench on the path and places a nickel on the seat beside him.

Seldin stands, providing cover from prying eyes as he watches his younger brawny friend motioning a finger above the coin. It takes him a minute to move the energy from his core, down through his fingers, and to the metal. The nickel slowly starts to angle up toward him as if caught in a weak magnetic field. An uncomfortable tingle of fatigue builds in his arm, and Leon then drops the connection. The coin falls flat. He sits back satisfied with himself despite his panting huffs.

"See," he says.

Seldin grins with pride. "That's very good. Now that you're moving stuff, you should try lifting heavier things. Weights help."

The bell rings, signaling the start of the first class of the day.

"I gotta go. I'll see ya later," Seldin says.

…

"Roe was the Guardian of Knowledge. Everything it knew about matters of energy and the universe are inscribed in that book," Lamryl explains.

Theresa makes a puzzled face. "It?"

Lamryl nods. "According to the text, Roe ascended from a unary race. They are… genderless."

"Ah…" Theresa nods. "Is Roe stronger than Khyrah?" she asks.

"No. The God of Chaos proved far too powerful for our beloved guardian, but the secrets Roe left, grant us access to a depth of magic far beyond what Khyrah would ever offer. Study it; make it yours."

Theresa nods.

"Do keep me appraised of your initiates," Lamryl says.

"Yes, I'll put the word out and start recruiting right away," Theresa says.

"Be selective of course—oh! An important detail I neglected to mention." Lamryl taps a finger to the book in Theresa's hands. "Keep this out of the reach of others. If someone were to touch it without the training you've had, they would die."

…

Seldin looks around as he enters what could be described as the campus' game room. There are sounds of rustling, chattering, and clacking with ping pong, billiards, and the like filling the space.

He scans the room, looking for familiar faces and any games of interest when he spots Neil, the tall one with dark fluffy hair, glasses, and a birthmark on his neck, which resembles a permanent hickey, playing air hockey with his girlfriend, Elma. Seldin decides to walk over.

"Sup, wielder?" Neil greets with a subtle tone in his voice as he smacks the puck.

"Not much, caster," Seldin replies, watching the game as Elma returns the puck with a quick deflection back toward Neil, who gets ready to line up a shot.

Seldin offers a subtle flick of his index finger, curving the motion of the puck as it maneuvers around Neil's paddle and into his goal.

Neil looks up with an annoyed though perplexed expression on his face. He then sighs and sets his eyes on Seldin.

"You... asshole."

Elma laughs.

"Sorry, I thought you'd block it," Seldin says with a chuckle.

Neil then steps around the air hockey table and approaches Seldin with an angered demeanor. He stands there towering over him and posturing for a second or two before swinging a right hand toward Seldin, who catches the deceptive high five.

"Nice to see ya. Want a game?" Neil asks, cracking a smile.

"Sure."

"No aether," Neil says.

"No spells," Seldin replies.

They take their positions, and Neil leads off with a fast serve. Elma leans comfortably beside him, watching and listening to the sounds of pucks and paddles clacking.

"Did you hear? Theresa just got promoted to priestess," Neil says.

Seldin shakes his head. "We... haven't been keeping up."

"Then I guess you'd have to have been there. It was a nice ceremony. She'll be at the beach tonight if you... want to apologize," Elma says.

"We merely have a difference in opinion in the ways of energy," Seldin says.

Elma shrugs. "That's not what she thinks."

"I bet she'll be recruiting soon: all the higher levels get to form a coven. What do you think about abandoning the complexities of aether for something… simpler?" Neil offers when he nails the puck hard, slamming it past Seldin's guard. The buzzer sounds and the three of them pause with a look to the score: Neil 7, Seldin 4.

"Looks like you beat me," Seldin says with a half-smile before walking off.

Chapter 3

"Guardians"

The blackened sky over Clearwater Beach is alive with vibrant flickers of whirling flames from fire eaters, spinners, and twirlers alike, while the air is a hum with a gentle tune and the beat of the drums and chanters speaking in tongues. There are show-boaters walking on coals to demonstrate their faith, and benders pressing iron rods between one another in a display of strength. Most of it is charismatic performance art to tame the masses and distract them from the real goings-on.

Arriving fashionably late, Seldin is pleased to see his friends are already here. Dean, the stocky bearded one with obvious signs of the Irishman in him, is off to the side speaking with some hooded figure in a black cloak. Everyone goes goth these days, Seldin thinks to himself, while looking around the area to see who else is here.

There's Theresa in the middle of the drum circle, drumming with Jasra, while Simon is off talking shop with Arius: the average figure with long white hair, also darkly dressed, though in the finest of English attire.

Seldin waves to them as he heads over to see Dean, who he greets with a firm handshake.

"Evening, Dean," he says.

"Hi Sei, great party!" he replies with a heavy Irish accent.

"Who was that?" Seldin looks past trying to get a better glimpse of the fellow.

"Oh, *him?*" Dean emphasizes with a playful grunt, "Just an hombre," he says.

To that, Seldin lets out a laugh, "Ha, still practicing your Spanish?" he asks.

"You know it! Haha—actually, he's an old friend. We go way back. So, what's new with you?" Dean asks.

Seldin makes a circular gesture with his hand. "As soon as I round everyone up, I'll fill you in," he says, stepping away.

. . .

Theresa's eyes lock to Seldin as he moves about, while the chattering voices of Elma and Jasra fade into the background.

"Earth to Theresa," Jasra says, catching her as she drifts away. She can feel something's off about her aura tonight—something she didn't feel the last time they hung out. Curious, Jasra deepens her senses to scan for momentary tangents in the present and answers to questions she has yet to ask. She smiles softly before rubbing away the mental strain that only a few seconds brings.

"You, ok?" Jasra asks again.

"Mm-Hmm." Theresa's attention returns.

"So, High Priestess, what's it like with all that power?" Elma asks.

"Yeah, how's your first day on the throne?" Jasra prompts.

Theresa smiles. "It's just *'Priestess'*, but there are some nice perks that come with the job."

"Like having your own initiates?" Jasra asks, and Theresa nods.

"More than that. Why, you want in?"

Elma perks up. "Me and Neil want in—you know, officially." She smiles.

"Well, there's a ritual, officially," Theresa says to her.

Jasra shakes her head. "I couldn't live at a monastery." She looks off toward Simon, who is busy tinkering with his eyewear.

"It's a cathedral, but yeah… it does make romance harder," she says.

"You sure about that?" Jasra teases, knowingly, and Theresa blushes, looking down.

"Honestly, I wouldn't know," Jasra adds.

"Are you having problems?" Elma asks.

Jasra sighs. "I… just wish he'd show some affection sometimes. You know, we've been together three years, and he's never once said that he loves me?"

. . .

Not far from the drum circle, Seldin is moving through the crowd when he spots a slouching figure hunched over his own knees, sitting on a log in front of the bonfire.

"Hey, Lee, what are you looking so glum about?" Seldin asks him.

Leon glances up at him. "Eh… it's my father—err—stepfather, Ryan. He insisted on coming out here tonight to meet all of my *funny friends'*—particularly you. He thinks you're a bad influence and wants to have words with you." Leon rolls his eyes before pointing to the buffoon dressed like a pirate, out watching the performers.

"Watch out for him, Sei: he practices magic. I can't sense his power, but you always said spell casters were hard to read," he warns.

Seldin nods, looking over at him, and not getting much of a sense for him either. "I'll avoid him for now; I wouldn't want to make things more complicated for you at home. Although I am curious as to why he's so interested in me now. I mean, I've known you for over a year," he says.

"Yeah, he's an off-again, on-again, role model that my mother picked out. He's not around often, but when he is, it's a total hell," he says.

"Sorry," Seldin says.

"On the bright side, I think I'm getting better," Leon says, while telekinetically writing his name in the sand.

Seldin smiles with a hint of pride for his younger friend. "Very good," he says with a swipe of his right hand, telekinetically erasing his work.

In turn, Leon swipes back, initiating a telekinetic sand toss between them. The two play and laugh for moment when Seldin notices the disapproving eyes of Theresa aimed their way. He stares back and she looks off. He then catches the motion of Simon's hand just past her, waving for him to come over.

"Hey, I'll be right back," he tells Leon before walking off to chat with his best friend.

The sound of the drums picks up as the level of theatricality increases on the beach. Fire dancers twirl their flaming poles, breathers spit their flames, and some of those, who are skilled in sorcery, as well as the martial arts, begin to display their techniques in a friendly show of combat.

Seldin looks around, stopping for a minute. He can't help but observe—the warrior within calling him to study the movements of a potential enemy. In this case, Leon's stepfather, Ryan, who lands a solid side kick to Neil's midsection.

"Ooof!" Neil grunts and stumbles back as he recovers.

Ryan dives and rolls on his shoulder before posturing in tiger stance. He brings his hands together in a circling motion like rolling dough.

"Ring of fire, arc of light," Ryan chants; sparks pop and emanate from between his hands.

Seldin opens his mind to gauge Ryan's strength, but there's no flow to the aether in his aura; his meridians are empty, and his core is misaligned. The energy he's gathering is clearly not his own.

The same goes for Neil, who begins chanting as well, while tracing his hands out front in a diamond pattern. "North, south, east, west—" a series of Celtic runes appear in gold magical light along the invisible shape.

"May my enemy fall tonight!" Ryan thrusts his hands forward, releasing a fireball aimed at Neil, whose chant finishes in the nick of time.

"Shield me from my foes best!" The diamond shape solidifies just as the fireball collides in a shimmering explosion.

Seldin glances back at Leon, who is busy watching, before he continues toward Simon.

"How's the experiment going?" Seldin asks as he approaches.

Simon glances his way, offering a subtle smirk of amusement as he, too, watches the free source of entertainment.

"Pretty good. You were right: spell casters average around a hundred joules," he says.

Seldin shrugs with a bit of a face. "That's not so surprising, considering they don't use their own power. The body consumes about that much energy a day just living," he comments.

Simon then leans his way. "Yeah… you know how everyone's aura feels different?"

Seldin nods. "Mm-hm."

"Well, based on these scans, everybody's energy vibrates at a different frequency," he claims.

"That certainly explains a lot," Seldin notes.

"Yeah, but check this out." Simon removes his goggles, holding them out so both of them can see as he points to Leon. "I noticed this earlier: Leon's energy vibrates at the exact same frequency as the Earth's magnetic field."

Seldin looks while comparing his senses to Simon's readings. "You're right," he says, the curiosity occupies his mind before Simon interrupts.

"Your field," Simon says, turning to face Seldin, "changes based on whomever you're talking to. Like… it attunes to them."

"For real?" Seldin questions.

Simon nods. "I was watching when you said *'hi'* to Dean; your signal changed to match his. The same thing happened when you went over to Leon. It must be subconscious if you didn't notice."

Seldin shakes his head. "No, I didn't."

"Guardian of Life," Simon confirms, and Seldin pauses in thought.

"What about yours?" he asks.

"Mine has an affinity for the devices I interact with. It makes sense when you think about it. I haven't been able to figure out everybody, though. Dean's energy seems to match the environment but the signal fades in and out. Jasra's, on the other hand, is stable, yet I can't pin down the frequency. And Arius—" Simon points.

"Wait, go back to her," Seldin instructs as he looks through the lenses, while feeling her energy push back against his own. "There's almost like a pulse to it… one-Mississippi… two-Miss—" his eyes widen as he looks to Simon. "Let me see your watch," he says before looking between it and Jasra. "One second intervals… almost as if—"

"Synchronized with time," Simon comments aloud. "Are you thinking what I'm thinking?" He looks to Seldin, who makes a face of intrigue.

"With her gift of foresight?" He smiles with a nodding gesture toward the drum circle. "Have you said anything?" Seldin asks as they walk.

"To Jassie? No, I didn't want to steal your thunder, but you know her, she's been dropping hints all day." Simon quietly replies before the two of them take their seats amidst the group of their closest friends.

"Ok…" Seldin hesitates in the moment, thinking of what he's going to say. It's something he hasn't told anyone, other than his best friend. "Thank you all for coming, I've asked you here today—"

"In this state of holy matrimony…" Simon teases in a sarcastic tone. The others snicker, as does Seldin before glaring back at Simon, while waiting for the chatter to cease.

"We can all tap into the aether, wield it in our own ways. Five years ago, we would have said it was impossible, yet here we are, capable of doing what only a select few have ever accomplished and what so many others refuse to believe—even the spell casters." His eyes shift to Theresa, who looks away with a disapproving sigh. "Lately, I've had this drive to push myself… like I've never done before. I can't help the feeling that this… is just the tip of the iceberg." He looks down with a heavy breath. "For all of us."

"Go on, Sei." Dean ushers with a supportive nod just as Jasra's hand reaches his back. Her long auburn hair and emerald eyes catch Seldin as his gaze pans the group.

"I believe we're meant for more, and I'm going off to train. You should too," he says.

"Train for what?" Leon asks.

"To be guardians," Seldin says, firmly, with his eyes reaching each of them.

"I had the same thought," Simon tells them.

"Me, too," Jasra adds.

Right then Elma chimes in. "But guardians are a myth…" she quietly looks around as they all stare at her, "…aren't they?"

"What kind of guardians?" Leon asks.

Seldin looks to him. "I have a feeling you may already know," he answers, then points to himself. "Life." His eyes then move to Simon.

"Technology," Simon says with a glance to Jasra, who gazes down for a second to search inward.

"Time."

"Lee?" Seldin looks to him, but Leon hesitates just as Ryan and Neil make their way over, while carrying on amongst themselves.

"You're pretty good," Ryan comments on the young man's ability. "You should join my coven," he offers as they catch wind of the other group's conversation.

"Sei, how come you didn't wait for me?" Neil asks with disappointment in his voice.

"You don't practice aether; I didn't think you'd mind," he answers.

"So, you're Sei?" Ryan looks down at him sitting there on the log.

"I am," he replies.

"You're the one filling my boy's head with all this aether nonsense, huh?" he scowls with a mocking tone.

"It's only nonsense to the closed minded," Seldin replies.

Ryan laughs with a hint of arrogance. "At least sorcery works when you use it," he taunts.

Seldin just shakes his head. "Well, I'm sorry that it's more complicated than reciting a few rhymes. *'I am chanting my words harder than you, Potter,'*" he mocks with a squinty face, while twirling a finger like a wand in his direction, and some of the other sorcerers take offense—including Neil, Elma, and Theresa.

"Why don't you put your money where your mouth is, boy?" Ryan challenges.

Seldin breaks eye contact, gazing amongst his group. He doesn't want to stir up trouble for Leon, yet he really wants to accept. The others return his stare, specifically Arius and Dean, who have a look of approval in their eyes. Leon, on the other hand, doesn't seem too thrilled.

"Lee, it's up to you," Seldin says.

Ryan shrugs, making a gesture out of frustration. "Oh, come on, you're just afraid to lose!" he shouts.

"No. I'm afraid to win," he retorts.

"Go for it," Leon permits at the sound of his stepdad's annoying laugh.

Seldin opens his hand, while focusing aether through himself, and as his fingers fan out from his palm, they feel hot. The pressure builds within them until a bluish-white arc of light dances between the tips, crackling and popping the air with an electrifying hum.

Ryan backs away. "What the?" he gawks in disbelief with a look to Neil.

"I don't need spells to use energy; none of us do," Seldin says, drawing the power back in before dismissively averting his gaze, facing his friends once again.

Ryan shakes his head, turning away. "You're lucky I didn't kick your ass," he says as he walks off with Neil following behind; moments later, Elma runs to catch up with them.

"I wish you would have fought him; he acts like my dad," Leon scowls.

"The best fights are the ones we don't have to be in," Seldin comments, while discreetly rubbing the still-present singe from his fingers.

Dean and Arius glance between one another at that before Theresa turns to Seldin.

"Why do you hate sorcerers so much?" she asks.

Seldin sighs. "I… I don't. I just can't understand worshiping a god that I've never seen for favors that might cost my soul," he answers.

Theresa shakes her head at that notion. "But aether is so much harder," she replies.

"Aether requires a disciplined mind and a honed body to handle its forces. The tradeoff is the energy is mine. Plus, it exists in everything—even the spells you cast. Personally, I like skipping the middleman. Will you be ready when that god comes for a three-fold payment?" he asks, and Theresa scoffs at him before walking away as well.

"What's with her?" Seldin asks.

Jasra flicks her eyes his way. "You're being a jerk," she comments.

"So, we're all going to be guardians, then?" Leon asks.

"If you want to be, but you'll have to work at it," Seldin says.

"Well, I'm in," Jasra says.

"Me, too," says Simon.

"And me," Dean smiles.

Right then, Arius stands. "I'll practice." His muddled accent sounds thick and hoarse. "But I won't be a guardian," the white-haired man says as he walks off toward the shoreline.

"Should we…?" Leon asks.

"I got it," Dean follows.

Simon then looks to Leon. "So, how goes practice?" he asks.

"Ask my teacher." Leon nods to Seldin.

"Oh right—well then, this should be easy." Simon smirks.

"Wanna go?" Leon smiles at the chance to spar with Simon. The two of them then move out a distance before taking their stances.

Seldin then leans close to Jasra. "There's something odd about Theresa's aura, almost like there's two signals. Have you noticed?" he asks.

Jasra just rolls her eyes at him. "She's pregnant, genius."

"Wait, what? When did this happen? Who's the father?" he asks.

She shrugs. "Don't know, never met him. But don't worry, I still love you." Jasra smiles.

Seldin shakes his head at her comment. "You already have a boyfriend," he teases.

Jasra sighs before looking out at Simon as he spars with Leon. "Yes... I do."

. . .

Arius stares out over the darkened sea, not really watching as the waves crest then crash onto the shore at his feet with the moon glistening and the water dissipating into scintillating speckles.

To him, it's the asteroid belt all over again with the sun far off in the distance and nothing but a vast ocean of stars in sight as he drifts—too weak to move and powerless to help.

The cheers on the beach behind him bring chilling echoes of the screams he's tried so hard to shut out.

Dean steps up beside him as Arius wipes his eyes. "What was that back there?" he asks.

"I will not be a guardian again!" he scorns.

"Listen to me, this mission is important—"

"It's a mistake, Dean; this path can only lead to their deaths," Arius says.

Dean nods softly. "Perhaps, but in four centuries, we haven't seen true wielders—this is what we've been searching for!" He gestures to them.

Arius turns to him. "On a planet that worships Khyrah! She'll destroy them all if discovered! Encouraging their development will only serve to bring her here. Can't you see that?"

"And to what alternative? They're no use to us as mortals—their ascension is all that matters! We must proceed with Death's plan!" Dean shouts.

"Tillman doesn't care about them!" Arius scoffs at the idea, gazing out at Seldin and his friends. "These last few years we've lived among them… guided them." He pauses with a sigh. "I feel I know them quite well."

Arius then turns to Dean again. "The last time we faced Khyrah, we had an army. What the hell is a handful of children supposed to do against a demigod?"

Dean lowers his eyes before looking out at them. "At least with them awakened, we have a chance to rebuild and restore the balance of nature. But until they are ready to meet the Guardian of Death, we have orders. Follow them," he says.

…

"Not bad!" Simon grunts, dodging out of Leon's front sweep before springing back into a half flip-kick that nearly cuts across his nose. Leon can feel the wind and sand splashing his face.

"Oof!" he turns left, brushing away the grit. Before Leon can recover, Simon darts forward then slides like a baseball player coming into home to scissor his opponent's legs. With a quick twist, Leon is on his back, and Simon kips to his feet, taking a low cat-stance. There's hardly a sound when a pair of arms brace him from behind.

"Look at these pussies!" Ryan says to Neil, while squeezing Simon. "They think they can fight. This is called *'bear hugs the tree,'*" Ryan says to Simon.

Leon attempts to scuttle to his feet when the instep of Neil's right foot greets the left side of his face.

"That's called the *'flutterby,'*" Neil says, while turning in his stance to face the struggling Simon caught in Ryan's grasp. "And this is called *'rising tiger takes a breath.'*" Neil's knee rams his sternum. Simon collapses with a spit-spraying gasp.

"Where's that aether, wielder?" Ryan taunts into his ear before thrusting him to the ground with a push-kick to the back.

With them both in view, Ryan sets up with a hand forward. "A pulse within, quick and easy, on your knees, you feel queasy!" he chants and suddenly Simon and Leon hunch forward, puking all over themselves. The beach sand sticks to them in their own mess; it's gross and humiliating. The two boys are hot from fury and covered in nasty.

Neil laughs, while stepping up to kick more sand at them. As the spell runs its course, Simon shakes himself of the sick and wipes his mouth. The shimmer of Ryan's wristwatch grabs his intrigue. Rolling to all fours, his eyes stay locked with Ryan's before he leaps at an angle, driving his shoulder into Neil's gut, for he is closer and off to his right. The two of them struggle for a moment. Surprised by the sudden change in direction, Ryan arches forward to rush in.

Right then, Leon casts his hands toward him in a sweeping motion, using the aether to shower his occasional father figure with a blinding plume of sand and vomit.

Simon then takes Neil by the wrist, twists around and behind him, and bars his arm to his back, while forcing him to his knees. In that same moment, he opens his mind to feel for that delicate charge of direct current circuitry and those ticking gears at a distance. It's like music to him, and only him. With his focus ready and his awareness inside that watch, he culls the aether there in a surge that overloads it.

"Bah!" Ryan's body jolts at the paralyzing shock and he grabs his wrist. Likewise, the strain on Neil's shoulder causes him to howl loudly as Simon increases the pressure on the joint, one newton at a time.

In the few seconds that transpired, Simon has gained control. The sounds of commotion and the yowling screams draw Seldin and the others over.

"Simon, that's enough!" he exclaims.

"They started it," he says, "that guy and this traitor ambushed us, like a couple of cowards!" Simon adds a quarter turn more to Neil's shoulder.

Leon then gives his two cents. "It's true!" he shouts, and Neil's cries grow louder with a pop in his arm.

Seldin runs to Simon, "Let him... go... you're going to... break it!" He grapples with Simon's grip to get him to ease off.

Simon drops the hold, and then kicks Neil in the ribs before allowing the electricity to drain from Ryan's watch.

"Fine!" Simon huffs. "Take their side if you want to." He steps away.

"I just don't want people getting hurt," Seldin replies.

Simon gestures to himself and Leon still covered in bile. "And this is okay, getting jumped by spell casters?" Simon argues.

Sighing, Seldin glances to Leon, then to Neil, and then Ryan. Nodding, he concedes to the situation.

"You're right. If it's a fight he wants…" He readies himself, but Ryan shakes his head, while peeling the watch from his wrist to rub at the burned skin. He then gets up, pushing past Seldin and the others as he walks off without a word.

Dean and Arius once again look between one another in the moment.

"He handled that well," Arius whispers, and Dean nods in agreement.

Chapter 4

"Cooling off Period"

"Jesus, Sei, what's your problem?" Simon scoffs as they step into his apartment. Leon and Jasra follow behind. The drive back from the beach was short but tense.

"Simon, you could have broken his arm!" he continues to argue.

"I heard you the first time! And you know what? I should have done more than that!" Simon moves into the living room.

Jasra reaches out. "Hun, don't sit on the—"

Simon plops down on the couch, getting foul sand everywhere.

"—couch…" She sighs. "Will you get cleaned up?" she scolds.

"Eh, guys, do you mind if I crash here? I don't want to go home with Ryan there," Leon says.

Jasra nods. "Sure," she says softly.

"Lee, you can come back with me if you want. I might have clothes that'll fit ya," Seldin says.

Simon gets up, still heated with his brow scrunched into a tight furrow as he paces the living room like a caged lion. "You know what we should do?"

Seldin sighs. "Simon… let it go. You already won the fight. What else is there?"

"How about standing up and showing they can't just knock us around?" Simon barks.

"We did that." Seldin gestures to himself, Simon, and Leon. "You guys fought them off. They saw what we can do. Kicking them when they're already down will just make things worse."

Jasra nods, speaking softly under her breath. "He's right, hun."

"Man…" Simon shakes his head, staring Seldin down. "You don't get it." His eyes move to Jasra and Leon. They all stare back, waiting. "To hell with it." He scoffs, then storms down the hall, slamming his workroom door.

…

Once home, Ryan staggers into the bathroom and switches on the light. He winces as he turns his left wrist to examine the second-degree burn where his watch once was. A circular blister of charred, jagged skin surrounds an inner red and white patch that has broken open.

"Argh, damn that kid," he grunts.

The commotion in the bathroom wakes Leon's mother, Sarah, who peers into the cracked doorway.

"What are you making all this noise for?" she barks.

Ryan glances at her. "Just cleanin some road rash, is all," he says, searching for supplies in the bottom cabinet under the sink.

"Ugh," Sarah groans, "Out of the way, you're making a mess." She scoots him aside, then reaches into the cabinet to grab some gauze and peroxide. "Where's Leon?" she asks.

"What? Oh, that freakin kid? Doesn't listen to anything. Ran off with his friends."

"I told you to—"

"What I just say? The kid doesn't listen."

"Yeah, well, when he gets home, he'll get an earful! Now hold still!" She grabs his wrist and starts wrapping it.

Ryan winces. "Argh!"

"Did you have your talk with Seldin, or did you screw that up too?" Sarah asks.

"Oh, I talked to the little prick. He tried to show me up with his aether—like that shit works," Ryan scoffs, "I kicked his ass." He laughs.

Sarah sighs, taping the gauze. "Honestly, what kind of parents let their kid run around touting about energy in the air? Ridiculous."

Ryan leans in for a kiss. "Tell me about it."

. . .

"Ahhhh!" Neil screams, lying face down on a long altar as Theresa examines his shoulder. She runs her fingers along his collarbone, following the bruising and checking for breaks or any separation before pressing into the joint.

Neil howls again. "Aahh!"

Elma winces and gasps, sympathetically.

Theresa then looks to Elma. "I need you to raise his arm," she says, while holding a round, faceted emerald over Neil's shoulder. She peers at him through the flat side and chants, "Flesh to bone, blood to vein, show me the source of pain." The emerald glows, and through it, she sees an x-ray view of the underlying tissue and bone.

Elma's eyes widen. She stares, stunned. "W-what is this magic?"

Theresa gestures with a finger. "Up."

Elma nods and lifts Neil's arm. There's a loud pop and Neil screams.

"Arrgh-ahhh!"

Elma grimaces at his cries. "You'll be ok, Neil." She then looks to Theresa with hopeful eyes.

"Alright, let his arm down," she says.

"Ok." Elma eases his arm down to the altar.

"Easy, easy…" Theresa says.

There's another pop and Neil howls, "Ow!"

"You've got a torn rotator cuff," Theresa tells him, while letting Elma have a look through the emerald.

"Can't you just use a spell?" Elma asks.

"That's not the best option," Theresa turns to prepare a kettle. "Spells shouldn't be used for healing wounds directly," she says, setting the kettle on the burner.

Elma makes a confused face; she's used spells to repair jewelry before. How is this any different?

"Why not?" she asks as Theresa begins mixing various herbs into a mortar and pestle.

Theresa shrugs, grinding the herbs. "Spells are too… abrupt. Too… forceful; healing requires a gentler touch with sustained energy over time. The suddenness of a spell yields, well…" she pauses, making a face that suggests she's seen more than is apparent for her age, "unpleasant results," she says.

The kettle whistles, and Theresa pours the scalding liquid into a teacup, while stirring in the powdered herbs as she chants, "Three days hence, day through night, heal the shoulder on the right."

The tea shimmers with a brief yellow glow that quickly fades into a normal looking tan liquid.

"Sit him up," Theresa says. She and Elma help Neil into a sitting position before handing him the cup of herbal tea. "Drink up. It should be good in a few days. How'd this happen?"

Neil takes a steaming sip before replying with a panting huff, "Seeiii."

Theresa shakes her head in disbelief. "Sei wouldn't do this; he'll defend himself, but he wouldn't hurt you."

Elma is taken aback. "How can you defend him after all that?" she asks.

Theresa looks into Elma's eyes and then Neil's. "I will make this very clear: if you want to be in my coven, don't think you can lie to me."

Elma looks down, nodding obediently.

Neil scoffs. "His friend then—but it doesn't matter, they're all guilty!"

Theresa sighs. "That's not how we do things, Neil. We don't blame unjustly. I'm very disappointed in you two."

Chapter 5

"Graduation Day"

The crowd is growing at Mangrove Stadium as students, families, and visitors pile in for graduation.

Simon and Jasra have already taken their seats in the stands when they see Seldin's dad and Leon searching for a place to sit, a few rows down.

Jasra stands and waves her hands, "Mr. Gardane, Leon! Up here!"

"Hey, what are you two doing here?" Morgan asks as he and Leon make it to their row.

Simon shrugs. "Same as you."

"After last night I didn't think you would show," Leon says.

Morgan looks between them. "What happened last night?"

Jasra shakes her head. "Oh, nothing; the boys just had an argument."

"Jeez, you two," Morgan says.

Simon leans back in his chair and gestures with hand. "Water under the bridge—say, where's Sei at anyway?" he asks.

Morgan turns and points to the middle of the line near the stage though Seldin is on the other side out of view.

Down by the stage, Seldin spots Neil and Elma preparing to get in line when he notices Neil's arm in a sling. Concerned, he heads over.

"Hey Neil! Neil!" Seldin shouts.

Neil looks over with a sour face as Seldin steps up.

"How's the arm?" Seldin asks.

"Piss off, wielder," Neil scowls.

"Yeah, piss off!" Elma says.

Seldin's expression softens. "Look, guys, I'm sorry about what happ—"

Neil turns to face him, staring down from his taller stature. "Yeah, well, I'm not. It's about time someone took a swing at you wielders. My only regret is you weren't in the fight." He forcibly taps Seldin's shoulder with his left hand.

There's a shimmer of blue in Seldin's eyes and the hairs on his arms start to stand.

Right then, an usher steps in. "Break it up, you two! Where are you supposed to be? Last name?" she demands, pointing to Neil.

"Beyer. I'm the salutatorian," he replies.

"Then you should be on stage, not back here picking fights." She then gestures for Neil to get on stage before turning to face Seldin.

At about that time, the loudspeakers come on with the principal testing the sound.

"Good morning and thank you all for coming to support our scholars in this shining moment of achievement. In just a few minutes, we'll begin awarding their diplomas, but first I'd like you all to hear the inspiring words of this year's valedictorian, Cassie Manchester and salutatorian, Neil Beyer.

Simon's ears perk up, hearing Neils name. His eyes get to work searching the line when he spots him entering stage left. A smirk stretches across his lips.

"Well, shit." Simon grins.

Cassie, a tall thin girl, walks up to the podium. She shuffles some papers, taps the microphone, which squeaks and squeals for a second. "Good morning," she begins, pushing up her thin glasses, "teachers, faculty, Mom and Dad. Like you, I started on this journey not knowing who I was or what I wanted to be…"

In the back hall behind the stage, Seldin's ears perk up, listening as Cassie speaks, while he waits in line.

"The future, as I saw it, was both mysterious and terrifying. It was because of teachers like Mrs. Gellesko and Mr. Ramsey, that I was able to find my confidence…"

Her words make Seldin thinks about his own future, the one his dad wants for him. A knot of unease forms in his stomach. He sighs.

Simon leans back in his chair with his arms folded across his chest, not really listening. The gears in his mind tick with his eyes fixated on Neil as he waits for Cassie's speech to end.

Cassie continues: "They helped me find my path. There are no chosen ones in life. There's nothing preordained. There's just what we choose for ourselves. To my fellow classmates, I wish you the courage to choose. Thank you."

The crowd roars with applause. Cassie steps away from the podium as Neil steps up to it.

Simon smirks and surreptitiously angles his hand forward, aiming for the microphone as he concentrates.

"Good morning. My name's Neil, and I—"

"—am a backstabbing weasel who likes licking his own asshole."

Jasra snaps to her right. "Simon!" she scolds with a loud whisper. He and Leon break into hysterical laughter.

Neil stares out at the crowd, mortified.

Seldin covers his face as boos roar from the crowd. "Oh, Simon." He sighs.

"Wow, that kid's got a filthy mouth," Morgan says.

Neil backs away from the microphone and turns. "I… I didn't say that!"

The principal gathers some ushers and points at Neil. "Get him off the stage!"

"No! No! Wait!" Neil grabs the microphone in a panic—desperately trying to speak. "Principal Jones touched my naughty place!" He gasps in shock then tries again. "I… I love hentai!"

The ushers grab him.

"No! No! Noooooo!" Neil tries to hold onto the podium as they drag him away in tears. "It wasn't me! I didn't say thaaaat!" he cries.

...

After the ceremony, Simon, Jasra, Leon, and Morgan are walking through the crowd on their way to the exit.

"Hey, Mr. Gardane, is it cool if Sei rides back with us?" he asks.

"Sure, just don't keep him out too late. He's got a plane to catch tomorrow," he says.

"No problem." Simon waves as Morgan heads out.

"Simon!" Seldin yells as he approaches them, ready to give him a piece of his mind, and Simon turns to face him.

"Hey, there he is. It's official now." Simon smiles.

Seldin scowls. "I thought we agreed to let things go."

Simon straightens up. "No. You," he points to him, Jasra, and Leon, "agreed to let it go," he says just as Neil rushes out from the crowd and shoves Seldin from behind.

Seldin stumbles forward a bit then turns around to see the hurt faces of Elma and Neil.

"They won't release my diploma now— they're expelling me because of you!" Neil yells with tears in his eyes.

Seldin looks sorrowful. "Neil... I... had nothing to do—"

"Save it! You're all a bunch of assholes!" He and Elma storm off.

Seldin watches them leave, and then sets his sights on Simon. "One day, we will be revealed to the world. How are they supposed to accept us… when we do things like this?" he asks, turning toward the exit.

Simon makes a shrugging gesture of confusion. "Wha—Sei…" he tries to stop him as he walks out. "Seldin!" he shouts with a look to Jasra and Leon. "What's his deal?"

Jasra looks at him with sigh. "You couldn't just let it go, huh?" she asks.

"Yeah, that wasn't cool, man," Leon adds, while trying not to laugh.

"Shut up," he says to Leon. "I didn't see you try to stop me." He then steps outside with Jasra and Leon following behind, but Seldin has already made it halfway across the parking lot.

"What now?" Leon asks.

"Get in the car," Simon says.

…

Theresa is sitting at her altar with her eyes intently scanning the obscure passages of the Book of Roe. Each page is intricate, almost holographic in nature, with the way the layers of text appear to meld and shift like a kaleidoscope of sorts.

She turns the page and stops at a section, which piques her interest.

"One-line spells?" she asks, reading aloud. "Hmm. How is that possible?" She pauses to think about it before continuing.

"The rhythmic cadence of lower magic makes its use slow and cumbersome and borrows energy from higher beings, taxed threefold. These restrictions, though few, makes accessing the universe's secrets a questionable tradeoff for mortals."

Theresa sets the book down with a heavy sigh. "I know this already. What else do you got?" she says then flips to the next page.

"The universe, however, lends itself to all inhabitants provided that two conditions are met: the first is the caster's core must be aligned to allow the flow of aether. The drawback is, like wielders, their body acts as the conduit and takes the brunt of the aetheral forces. For this reason, smaller spells are preferable. The second condition is the spell must be written or spoken in the Language of the Gods. The length of the incantation doesn't matter as long as the conditions are met and the intent is there."

Intrigued by this, Theresa sits back and thinks about it for a moment or two. She then looks to an expired candle on her altar.

"Dobsnich," she says, but nothing happens. Theresa straightens up, focuses on the wick, and aims a hand at the candle, then tries again.

"Dobsnich." There's a subtle pop and the wick ignites. A laugh of amazement escapes her. Right then, her phone rings.

"Hello? Neil what's wrong?" Theresa asks with concern, hearing his sobs. "When?"

. . .

About a block from Mangrove Stadium, Seldin continues to walk off his frustration. His thoughts fixate on his best friend's callous actions and his own inaction.

"Maybe I could have done something," he says to himself when he hears the sweet voice of Jasra on his left.

"Hey handsome, need a ride?" she asks, and he looks to her standing partway out the sunroof of Simon's Jeep. He tries not to smile as they follow at his walking pace.

Simon leans forward, looking past Jasra's legs to make eye contact with him. "Listen, things got out of hand back there. I'm sorry," he says.

Seldin sighs, facing forward just as the light ahead turns red, and he stops at the orange hand of the crosswalk before pressing the button.

"C'mon, you gonna stay mad at me all day?" Simon hollers.

Seldin impatiently presses the button on the crosswalk again.

"I said I was sorry," Simon says.

Seldin tries to ignore him, but his ears fall to the lack of traffic, and his eyes scan the lights, which are red on both sides. He sighs, then turns with an annoyed look of defeat to Simon, who grins as he walks toward the Jeep.

…

"High Priestess! High Priestess!" Theresa shouts as she runs down the main hall toward Lamryl.

Lamryl stops and turns to address her apprentice. "Theresa?"

"I… need your guidance," Theresa pants.

"Have you been reading the book?" she asks.

Theresa nods. "Yes, some—it, it's doesn't appear to be arranged in any particular order," she says.

Lamryl smiles. "It can be a difficult read. The book is an imprint of Roe's mind and employs a technique learned from the Guardian of Dimension to compress so much information into such a confined space. As you delve deeper, you'll start to see how each page is more like an onion."

"Ma'am, no disrespect, but I didn't run all the way down here to discuss Roe's mind. One of my initiates has been attacked by wielders. I need to know what to do," Theresa says.

"Do you know who… started the confrontation?" Lamryl prompts.

Theresa shakes her head. "Does that matter?"

"Of course. There are always three sides to every story: your side, their side, and—"

"The truth," they both say together.

"I know, but—" Theresa begins.

"Eh-te-tet," Lamryl interrupts, "You are right to want to stand up for your initiates. Just be mindful... even if you win the fight, there is still pain."

...

A few blocks south of Simon's apartment is a medium-sized warehouse on an otherwise vacant industrial lot. The hyphenated name, "Sim-Antics" looms over the front of the building in large metal letters.

To the left of the compound is Kane's Lumberyard, and to the right is Nelson's Glass Factory. All three buildings, spaced a good distance from one another, face a small road with hardly any traffic.

Inside the lobby is a desk with no one at it. Drapes of plastic sheets block any direct view into the back of the warehouse. Much of which is in varying stages of construction.

Leon is wandering around the large, mostly empty room, while Seldin helps Simon repair his goggles.

Seldin holds a lens in place. "You got it?" he asks.

"Yeah," Simon replies, tightening a screw on the interior housing.

"So, when are you gonna make it right?" Seldin asks, and Simon glances away from his work with a sigh.

"Are you still on that—" There's a soft metallic thud. "Damn it!"

"What?"

"I dropped the screw." Simon looks around.

Seldin moves the goggles out of the way and there's a metallic/plastic rattling sound inside.

"No," Simon takes the goggles, "it's between the plastic.

"Well, if you—just—" Seldin tries to help when Simon pulls away and holds the goggles in one hand while focusing and aiming with his loose fingers. The screw can be heard scraping around inside the plastic housing. After a minute or two, it lifts out with Simon holding it telekinetically. He takes a breath.

Seldin reaches for the goggles, but Simon shakes his head.

"No. I can see it," he says.

"Huh?"

"The circuits—oh that's cool." Simon's gaze penetrates through the layers of material.

Leon walks over, curious about what's going on.

Seldin smiles at Simon. "Are you gonna?"

Simon nods. In his mind's eye, he can clearly see the slot for the screw on the circuit board. He concentrates, easing the screw closer. They can all hear it bumping around as he misses. It's like threading the eye of a needle without a guide.

"Come on, you…" Simon whispers.

"You've got this," Seldin says.

Leon watches intently, and just as the screw slides into position, it slips out of place.

Simon sets the device down and drops his telekinetic connection, while taking deep labored breaths.

"Aww, so close," Leon says.

Seldin reaches for the device.

"Hey, I'm not done with that!" Simon snatches it up.

"Oh, come on, you had a go!" he says, and Simon scoffs then slides the goggles his way.

Seldin grins as he takes them up and goes for his attempt. "Ok…" He let's his mind fall into the plastic, reaching for the screw. "You said you could see it?"

Simon nods. "Yeah, I was looking at it but not with my eyes. It was more of a—"

"A feeling," Seldin says, finishing Simon's sentence. He concentrates, letting his eyes fall out of focus, working his senses through the plastic. In his mind's eye, it's hazy at first, but then… "I see it," he says with a soft smile. The screw comes into view with the weight of it tugging at his pointed fingers.

Tap, tap, the screw clicks and clanks around inside as he tries to work it into place.

"Ugghh." Seldin sits back, taking a rest before handing the device to Leon, who declines.

"Nah, I'm still struggling to lift a nickel, guys," he says.

"It's not the weight," Simon says.

"It's the precision," Seldin answers. "Not to mention, the circuits are likely catching the energy and interfering," he adds.

Simon scoffs, "Maybe your energy, but I am the Guardian of Technology." He telekinetically pulls the goggles to himself and tries again. He makes a face of extreme concentration. The screw taps here and there, and then...

"I got it!" Simon exclaims. "Now, if I can just..." He tries to tighten it, fighting the strain as it gets more and more difficult with each revolution.

"There," Simon says, sitting back in his accomplishment.

"Nice!" Seldin grins.

"Good job," Leon says.

Simon then looks to Seldin. "You ready?"

Seldin nods, then walks out toward the center of the lab and steps onto a metal platform. Above it is foil canopy with cables running from both it and the floor plate to a large computer station.

Leon looks confused. "Ready for what?"

"Calibration," Seldin answers.

Simon puts on the goggles. "Ok, slow burn at first," he says, then reaches out to the computer to activate it telekinetically.

Seldin bends his knees, getting ready. He holds his arms loosely out front with his palms facing inward as he concentrates, moving energy from his core, up his spine, and down his chest in a circular fashion. It's slow at first, then faster. The hairs on his arms, legs, and head stand on end as he builds a charge.

The readout on the main computer shows a diagram of the human body with the point just below the navel labelled as the core. Seldin's starts at around 450 joules, then slowly rises.

Leon looks on in astonishment. "Is that his energy?" He walks up to the readout.

Simon nods with a grin. "Yeah."

Seldin doesn't break a sweat as the readout passes 980 joules, then 1,000, and then 1,100. The colored indicator bar moves from green to yellow.

Simon taps a button on the side of his goggles to compare the readings. There's a slight variance of 100 joules that he manages to calibrate out with a small dial.

"Alright, bring it down some. You're a little high," Simon says.

"Is it me or the device?" Seldin asks.

"No, it's you. Bring it down."

Sparks shoot off as little arcs of electricity pop and dance around Seldin's body. The indicator on the readout moves into red as his core reaches 1,300 joules.

"Jesus, do you feel that heat?" Leon shouts, backing away from Seldin and the computer.

Simon's face grows to concern. "Sei, you're hitting the redline! You need to take it down!"

Seldin grunts. "Uggh, you said… 1,300 the the other night, right? Let's see… how far I… can push it!" He grits his teeth and braces himself in horse stance. There's notable strain on his body. His skin reddens as veins bulge with sweat running down his face. Loose equipment gets pushed away, while papers spiral around.

"Uggghh!" Seldin's core passes 1,350 joules, and the readout hits deep red.

"Sei!" Simon shouts.

Seldin stops, dropping to his knees, while panting and gasping. Simon and Leon rush over.

"Are you insane?" Simon questions.

"Now… we… know," Seldin says with gasping breaths.

"Know what?" Leon asks.

Simon lets out a half chuckle and shakes his head, "The edge of the safe zone."

Seldin looks to Leon. "We've always suspected it but have never been strong enough for overloading to be dangerous. Based on this, I predict that as we get stronger, anything over three times our base core will be—"

"Catastrophic," Simon finishes his sentence, and Seldin nods.

. . .

Out in the cathedral courtyard, Theresa is sitting in the shade by the koi pond with Neil and Elma.

"How could they do this to me? They ruined my whole life!" Neil sobs.

Elma holds Neil with her eyes locked on Theresa. "They've gone too far this time! What are you gonna do?"

Theresa sighs. "We're gonna fight back. But first, we need to know who did it."

Elma makes a face. "But why? They're all guilty!"

"Because," Theresa pauses, "even if we win the fight there will be pain. It's important that we direct it to the right person, so others don't get hurt in the process. Who else was there?" she asks.

"Um…" Elma thinks for a second. "There was Jasra, Simon, and um…" She snaps her fingers, "What's his name?"

Neil speaks up. "Leon, he's Sei's student."

Theresa nods. "Ok. I know Jasra pretty well. I don't think she'd do this, and it isn't really Sei's way of handling things either. He'll hold his ground but he's not one to pick fights."

"What about Leon?" Elma asks, and Theresa shakers her head.

"My money is on Simon; he has both the strength and the ability. Not to mention, you two already had a scuffle," she says.

Neil looks to her with teary eyes. "Is there any way to know for sure?"

Theresa gently wipes one of Neil's tears with a finger, then moves to the koi pond. With a gesture of a hand, she chants.

"Tears of weakness, scars of pain, reveal to us the one to blame." She dips the tear into the water, which ripples, and an image of Simon appears.

"I thought so," she says.

Elma and Neil look into the pond, and Neil's face contorts with anger.

"That son of a bitch!" He turns away, heading toward the exit.

"Neil!" Theresa shouts, and he stops immediately.

"We're not ready. Your shoulder still needs to heal, and our circle is incomplete," Theresa says.

"What do you suggest?" Elma asks.

"We need at least one more member to form a circle. Find our fourth member, and then we can perform the initiate's ritual and combine our strengths.

Chapter 6

"Long Goodbyes"

"Oh—come on! How do you control these things? It's nothing like a real car!" Seldin complains, while angling the video game controller as he leans with the racecar on screen.

Simon chuckles, sitting forward on the couch. "Maybe you should learn to drive," he gloats as his car crosses the finish line. "Yes!" He throws the controller.

Leon sighs. "GG."

Seldin sits back, annoyed, then pans his eyes around the apartment. "You got anything that doesn't rely on broken physics?" He spots the chessboard in the corner. "How about chess?"

"Nah." Simon gets up. "I got a better game. Be prepared to lose some money," he says on his way to the closet at the end of the hall to left of the living room. After a few seconds, he returns with a silver poker case and sets it on the kitchen table.

"Alright, boys, the game's five card stud—nothing wild—"

"Uh, guys, I don't know how to play cards," Leon says as he and Seldin take seats around the table.

"It's easy; we'll teach you," Seldin says, while handing Simon two $10 bills.

Leon makes a face. "Real money?"

Simon smirks. "Makes it interesting," he says, then hands them each a stack of chips.

Seldin leans to Leon. "You know who's really good? Jasra," he says.

"Only because she cheats," Simon quickly follows up, while shuffling the cards.

"Remember that time your dad tried taking her to the casino?" Seldin asks with a chuckle.

Leon looks to Simon. "I thought your dad didn't believe in this stuff," he says.

Simon shrugs as he deals. "He doesn't, but anything for a buck," he says.

"I hear ya." Seldin sighs. "My dad's played the same lottery numbers since I can remember."

"Yeah, but at least your dad never dragged you to court to get what wasn't his," Simon says.

Seldin whispers to Leon, "His mom got everything in the divorce and left it to him when she passed," he tells him.

"Alright, anti-up," Simon says.

Seldin reaches to Leon's stack of plastic chips. "Put in two chips; the white ones are pennies, the reds are five cents, the blues ten, greens are a quarter, and blacks are a dollar," he instructs, tossing in two white chips just as the door opens with Jasra toting bags of whatnot.

"Bye, mom. Love you," she turns to close the door before greeting the boys and heading around the kitchen table to set the bags on the counter.

"Anyone want sushi?" she asks.

"Yes!" Simon answers without hesitation, hopping up to get a plate.

Leon nods. "I'll take some!"

Seldin makes a sour face. "Eh, no fish for me, thanks. I'll just take a Gatorade," he says.

Jasra peers into the fridge. "Orange or blue?" she asks.

Seldin shrugs "Doesn't matter." And she tosses him an orange one.

"What'cha all playing?" she asks.

"Poker," Leon replies with his mouth full.

Jasra smiles, "Deal me in!" she says.

Simon quickly comes around to his seat with a plate of crunchy rolls and spicy tuna. "Ohh, no, house rules—no psychics at the table!

Jasra kisses his cheek, then sits at the kitchen table anyway.

"He's just mad that he can't win when you're around," Seldin laughs.

Simon stuffs his face. "Alright, alright, but don't come crying to me when you leave broke," he says with his mouth smacking as he chews before dealing her in.

. . .

"Where are we gonna find another sorcerer?" Neil asks Elma, in a sort of pouting voice, while they walk down the long stone stairway of Watcher's Keep.

Elma shrugs with a gesture toward the cathedral behind them. "We can always ask someone here," she says, but Neil shakes his head.

"No, they're all already taken," he says.

"We weren't," she comments with a shrug, then suddenly turns to him. "Hey, what about Bonnie and Michael?" she asks.

Neil sighs. "Bonnie's a dip and Michael couldn't fight his way out of a wet paper bag. We need someone good," he says.

"Hmm…" Elma thinks. "Let's try Relics and Runes, there's always somebody there," she says as they take a right onto the sidewalk to head downtown.

…

Laughter fills the kitchen with Leon throwing his cards face down on the table. Jasra is winning, having most of the chips. Simon is in second place with Seldin trailing pitifully in third, though he's not doing as bad as Leon.

"How do you do it?" Leon asks.

Jasra playfully shrugs. "I don't know, it just comes to me," she says, calming her laughter. "It's not even good information half the time."

"What do you mean?" he asks.

"Like," Jasra looks up gathering her thoughts, "sometimes it's useless, like knowing Simon's about to snee—"

"Aauchhewww!" Simon bellows, then grabs a napkin to wipe his face. "Well, that would have been nice to know." He blows his nose.

"Other times it's a weird dream that I have to decipher, or um… something that won't even happen for years without a clear idea of when," she explains.

"Can you control it?" Seldin asks.

Jasra shrugs with a soft nod. "Well, yeah, a little," she says.

"I think that's obvious, Sei," Simon says with a gesture to the game.

"No, I mean like—" Seldin tries to rephrase when Leon reaches across the table, drawing a card from the deck.

"What do I got?" he prompts.

Jasra smiles, being put on the spot. "Um…" she focuses on the moment, which plays out in a quasi-accelerated fashion with Leon revealing the card to her before rewinding to the present.

"Two of clubs," she answers to his astonishment, and just like in her vision, he reveals his card to her.

"That's cool," Leon says with a laugh.

"Incredible," Seldin says.

Simon then takes a card from the deck and holds it up. "How about this one?"

"Queen of Diamonds," Jasra says.

Seldin looks to her. "So can you pick any moment in time?" he asks.

Jasra makes an inquisitive face. "You mean like, can I get the lottery numbers for tomorrow?"

Seldin shrugs. "Sure."

"Mm, no—not unless it came to me in a dream or something; it's too far," she says, shaking her head.

"Well, how far can you see?" Seldin asks.

"Consciously?" Jasra asks.

Seldin nods. "Mm-hm."

"Um…" Jasra starts the first of two watches on her right wrist. It beeps; the timer ticks rapidly in her view—1:18, 1:19, 1:20—the various layers of her vision start to blur and twist. She brings a hand to her temple, pushing past the strain—1:27, 1:28—the moment collapses. She stops the watch and she rubs her forehead. To everyone else, the two beeps were back to back.

"Mm… a little over a minute," she answers.

"Interesting," Seldin says, thinking.

"That's it?" Leon makes a questioning face.

Jasra shrugs. "Well, that's farther than I could see last week, and much farther than a year ago," she says.

A thought comes to Seldin, and he draws a card. "So, if I were to hold this for say… two minutes, you couldn't tell me what it is?" he asks with a curious smirk.

Jasra's mouth hangs open in stunned silence, and Simon and Leon lean forward on the table, watching intently.

Seldin holds the card up, waiting.

Jasra smiles, embarrassed. She covers her mouth with a hand, while staring at him and the card. The moment stretches on until finally, she reaches across the table. "Give me that!"

Seldin pulls it away, and they all laugh.

...

There's a soft chime as Neil and Elma step into Relics and Runes—a small sorcery shop, just off the main strip in downtown Clearwater.

Neil frowns, seeing an utter lack of patrons. "Seriously?" He sighs.

"We can always check the square," Elma says before breaking off into a separate aisle, following her nose to the smell of burning incense.

"Mm... maybe—oh cool, an engraver!" Neil exclaims, picking up a metallic pen-shaped instrument with a diamond tip when a woman's voice comes from over the counter in the far corner of the store.

"It's for writing enchantments," she says.

Neil and Elma jump then look up at Madam Nadine.

"Sorry, didn't mean to startle you," she says with a soft smile. "Do you know how to use that?"

Neil nods. "Uh, yeah, it's sort of my specialty," he says with a look to Elma, who joins him as he approaches the counter. She presents a small diamond-shaped pendant on her necklace with an amethyst crystal in the center and runes engraved along the perimeter.

Madam Nadine examines it. "Auhh… you made this for protection?" she asks, knowingly.

"Mm-hm," Neil replies.

"The crystal's my touch," Elma says.

"North, south, east, and west, shield me from my foes best. Very impressive," Nadine complements.

"Thanks," Neil says.

"We serve Priestess Theresa of Watcher's Keep," Elma says.

"Oh?" Madam Nadine responds.

"That's actually why we're here; she asked us to find our fourth," Neil says.

"Would you be interested?" Elma asks.

Madam Nadine shakes her head. "No, I have responsibilities elsewhere, but you might find someone in the square," she suggests.

Elma turns to Neil. "That's what I said."

"It gets pretty dead around 7:30, gives our kind a chance to mingle without prying eyes," Madam Nadine says with a smile.

"Thanks, we'll check it out," Elma says.

Neil places the engraver on the counter and pulls out his wallet. "How much?"

"$15," Madam Nadine replies, then rings him up.

...

"Go! Go! Go!" Seldin, Jasra, and Simon cheer as Leon steps up onto the first Styrofoam cup in a row of three, arranged like stairs stacked three high. He gently lowers the ball of his foot to the top of the cup, while focuses aether below himself.

The cup sinks a little into the carpet and Leon wobbles a bit.

"Ugh!" he huffs.

"Oh-oh!" Jasra lets out.

Leon steadies himself, balancing with his arms out like a tightrope walker.

Simon grins with a sigh, slipping Seldin a dollar bill as the cup holds firm.

"You got this, Lee!" Seldin cheers.

Leon slowly takes a breath before bringing his other foot up to the top of the second cup. The Styrofoam whines a little, sinking down some, but it feels solid as he presses. He shifts his weight forward, taking up his back foot—schwomp—the cup crushes and Leon falls back onto the living room floor.

"Oaf!" Leon thuds.

"Aw-man! So close!" Seldin shouts before nudging Simon with an elbow. "You're up," he says.

"Yeah, see if you can beat one cup," Jasra says, being snarky.

Simon groans and places a fresh row of cups on the floor. He then takes position and focuses, while lightly bringing his foot to the top of the first cup.

"Do you think he'll do it?" Seldin whispers to Jasra, who smiles with a wink.

Simon presses his weight down, then lifts his back foot—crush—thud—he hits the floor.

"Damn!" he swipes the cups away, hearing Seldin laugh.

"Haha, you suck!" Seldin says.

"Oh, yeah—you try it!" Simon gets up, rubbing his left hip.

"Set it up," Seldin says with a gesture to the cups, and Simon does.

Seldin gets ready. He closes his eyes to center himself, then brings his right foot down onto the first cup.

Simon whispers to Leon. "Five bucks says he falls," he says.

"No way," Leon rebuts.

"I'll take that bet," Jasra says, reaching out to shake Simon's hand.

The first cup whines as Seldin balances, but it holds. He gently brings his left foot up to the second cup. His mind focuses past the layers of Styrofoam as he feels out the floor beneath. There's a soft creek of the spongy material sinking as he shifts all his weight to it.

"Darn, I should have taken the bet," Leon sighs, watching Seldin balance just fine.

Jasra claims her five dollars from Simon.

Seldin then places his right foot onto the third cup. Everyone holds their breath. He slowly shifts his weight before crashing down onto his back with a sharp gasp and a cough.

"Oaf!" Seldin rolls to his side, catching his breath, while hearing Simon laugh. "Still farther than you," he says with a raspy chuckle.

"Jassie, you're up," Leon says, stacking the cups for her.

"Alright," she says before focusing on the moment. A version of herself steps down flat through the cup; she tries again. The moment backs up to just before, and she adjusts her footing—crunch! Jasra takes a breath as she concentrates, lifting herself up onto the first cup.

The Jasra ahead of her falls as she tries for the second cup. "Not that way," she whispers to herself, making the necessary correction to the placement of her foot, then steps onto the second cup. There's a soft creak as it carries her weight.

Jasra reaches out to the third.

"No way," Leon whispers, watching as she shifts forward.

Simon and Seldin stare, practically holding their breath as the toes of her back foot lift off.

"Yeah!" Simon cheers, breaking her concentration, and she falls back with a yelp.

Seldin dives to catch her—crash—they smash through the coffee table, and they all laugh.

. . .

Seldin steps out onto the balcony of Simon's apartment, closing the sliding glass door over the sound of muffled voices and laughter. He then stares out over the guardrail to Cedar Park—their humble battleground—lit by a single faded orange streetlight and the pale glow of the whirling vortex.

He sighs, thinking about his future, his friends, and what he'll have to leave behind. His eyes drift northward to the feeling pulling him that way.

"Sseellddiin!" That low gravelly voice enters his mind once again with a superimposed view of a grassy clearing featuring a small boulder shadowed by two large trees spaced like an entrance into a deeper wooded area. A strange rose-like flower sits atop the rock. *"Get here,"* it says, and he creeps toward it, preparing to climb over the guardrail.

The sound of the sliding door behind him grabs his attention, and he glances back with a startled breath to see Jasra stepping out.

"Why are you hiding out here?" she asks.

Seldin shrugs. "Eh, just… thinking," he says, turning his gaze northward again.

"About your future?" she asks.

Seldin nods. "I feel something," he gestures, "out there—calling to me." He looks to her. "I heard a voice," he says.

"For real—l-like, in your head?" she asks.

"Yeah… have you?" he asks.

Jasra shakes her head, then rests her arms on the railing beside him. "Heard voices? No. What do you think it is?" She looks to him.

"I don't know." He looks down. "But I know I have to leave," he says.

"Are you scared?" she asks, and Seldin shakes his head.

"I'm… m-more afraid of… what my life will become if I don't go," he answers.

Jasra places an arm around him, and he looks down in thought for a long while.

"My mom left when I was two," he says out of the blue, "never looked back. Simon's mom was the only mother I had. When she got sick, I tried to heal her; it didn't work, but my dad saw it as an opportunity to make money—heh… I had to convince him it wasn't real."

"I'm sorry." Jasra rubs his back. "Are you… not going to tell him?" she asks.

Seldin looks into her eyes. "What do you want?" he asks with a pause, "M-more than anything in the world?"

Jasra looks down and away with a half-smile that fades out of his view. She covers her mouth as she thinks before looking back, avoiding eye contact.

"To see my dad again." She sighs. "He died when I was thirteen. And… to have a… someone, who loves me as much as I love them," she says, her eyes looking into a future too far to see.

"If strengthening your gift could get you that, would you do it—even if… it meant giving up everything else?" he asks.

Jasra looks into his eyes. "I don't know that I could," she answers, and Seldin looks north with a soft nod.

…

Clack—clang—ping—tong! The cadence of swords clashing, echoes throughout Clearwater Square as Neil and Elma make their way over to a small crowd gathered around a dueling pair, fencing within a sorcerer's circle etched by magic into the redbrick ground.

"Excuse me," Elma nudges one of the observers, "Would you like to join our circle?" she asks, and the young woman shakes her head before cheering.

"Come on, Rico!" she shouts as Rico blocks upward, locking his blade with his opponent's downward strike. He grits his teeth, trying to out-muscle him.

Neil moves around the crowd in the opposite direction. "Anyone want to join a circle? Hello? Anyone? We're recruiting for Priestess Theresa of Watcher's Keep," he says, but no one pays him much mind.

"Cory! Get him—get him!" some guy cheers, and Cory grunts, pushing his blade down against Rico's.

Rico sees an opportunity: "Quick and sharp, small and narrow, this I cast, a magic arrow." He flicks his wrist with an open palm, and a golden arrow fires at Cory—whoosh—he dodges with a twist and delivers a front kick to Rico's chest just as the arrow wizzes past him.

Neil whips his head, following the arrow's path as it soars into the crowd. Spectators duck, dive, and dodge, but Elma stares wide-eyed and frozen.

"Elma!" Neil shouts and darts forward.

She gasps with a flinching yelp, bringing her hands up just as the arrow crashes into a translucent diamond-shaped barrier of orange light that ripples on impact as it appears before her—the pendent on her necklace glows brightly.

The crowd cheers!

"Are you ok?" Neil asks, running up to her, and Elma nods despite the panicked throb in her chest.

"Yeah," she says.

Swoosh—swoop—ting! Cory attacks with fury—down strike, down strike—he brings his sword up; the runes along the edges start to glow from guard to tip as he brings it down through Rico's blade—slice!

"Agh!"—Clink! Rico falls back when his sword splits in two, and he narrowly dodges the tip of Cory's blade, which nicks his shoulder.

Cory quickly sets up another strike, raising his sword high, once more. There's a sharp gasp from the crowd.

Rico holds out a hand. "Wait—wait! I yield!" he exclaims to the mixed sound of cheers, laughter, and boos from all around.

As the crowd dissipates, Neil and Elma push through to the sorcerer's circle where Cory is packing up his gear. They clap.

"Amazing!" Neil says.

"Well done!" Elma follows up.

Cory gives them an odd look. "Uh, thanks," he says, while toweling the sweat from his hair.

"Are you in a coven?" Elma asks.

Cory smiles. "Yeah." He then looks over his shoulder. "Hey, Ryan!" he calls out, and Neil and Elma follow his eyeline to a familiar face as Ryan, Rico, and Joanne close in.

"Sup, Cory?" Ryan asks.

"I think these guys wanna join," Cory says.

Ryan looks to Elma, and then Neil before grinning. "Hey—um, what are the odds? Neil, right?" He extends his hand.

Neil shakes it. "Yeah, that's right."

"And, uh, sorry I don't remember your name." Ryan points to Elma.

"Um, my girlfriend, Elma," Neil says.

"Right, right, um… well, look, if you want to join, step into the circle, and we'll do a proper strength test," Ryan says with a gesture to the sorcerer's circle, and then looks back. "What are your talents?"

"Actually, we're recruiting for Priestess Theresa," Elma says.

Ryan's pleasant demeanor changes with a look to her, and then Neil. "You trying to bogart my guys?" He shoves Neil's chest.

"No," Neil says.

Ryan shoves him again and grabs the collar of his shirt. Elma tries to stop him, but Rico, Joanne, and Cory block her.

"No! No! Wait!" Neil grabs his hand. "How would you like to get even with those douchebags from the beach?" he asks in a panic.

Ryan eases up. "I'm listening."

. . .

It's Sunday morning and Seldin is packing for his long journey, while Leon and Simon help load up the Jeep. A sleeping bag, meal bars, and a couple of canteens are among his things.

"Did you put the rough sack and sleeping bag in the car?" Seldin asks Simon and Leon as they reenter the room.

"Yeah, you're good." Simon nods.

"Your dad didn't see us," Leon says.

Seldin looks to Simon. "Are you gonna fix things with Neil?" he asks.

Simon groans. "Don't push it, Sei," he says.

Seldin sighs, then takes a couple jars with sewing needles suspended inside, wraps them in a towel and places them into his bag.

"You're taking those but not a computer?" Simon asks, while telekinetically playing with the needle in another jar on his desk.

"This isn't a vacation, Simy; it's work. The goal is to rely on my senses," Seldin says.

Simon shrugs. "That's all good until something misaligns your core," he says.

Leon looks to Simon with surprised confusion. "That can happen?" he asks just as Seldin's dad steps into the doorway.

"Are you all packed up? We gotta leave soon," Morgan says.

Seldin looks up at his dad. "Um, I was going to have Simon drive me. I… hate long goodbyes," he says.

Morgan looks a little disappointed. "Oh." He sighs, then gestures for his son to come out into the living room. Seldin does.

"Look, uh," Morgan look's into Seldin's eyes, "I just want to say that I'm proud of you," he says.

Seldin looks down. "Um, Dad," he hesitates, "about college—"

"Right—" Morgan searches himself before presenting an envelope. "Here."

"What's this?" Seldin asks, looking inside; it's money.

"It isn't much, but—"

Seldin hands it back. "I can't."

"No," Morgan insists, "you can. I've been saving a long time," he says, and Seldin's heart sinks a little.

"I, uh… got a scholarship, remember? I'm paid for. You keep this," Seldin says, then pulls his dad in for an impromptu hug. Morgan hugs back, then begrudgingly takes the envelope.

"This will be here for you, if you need it," he says, putting it back in his pocket.

Right then, Simon and Leon come out, toting Seldin's bags.

"Hey, Sei, we're gonna miss the plane," Simon says.

"I love you," Morgan says to Seldin.

"You too," Seldin replies.

…

Dean, Arius, and Jasra are standing in the parking lot of Simon's apartment complex when he pulls up with Seldin and Leon.

Seldin smiles. "What are you doing here?"

"We've come to see you off—this one arranged it," Dean says with a gesturing thumb to Jasra as Seldin hops out of the jeep to shake his hand. They embrace for a second. "Good luck, Sei."

"Thanks," Seldin says, then turns to shake Arius's hand. "I hope you train," he says to Arius.

"I will. You have my word," Arius says.

Jasra then hugs Seldin when he turns to her. "Take care of yourself," she says.

"You, too. Don't let this one get out of line," Seldin gestures to Simon before offering him an open hand.

"I'm not hugging you," Simon says, returning only a fist bump.

"I didn't think you would." Seldin smiles.

"But I will kick your ass." Simon quickly feigns a readied stance to get him to flinch, and they laugh.

"I expect a good fight when I get back," Seldin says before turning to Leon. "Lee." He shakes his hand.

"Train hard," Leon says.

"You too," Seldin replies. He then grabs his gear from the Jeep and faces north.

"Are you really going to run the whole way?" Jasra asks.

Dean slaps Seldin's shoulder. "Of course, he is," he says.

"Do you know where you're headed?" Arius asks.

Seldin nods. "North; that's where I feel… whatever it is," he says.

"I don't feel anything," Simon comments and Jasra gives him a soft elbow to the ribs.

"Well," Seldin looks to them one last time, "see ya." He takes off into a steady run.

...

High in the sky over Florida, Dean, Arius, and a darkly dressed hooded figure hover, while watching Seldin as he runs.

"Is it in place?" the dark one asks.

Arius nods. "Yes. I've done as you asked."

"Good." the dark one says with a look to Dean. "So, this… is the new Guardian of Life?" he asks in a questioning tone. The boy has strength. He can sense that, but there's weakness in his heart.

Dean gives a reluctant nod to the Guardian of Death. "If he survives; you know as well as I do, Tillman, they all have to walk their own path."

Chapter 7

"Leon's Apprentice"

"Is this legal?" Almir whispers, peeking over the brawny shoulders of his mentor to the coin machine in the far corner of the small convenient store.

Leon responds with only a sideways glance. It wasn't a hard question, but he needs to stay focused for this to work. Legal or not, it's about the challenge.

His eyes then fall back to the task at hand and the reciprocating motion of the plate pushing the mountain of quarters forward. He doesn't need to grab them all—just one.

Allowing his body to relax, Leon extends his mind down into his core. His hands are poised with his palms and his focus aimed through the glass. A deep breath pulls air in until a sensation of pressure and warmth forms at his center. He can feel it building, moving through his body, and the glass resisting his intent—cha-ching! The bells ring and the buzzers sound with the jolly sirens of a winner as he collects his booty.

"Seldin teach you that?" Almir asks with a look of amazement.

"Not exactly," Leon replies with a bloated, prideful grin as they leave the confines of the convenient mart.

"So, when are you gonna let me meet this Seldin guy, anyway?" the youngling pesters, though he's not much younger than Leon.

"When you are ready," he answers with a hint of smugness in his voice as they walk. Leon has always looked up to Seldin. For the longest time he strived to be exactly like him—perhaps even to the extreme. The same clothes, the same haircut, but now with his best friend gone, Leon has taken to finding his own way, and with that, his own student.

He met Almir, a sophomore placed in his junior English class, earlier in the school year, and has been feeding him secrets—a controlled shock here, moving a pencil there—the ways of aether, much like Seldin had for Leon all that time ago.

Out of nowhere comes a young, though familiar voice, "Hey, Lee! You better get home. Dad's been looking for you."

Both Leon and Almir glance to the little brother approaching from the left.

"He's not our dad, Chad. The sooner you realize that, the better," Leon says as they continue to walk past him.

"I'm going to tell him you said that," the twelve-year-old replies as he enters the store.

The teens then head off to practice at their favorite park, as they typically do, entering into their daily ritual of partial concussions and deep bruises. The brutality of their antics drives their strengths to new heights each day, and without

Seldin, Leon is determined more than ever to surpass him—to become a guardian in his own right.

Exchanging blows, Leon does what any good teacher should for his student—he demonstrates the value of his lessons through application.

"Hu-argh!" Almir grunts as his shin just grazes past the head of his opponent, who ducks out of the way. Leon returns swiftly, rolling out of the dodge and ricocheting off his right palm, launching into a one-handed mule-kick that connects as he counters.

"Remember, attack and defend simultaneously," Leon instructs, springing onto his feet.

Almir pops out of a kip-up and charges at him, attacking from a standing front sweep with his left leg, followed up by his right, switching off one after the other while Leon steps casually out of each move.

Smack—a beet-red hue anoints Almir's face, forming the shape of a palm.

"You're looking at my feet. Keep eye contact at all times and use your peripheral vision for targeting. If you look where you strike, you narrow your vision and give yourself away," Leon says, twisting Almir, while dodging a punch that clips the random peaks of his buzzed hair.

With a swift push, Almir goes forward and stumbles to regain his balance, and once he does, he drops into a perfect horse stance, then pushes his hands outward and up thirty degrees with his palms formed in tiger claw.

Leon rests in his stance, offering a prickish smirk, and then lowers his eyes while giving a subtle shake of his head. "You're doing it wro…" He then notices the shift in the air. "Oh, you're learning," he says with pride. Almir's core is heating up, and Leon can feel his power growing.

"Steady it, that's good," Leon says, then shifts his rear foot, bending his knee slightly as he begins concentrating to match his student.

Staring each other down, the two relish the excitement of the challenge. For Leon especially, there's something about passing one's knowledge on. He wonders if this is how Seldin felt. With his posture ready, he leaps forward.

Seeing his teacher charging at him, Almir's mind races, *'If only he would look away, look away!'* he thinks to himself, hoping for a perfect opportunity.

Leon then pushes energy ahead of himself to cushion the shoulder-ram into Almir's guarded stance, but then, abruptly, he stops, feeling an overwhelming urge to gaze over his shoulder. Immediately, Almir does a quick hop left, turns himself ninety degrees, and places his palms out. There is a low, muffled boom like a firecracker exploding under water as he releases his storage; it isn't much, but it is enough to surprise his mentor and provide an opportunity for a knee to the gut.

Leon falls, defensively rolling a short distance, and then rests on his knees to regain his wind, which has been knocked out of him. Working to conceal his breath, Leon is tapped out. That one well-placed blow numbed him good. For a moment, as Almir presses on with his attack, Leon is lost in uncertainty.

As if coming from instinct, Leon slaps his palms to the ground. Suddenly the Earth shakes and then cracks beneath Almir, who is hoisted upward.

"Whoa! What did you do?" Almir gasps, clinging desperately to the twelve-foot-tall rocky spire that had somehow sprouted from out of nowhere. Pulling his hands away from the base of the pillar, Leon stares at his soiled, sweaty palms. The tingling sensation of aether still present within them.

"I don't know," he replies.

. . .

Ten hours on the road can be a challenge for any long-distance runner, and Seldin is no exception. Even with the aether to fuel him, twenty-two miles per hour just doesn't get you very far very fast, and his concentration is starting to wane just 130 miles from Georgia's border.

Seldin presses on, shaking the drowsy feeling from his head as he tries to regain focus on the northward presence still so very far away. The wooded areas he clings to keeps him off the public radar and forces him to rely entirely on his senses for navigation.

"Ugh…" Seldin sighs with exhaustion and slows to a stumbling wander before bending over his knees to catch his breath.

There's a soft rumble of thunder from overhead and he glances up, still panting, as drops start to fall.

"Great," he says, then pulls a power bar from his pack for a quick bite and sips some water from his canteen.

—*"Seldin!"*—a voice calls inside his head and he snaps his gaze north again before darting that way, jumping a narrow brook as he continues onward.

…

Leon creeps up to the tattered wooden fence of his backyard with a cautious peek through the broken slats. He dreads the idea of coming home, but where else can he go? Simon isn't really his friend, he sighs, and Seldin is gone.

"Huh-ummph!" He jumps over the fence in a single leap and lands hard on his hands and knees in the sandy sandspur infested patches of Florida grass.

"Ah—damn," he winces under his breath, picking a few sandspurs from his palm when he hears the murmuring voices of his mom, Ryan, and Chad through the open kitchen window. His stomach twists as he approaches the back door. He stops with a hesitant hand at the knob, then sighs with a soft shake of his head as he eases back and turns away.

"Maybe I can crash with Almir?" he whispers to himself.

"Leon!" squawks the chilling sound of his mother's ear-piercing voice. "Get in here!" she shouts through the house to the backyard.

His heart sinks immediately with a thump in his chest. "Damn," he says with a groan before adhering to her summons. The aroma of a peculiar southern herb fills the house, and he curls his nose to it as he steps inside.

"Where the hell have you been for the past two days?" Sarah scowls, taking a drag from a joint before passing it to Ryan, who takes a puff then hands it off to Leon's younger brother, Chad. Leon stands there holding his breath, while offering no reply.

"Nothing to say, huh? Well, Chad tells me you've been out fighting again—beating up on that Almir kid! What did I tell you about that martial arts nonsense?" she yells.

"Ryan practices," Leon responds.

"He has years of real experience from a real instructor," his mother says.

Leon scoffs. "Didn't help him on the beach," he says under his breath.

"I heard that." Ryan points his two joint-holding-fingers at him before handing it off again. "You think your friend Seldin knows everything, yet he was too chicken-shit to fight me because he knows his so-called skills are crap and practicing aether is a waste of time."

"You're the one who walked away, not him," Leon argues.

"You and his friends jumped me," Ryan claims, "I had to be the bigger man and walk away before somebody got hurt."

Sarah looks to her boyfriend, then back to her eldest son. "Is that what happened, Leo, you jumped your father?"

"No, that's bull—"

"I don't wanna hear another word. From now on, you are forbidden to practice that garbage!" she commands.

"But he's lying!" he shouts back.

"What'd I just say? Now get the hell out of my sight and do your goddamn chores!" She gives him a stern look, then points to the kitchen.

Leon grumbles and walks into the kitchen; he's so fired up he could hit something. He paces on the peeling linoleum floor like a lion scouring a cage.

"Ugh! That woman is sooo ssstuuupppiid!" he snarls, while glaring at the mess of pots on the stove and dishes in the overfilled sink. The aether within him responds to his emotions. He feels hot, and the water in the sink begins to boil.

His home life has always been like this, at least, ever since his father died—his real father. His mother became a ranting tyrant, and Chad, her little lapdog. Come to think of it, he's not even sure the last time he and Chad did anything that closely resembled brotherly.

As for his mother, it would take a psychiatrist years of regression to find a happy memory. The only good thing in his life this past year has been Seldin. He gave Leon an escape—a way out. Being a guardian is a hundred—no, a million times better than being his mother's bitch.

In that time after his father's death and before Seldin came along, Leon severely lacked confidence in himself and rarely conveyed his own thoughts or stated his own opinions. He was in a slump, but for obvious reasons. The only thing he seemed to care about at the time was the martial arts, and the only one he could learn from was Ryan. But one day, that changed.

It was four o'clock as Leon waited for the bus to arrive and take him home. He had only been in Florida a few weeks, the fourth term had just started, and Massachusetts was still home in his mind. As he waited there, practicing his forms in the shade, a teenaged boy a little older than him strolled by just as he shifted out of a T-stance into a right bow-stance.

"Hey, I know that one," the boy said. "Can you do this?" He jumped into a one-handed cartwheel, then into a jumping spin kick.

"No," the young Leon answered, "but I can do this." He pointed his hand to the abundance of leaves in the grass. "Wind and air, swirl and tease, spin them fast, spin the leaves." The air did just that, swooped down like a miniature cyclone and spun the loose particles for a short second before dropping the debris to the ground.

Seldin smiled. "Cool! Can you do it without the spells?" he asked.

Leon furrowed a brow—was that even possible? He wondered.

"Look." Seldin held out his arms like a tree bathing in the sun. The rustling of air through the trees grew louder as the energies around them moved to his core. With a quick turn of his wrist, he opened his palm to the pile of leaves and blew them away.

Leon hadn't seen anything like that before; no one he knew could do it without the words.

"It's called aether," Seldin presented this strange new word. "You should come hang out sometime, I'll show you more," he offered, and of course, Leon accepted.

His friend opened a door for him with a span of vastly new ideas, strategies, techniques, energy control, and the prospect of being greater— the legends of the guardians of old, and the potential of wielders. Maybe it was the way Seldin carried himself, or perhaps the way Leon carried himself around him. From that day forward, things started to change.

Leon couldn't wait to tell everyone about his newfound friend. The smile on his face and the joy in his heart made him glow, but his mother hardly felt the same. Sarah hated Seldin the very moment she set eyes on him. Maybe it was what he stood for that she despised so much, or maybe she saw him as a threat that would one day take her boy away from her. Whatever the reason, things grew more chaotic at home. Today isn't faring any better.

With his anger boiling to its max, he feels something strange—a pull, or a tug on him toward the sink and the faucet. There's a similar sensation coming from the stove and the pot of stagnant water with hotdogs still floating about, coated with a milky-white film.

Suddenly, there's a whistling sound of steam coming from the faucet. Looking to it, he then hears a rumbling rolling boil from the stove. Bsssssssssssssssssssssshhhhhhhhhhhhhh! The faucet bursts. Leon rushes over to it, fiddling with the knobs to calm the scalding flow, and as his heart shifts from an angered beat to a flutter of concern, the boiling ceases.

"I," he takes in what just happened, "did that?" Leon looks around at the mess of water on the floor, ceiling, and walls. He can still feel himself shaking from buried angler, the tingling pressure of aether in his meridians, and he sighs, resting with his hands on the edge of the sink to compose himself before starting to clean.

Chapter 8

"A Common Enemy"

Day breaks with faded puffs of white smoke trailing up into the morning sky from the dying campfire, while Seldin sits, meditating, his mind elsewhere despite the pleasant chirp of the birds singing in the trees.

—*"Seldin!"*—He hears that voice again and opens his eyes with a startled gasp—he's suddenly standing in a field with great jagged columns like termite mounds towering in the distant haze of a violet sky.

"Ugh!" Seldin jerks, shaking himself from the vivid vision. "I must be getting closer," he says before sensing something in the trees behind him. Immediately, he stands and turns, panning his gaze across the tree line.

"Hello?" He scans for anything that matches his senses; he could have sworn it was a person with the way the energy pushed against his own. After a few seconds of nothing, he sighs, figuring he's just on edge. Seldin then turns away to start packing his gear.

. . .

Tossing and turning, Leon struggles to find a comfortable spot on his tattered foam mattress, which lies directly on his cluttered bedroom floor and flattened like a squashed loaf of bread under his muscular frame. His hips sink right down to the thin layer of decades-old carpet.

He groans at the light coming through the broken horizontal blinds over his window to the backyard, and he rolls to his side, turning his face under the shade of his arm.

There's a swift kick to Leon's ribs and he quickly turns with a hand holding his side when he sees Ryan staring down at him.

"Get your ass up!" Ryan barks, then snaps his fingers. "Your mom wants you to mow the lawn and clean out the garage. My advice: start with the kitchen."

Leon's eyes follow Ryan as he steps out, and he listens to his footsteps and the sound of him walking out the back door before getting up. He sits there rubbing his groggy face for a minute or two, and then stands to peek out to the backyard; his mom is sunbathing like a beached whale in a lawn chair, while Chad practices sorcery. Ryan gives Sarah a quick peck on the cheek.

"I got someplace to be," Leon hears him say. He sighs, and then walks out to find the dining room table stacked with plates, cups, and half-eaten breakfasts; the kitchen is much the same with pans on the stove and dishes, once again, piled into the sink. Leon stands there in his tank top and boxer shorts, while trying to hold back the anger he feels filling his aura.

...

Within the inner sanctum of Watcher's Keep, Theresa kneels before a circular stone altar, which arcs around a whirling vortex of luminescent energy—much like the one at Cedar Park— recessed into a wall that was built around it like a mystical fireplace.

The Book of Roe is open beside her as she reads silently, tracing the lines of text with a finger, while placing various crystals onto the altar. Theresa then closes her eyes in prayer and mouths an incantation. In time, the crystals start to glow, and she picks up a small emerald for inspection.

There's a sudden grinding clank of the large double doors behind her, and she turns to see Neil and Elma barging in with four strangers: Ryan, Cory, Rico, and Joanne.

"Priestess!" Neil shouts.

"We've brought recruits!" Elma says with excitement.

Theresa stands with a look of irritation on her face. "This hall is sacred. How dare you bring uninitiates in here," she scolds.

Neil and Elma bow to their knees. "We're sorry, Priestess; it won't happen again," they plead.

Ryan makes a face. "Wait, I know you— you're that chick from at the beach," he scoffs with a brief look to his coven. "Aren't you a little young to be a priestess?"

"Aren't you old enough to know respect?" She points to the ground. "Ni etche," she chants in the Language of the Gods, forcing Ryan to his knees. He's surprised at first, then bows his head willingly before glancing back to Rico, Joanne, and Cory.

"On your knees, stupid!" Ryan shouts, and they promptly comply.

Theresa steps around them, "I asked for initiates, and this is what you bring? A fool and his followers? He already led you once, unprepared against two wielders, and for that you hurt your shoulder," she scolds them.

"I am not a fool, Priestess," Ryan says.

"No?" She turns and looks down at him. "Then tell me what you know about aether."

"Wha…" Ryan looks up with hesitation, confused by the question. "It… it's useless," he says.

"Useless?" She kneels, then takes his left wrist and turns his bandaged burn to the light.

"Ahh!" Ryan winces.

Theresa looks into his eyes. "I thought you said you weren't a fool," she says with a disappointed stare before standing.

"S-so, so they got lucky. So, what?" he questions.

Theresa walks to the altar and picks up the Book of Roe, then turns back to him. "What if I told you the greatest sorcerers in history—Merlin, Seimei, Bezalei—used aether and sorcery together?" she asks, and Ryan looks up at her with intrigue.

She continues: "Those secrets are in this book," she says, opening its pages for Ryan to see, and he stares with astonishment at the intricate layers of esoteric writing, unable to decipher the symbols.

"But—" Theresa closes it. "You need a connection to aether to read it." She turns her back to him and sighs. "Get out. You're no use to us," she says.

Ryan reaches out. "Wait!" He gathers his thoughts before speaking. "We s-share a common enemy, Priestess Theresa." He then looks to his followers. "We… know little about a-aether, but we're strong sorceress. M-maybe we can work together?" he presents with a bow of his head.

Theresa paces, mulling it over. "To defeat the wielders, you need to understand their power." She turns her gaze to Ryan. "Your son, Leon, is a wielder, correct?" she asks.

Ryan nods, hesitantly.

"He could be useful," Theresa says.

…

Outside the cathedral, Ryan slowly steps down the long stone stairs with his gang following behind. He seems distracted despite all the talking going on around him; his thoughts are fixated on the things Theresa said and her raw display of power. He's never seen sorcery used so effortlessly.

"I can't believe you let her talk to us like that," Rico says, but Ryan doesn't respond.

Cory looks to his friends. "I don't know about you, but I'd like to get my hands on that book," he says.

"I second that," Rico says.

"Yeah," Joanne agrees.

Right then, Neil comes running out. "Hey, Ryan!" he shouts after him. Cory taps Ryan's shoulder.

"Hmm?" Ryan looks to Neil.

"You guys comin back?" he asks.

"Uh, I don't know, we gotta think about it," he says before waving him off as they reach the sidewalk.

Neil sighs, then goes back inside.

Cory steps up beside Ryan. "Hey, wait— Ryan… come on, y-you're not really thinking of joining them?" he questions.

Ryan shrugs. "Maybe. You all saw what I saw; there's a real opportunity here," he says before walking off.

...

In the Sim-Antics lab, Simon connects an intravenous line to his wrist then presses a button on his computer. The screen heading shows a message: "Sim-Bots—version 1.5—dispensing." A clear metallic fluid flows through the tube into him.

Simon watches the percentage on the readout creep up to 100%.

"Initiate sequence," he says, and a digitized feminine voice responds.

"Aether test in 10… 9… 8…"

Simon unhooks himself from the console and takes a position out on the center floor.

"3… 2… 1…"

Simon grits his teeth, while focusing aether from his core to his aura. "Grr—aarruuhhh!" he grunts. The console shows the energy levels of the bots, and he can feel a burning sensation in his veins.

"Warning: power exceeding 1,127 joules," the computer says.

"Huuaarrrghhh!" he howls.

—Psssshhh! "Augh!" Simon yells as capillaries burst on his hands, arms, shoulders, and legs, and he drops down to a knee as he relaxes his core. A warning alarm sounds from the console, showing the microscopic bots overloading.

Simon winces, while examining the bloody and burned ruptures his hands. Dark veins move over the surface of his skin as the remaining bots work to repair the damage.

"Ugh…" He stumbles to his seat. The peak power reading shows a high of 1,163 joules.

"Show me last week's reading," Simon says, and the image on the screen divides into a side-by-side display showing the requested information: 970 joules. A smile stretches across his lips.

"That's progress," he starts typing, "but I've gotta find a way to manage the energy—" Simon reaches to the intravenous line and accidentally knocks a coil of copper wire from his desk. He picks it up and pauses in thought, examining it for a moment. "Hmm…"

…

Leon shuffles as he walks from the garage, lugging two overstuffed garbage bags—one in each hand—to the overfilled trashcans on the side of the house. He turns his head to the sound of laughter coming from the backyard, and he sighs, seeing Chad and his mom playing in the fading evening sun. His eyes trail down to the open trashcan before he crams the bags in and goes back to the garage.

There's a soft creak of the side door opening with his stepdad popping in. "Yo, Lee," Ryan says, approaching.

Leon turns to him, still heated from earlier, and he braces himself against the dusty wood table behind him. *'C'mon…'* Leon thinks, *'…just give me a reason,'* his mind races, but then something happens that he did not expect: Ryan's tone softens.

"Listen, your ma and I were talking, and she and I think maybe… we'll get along better if we spend more time together, like we used to. What do you think?" he asks.

This is the moment, Leon feels, a chance to be blunt. His head sways, as if to answer with his body language. "I don't like you, Ryan," he tells him honestly.

"Hey, don't be like that. To be honest, I don't much care for you, either. I think you're a smart-ass little punk, to tell you the truth, but for the sake of making this whole," he gestures with a motion of his hand, "family thing work, I'm willing to be a man and set my personal feelings aside to work things out."

Leon looks down, thinking.

"Why don't you come out with me and my buddies tonight? We can sit around, have a few drinks, and shoot the breeze. Hell, we can even talk martial arts. What do you say?" Ryan asks.

Leon just huffs, turning his back to him; there's no way he can replace his father, and surely, one night isn't going to make up for the last few years of discord.

"What would Sei do?" he asks himself.

...

The rapid cadence of Seldin's aether-powered steps echoes throughout the woods. He's close; he can feel it. The presence of whatever it is, is strong in his mind—and now… he's right on top of it.

Coming up on a small open field, Seldin leaps with a strong kick off a fallen log, and he twists into a half flip before landing in a crouching stance. He pants, catching his breath, then sits back on his rear. His hands press into the soft grass behind him with the unpleasantness of the hot summer sun beating down in the already humid heat.

He gets up, panning his gaze around to the arching trees that lead into the woods and a stone slab that looks somehow different from his vision. As if… something's missing.

"I'm… here," Seldin says, while scanning the immediate area with his eyes. "Where are you?"

Suddenly, a vine-like root wraps around his right wrist, and then…

Chapter 9

"The Initiates' Ritual"

The ride from Kenneth City to Clearwater Beach is a decent stretch, allowing for emotions to simmer down and thoughts to gather into something resembling the beginning of a conversation. Leon isn't certain of what to make of this change his mother and stepfather are employing. Maybe she really does wish for them to just get along as one big happy family, or maybe Ryan is just looking for a way in.

Seldin once told him to always be on guard with his senses sharp. With that in mind, Leon scans his surroundings, but nothing in the air or the even color of Ryan's aura seems out of place. Currently, he's running a smooth yellowish glow with hints of mauve to suggest that he's mostly content though slightly uneasy, perhaps as much as Leon. The other bodies in the car appear to be showing signs of intrigue, as if they're surprised or even curious that he is on board.

Leon tries to ignore the awkward glances coming from Joanne and Rico, who sit on either side of him in the back seat, and the occasional peeks from Ryan and Cory in the rearview mirror.

"So..." Joanne breaks the ice, angling herself more toward him, "...you practice aether?"

Leon tries to scoot back some, but there's nowhere to go with Rico so close on his other side.

"Uhh…" he looks to him staring, then back to her "…yeah," he says.

"Can you show us?" Rico asks.

Leon shies, uncomfortably. "Um…"

Ryan looks back at him through the rearview mirror as he drives. "It's ok, they're just curious," he says, with tone of uncharacteristic encouragement.

Cory then shifts in the front passenger seat to look back at Leon. "Yeah, you're the first wielder we've ever met."

"Well, first real one," Joanne interjects, "there are a lot of posers out there."

"But Ryan says you can really do it," Cory says with a raised brow, and Leon makes a suspicious face.

"Ok, now I know something's going on." Leon shifts his eyes between them.

"Haha," Ryan chuckles. "We're just trying to get to know you," he says.

"Come on, show us," Joanne says, sweetly.

Leon sighs, then looks around the car for something he can move—a crumpled wrapper, a coin—he then spots the pentagram charm on Joanne's necklace.

"Hold still," he says, bringing a hand up and aiming his open fingers toward it.

Joanne looks down at her necklace. Leon concentrates, feeling the metallic energy of the charm dancing on his fingers and the pressure building in his core. There's a sense of tingling warmth that moves from his abdomen up through his arm to his fingertips, and slowly, the charm rises with gentle tug on the silver chain around her neck.

"Oh, cool," Rico says with wide eyes.

Cory taps Ryan's arm. "Ryan, do you see this?" he asks, and Ryan glances back through the rearview mirror, while trying not to look surprised.

Joanne stares with astonishment, her mouth open at the sight of her charm floating in front of her face. "You really… can do it," she says with a hesitant smile.

Leon begins to feel a shift in the air and an unsteadiness in the flowing aether of the night as they approach the beach. He drops the connection to the necklace and looks around when he hears a dull monotone cadence.

"What's that sound?" he asks.

"Sorcerers chanting," Ryan answers.

At first, it's indistinct—a muddled jumble of layered voices and pounding drums of a similar note. However, in time, the strange chorus finds its way into the car with Rico, Cory, Joanne, and even Ryan humming it. Their auras shift to a more focused, excited hue, and as they get nearer, Leon starts to hear a more distinguishable set of syllables.

"Ka-rah! Ka-rah! Ka-rah!" Chanters all around the beach form up at the water's edge. Many of them rest on their knees along the shoreline, doing the traditional bowing of their arms and heads in open prayer, while others sway and dance. The sound of their combined voices creates a low resonating hum with each major syllable correlating with the tapping of a drum.

"Ka-rah! Ka-rah! Ka-rah!" they chant, again and again.

"I guess you've never been to a reiking ceremony," Joanne comments, watching him trying to make sense of it.

Leon makes a questioning face. "A what?"

"It's cooler if you see it," Cory says.

"See, Lee, sorcery isn't a bad thing like your friend claims. Look out there, what do you see?" Ryan asks.

Leon does as asked and gazes over the ever-growing crowd. "A bunch of people chanting and dancing," he answers.

"A bunch of people in unison, harmonizing. We're united as a group—a congregation of folks from all around, uniting here, right here for one single purpose."

Joanne smiles. "It's actually quite beautiful," she says.

Looking again, Leon ponders it, wondering if maybe Seldin was wrong about sorcery. The auras he sees flowing over the crowd seem to meld into a single bubble of emerald, steady and triumphant in whatever it is that they believe. Everyone here looks healthy, with no signs of their spirits being vamped. Still, he can't read their cores very well. Most of them feel normal, while others feel like voids. Wherever the energy that feeds their auras is coming from, he's not sure.

"What is that they're saying?" Leon asks.

"Kh-y-rah," Cory enunciates.

"It's the prayer for the god of chaos," Ryan says.

"Chaos?" Leon asks with a tone of concern.

Rico chimes in. "Unpredictability," he says, "through chaos comes order."

Joanne looks to Leon. "Our universe is governed by seemingly random or chaotic events—the way particles move or how galaxies form. Khyrah oversees them," she tells him.

"And us," Cory adds.

Ryan looks through the rearview mirror at Leon. "And by praying to her, she grants us favors in the form of spells," he says.

"It sounds like a cult," Leon smarts.

Rico turns abruptly in his seat, "Organized religion is merely a cult with more members," he states and Joanne snickers with an agreeing nod.

"Except our god exists," she comments.

"So you say," Leon rebuts.

"Look around you, Leon, the religions of the world are a dead cause. Otherwise, the planet wouldn't be in such a corrupt state," she says.

"So, their beliefs don't matter?" Leon asks.

Ryan laughs, "Their gods may have existed at one time, but Khyrah is the only god in this universe now," he claims.

As the car stops, the group exits and approaches the shore. "Come on," Ryan says, "you don't want to miss the light show."

"What light show?" Leon asks as the others look knowingly between themselves.

"I bet your friend has never seen anything like this." Ryan offers a tilt of his head to the sky at the darkened horizon where it looks like an aurora is taking place. Colors of all sorts shimmer and streak across the blackness like wispy swirling clouds.

With the chants growing louder, and Cory, Rico, Joanne, and Ryan joining them, the colorful streams begin to settle to an eerie arc of emerald, much like the crowd. The sky over the water lights up like a grid—a lattice, brighter at its intersecting points than at the braces but present, nonetheless. Ryan is right: he's never seen anything like it.

"Beautiful, isn't it?" A voice startles him, and Leon looks to Theresa approaching from his left. She smiles warmly with a strange book cradled in her arms. "I'm surprised to see you here," she adds.

"Eh… yeah… my um, mom wanted us to spend some…" he sighs at the thought, "…quality time together." Leon thumbs in the direction of Ryan and looks his way for a second or two before returning his gaze to the sky.

"I see," she says.

"What is this?" he asks.

"A reiking ceremony," Theresa answers, stepping closer to him.

"You mean, like… Chinese healing?" he asks, and Theresa shakes her head, while letting out a soft laugh.

"No, um… a reik—the earth is surrounded by an energy field we call the '*Reik*'—"

Leon nods. "Right, the magnetic field."

"No," Theresa shakes her head, "this is special: once a month, sorcerers around the world gather and offer their energy to charge it," she says.

Leon looks to her, confused. "But… I thought you had strict rules against people seeing magic," he says.

Theresa smiles. "They think it's the aurora, and we move around," she says.

"I didn't know," Leon says, watching the sky again.

"I'm sure there are a lot of things Sei hasn't told you," she comments, and Leon looks to her again. "We used to train together, you know?" she adds.

Leon nods. "He said you…" he lowers his eyes, "…only cared about sorcery and were dismissive of aether," he says.

Theresa's face reddens. "He was the dismissive one—wrote off sorcery out of fear!" she abruptly scolds, then composes herself.

"Sei's not afraid of sorcery, he just doesn't want to give his soul to that thing you worship," he says.

Theresa rubs her face. "But that's not..." she sighs. "In exchange for some energy, Khyrah offers us power and protection," she clarifies.

"But what are you really gaining? I mean, can you feel the energy in the air or sense the auras of others?" Leon asks.

"This..." Theresa gestures between them, "...is why me and Sei don't talk anymore." She shakes her head and walks away.

...

Gasping, Jasra clutches her throat as she wakes from a nightmare, letting out a heart-pounding, ear-piercing scream. It takes her a second to realize where she is. Ghosted images of terrifying plant-like creatures linger in her view, slowly fading softly into the dark bedroom.

"What was that?" she asks herself, attempting to put the pieces together. Her eyes then meander, falling to an empty room. "If only he'd come to bed." She sighs sadly before reaching to her nightstand for one of her many watches. Beep-beep! She sets it back down, disappointed. "I guess he's not coming back tonight." She shakes her head, listening to the sounds of his tools coming from the other room as she lies back, staring up at the darkened ceiling.

The blackness acts as a backdrop for the images, which seemingly project, as if mentally, in her field of view. She sees clouds billowing and fire encasing a large cigar-shaped body that penetrates the atmosphere with immeasurable force. It then opens, fanning out its petal-like structures as the clouds melt away, and it draws in the light of the sun.

"Dear God, what is this?" She rubs her eyes, pushing out what she thought was a terrible dream and then the woeful gaze of a friend catches her sight. The scene in her mind draws back, as if to dolly out like a camera, to offer a full view of the well-built man in white garb hovering before her. She barely recognizes him at first glance but her heart flutters in knowing who it is, and she offers a comforting hand to his shoulder as he stares out at the vessel, facing away from her. Her hand presses into the fabric, feeling the detail of the material and the firm muscle that lies beneath, as if he were really there.

"Sei?" Her voice trails in a paralyzing moment of disbelief, but then the tears in his eyes soften her beats as he glances back to her.

"I'm sorry," he says.

...

Out in the courtyard of Watcher's Keep under the full moon's light, Theresa, Neil, Elma, Ryan, Rico, Joanne, and Cory gather around a small altar resting on a ceremonial dressing on the ground.

Theresa sets the Book of Roe beside her, along with a gilded chalice, a decorated dagger, and a bottle of red wine.

Ryan glances to her, watching as she prepares for the ritual. He had been quiet since the beach; things didn't go quite as planned.

"I'm sorry about Lee," he lets out, genuinely worried about disappointing her.

"It's fine," Theresa says, without a look, "he just needs time to warm up to us. For now, we'll rely on what we know." She opens the Book of Roe to a section on coven binding, which gets a strange stare from Cory.

Neil and Elma grin widely at each other.

"We're really doing it!" Neil says with excitement.

"Yes!" They hug.

Cory gestures to the book. "Where'd you get that?" he asks Theresa.

Joanne and Rico, take interest.

"It was a gift from the Guardian of Knowledge," she answers.

Joanne shakes her head dismissively, and Rico looks off.

"Ugh," Cory scoffs, "guardians aren't real," he retorts, and Theresa rolls her eyes.

Suddenly, Joanne reaches for it.

"No!" Theresa pins her hand to the ground and stares into her eyes for a few seconds to calm herself. "It will kill you," she says.

Joanne stares back. "Yeeaah riight," she says, pulling her hand away.

There's a snicker from Neil. "You should throw it at Simon," he smarts, and Elma elbows him in the ribs. "Ow!" He looks to her. "What?" He then looks to Theresa. "I can't wait to see his stupid face."

Ryan nods in agreement. "Yeah, let's see how his aether holds up to a coven," he says.

"Yeah!" Cory high fives his friends, excited for a real fight.

Elma looks to Theresa. "What about Jasra?" she asks with concern.

"Who's that?" Joanne asks.

"Simon's girlfriend," Neil answers.

"Wielder?" Ryan looks to Theresa, who nods. "Then she goes down, too," he says.

Theresa shakes her head. "Jasra is innocent in this; we can't hurt bystanders, and at no point can we expose real magic to the public. We need to be careful," she says.

Rico speaks up. "I have a concealment spell that should work for any prying eyes, but the fewer people, the better. Where are we doing this, anyway?" he asks.

Theresa looks among the group. "That's a good question. Any suggestions?" she asks.

"How about the mall?" Elma suggests.

Joanne shakes her head. "Too crowded."

"What about the beach? Sorcerers practice there all the time," Ryan says.

"Or the square," Cory adds.

Theresa sighs. "Crowds, guys—and how often do you see wielders at either of those places?"

"Riight, right," Ryan says.

"Uh, wait…" Neil holds up a finger, "…doesn't Simon have that warehouse?" he asks.

Elma thinks but doesn't answer.

"Warehouse?" Cory looks to him.

"Yeah, I went out there with Sei, once; it… it's a block from their apartment. That's where Simon runs his business," Neil says.

Theresa shakes her head. "If it's a business, then he's got employees," she says.

"No, I think it's all automated," Neil says.

"Just him?" Ryan asks.

"I'm pretty sure, yeah," Neil replies.

Theresa nods. "That… actually makes sense," she says, thinking about what she knows of Simon.

Joanne flicks her eyes her way. "So, Priestess, what are we up against?" she asks with a tone.

"All I can tell you is what I know, what I've learned." She pauses in thought. "Wielders don't pray to Khyrah like we do; they draw their power from inside." She taps her lower abdomen. "They call it the core," she says.

"Sounds like bullshit to me," Cory scoffs, fiddling with his sword.

"It's not," Theresa states, placing a hand on his arm. There's a hint of discomfort on her face when a sudden electrical surge flows through like he's being tazed.

"Ah—shit!" He quickly pulls away, rubbing his arm.

Neil backs up with wide eyes. "You can?" He gestures to Cory.

"I had training," Theresa says with a glance to Neil.

"If you can do that, why not teach us?" Ryan asks with yeahs from his group.

"I know enough to make me a better sorcerer but to teach it…" she sighs and shakes her head, "…for that you'll want a wielder." Theresa's gaze sinks. "I was lucky to have a mentor—and even then, it took me months," she says.

"Heh-heh, and you think my shit-stain of a stepson can do that?" Ryan laughs.

"I was hoping he'd be more willing, but yes," Theresa replies.

Cory speaks up. "Leo showed off his aether in the car; it wasn't that impressive, to be honest."

Theresa shrugs. "He can project it, even I can't do that," she says.

"Can Ss—what's his name?" Joanne asks.

"As far as I know, they all can to some degree, but every wielder is different… no two are alike, but…" Theresa sighs. It feels wrong sharing these secrets—secrets earned from her haloed position—or perhaps it's more that she's betraying old friends. She continues.

"They each have a specialty—something that comes natural or easy for them," she says.

"Like what?" Rico asks.

"Jasra can see things before they happen," she says and they all look to her, intently.

"Are you serious?" Cory asks.

"No way," Joanne says in disbelief.

"That's another reason we don't want her in the fight; she's not as strong as her friends, but it's hard to beat someone who knows what's coming."

"Simon's is gadgets, isn't it?" Neil asks.

Ryan silently rubs his wrist.

Theresa nods. "Electronics, I think; tech stuff," she says.

Neil's eyes drift down. "Like the microphone," he says, softly.

Ryan looks to Theresa. "What about Sei?"

Theresa shakes her head. "Mm, I don't think we need to worry about him; he told me he was leaving for college after graduation," she says.

"Damn," Ryan sighs, "I was hoping to take a swing," he says despite Theresa's disapproving glare.

"We need to stay focused on our target. No casualties," Theresa says.

Ryan nods. "Right. Simon," he says.

"Simon," Theresa responds.

Neil, Elma, Cory, Rico, and Joanne all say in unison, "Simon."

"Well, then, it's settled. Are we ready?" Theresa asks the group, and they all nod. "Then let us pray." She fills the golden chalice with red wine, and then holds it up before setting it on the altar.

"With this, my brothers and sisters," Theresa pricks her finger with a small, decorated dagger and squeezes a few drops of blood into the cup, "we shall be united by spirit and bound by blood." She passes the chalice and blade to Neil, who does the same before passing it on to Elma.

Theresa continues: "May this pact of our coven bring us knowledge, protection, and strength," she says.

The chalice makes its way back around to Theresa, who holds it up, and then chants: "My body, my blood, my spirit, my mind, my coven, my life, this I bind." The cup glows, and she takes a sip before passing it back to Neil.

He takes it with a soft bow of his head, then holds it up. "My body, my blood, my spirit, my mind, my coven, my life, this I bind," he chants, then sips, and then passes it on to Elma.

Looking down from the third-story walkway, Lamryl watches over the young priestess and her followers sipping and chanting below. A darkly dressed figure stands beside her.

"Are you sure about this, Master Guardian?" she asks with concern.

Tillman nods.

Chapter 10

"Best Served Cold"

There's a soft hum of a sewing machine in the living room as Jasra stitches sections of green fabric into the shape of a form-fitting, athletic romper—a one-piece body suit with shorts, short sleeves, a buttoned chest, and a folded collar. She carefully checks and rechecks the hand-drawn design sketched and measured out on the coffee table.

Beside the table is a pair of green knee-high riding-style boots, open on the sides from ankle to top and held together front to back with faux leather straps. Burgundy knee-high socks lay draped over them, but the most important part—Jasra whips a large piece of green cloth, letting the ends flutter in the air—is the cape.

Excitement fills her, and she gets up to try it on and test the fit before walking to the bedroom to admire herself in front of a large vanity mirror. Her reddish-brown hair makes for a striking contrast with the green of the outfit.

"Guardian of Time," Jasra says with her left hand out toward the mirror. She snickers, then looks down at her pasty bare thighs. She lightly slaps them. "Hmm, something's missing. Should I do a skirt or tights? I could definitely use a belt.

What about gloves?" she ponders, when suddenly, there's a knock at the door.

Jasra directs her keen senses that way with a puzzled look on her face. "What's she doing here?" she asks herself before walking out to the living room to open the door.

Theresa smiles falsely; she's obviously uncomfortable. "Hi," she says.

Jasra's face shifts to confusion. "Hi," she replies. "This is… unexpected."

"May I come in?" Theresa asks.

Jasra nods, letting her inside.

"You look good," Theresa says.

Jasra blushes. "Oh, thanks," she looks down at herself, a little embarrassed, "it's, uh… wh-why are you here?" she asks.

"To keep you out of the fight," Theresa says before presenting an emerald, which shimmers with green light—the moment distorts, returning to just before she opened the door.

Jasra stops, her hand shaking over the knob; her mind races to make sense of it all. "Simon," she mutters to herself before darting out the balcony door and leaping over the railing. She focuses, projecting aether to cushion her two-story descent—kathump!

"Ugh!" She hits the ground harder than expected, lightly cracking the concrete as she lands on her hands and knees before taking to an aether-powered sprint south toward Simon's lab.

Theresa knocks on the door again. "Hello?" she calls out, "Jasra?" she calls again, then tries to sense through the door. Her mind strains in the effort, and she looks down the hall to Elma, who is standing guard by the stairwell. *"She's not there,"* she says telepathically with a hand to her temple.

Elma hears her voice in her mind. "That's so cool…" she says to herself, not sure she'll ever get used to it. She presses a finger to her temple. *"Neil, careful, Jasra's not here,"* she out loud, but like her, he receives the message telepathically.

"Right, I gotcha," he replies, just as Ryan pulls into the Sim-Antics' parking lot with only Simon's jeep in attendance. Ryan, Neil, Rico, Joanne, and Cory get out of the car and head toward the main entrance.

Rico begins to gesture, tracing the perimeter with his eyes as he points to the corners of the compound. "Make this space, I've defined, a secret place for none to find," he chants, and from the outside of the parking lot looking in, Rico and his comrades appear to vanish.

Inside the lab, Simon is busy running lines of copper wire through layers of neoprene when a familiar computerized voice alerts him.

"Unscheduled visitors approaching," it says, showing security footage on his main monitor.

Simon glances at it, not really paying attention at first, but then he snaps his gaze back to the monitor for a closer look when he realizes it's Neil and Ryan.

"Ohh, you're in the wrong back yard," he grins with a rush of panicked excitement as he quickly attaches the nanite injector to his wrist and hits the start button; version 1.7 begins to flow into him. The readout on the screen shows: "Warning: Untested," and Simon grits his teeth then braces himself against a chair as dark veins of nanites spread out over his graying skin.

Outside in the parking lot, Ryan, Neil, and the other sorcerers form up at the main entrance, and peer through the glass doors into the empty office space that shields the lab and production areas from view.

"Yo, Simon!" Neil shouts.

Ryan tries the door; it's locked. He turns to Cory. "Open it," he says with a tilt of his head to the door.

Cory nods, then takes a stance, waving his hands over the glass as he prepares a spell. Ryan and the others clear a path.

"Quick and sharp, small and narrow," golden energy starts to emerge, "this I cast, a magic—ooaaff!"—A sandaled foot smashes his face, sending him to the ground at his friends' feet as Simon lands from an open second-story window.

"Oh, I'm sorry, were you saying something?" Simon laughs.

Ryan and Neil quickly take protective stances in front of Cory, while Rico and Joanne help him up.

"You're gonna pay for that!" Neil grunts.

"Me? And here I was about undo your expulsion," Simon says to Neil.

"You liar!" Neil exclaims, about to charge him, when Ryan holds him back.

Simon shrugs. "Guess you'll never know," he says, then looks to Ryan with a gesture of his eyes to his left wrist. "Nice burn. One ass-whoopin wasn't enough, huh?"

Ryan scoffs with a look to his friends. "Do you believe this guy? He gets lucky with a little aether, and he thinks he can take us all. Open your eyes, dumbass, you're outnumbered," he says.

"Oh, I have." Simon scans each of them through his goggles. "Five powerful sorcerers against one pathetic wielder—huh," he brings a hand to his chin, "I'm actually kind of flattered," he says with a smirk.

"That's it!" Neil throws his hands down to break free of Ryan's hold and rushes at Simon, swinging a wild right fist to his face.

Simon slips inside his guard and deflects Neil's strike with his forearm, while wrapping his wrist around his, and he turns, lining him up with the glass door before sending him through it with a straight fist to his chest—crash! The glass shatters and Neil smashes into the empty receptionist desk.

"And that was called," Simon mocks, cracking up, "why I'll never graduate!" he gloats just as Ryan, Rico, and Cory grab him from all sides, and he twists and turns to center himself. His movements pull and drag them along; to them, it's like trying to wrangle a bull.

While they struggle, Joanne sees an opportunity. She begins to chant: "Skies above and ground below," clouds start to form overhead with flashes of lightning and pops of thunder.

"Not this time!" Simon yanks his hands in close to his chest, gathering aether. Ryan and Cory, who each have one of his arms, get slammed together.

"Huarrrgghh!" Simon howls, thrusting his hands out, while releasing energy in all directions—throwing his enemies back.

"Ohhgg!"

"Ahh!"

"Oaf!"

Ryan and Cory meet the pavement, while Rico becomes friends with the warehouse wall behind him, knocking himself cold.

Simon then turns with a backhanded motion to Joanne, telekinetically slapping her across the mouth, midsentence.

"Argh!" She falls back on her rear with her hand on her busted lip.

Cory grits his teeth as he rolls to his side and draws his sword. "Son of a bitch!" He pushes himself from the ground and charges in, swinging low, then high, and then across.

Simon strafes and ducks out of his opponent's attacks, while watching through his goggles. Cory's core is only 140 joules, which shouldn't be a problem, but his own energy is fluctuating sporadically with spikes over 2,200 and dips as low as 30. Small dark veins start to appear on his skin as failing bots pool beneath the surface, and he stumbles weakly right as Cory lands a successful hit—grazing him with a diagonal slice across his chest.

"Mmph!" Simon grunts, clutching the wound before dropping down to a knee with a retching cough of a clear gray fluid into his hand.

"Ugh, that's not good," he pants with a gritty sensation in his teeth and a metallic taste in his mouth—but there's no time to focus on that— his goggles signal a warning, and he looks up at Cory swinging down at him.

"Haahhh!" Cory howls with fury— clatink—"Huh?" He looks and is surprised to see the blade caught in Simon's hand.

Simon closes his fist, squeezing blood out from around the sword, which Cory wiggles and twists, trying to break it free. Nanites move through the torn flesh of Simon's palm and fingers to heal the cuts and shield him from the razor-sharp edge.

"Grr!" Cory grunts and tries to force the sword down with all his strength; the runes along the blade start to glow.

Simon's hand heats up. He focuses with a grimace and grabs the blade with both hands.

Ryan shakes the daze from his head, then slowly pushes himself up from the glass-covered ground. "Ugh…" He looks out to the sounds of the scuffle before taking position, catercorner to Simon.

"Weak and weary," Ryan begins the chant, while waving his hands about.

Simon snaps his gaze to him, then pushes him back with a telekinetic shove.

"Oaf!" Ryan stumbles back.

Joanne follows Ryan's lead on the opposite side, continuing the chant. "Slowing down!"

…

Jasra doesn't see or hear anything as she approaches the lab; to her, it's as if no battle is taking place. There are no sorcerers, no screams, and the building is intact. That changes, however, the moment she sets foot on the parking lot. Like crossing some invisible barrier, the veil is lifted, and she gasps at the sight of Simon holding back Cory's glowing sword with a bloody hand, while trying to telekinetically fend off Ryan and Joanne.

"Simon!" she yells at the top of her lungs, and Cory, Ryan, and Joanne snap her way as she makes a beeline toward Cory, who immediately front kicks Simon in the chest, knocking him back on his pride, before taking a swinging slash across Jasra's midsection.

Jasra ducks back, cushioning herself with aether as she slides on her knees under the blade, and then twists with a sweep of her right heel to the back Cory's ankle, flinging his foot over his head, causing him to torque up off the ground before landing flat-back on the pavement.

"Ah—huuughhh!" Cory's breath leaves him with a thud.

There's a tinge of relief in Simon's heart when Jasra takes a defensive stance between him and the two remaining sorcerers—her aura is steady at just over 600 joules—with a hand aimed at each of them.

"Back… off," Jasra says sternly to Ryan and Joanne, who each show their empty hands and stop chanting. Her eyes shift to Simon. "You, ok?" she asks as she stands down and turns to him, finally getting a good look at his pale tone. "Why the fuck are you gray?"

"What the fuck are you wearing?" he rebuts.

Screeching tires skid into the parking lot as an old burgundy sedan comes to a halt. Theresa hops out of the car, carrying a walking staff with a large ruby on top. Elma follows behind.

Simon gets to his feet and takes a stance beside his girlfriend.

Ryan makes a gloating face as his friends walk up. "You're in for it now," he says to Simon and Jasra.

"Shit, we're late," Theresa says, while taking in the scene with Cory and Rico laid out.

Elma scans with concern. "Where's Neil?"

Simon gestures with a tilt of his head behind and to his left, and Elma's eyes follow the trail of broken glass through the shattered doors to her bloodied boyfriend lying face down, whimpering.

"Neil!" she screams and goes to rush in.

"Auh-auh!" Simon raises his hands, levitating the shards of glass around himself and Jasra in a threatening posture. "You can have your man when you stand down," he says.

Schling—Cory's sword tings as Joanne picks it up from the ground. "Liiike hellll!" she yells with a stabbing thrust toward Simon. There's a sudden beep-beep of a watch when Jasra crescent-kicks the sword, hooking the blade with the outside of her boot as she slams it to the pavement under her foot. This abrupt redirection pulls Joanne along with the sword, lining her up for a roundhouse to the face.

"Uugh!" She spits blood, drops the sword, and the two square off. Joanne leads with a punch, round kick, and spinning back kick, while Jasra slips, steps, and dodges easily with minimal movement as she replies with counter attacks of her own: a left hook to the ribs, a right cross to the chest, and a front kick to the gut.

Joanne stumbles back and tries again, but she can't seem to land a single hit despite her best efforts; it's like everything she tries, gets herself tagged several times.

In that moment, Simon sends shards of glass hurling toward Theresa, Elma, and Ryan. Ryan dives to the ground, leaving them to fend for themselves, and Elma flinches with a loud shriek when she sees the volley of jagged edges. She quickly brings her arms up to cover her face.

Bwoosh—bwoosh—the pieces of glass collide with a shimmering orange barrier that envelops the three of them. The diamond-shaped pendant on Elma's neck lights up with the center gem and edge runes glowing in sync with each shard that splashes into the rippling force field of magical energy.

Simon doesn't let up. He continues showering them with chunks, fragments, and slivers like a gatling gun of broken glass as his optics feed him precious information about each strike; the more aether he puts in, the harder Elma's pendant counters—that's it—he realizes.

His goggles lock onto the gemstone with the analysis appearing on the screen in plain lines of superimposed text: "Material: Amethyst. Mass: 78.64 grams. Frequency: 7.5×10^{14} Hz. Aether Output: 489.91 joules/second."

With his mind, he switches the view in his goggles to the warnings of his own sporadic energy—the nanites are down 50%, while his core struggles to maintain a reliable output. As much as it pains him, he makes the decision to disable the remaining bots. Immediately, his core stabilizes to his natural baseline of 639—and he refocuses—pushing it threefold to 1,917. There's a loud warning as he redlines. Small gashes start to sprout on his skin

"Aaarrgghhh!" he exclaims—overloading the barrier. The energy fluctuates violently, and the pendant shatters. Elma falls back, tripping over Ryan, just as Simon rushes in with a right roundhouse to the left side of her face—swoosh—he barely misses before she hits the paved ground.

Simon then follows through with the momentum and twists to deliver a fierce spinning back kick aimed at Theresa's abdomen. Suddenly, a force out of nowhere knocks his leg off target, causing him to stumble. He settles into in an awkward stance with his back to Theresa.

Dean casts a surprised gaze to the Guardian of Death, who calmly lowers a hand aimed at Simon. "That's not like you," Dean says, and Tillman merely angles a sideways glance at him.

"No need for an innocent death," he says to the Guardian of Dimension as they continue to observe from their dimensional duck blind.

"Hmph," Dean lets out a reptilian snort; his skin briefly shifts into something scaly.

With Simon's back to her, Theresa aims the ruby of her staff. "Bae robell!" She fires a red energy bolt at him.

Jasra focuses and quickly swipes her hands to the right, using aether to deflect the blast—kaboom—it blows a chunk out of the building.

Simon lets out a startled breath in realizing how close that was; the energy reading in his goggles recorded Theresa's attack at over 400 joules despite her core of 234, which is more than he ever expected from a sorcerer. With that in mind, he scans Ryan, Joanne, and Elma, who are 161, 137, and 112, respectfully.

"Are you trying to kill us—what the hell's wrong with you?" Jasra scolds with a gesture to the devastation.

"That's what you get when you mess with sorcerers!" Ryan shouts as he and Elma get up.

Jasra makes a face of disgust. "Who's messing with who, here? You started the fight on the beach," she points to Ryan, "and you led the attack here!" She points to Theresa.

Elma steps up, feeling defensive. "Well, Simon got Neil expelled!" she shouts.

"Because he jumped me!" Simon retorts.

"Enough!" Jasra screams, then looks to Theresa. "Is this the kind of leader you want to be?" she asks, holding back the pressure behind her eyes.

Theresa looks down with a sigh of shame.

Jasra wipes away angry tears. "Sei was right about you," she sniffles, "our friendship is over," she says to her, then places a hand on Simon's shoulder with a stern look into his eyes. He nods, letting the glass shards fall to the ground.

Elma runs into the mangled office to help Neil, who yelps as she lifts him. "Help me!" she shouts, and Ryan gives her a hand.

Joanne turns her bruised and bloodied face to Theresa. "Their guard's down; let's rush them," she suggests, taking a stance.

Theresa's eyes stay low as she shakes her head without a glance to Joanne. She simply gestures with an open hand for her to stand down.

"Heh-wha—are you afraid of her?" Joanne gestures to Jasra in disbelief.

"Try me, because I can see everything you do before you do it." Jasra brandishes the two watches on her right wrist, while readying her left hand to the timers.

Given what Joanne's experienced already, and what Theresa has told her, perhaps it's true. She makes a sneering face, while looking over the petite girl with her flowy reddish-brown hair and green outfit. Her eyes fall to the hourglass-shaped patch on her chest. "And what are you supposed to be?" she scoffs, holding back a laugh.

Jasra's eyes stay locked with Joanne's. "I'm the Guardian of Time," she answers.

Dean crosses his arms and casually strokes his scaly beard with a glimmer of hopeful pride in his eyes. "They're getting stronger," he says.

Tillman doesn't break from his thoughtful gaze. "Still… no match for what's coming."

Chapter 11

"Signs of Fray"

"Aaarrrgghhh!" Joanne screams into a mirror at the sight of her nose busted and her face bruised to a ripe shade of purple. "Damn her!"

Ryan glances through the half-opened door of Theresa's bathroom and makes a face at the not-so-pretty sight of blood-soaked cotton balls sticking out of Joanne's nose as she patches herself up. They're all licking their wounds, of course.

Rico sits, holding an icepack to his bandaged head, while Ryan tapes Cory's ribs.

Theresa tries to ignore her; she feels bad enough about the outcome. Carefully, she pulls glass from Neil's arms with Elma's help. Neil winces with a wide grimace. Some of the shards are quite long.

Staring at her reflection, Joanne gently rubs her cheek, stretching the skin, while pressing to feel how deep the bruises go. "Soft and supple, clear and free, take these bruises away from me," she chants, but the bruises don't fade; instead, they grow larger and deeper.

A loud, wrenching scream comes from the bathroom. They all look that way, and Theresa sighs, seeing Joanne's face as she peers out.

"What the hell?" Joanne shrieks.

Cory gets up with a wince to check on her.

"You can't use spells for healing. Here." Theresa passes her a cup of herbal tea—smack! Joanne knocks it away. The cup shatters, and Neil twitches at the sight of more broken glass.

"Ugh," he lets out.

"I don't want your advice or your help! It's because of you, I look like this!" she yells.

"I warned you about Jasra!" Theresa shouts back at her.

"Yeah, well, how do you think we did today, Highness?" Joanne gestures to her friends, who are equally broken and battered.

Theresa's gaze moves across them. "Worse than I thought. Better than I hoped," she says, softly with strong stares from Joanne, Cory, Rico, and Ryan.

"Heh," Cory scoffs, "what the hell's that supposed to mean?" he asks.

"We broke even—"

"Even? You call this breaking even?" She gestures to their injuries. "We got our asses kicked because of you! You were supposed to lead us to victory!" Joanne shouts, then grabs her things. "Let's go, guys," she says to her friends.

Cory and Rico get up, but Ryan seems hesitant. He sighs, thinking for a few seconds before following them.

Theresa looks at Neil and Elma as she applies the last of his bandages. "You should go too," she says with her eyes low.

...

Winding gears and whining electric motors are buzzing loudly and humming up the room. Simon has been rather busy the last few days, burning the midnight oil long into the night, testing, calibrating, and retesting again and again. Time seems to pass him by as he tinkers.

Vzz-rr-rr-vzz sounds the micro drill, tightening a screw. Reaching for a small capacitor, he then maneuvers his head to see through the mountain of debris cluttering his workstation; microchips, tools, and various computer parts are all scattered about the place.

Chuckling to himself, he thinks about the future—the way he'll handle things the next time sorcerers come to his door—and the crap he'll pull when Seldin returns. His mind drifts to the absence of his best friend, and for a moment, he considers how wrong they were in their previous assumptions with a glance to the most recent data.

With his focus so involved in his work, he doesn't even hear Jasra come into the room. She was asleep, but the crack of light and the annoying sounds of his tools woke her. She steps around the cluttered mess of his overcrowded workroom, now filled with boxes, supplies, and equipment salvaged from the lab.

"Come to bed," she lets out softly, while nestling her head gently and pressing her chest against Simon's back.

He turns with a soft sigh. "I'm working. Besides, I know he's working just as hard," he says.

"Speaking of…" she starts to say with her head resting on his shoulder, "…I don't feel him anymore. I haven't felt him for a few days now; it worries me."

Simon shrugs, offering a soft kiss. "He's probably just out of range. I wouldn't worry. Sei can handle himself. Go back to sleep," he says, while running his fingers affectionately through her hair.

"But I want you to come with me. Your projects will still be there in the morning," she says, tightening her hug around him.

Shaking his head, Simon lets out, "I can't Hun; the data I got from the fight has been invaluable. I'm so close to getting this prototype ready. I can't stop now," he says, turning his gaze back to the project at hand and pulling the tiny magnification device on the head-mount over his eye.

Jasra feels annoyed; she has her own passions for their training, but not now. She wants her boyfriend to at least spend a few hours with her, even if it meant only sleeping. She crosses her arms and sighs out of frustration, sitting down beside him while grazing his arm with her emerald nightgown.

"What exactly are you working on that can't wait till tomorrow?" she inquires, then touches the spongy material on his desk.

Simon grins widely, staring through the magnified view. "It's a bio-suit. I finished coding the software a couple hours ago. Now I'm working on the hardware," he answers.

Jasra shrugs. "Well, it looks like diving gear to me," she comments, while picking at it.

Simon displays the fabric, peeling back the layers. "I guess it could look like a scuba suit. On the outside, it's neoprene for flexibility and comfort, between the layers of neoprene are several layers of spectra-shield to redirect the energy from blunt force attacks; the electronics will draw that energy in to benefit me," he laughs, imagining a scuffle. "Then, on the inside, there's a bio-synthetic gel to keep me well insulated, warm, and prevent itching. It will also help carry nerve signals so that I can feel the material as if it were a second skin, basically," he explains.

Jasra yawns, making a tired face. "That's so cool," she comments. "So, if I were to touch you, you would feel it?"

"Right," he answers.

"And if I tried to hit you, the suit would just steal my energy?" she asks.

Shaking his head, he responds, "No, it won't pull your energy out of you, it just takes the force of the impact and converts it into energy, then gives me a charge. I can't wait to use it on Sei. Can you imagine how pissed he'd be when he realizes he can't hurt me?" Simon chuckles.

She smiles back, and snickers at the idea, if only halfheartedly. They are all very competitive with each other, so anything to tip the scale, even a dick-move like this, is always a source of amusement. Simon keeps on talking for a while about his grand scheme and how this suit will enable him to realize his goal of becoming the Guardian of Technology.

"Mmm." She exhales, while listening and resting her chin in her hand propped with an elbow on his desk. Simon continues to fiddle with the material, attaching one odd instrument to it after another.

"And what are these things?" she questions, feathering the thin metallic barbs protruding from the inside of the spine of the material.

Simon gestures, "They burrow down into my meridians and help carry aether from my core, making me faster when it comes to using energy abilities. While we are on the subject, how's your training going? I see you added another watch," he comments, noticing the three watches trailing up her right wrist just under the sleeve of her nightgown.

Smiling, she brushes her left hand over her right arm, feeling for them; she pauses, looking down at her arm in an attempt to avoid her initial reply, which she thinks will be too rude even for her. She wants to tell him that if he had been spending time with her, he would probably know the answer, but instead she looks back up at him and says, "I'm getting better at foreshadowing and the watches give me a frame of reference between an episode and the event that comes after it. They've been occurring more and more frequently, sometimes on top of one another; the watches make it easier to keep track," she tells him.

"Ah... I see, but don't you mean foreseeing?" he asks in a corrective tone.

"Whatever!" she scoffs.

Laughing he says, "I'm just teasing."

Beep—sounds a watch as she presses the button. For her, the moment plays on for a little over two minutes—beep. She stops it.

"What's that?" Simon seems curious.

Jasra simply shakes her head, while making a childish squinty face.

"Well, I have something else I want to show you," he says, rummaging through the clutter of his desk. "Ah, here it is—fresh off the centrifuge." He presents a clear vial of liquid.

Jasra takes the sample and fiddles with it for a moment as she examines the solution. "Nanites, version two," she says calmly with a smirk.

Simon draws back in his chair for a second, returning her a puzzled look. "And how did you know that, dear?" he asks.

"Like I said, I've been working on my foresight," she answers allowing her inner child to come out once again as she playfully blows him a raspberry.

Chapter 12

"Hunger Pangs"

Enveloping him, it wraps its leafy extremities, vine-like as they are, around his limp, almost lifeless body, nestling firmly, close to his flesh like the giant squid that entangled Captain Nemo's submarine. It feeds on his very living essence as he lies helplessly, trapped within the vessel of his own comatose body.

He feels no pain, and although he is consciously unaware of the danger, a lingering presence exists in his mind. Flashes of red and black flood his dreams with images of a terrifying creature. It stands like a man, though its movements are shifty and awkward; it shuffles as it walks, swaying from side to side, and has greenish-brown coloring like a lizard, yet its limbs are twisted and tangled with layers of tightly wrapped foliage, fluttery and leafy like a tree with sharp tooth-like thorny protrusions where a mouth should be.

Seldin curses at it harshly—shouting obscenities—in an attempt to summon up anger from deep within himself to bury his fear and convert it into something more useful. The energy pushes out from the core of his being, radiating through his skin and into his aura. With a grunting groan, he heaves, generating a defensive matrix, but the creature does not budge; it latches on even tighter than before, allowing itself to be bathed in the energy he freely gives up, unintentionally satisfying its raging and undying hunger.

And that's how it went for a while. For several days now, he's experienced this hellish limbo, unable to escape. The entity continues to feed, bringing him to the brink and back—over and over—but it won't kill him. Instead, it brings him to within an inch of his life, then releases its grip long enough for him to regain his strength so it can start feeding again.

But then, it stops.

As the rain comes and the weather changes, the air grows colder. The sunlight recedes from the crest of the canopy overhead as the clouds steadily move in, bringing the whooshing roar of the downpour—spewing forth tiny sparkling beads that pelt the trees and the surrounding vegetation, while filling the air with an intense rumbling rhythm that drowns out the majority of the ambient woodland sounds. And for the first time in days, Seldin's eyes open as he awakens to the cool sensation of the drops running down his face, clinging to what feels like a week's worth of growth. He looks up at the falling rain as he rises from his back then presses his right hand into the moistened soil beneath him, using what strength he has to reach a half-seated position. His eyes then catch their first real glimpse of the terrible attacker, the thing that has kept him hostage these last few days. It isn't a giant squid or even a ferocious plant monster for that matter; in fact, there is nothing frightening about it—just a tiny rose flower rooted to the middle of his chest with a white ball of fluff, like a dandelion, in the center of its blooming bulb.

As he goes to touch it, the flower twitches and startles him. The bulb then closes up, while the vine-like roots retract, and the small plant drops off, falling to his lap. He reaches behind himself, slinging his duffle bag to his side and quickly pulls out a jar with a sewing needle suspended from the inside of the lid by a string. Popping the jar open, he removes the trinket, packs in a few handfuls of moistened dirt, then quickly sets the flower inside.

"What the hell are you?" he asks aloud, examining it through the glass. A clap of thunder steals his attention with an ear-shattering boom that soon fades, swallowed up by the sound of the rain. He knows he can't stay out here—cold and soaked to the bone—and sitting in almost an inch of mud. Food and shelter are his priority now, for he will need to regain his strength before he can press on. His curiosity will have to wait. Putting his things in his bag, he then looks for a place to shield himself from the weather.

This little patch of woods is pretty big for what it is, about a hundred acres or so, and the closest thing to being in the wilderness he has ever been. Woods this thick don't come often in Florida, where he grew up, but this isn't Florida—Virginia, maybe? Or perhaps one of the Carolinas? Seldin isn't sure. The distance gone and the time traveled are still a blur and it doesn't help that he stayed off the main roads. With his head still in a fog and the rain still hitting hard, he feels it's best to simply wait it out.

He spends the bulk of his first day hunkered under a narrow cliff face that protrudes out some fifteen feet from the side of the mountain's west wall. It serves as good cover and not far from there is a river that brings—or so he hopes—a potential food source. With fruit scarce and berries uncertain, he refrains from trying the unknown, but he'll have to venture out soon. The provisions he packed have withered during his unconsciousness; they're not good for anything now except maybe bait.

Seldin thinks for a while about what might be out there, what sort of traps he can set. Though he wouldn't dare kill anything himself, hunger can be a powerful motivator. Still, he just can't bring himself to do that just yet, but soon he might have to. For the most part, he feels his time in the wilderness is going well. Despite his run-in with a carnivorous plant, the worst experience was answering the call of nature. But he managed.

Resting for a while, Seldin naps nude to the sound of the rain and the rhythmic drumbeat of the thunderous storm. His wet, muddy clothes sway on the drying line that he brought along and stretched across the crevice where he hides. There isn't much to do with the way things are except to rest up for what lies ahead. He's still unsure of why he's here, and he can only guess at how much power he's lost.

Physically, he feels fine—a little tired, groggy—but he fears his core is misaligned, given his weakness and poor senses. Perhaps it's the result of being drained by a ravenous flower, which lays shriveled and un-blooming in the jar across from him. He can barely move the needles in the other jars he brought with him for telekinetic practice. Normally he can make them point to him like the hand of a compass aligning in the Earth's magnetic field, but he can hardly make them jiggle now with the aether in his meridians so low.

Opening his eyes, he peeks out at the flower with its bulbous bud slumped over a thorny stem that rests against the inside of the jar and shrouded by the frosted presence of condensation that perspired thanks to the rain and the muggy humidity. He wonders why it won't bloom, and it hasn't since it dropped off the day before, or the night thereafter, and now. Perhaps it is the lack of sunlight, the thought occurs to him. Flowers rarely bloom in gloom. Then again, it isn't the sort of thing you'd find at the local florist.

Standing just long enough to take the few steps forward, Seldin brushes the sand and grit from his backside then kneels by the container sitting on the edge of a stone slab, and he gently taps at the glass in an attempt to rouse it. He then scoffs at himself.

"It's just a plant," he comments on his own actions; for a moment he expected it to move, but why would it? Shaking his head, he turns about, heading back to the comfort of his spot. Then, a barely audible single tap catches his attention. As he looks back to check, he is amazed at what he sees: one vine-like root has reached out and touched at the stain of his fingerprint, pressing up against it from the inside of the glass container.

Tapping at it a second time, he runs his index finger along the outside of the jar. The little rose follows suit, mimicking him in his motion. He laughs, unable to hold in his astonishment. He then pulls his finger back and goes in for a third attempt, which yields a similar result.

"Ha—fascinating," he says with a soft chuckle, "you're attracted to my energy." He closes his fists to test the flow of aether in his hands and fingers. "What little I have left, anyway." Seldin then sighs and peers out into the wet woods. He takes a breath and closes his eyes to focus through the dark view of nothing in his mind's eye.

"I don't know where I am." He thinks for a moment, trying to remember if he saw anything— a sign or… something—he yawns deeply and shakes the grogginess from his head. "You called it, Simon. I've gotta get my core realigned."

With that, he gets up and heads back to his spot against the rock wall across from the plant and takes a cross-legged seat on the hard ground with his hands resting, palms slightly open on his knees. He closes his eyes and takes in several deep, relaxing breaths, while trying to focus on the path from his core, down through his perineum, up his spine, over his head, and down his chest. Steadily, he works the flow of his energy with his consciousness, which weakens as he drifts off to sleep.

…

The low evening sun beams through the curtains of Theresa's quarters. She sits on her bed with the covers undrawn and still wearing her pajamas. The loss of her coven was painful enough, but it's Jasra's last words to her that sting the most. Not only did they not win the fight, but there was considerable pain.

"How could I be so reckless?" she asks herself in a quiet, barely audible, cracking voice.

Her mind drifts to over a month ago now, when Seldin came to see her—as he had been for several months. He stood with his chest to her back, his left hand to her spine, and his right under hers, guiding her aim to a set of candles on her altar.

"Focus. Feel the wick in your mind. Remember the order," he said to her, and she thought back to the first time he came out. He was gentle with her—though he always was. The first place he touched was just below her belly button.

"Core," he said as he did, and a strong sensation of tingling warmth appeared there. She had never noticed it before, yet from just his touch she could feel a force swirling and spinning in all directions. He then moved behind her.

"I promise I'm not being fresh," he said with a gentle though precise touch between her legs to her perineum. At once, the swirling presence in her belly became less random with some of the energy now traveling there. The next spot he touched was her lower back where the spine meets the pelvis, then her middle back below her shoulder blades, and then the base of her neck.

Each place he touched felt like it had lit up like a solstice tree with the energy in her belly reaching out in a line. The farther it reached, the more stable the churning at her center became.

"Neck, back of the head, crown, third eye," he touched those places, "mouth, throat, chest," he drew a finger down to the crook of her breastbone, "and finally back to the core," he said.

But the last day he was with her, things turned sour. The candle he aimed at lit up with a soft pop; hers didn't.

Seldin let out a sigh, and then stepped back from her. Theresa half turned to look back and saw the disappointment in his eyes.

"You haven't been practicing." He shook his head, then went for the door.

Immediately, she reached out for him. "Wait, wait—maybe we can just… do sorcery," she suggested.

He snapped back at once. "I am not giving my lifeforce to that thing. Look… you asked me to teach you this—and yet it's the same every week. You don't put in the effort."

"But Sei—"

"Core alignment is crucial; it's a waste of time when you don't practice," he said with the door closing hard behind him.

. . .

Sleeping off the remainder of the day before and clear through the night, Seldin wakes feeling somewhat refreshed. His attempt to meditate wasn't a complete failure after all, it seems, as a portion of his strength has returned.

The breathing exercise just before he nodded off must have set up alternating micro and macro cycles—the internal flow between the central chakras and the external flow in the aura, which are necessary for aligning the core. It feels good to be in tune with things again. He knows exactly where he is now, able to affix his bearing to and feel the Earth's magnetic field in the clearness of his mind. "South Carolina." He smiles, taking in the moment.

He isn't at a hundred percent just yet, but even the rose can feel his renewed strength, for it too is awake in full bloom, perked, poised, and ready. If it had eyes, its casual gaze would be a stare cast from the parabola of its petals. Seldin gets up sprightly to greet his little companion, teasing with his finger.

"After breakfast, my friend," he says while peeking out at the gray sky from the confines of the crevice, "there are some experiments that I will try." He then pulls his clothes off the line.

"At least it's lightened up a bit." He steps out, sloshing through the soggy landscape of fallen forestry debris. The little bit of light coming through leaves radiant beams of brilliant gold, which stream slightly angled toward their origin in the sky. A veritable kaleidoscope before him, he reserves a moment for the spectacle on his morning forage, smiling at the sight of its awesomeness. The subtle break in his pace awards his senses with a narrow trail just off kilter of his initial direction. Looking there, he decides to follow. Seldin maps the area mentally, keeping a tether on his camp, which he focuses on like a beacon so as to not lose his way.

Whoosh, swoosh, the leaves and fronds of various shrubs fan past him with violent, springy rebound as he brushes them aside to clear his path. They sprinkle beads of wetness that chill his skin, despite the rain and the ominous, hazy forest fog. With his stomach growling, he continues moving through the woods, and in the distance, he hears a rolling, roaring tide. Excited, he takes to a sprint before entering a clearing and stopping just before the edge of the bank. His eyes widen at the magnificence of the energetic rapids that slap the protruding rocks beneath the water's surface.

Hearing a rumble from within, he kneels, peering through the rushing current in hopes of a morsel when a sudden crack from above brings down the heavy rain once again. Cold and already soaked, his shivers draw no comfort from the emptiness of the water. Sadly, he relinquishes a breath of disappointment, unable to forage any farther, for the weather has stolen any chance of satisfying his hunger.

With the little strength he has, he concentrates, drawing in the aether in an effort to shield himself in a blanket of warmth as he meanders back to camp, all the while pondering the prospect of food. With his mind filled to the brim, he takes a seat with his back rested against the stony protrusion that supports his little companion.

Grrrrgllll. "Ugh… I'm so hungry," he moans along with his stomach, which he cups with a hand to muffle the growl. Suddenly, he hears a clinking sound just off to his right and finds the jar rolling up beside him. Bringing it up to eye level, he offers the little flower a quaint, dissatisfied smile.

"You're hungry too, aren't you, little fella?" His eyes follow the enchanting rhythm of the plant's swaying motion. A single viny structure presses against the glass, reaching for him, squeegeeing the inside of the container.

"I'm sorry, I just don't think I have enough energy to share," he says while tracing a finger over the jar and following the motion of the little vine.

Unscrewing the cap, he presents a finger. The plant's bud blooms at the introduction of fresh air. Seldin touches the petals, then the stem. The flower stays placid, swaying contently.

"Nah, you can tell there's none left, can't you?" he asks without really expecting an answer—wham! It latches a vine around his finger, and he drops the jar immediately, startled as he is. It only held on for a brief second, yet it was enough. Scurrying away, he steps back and stares at the organism. The last time it touched him, it left him drained and in a weakened state. Yet for all the excitement, he feels… alright.

Cautiously and slowly, he inches his way back into his den while peering around the stony structure. Out from the base stretches a single root-like vine that gives a hint of that which hides around the corner. As Seldin steps closer, he kneels to take up the container. Clink, echoes the glass of the jar as it grazes the hard floor. The sound causes the plant to flicker, and he jumps back.

"Damn it," he huffs a startled breath before braving the distance with a leap forward, pouncing over the rock as he slams the jar down like catching a fleeing mouse.

"Gotcha!" He smirks proudly in his success while carefully scooping the rest of the rose into the jar before firmly securing the lid. Catching his breath, he sets the jar down, and then peers out into the wetness of the woods, scanning for signs of life.

"If I don't find food soon, there won't be anything left of me for you to eat," he mumbles with a glare back to the rose.

Venturing out once more despite the rain, he decides to forage for materials. The stream he saw earlier had no fish to fry, literally, and he knows that unless he is willing to eat his own arm, he'll have to try something else. Picking up strands of vine as he goes, he braids them to the spare lengths of line from his pack then loops one end of it around the branch of a tree. Seldin draws the line tightly before covering it with leaves and placing bits of a spoiled honey and nut bar in position.

Making a face at the moldy nuts, Seldin looks at the wrapper. "Store in a cool, dry place. Shelf life: 6 to 12 months." He sighs, shaking his head. "So much for that." His stomach growls.

Fashioning a few more snares, he places each only a few paces away from camp, though far enough to keep his scent away, or so he hopes.

"Now, I wait," he says, marching back to his crevice. Sitting in his usual corner, Seldin stares at the plant for a few seconds, and then once again attempts to meditate, for it is the only training his body can endure, given his strength.

As the breathing cycles start, he begins to feel relaxed. On the inhale, he counts to four seconds, while on the exhale, he counts six until the rhythm becomes natural and he can focus on the flow of his energy. Like a beacon, he opens himself to his surroundings, allowing the life around him to be felt as the pull of their auras tug against his.

'So, there are animals here.' His mind discovers, seeing intuitively what his eyes could

not. But there is something else that he can feel: a force stronger than the neighboring wildlife and it is right in front of him. With a shocking gasp, he opens his eyes, overwhelmed by what he sees.

The light of the land shimmers with brilliant violet hues, which appear to tint all that is visible, like the shades he'd wear on a bright summer day.

There are animals and plants all around him, familiar in design yet distinct enough for him to know something's out of place—namely him. He stands in the heart of the plains that span for miles to a backdrop of a mountainous landscape.

In the distance, there are structures of a sort that stretch so tall they could likely touch the sky. And as his gaze follows the trail of the towering peaks, his eyes widen at the massiveness of a neighboring body—a moon perhaps. It's so much larger in his view while silhouetting a glaring spectacle adjacent of the mass and shining through from just behind, blindingly-so, despite the purple haze, with greenish rays of a star that gives life to the system.

Seldin simply cannot believe it. What a wonderful dream. With lucid thoughts dancing in his mind, he takes in the scene as an experience to be had, and like a child, he races on toward the enormous mounds of what look like spires of papier-mâché.

In spite of his excitement, he finds himself to be remarkably rejuvenated in this place, for each unlabored breath he takes as he runs empowers him with the heavily enriched, oxygenated air. It is clean, virtually unpolluted, while the gravity that anchors him makes him feel light and free. He could easily jump forty feet and land just as softly.

When he finally reaches the area that he can only describe as a village, he pauses in search of any patrons. With none in sight, he approaches one of the many adjoining constructs and touches the outside of the wall. It has a grainy texture—a secreted resin of some sort, akin to that of a termite mound or a wasp nest with a seemingly cool metallic feel.

Suddenly there is movement from his side, and he jumps defensively at the sight of the gigantic creature to his left. It is nearly twice his height with a slightly elongated body. Standing on four legs, it is insect-like in appearance with its remaining two limbs positioned at its front, like arms. It has large, almost front-facing eyes, antennae, and a carapace with a skin that ripples almost fluid-like as the being moves. The wasp-like beast approaches him, and as his heart sinks in the fear of it, Seldin backs away.

"What are you?" he lets out.

"Suka." A sound echoes within his mind— a familiar gravelly voice.

"It's you…" Astonished, he utters a reply. "Did you bring me here?" he asks it.

It nods.

"Why?"

It then slinks forward, looking into his eyes and with a gentle upturn of its right forelimb, it extends a fingerlike digit, and then presses it briefly over his left breast. The suka then breaks its gaze and looks upward and past him. Seldin then turns, looking up and back over his shoulder. At first, he doesn't know what to think, but then he sees them through the overcast sky.

Pods, endless pods, falling from the heavens like the seeds of a dandelion blowing in the wind. They corrupt everything they touch, rooting into the ground as they land, while tormenting the unfamiliar forms that he sees there. Ravenous and unrelenting, the sprouts that spawn from the spores overrun the world and feed on the life of whatever they encounter.

The suka's eyes widen in the chaos, and then it looks to Seldin. With a flick of its wrist, it fires off a spine, like the quill of a porcupine. Seldin turns to defend himself, and as he does, the spine grazes his shoulder, stabbing through the heart of a spore. Stunned, he offers a surprised look of gratitude before joining in the fight.

Within minutes, the surrounding vegetation has been replaced by these new things that resemble what was once there, despite being something else. Where tranquility once stood is now war as the suka's brethren scurry to the surface from their burrows to combat the menace. Futile the attempt, for soon it is suka pitted against suka. Their fallen have risen as the spores latch on, drain them of their very life force, and copy their form. This new breed holds their own, despite being plant-like. The spores grow to resemble their host, taking their strength and nearly tripling it.

The overrun is fast. Seldin does what he can to fight, dodging the spores left and right; he charges his body like an electric eel. The spores that touch him seem to relish in doing so, unfettered by his defensive matrix. Although he is able to brush them off, each still sprouts into an opponent like no other. They look like him, and worse, can hurt him with his own skills. A great teacher once told him that his fiercest enemy would be himself and these things are putting that to the test. They have no weaknesses to speak of and possess overwhelming and unwavering strength.

He combats them fiercely, employing every asset that he has and every technique he's ever learned. Though try as he might, they have no joints to lock, no bones to break, and the limbs he manages to tear from their viny bodies grow back almost as quickly. While the saplings that spawn from his fallen friends are easier to blemish than those that come from him, his brute-force method yields little result against their numbers, and those that he welts soon heal, only to join the fight again. To make matters worse, the benefits to his strength, which he draws from the atmosphere, seem to pass on in the spores that attach to him. Regardless, he starts to believe his strength to be the reason the suka brought him to this place, for he is stronger than the natives, and that must give them hope.

Dropping to his knees, Seldin plants himself, grabbing at the dirt. He then looks to his companion before clasping his hands together, inverting the orientation of his palms so that his fingers point in opposite directions, purposefully misaligning his poles. He then begins pushing his energy into his hands, slowly sliding his palms across one another as he chants.

"Haa-niih." His hands begin to heat up intensely. He sandbagged the technique for good reason: it's slow and it's taxing. Yet as the power builds and his hands start to burn, the air around them ripples with waves of heat. He feels it's ready, though not a moment too soon, for a doppelganger charges at him. "Spiiiiiihhhhhhaaaaa!" he chants loudly, slapping his palms to the chest of the beast as he releases the energy in a bright beam of light.

The creature shrills as it stumbles back, clasping itself as its leafy skin turns white from the intense radiant glow. Seldin smiles at its apparent dismay, but as the light dims, the monster glares at him, then exhales a steamy breath before licking its thorny teeth.

"Oh, shi—"

It rears back, thrusts its hands forward, and then projects a beam that strikes him to the ground, knocking him into a daze. Seldin looks up at the mistake he has made as it stands over him ready to use the strength that he gave it. It stares into him despite its lack of eyes, and he can hear the terrible things projected into his mind. Its thoughts are primal, unorganized, yet he can sense another presence within the creature—a mind separate though interconnected and in control. As he looks deeper, he shudders in an attempt to block out the image of something monstrous yet rose-like.

Then in that moment, he feels a tear into his chest, and with a howl he exclaims, "But it's just a dream!" His mind fades. "I shouldn't feel the—"

With a shrieking gasp, he clutches his chest, crying out in agonizing fright. The shock to his consciousness plunges him awake in the crevice where he dozed. A sigh of relief flees his quivering lip then his gaze falls to the rose across the way, still sitting on the stony slab where he left it with its bud blooming intently at him.

"What the hell are you?" he asks with a stuttering breath.

Crash! There's a loud crack of a sound just off in the distance. The noise startles him, making him jump in the midst of his already risen anxiety. But then as he realizes the nature of the noise, his heart flutters with excitement as his stomach growls. Darting out of his dwelling, he races at top speed.

"Yes, finally!" he cheers just as he comes up on it, over a shy hill and through a set of crossed trees. But then his wide grin transitions into a grimace. Although his stomach rejoices in his discovery, he suddenly grows opposed to the idea.

"A fox?" he pants. "Oh, man, I don't know if I can do it. It's too much like a dog. Why couldn't it have been a rabbit, or a rat? At least then I wouldn't feel as bad. Well, maybe…" His mind wanders as he inches up to the small red and white bundle of fluff that whines and kicks at the snare entangling its hind legs. Reaching down to it, he jumps back as it snaps defensively at him.

"Kill it." He hears from a voice as he sees flashes of the gigantic rose.

"I can't." He pushes the thought out.

"Kill it." He hears again; the voice even louder this time.

"No!" he shouts, fighting the image of thorny teeth and vine-like limbs.

With his hunger compounding and his instincts high, he knows he needs it—needs what it has.

"You have to survive," the voice says.

Succumbing to the wisdom and influenced by a deeper yearning, Seldin kneels, pinning the animal with his left hand just behind the neck and away from its snapping jaws, while forcing its face into the ground. With his other hand, he grasps the nape.

He sighs, surprised at how soft the fur is. Pausing to caress the feathered locks, Seldin feels a shift in his heart as he starts to apply pressure. The animal squeals as he does so, which chills his bones. Before his sympathy can break into tears, he backs away.

"Whoa!" He tries to dodge as the fox lunges and snaps his hand.

"Gah!" Quickly, he moves to a safer distance, while cradling the painful bite in his left palm. Even with the adrenaline and the need to feed, Seldin resists the urge to strike back, for it was only defending itself.

"I can't," he lets out a whimper in a soft, saddened breath. "I caaaaaannnnn't!"

Fiendish images push into his mind again, forced in from the unknown. Seldin wrestles with them. Pitted against survival and humanity, he flails wildly, stumbling forward as his foot locks with the protruding roots at the forest floor, which sends him headlong into a rocky protrusion.

"Kill it!" the voice commands, even louder than before, and Seldin opens his eyes. The pain kicks in the moment he sees the creature leering over him with its thorny claws gouging his chest. Grabbing at the arm-like apertures, he uses all his might to force it back.

"Kill it, Seldin, we need you to fight—we need you alive!"

"But I don't know how," he lets out, baffled, for all his attempts seem in vain—and then he sees it: a white mass like a ball of cotton entombed within a wall of vines just beneath the leaves of a false sternum. He wonders how he had missed it before. All that time it had been there like a heart that all the extremities are tied into. In that fleeting thought comes a flash of recollection of how the suka's spiky barb had succeeded earlier.

Seldin slips the monster's arm aside with a snaking motion of his wrist and then spears his hand up through the veil of leaves, feeling for the mass as the thorns of the vines crowd in and grow longer in its defense, penetrating his fingers. Pushing through despite the pain, he grits his teeth and with each pounding beat of his own heart shaking him, he wraps his fist around the spore, soft and fragile as it is. Immediately it falls dead, and the body of the plant withers before his eyes.

Although this one victory is a triumph, he feels pity for his fallen foe and sorrow for what he has done. Sadly, for him, there is no time to forgive himself. The line ahead is long, and the next enemy is on its way.

Empowered with this new knowledge, Seldin slowly stands, bearing a remorseful grimace. He hates the idea of what he had to do, necessary or not. Pulling the aether from his surroundings, he draws it into his muscles. Although direct energy seems useless against his enemy, he believes that this alternative approach might just work. His very next punch tears through the relatively soft exterior of the creature like butter, striking the spore. It falls quickly. The following few drop fast as well, and much like their comrades, they wither as the energy they had stolen spills out of them.

One by one they drop like flies. Seldin's renewed strength seems to be tipping the scale in the suka's favor, for now he can defeat them within two strikes or less. He swats the spores that touch his skin as easily as mosquitoes in the summer's eve, giving them no chance to sprout.

Making headway, the defenders press on, turning the tides of battle. The apparent victory, however, weighs heavily on Seldin's heart. As a fighter he loves to win, yet at what cost? In his child-like naivety, he struggles to balance the world—a peace for all. But he can't befriend them, not after all they've done. Still, with each falling foe, he feels an ever-growing sense of anguish that fuels each devastating blow.

Without warning, a shadow falls over the land, blanketing the world in darkness as the second wave swarms in like locusts. The skies fill with specks of flailing bodies plummeting toward the ground like paratroopers dropping in. They swoop as they land, generating a cushioning billow of thrust by flapping the enormous petals, resembling a bisected pair of butterfly wings, which stem from a blossom rooted to the small of their backs. As each of them touches down, the flower that eased their descent retracts, shrinking down to about the size of a hibiscus blooming in the spring.

Although the creatures look not all that dissimilar from the other monsters in the horde, right away Seldin can tell that these are different in overall design. The layering of the leaves and vines cover the body more accurately and much denser, with thorns that run along the vines that wrap around as if to trace out an underlying form of muscles and bone. Unlike their counterparts, their bodies are solid, their movements are purposeful and strategic. They're able to anticipate his actions and counter his techniques. These new things encircle him. Having seen his earlier success, they want him stopped—or more to the point—they want him dead.

Seldin punches one of them in its elongated face, which looks like the closed bud of a flower. His strike doesn't penetrate the petals, instead, the thorns cut him, shredding his knuckles as he hits. Jumping back to parry, he draws in more energy then tries again with a similar result. His suka friend isn't faring much better. Its bladed arms barely cut them, and its barbs barely gouge.

While gathering energy together, Seldin strikes once again, this time with a volley of maneuvers to everything he knows to be a major weakness in a humanoid form: face, throat, solar plexus, groin, though all of his efforts leave him shredded.

'What the hell am I fighting, a cactus?' a baffled thought races in his mind as he looks over his wounds, but then it hits him—literally, when a sharp, stabbing pain enters his shoulders from behind, raking the skin as if with a steel brush.

"Gaw!" he rears back as he drops to his knees from the pain then rolls to break from its grasp and take its leg with a sweep before the others rush in.

Although their hands are oddly shaped, having only two fingers and a stubbed palm, retractable spines on the underside give them one hell of a piercing grip.

As the one creature falls from the sweeping of its leg, Seldin kips-up and leaps straight into the air, using the weak gravity to his advantage, avoiding being touched again.

"C'mon, Sei, there's gotta be something you can do," he says to himself. "This place enhances your abilities, maybe if I—dear God!" He looks up, reaching the height of his ascension. For the first time, he sees it: the source of the madness. It has a metallic luster, yet it is organic in appearance. The large, zeppelin-like form stretches for miles with an even greater floral body hovering in the distance beyond it. He can see more of them entering the atmosphere, each carrying thousands, maybe even millions of these foliates. In that brief moment, he loses all hope of winning, for the ships in the distance open up and unfold their petals, fanning them outward to dangle the spore spewing appendages over the land.

Looking down at the world as his ascent begins to decline, he catches a glimpse of his friend being overrun.

"No!" he shouts. Fearing the worst, he pools his energy then expels it, pushing himself like a rocket as he falls toward the vicinity of the suka. Barreling forward, he aims himself at an enemy and rams it into the ground as they collide. Seldin then springs forth with all his fury, pulling energy from around himself to aid his strength as he swings on the next foe. It dodges and blocks until his fist strikes with blinding speed, tearing the foliage from its face. And there beneath the layers is something Seldin did not expect: a long black eye that curves around the smooth gray skin of a different face. At first glance, he thinks it's a snake, yet it sneers at him while squinting from the light and showing its rows of rounded teeth.

Before he can react, the creature strikes him with the back of its hand across his face, tit for tat, knocking him flat. As Seldin's eyes close, he catches a last glimpse of its looming face as the leaves regrow to shroud it once again.

. . .

The koi seem rather active today, jumping at low-flying insects that stray too close to the pond's surface. Theresa, of course, doesn't notice despite her empty gaze from the courtyard bench. Her mind is stuck in the past, wallowing in could-haves and should-nots.

A sudden familiar voice catches her by surprise. "Here you are."

She looks. It's Lamryl, her face covered by the hood of her decorated cloak.

"Still neglecting your duties, I see," Lamryl says, taking a seat beside her with a sigh. She draws her hood back, letting the light of the sun dance on her old, wrinkled face. Her silvery hair, pulled tight into a bun, shimmers.

Theresa shakes her head with sad eyes. "I don't know if I should be on the council," she says.

Lamryl cants her head oddly with a strange expression on her face as if hiding a smile. "Why, because you failed?"

Theresa looks to her, stunned by her response.

"That's the problem with revenge: no one really wins," Lamryl says.

Sighing, Theresa looks down. "It was a test?" she asks, rhetorically, and Lamryl nods.

"Bu-but I lost my coven," Theresa adds.

Lamryl stands. "Then…" she puts her hood up over her head, "they weren't really yours to begin with," she says, walking away.

. . .

Seldin doesn't wake back in his crevice; instead, his eyes open to a tan-colored, oval-shaped den. The texture of the papier-mâché walls teases the light as the shadows cast from the rolling flames of the fireplace blanket them in amber hues. Upon his chest is a familiar little flower, which seems to dance in a sort of swaying cadence, following the fire. The suka creature looks over him. It doesn't speak, though it never had in the most common sense. Carefully assessing the boy's limbs, it moves around him.

With Seldin's wounds mended, the alien scoops up the flower then sets it down with the other five across the room. Seldin sits up to get a better view at the others, each identical to the one he found in the woods.

"Malnar." He hears the sound echo within as visions of various plants come to him: the shifty humanoid shapes, *"Boni"*, a flat butterfly-looking thing, *"Cepella"*, and the flower itself, the creature gestures them, *"Beljusa"*.

"So, this is where they come from?" he asks in an almost rhetorical tone before an image of the adjoining world flashes in his mind. He closes his eyes as more information pours in. Two worlds—tethered to each other like the Moon and the Earth—fill his mind with a view of their elliptical orbit around a large orange star that appears green through the rich atmosphere. While there are other planets in the system, these two are the only ones with life.

The concept of a binary orbit intrigues him. It fuels his curiosity, stirring more questions within him, which are followed up, almost immediately, by more answers, more images. The sister worlds are aware of each other and, as such, share in a symbiosis that has allowed the inhabitants to coexist peacefully for millions of years. Their relatively short proximity to one another makes it easy for the two dominant species to migrate. Rather than building technology, however, they grow it—evolving and altering themselves to suit their needs. Until the day the pulsari came.

"The pulsari!" Seldin jumps to his feet, seeing a mental flash of the thing beneath the leaves of the plant-like creature he now understands to be malnar. That face unsettles him. The eyes, those black jellybean-shaped eyes.

"Stop! You mean, that thing, that thing I saw? Why the hell are we down here? Why are we not fighting?" he exclaims, shouting at the suka.

"There's nothing left," it says to him.

"No…" He backs away, looking into the sad eyes of his friend. "That's not true! I refuse it!" he bellows before darting up the tunnel leading to the surface. He clenches his mind, forcing out the images the suka feeds him in an effort to stop him.

Seldin runs as fast and as furiously as he can. The five-mile span of the tunnel seems to go on endlessly, until he sees the radiant glow outlining the hatch to the outside. Suddenly he feels exhausted despite the short run. His body grows colder and colder the closer he gets. Placing his hands on the hatch, there is a crystalizing sound and a sudden pain. He jumps back immediately, turning his palms up. The skin is frozen with chunks stuck to the door. Taking in a deep breath, he pushes energy to his palms, grabs the hatch and endures the moment as he forces it. He can feel his heat leaving, smell the chill in the air as the moisture in his flesh flash freezes from contact with the door.

"Ahhh!" he howls with all his might. The light from the outside begins to spill in with the breeze, and at once, the hatch gives way as he finds himself in a field of icy glass under the fading pale green light.

The suka was right, for there is nothing left—absolutely nothing—no grass, no trees. The land appears torn between two extremes: boiling heat in direct sunlight, freezing cold everywhere else. What could possibly survive here now?

As the suka pulls him to safety, Seldin drifts in and out of consciousness. The flesh on his arms, face, and chest is frost-bitten to the bone. His breathing has become labored as he is once again at the mercy of his wounds. Once back in the den, the suka sets him on the bed, and then retrieves one of the malnar and places it on him. The roots burrow into him, and as they do, the suka opens a small hatch, which allows a portion of sunlight to beam in. The flower's petals bloom, drinking in the light.

When he finally regains consciousness, Seldin finds himself lying face down in his own crevice out in the woods. The fading light suggests that the day is ending. As he pushes himself to sit up, he feels a presence on his back and catches sight of the vines enveloping him and the remnants of the fox.

"Oh, God, no!" He takes up the withered animal then looks to the slab encrusted with pieces of broken glass. He flails in a panic, drops the corpse and reaches for the rose attached to the base of his neck. He grasps it, pulls it from himself, and in a fit of rage, throws it to the ground. It hits hard then rights itself as he scrambles for another jar. Pouring out the contents in a hurry, he reacquires the plant and slaps the jar back down on the stone slab before taking his usual seat across from it. He then weeps for the fox that he didn't want to kill.

Chapter 13

"Dissension Among the Ranks"

"No, I won't do it!" Ryan says to Joanne.

"What do you mean, you won't do it?" she asks, making a disgruntled face. The tings and tangs of Cory and Rico's swords clashing cease as they turn their ears to the sound of the argument going on at the edge of the square with Ryan, Joanne, Elma, and Neil.

"I mean, I won't do it." Ryan stands firm.

"What happened to you, Ryan? Sh-she waved her hand and your balls fell off?" she questions him, and Rico laughs, while polishing his sword. "Her power could be ours," Joanne argues.

Ryan looks amongst them. "We each swore an oath and gave our blood to the binding. Now, I'm a lot of things, but I will not betray my coven," he says.

"Neither will I," Neil says.

"Yeah, Theresa's our friend," Elma adds.

Cory crosses his arms. "We're your coven," he says to Ryan, "not her—not them!" he shouts, pointing at Elma and Neil, who each lower their eyes.

"Think about it, Ryan, her power comes from that book, and she's vulnerable now—all we gotta do is take it," Joanne says with favorable nods from Cory and Rico.

Shaking his head, Ryan sighs. "No."

With that, Joanne gestures to Rico and Cory. "Fine. To hell with you. Let's go boys," she says, and they walk away.

…

It's a little after midnight, yet the main hall of Watcher's Keep is alive with parishioners and sorcerers gathered into the rows of pews that line the nave, with their eyes fixed on the central altar where their priestess stands, speaking her truth.

"The phoenix, often revered for its resilience, is a testament to the trials of our own lives. None of us are free from the burdens placed on us through obligation, status, or even by our own hands, but it is how we rise from the crucible of those challenges that our true selves emerge."

Theresa looks out amongst them as they listen to her insightful words: the hard lessons she's learned, the wisdom of their elders… and their gods.

"In those moments it's so important that we do not falter or lose faith, for Khyrah, through her grace, offers us all the strength to stand together and as one. Let us pray. O Khyrah, God of Chaos, Bringer of Order and Peace, through you, I shall not hunger, shiver, or suffer…"

…

"Shh." Joanne presses a finger to her lips as she, Rico, and Cory move up the steps to the enormous wooden doors. They pause, hearing the cadence of muffled voices praying inside the Keep. Joanne motions for Rico to try the door. He nods, then grabs the large steel handle and gives it a gentle, though firm tug. It's locked.

Brushing him aside, Joanne then waves a hand in a circling motion around the lock. "What keeps us out, now herein, opens up and lets us in," she whispers, and there's a soft click.

Once inside, the three of them move to the edge of the main hall, ducking out of Lamryl and Theresa's eyeline behind the giant leg of Khyrah's marble statue.

Rico gestures, pointing out a path for them to follow. "Make this space, I've defined, a secret place, for none to find," he chants, and they appear to vanish from view. Slowly, they make their way along the far-right wall past the pews.

A parishioner looks at Cory and he stops, holding his hands out to signal Joanne and Rico to wait. He stands there, staring back as the gentlemen looks up and down the seemingly empty walkway before returning to prayer. The three of them sigh in relief then continue on.

There's an abrupt thudding clack of the main doors opening, and Theresa stops to see Ryan, Neil, and Elma barging through and running down the center aisle. The hall grows silent, save for their yelling.

"Priestess! Priestess!" Ryan, Neil, and Elma shout despite the gawking stares from the parishioners.

Lamryl crosses her arms beneath her robes, while offering a soft smile to Theresa, who looks on with mixed feelings.

"No manners, as usual," Theresa scoffs, and Lamryl turns her back to cover her amused face, but her eyes fall to the Guardian of Death, who steps up beside her, casting a serious expression to the visitors. She turns back with concern.

"F-forgive the intrusion, Priestesses, but it's urgent," Ryan pants, catching his breath, "Joanne took my car—she uhh—"

"We think she's here!" Neil shouts, panting.

"After your book," Elma adds with equal huffs. A look of dread grows on Theresa's face.

"My quarters…" she utters and rushes down the hall. Ryan, Neil, and Elma follow, but Tillman takes Lamryl's arm as she steps, and he offers her only a shake of his head.

Lamryl nods, then addresses the crowd. "It's alright, everyone. Let us continue with our prayers."

. . .

Slowly, the door of Theresa's quarters eases open, and the prize Joanne so desperately seeks comes into her view—the Book of Roe lies closed upon the foot of the bed.

"It's mine," Joanne lets out in a hesitant, yet excited breath.

Rico and Cory look at her. "It's ours," Rico says, and Joanne nods.

"Of course… ours," she confirms, when the sound of thudding footsteps echoes from down the hall with Theresa, Ryan, Neil, and Elma clambering through the doorway. From their point of view, the room is empty, but they've seen this trick before.

"Joanne?" Theresa shouts.

"Cory, Rico?" Ryan follows up.

Joanne, Rico, and Cory look to them, bewildered for a moment before nodding amongst themselves.

"They don't' see us," Joanne says, relieved. Grab it!" she shouts with each of them reaching for it. The runes on the cover start to glow an ominous blood red and reshape to a warning none of them can read. The moment they touch it, a blinding light fills the room, and the thieves become visible as the concealment spell breaks.

Joanne, Cory, and Rico laugh. "Haha! It's ours!" they cheer.

"No, put it down!" Theresa screams in horror, as the energy of the books starts to creep up their hands.

"What's happening?" Joanne screams.

"I can't leg go!" Cory shouts.

"It's got me!" Rico yells.

Theresa motions for Ryan, Neil, and Elma to back out of the doorway, and they cover their eyes from a sudden brilliant flash. Joanne, Cory, and Rico cry out—their voices drowned by a thunderous woosh of energy. The light dims, and the room falls silent and empty.

Chapter 14

"More Prosperous Grounds"

Three days have passed since Seldin's rude awakening, and although the energy he got from the fox has sustained him, he is once again on the verge of starvation. Still struggling to catch food, he decides to do the only rational thing any survivalist would and seek more prosperous grounds. He heads north, following the flow of the stream a few miles up until coming to an end at the base of the mountainside where it disappears, penetrating deep within a narrow crevice too small for him to pass.

"Damn!" he huffs, peeking through the opening to the cave that resides just beyond the wall. It looks as though it could go on for miles. Stepping back, he scans the area and the side of the mountain that bars his path.

"Well, so much for that. It's too steep to climb," he comments aloud, tugging at a few measly vines that offer little in the way of support. His mind then wanders to childish thoughts, reflecting on the prowess featured in his dreams. He imagines himself back on the plains of the suka's home world, where gravity was weak, and his power was strong. "If I were there, I could jump this," he says to himself, envisioning such a feat.

Setting his bag down, he steps away from the mountainside, gathers up some courage, pools some strength, and then goes for it. He builds up speed in a charging run and then leaps, springing as high as he possibly can. "Yes!" he exclaims then suddenly, "Whoa, whoa—oh shhhiiit!" He falls back as gravity takes hold, proving to not be his friend, and he slams to the ground, bruising his pride.

"Barely even ten feet," he chuckles before standing to brush the soreness from his backside and retrieve his bag—clink! The jar rolls out. He turns a puzzled, unexpecting gaze to the container and the flower that is staring up at him. As he reaches for it, he feels the presence of another mind, much like the one he felt in his dreams. It seats into his consciousness, rooting there as he resists. Cringing, he pushes out whatever that feeling is before grabbing the jar and zipping it securely in his pack.

It's obvious he can't go over the mountain and going around could take days—a luxury his starving body just doesn't have. The shortest route, he thinks, would be to go through it. The cave that lies beneath the wall must surely go clean to the other side, he figures, for the stream likely wouldn't flow otherwise. He ponders this for a few moments, thinking about just how to manage it.

"Maybe I could…" he says aloud with his eyes tilted up in thought before looking to his right hand and making a tight fist. Tapping his knuckles to the opening of the crevice to test the rock, he steps back, takes a breath and focuses. "Uhh—" he grunts, pushing aether into his meridians and concentrating the flow into his right hand. He can feel his body heating up and the strain as his muscles swell.

"Grrrr!" He pulls back a readied fist with a growling breath, and then, "Haaahh!"

Smack! "Augh-ohh—futhermucker!" he exclaims, turning about, while shouting obscenities, and messaging the smarting sting from his knuckles. After a moment or two of cursing, he composes himself long enough to check his work, finding only a chip for his troubles.

Even with the aether to maximize his strength, he now knows he can't punch through the rock, and the power he'd need to pull it off would likely overwhelm his body. He and Simon figured that much out in the lab.

Although one's ability to will energy is independent of their physical strength, each benefits and augments the other. The more developed the body, the more it can withstand the tidal forces of aether and vice versa. Still, everything is about balance, and anything greater than three times one's strength could cause the body to rupture as the energy destroys it from within.

"There is… another option," he whispers under his breath before placing his palms on the rocky surface at the edges of the small opening. With a deep breath, he focuses his energy into the rock then continues to breathe at a steady pace, running internal cycles to maintain a constant flow of aether between him and the structure. The wall beneath his hands begins to warm up, and then slowly it steams, turning red. "Gah!" he grunts, for the power feeds back, singeing his hands. Despite the resistance, he can feel the rock weakening, and he pushes harder. "Haanni… spiihhhaa!"

Wham! He plunges through, unexpectedly- so, when the wall gives way. "Haha, I can't believe that worked!" he laughs, while relishing in his accomplishment.

Dusting himself off, he stands then peers into the mouth of the vast darkness before him. The stream that cuts through runs along a central path, which meanders into the depths of the cave. He follows along, exploring until the backlight cast from the outside begins to fade from the winding tunnel. And when the light seems almost completely gone, he gapes at the scintillating beauty of the star-like speckles that glisten like glitter in all directions, creating an almost twilight effect while casting a radiant blue luster over the cave walls. It's peaceful there, tranquil, and as he marches on, he comes upon a basin—a pocket of water about the size of a backyard swimming pool. The crystal-clear water darkens in the depths of the blackness. Above the pond clings a large protrusion—a stalactite, perhaps? He can't really see it, given the poor visibility.

"I need more light," he comments before cupping his right hand as he concentrates. He can feel a strange pull all around him, adding resistance to the aether as he draws it in, and as the energy forms an orb of light, it jumps—leaping off as if sucked away by the structure beside him. Startled, his gaze follows it to a large crystal before it bounces to the next, ricocheting around the cave. The orb passes from crystal to crystal, leaving dimly glowing stalks behind until it cuts across his path, striking him forcibly in the shoulder and knocking him flat. The energy dissipates on impact, illuminating the cave as it vanishes, absorbed by the crystalline formations lining the walls. The room then grows cold and dark once again.

"Ugh…" Seldin huffs as he sits up, flicking at some broken shards of crystal. "That… explains the feeling in here. These things are screwing with my aura." He then kips-up, leaving his bag at his feet as he moves around the edge of the basin to get a better view of the enormous body draping down from the ceiling and now known to be a crystal. Reaching out toward it, he concentrates a steady stream of energy to the colorful formation of quartz, which absorbs his power without resistance. After a moment or two, the large crystal begins to glow rather brightly. His eyes widen at the sight of thousands and thousands of jagged stalks protruding from the walls. Blue, purple, clear, and white hues shimmer like a rainbow in the light.

"Now that is cool," he mutters.

And then, as he glances down, his heart leaps in his chest. "Food!" he exclaims, diving into the water, giving chase to the enormous fish that school in a place that no human has ever been. With a gasp, he splashes his head out from the surface to catch his breath and hoist a flopping feast to the rocky shore of his new dwelling.

Utilizing the same trick he had to light the cave, he heats up a collection of stones to cook the fish. As he prepares everything, he goes about setting up a camping spot complete with his sleeping bag, a clothesline, and of course, his flowery friend. Before he knows it, dinner is ready, and he takes that first mouthwatering bite.

"Mm…" He savors the moment with the flood of endorphins—the brain's natural reward for a successful hunt. Still, as his stomach grows all the more satisfied, he finds himself uneasy in the moment.

"I realize I have to…" he says softly, glancing at the flower, "…and even though it doesn't have a cute face or soft fur, it still bothers me to no end. What about its life? If I hadn't strolled in here, it would be alive. Yet, without it, I should surely perish. There has to be a way, Lucy," he glances to the extraterrestrial flower, "to preserve life without destroying it." He sighs, closing his tired eyes to the fading light overhead. And for the first night in almost two weeks, Seldin nods off with a full stomach.

Chapter 15

"The Secrets of the Beljusa"

"You're awake," the sentence forms in Seldin's mind. He rolls to his side, groaning as he does, catching the stare from his insectoid friend.

"It's you?" he asks in a groggy voice, surprised to see him, for he hasn't had this dream in days. As Seldin rubs his tired eyes, he pauses to look over himself. In a flash he remembers a terrible thing, but the frostbite is gone. The suka then, once again, removes the malnar from Seldin's chest and places it in a planter amongst the others.

"What happened?" he asks the creature. Then, as before, the answers come to him in flashes of images, like a movie playing in his head. He sees himself in the third person, looking over a white landscape blanketed by ice and a bright blinding light. The pulsari raped the world of everything, damaging the atmosphere in the process. Without the ability to hold in the heat, the world as they knew it began to freeze. Seldin felt the cold touch of the climate's death firsthand the very moment he stepped outside. With no hope in sight, the survivors of the planet sought refuge deep within its recesses, much like his friend did when he rescued him.

The suka goes on to explain that its insect-like race inhabits Binax-Beta, the smaller of the two binary worlds. Born to fulfill specific roles within the colony, each individual is bred to be either a worker, a fighter, or whatever else is needed, including living structures and conveyances. In that way, they share a similarity with their plant-like counterparts of their sister world. Even so, they could not have predicted how devastating the malnar would be in the hands of those like the pulsari.

"Wait… if you can evolve—" Seldin begins to question, but his mind becomes full again with images of a barren land and an absence of time. There simply aren't enough resources to do as he suggests, he realizes. Then something forms in his vision and simultaneously he and the suka glance over to their salvation—their only hope. Seldin sees the explanation that comes to him, an image of himself on an expedition, a voyage, to start the world again. Gathering the flowers, the suka hands them to him and then fills his head with places to go.

"I can't, I'll freeze," Seldin replies.

Taking one of the flowers, the suka then places it to the base of Seldin's neck. Suddenly, its vine-like roots envelope him and burrow down into the surface of his skin. In agony he drops, and the suka moves to stare into his eyes with a supportive gaze to help him endure the initial pain. It shows him the power of the malnar—how the pulsari used them to gain an advantage, and how they might be used to restore their world.

Slowly Seldin stands, enveloped by the beljusa—the rose that encases him. He can feel the change in himself and a link to its mind. In this state of symbiosis, they are one.

As he breaches the surface, the leaves that cover his body shuffle like solar panels, orienting themselves to the sun while the flower to his back blooms. Its strength courses through him, fueling him with the energy it absorbs while shielding him from the frigid air. Seldin then turns to face the mound that he came from, and then climbs to the top of it to plant one of the roses there. Its roots stretch out in all directions and penetrate the harsh, icy soil where it rests. The flower sprouts quickly, soaking in the light, and as it extends its tendrils like feelers across the land, Seldin gapes at the wonders it brings. The white powder begins to melt as rejuvenated soil spawns new life. He then darts, moving at blinding speed to the other side of the world.

With the malnar linked to him, he feels no fatigue, he doesn't tire or even need to breathe. The plant feeds him directly with the energy it draws from the sun, which is only a small percentage of what it needs for itself. The feeling is simply exhilarating—supercharged!

In a day's time, he makes it to the other side and sets the next plant down. As it begins to spawn, he leaps, then uses the petals at his back to form wings like the pulsari had, and sails through the sky to the next location.

"This is amazing, I can fly!" he laughs hysterically with excitement. From his vantage he can clearly see the spread of the growth sweeping across the globe like an atomic blast dropping shrubberies in its wake. By the time he reaches the northern hemisphere, the planet resembles a tennis ball with two-toned patches of green and white.

"Only four left," he says, setting the beljusa into the dirt. It has much the same result as the other two, with the overgrowth spreading radially from the center. The sky is looking better, too, he notices, for clouds are starting to roll in as the atmosphere replenishes.

For a moment, he takes a seat beneath the shade of the rose that grows monstrous in the sun. Willing the foliate-helmet around his face to recede, he takes a breath of the new air while feeling the warmth of the wind on his face. The sounds in the distance make it clear with cracks of thunder, a sign that the weather is starting to return to normal.

'It is simply amazing...' he thinks while looking at the living suit that he wears, *'...how one flower can make or break the world. It's no wonder the pulsari wanted them so badly, for they are truly a living weapon.'* That thought frightens him, causing a sinking feeling in his stomach. Quickly, he springs to his feet, jumps to the sky, and soars to drop off the remaining beljusas.

The suka is waiting outside the lair when he gets back. Seldin dives to the ground at blinding speed then cushions his descent with a thrusting pulse, mimicking the actions he once saw of his enemy.

"I, uh… I have a question. There's a… I found an unusual flower in the woods on my planet. It's a rose." He pants. "Is it?"

The suka lowers its eyes in a nodding motion. Seldin steps back.

"This… this isn't a dream?" he asks.

Again, the creature answers with a gesture, this time by shaking its head. Seldin just can't believe it. The idea is simply preposterous.

'How?' He wonders. "I have to get ba—" then, *"Three years,"* he hears in his mind.

"What?" He looks at his companion. The suka then aims a finger in a pointing gesture to the sky beyond. Seldin turns to look over his shoulder at a small yellow star, eons away. Eerily, he turns back to look into the eyes of the suka, but the effort is fleeting, for he gasps in mid-turn as if a pulse has struck his chest and he finds himself awake, surrounded by the sparkling twilight within the belly of the cave.

In his haze, Seldin turns a gaze to the jar beside him. Immediately he swipes it up, scurries to his feet, and then races outside. There, he stands in the light of the sun, pops the lid from the jar, and reaches in for it, hesitantly-so. Like a spider fleeing a cup, the rose scurries with viny limbs up the length of his arm. He panics at first, then braces for it once it reaches the spot on his neck.

"Argh!" He lets out, gritting his teeth as the vines lace around him and burrow into him, and he thinks back to his dream—searching for a way to dull the pain. As the moment subsides, he rights himself, looking over the form of the living suit and then takes a steady leap high into the sky before landing on the crest of the mountain with a powerful thud, cracking the rock beneath his feet.

Although Earth's gravity is much stronger than that of Binax-Beta, the malnar's reaction to the light of the yellow sun makes up for the difference in weight. Earth's sun is much younger, and so the light is brighter, purer. The flower laps it up like sweet nectar.

"Three years," he says aloud, peering downward from his vantage. "God, I hope it's long enough."

Chapter 16

"The Passage of Time"

A warm summer sea breeze soothes their skin from the smoldering sun overhead. With no clouds to shield them, they are at the mercy of the elements, but that's just fine for Leon, he can do this all day—dancing with forceful exchanges between him and his student, Almir. The sand that whips with each soaring kick sticks to their sweaty bodies, uncomfortably-so, but the wind that blows, certainly makes up for the unpleasantness of the beach.

"Jeeze, I can't believe it's been a year already," Almir comments while ducking a roundhouse kick from Leon.

"Yup, a whole year of training and yet all you seem to know how to do is dodge. Get inside my guard for once, land a hit, throw a punch. C'mon, be different. Make this a challenge!" Leon scolds boldly, egging Almir on and setting him up for a new technique.

"But you taught me to be a defensive fighter—O Wise One," Almir smarts off then takes a step back, rooting his feet into the soft sand. "Ugh!" he exclaims, while making a sour face at the grains seeping into his water shoes. "Remind me why you insisted on sparring at the beach again?" he complains, unaware of his friend's intent and his feet, which have also sunken into the softness.

"It's growing on me," Leon shrugs. "I've been practicing out here at night," he answers, then shifts his eyes left then right, checking the passers-by before doing a skipping hop backward. In the movement as he lands, he thrusts his hands downward. Suddenly, before Almir can respond, the sand beneath him sinks, opening into a hole, which swallows him up to his knees before closing.

"Oh, shit!" Almir exclaims just as Leon thrusts his hands forward and a billow of sand strikes Almir in the face like a fist.

Offering a hand to his downed and coughing student, Leon reaches out to help him to his feet. "What do you think of that move?" he asks him.

"What? You did that?" Almir looks to him, dumbfounded.

Leon shakes his head in a bewildered sigh. "You still haven't grasped the use of aether?" he counters, sounding disappointed.

His student shrugs defensively, "Sure I know a little bit but…"

"See, you don't practice enou—whoa!" Leon topples forward, feeling his leg give way. He turns as he falls, finding himself seemingly knee deep in sand. Turning about, he reaches back to support himself, only to sink shoulder-deep. "Pull me up!" Leon panics, and Almir scrambles to drag him to solid ground.

"Are you alright, Lee?" he asks, placing his friend on the boardwalk.

"It felt like I was made of sand a second ago," he states, trying to grasp the moment. Leon sits up then creeps to the edge of the wooden platform, reaching ever-so slowly over the edge. As he places his hand to the sandy ground, he presses in only to be astonished as it seems to be devoured by the Earth. Quickly, he pulls back, looking himself over before trying again with only a finger, which disappears much like his arm did a moment ago.

"That's cool," Almir lets out. "So, that's what you've been practicing?" he asks.

Leon rests there flabbergasted by the experience. "I guess so."

. . .

Beep—sounds the first of her three wristwatches, just as Simon steps out onto the patio of their apartment to catch her staring off into the evening sky. There's a quaint little smile on her face as she gazes into the north-westward direction of the fading sun.

"Guess what?" Simon whispers—there's only one possibility: the flow of this moment, and she smiles while teasing at the strings of time that she plucks delicately-so like the chords of her hummingbird guitar, resting in her lap.

"What?" she replies to his query playfully, for it's so unlike him to be so subtle.

"My suit is done. I want to show it to you," he says just as her scene ripples, growing unsteady as the event collapses; the light twists, reverting back to the way it was a few moments ago—beep!

"Jasra!" She hears him shouting for her.

"That's more like it." She smirks, closing her eyes before turning to see an overly excited Simon coming out the door behind her.

"Let me guess, you're ready to test your new toy?" she presents. Simon stops in his tracks, dropping his gaping grin.

"Well, yeah, but…" He realizes. "Stop that!" he exclaims, and she laughs.

"I can't help it. I've been watching this very moment play out ten different ways for the last few minutes," she tells him.

"Wait, so are we here now, or is it then?" he asks with a puzzled look.

"Don't worry about it; we're in now, now. But I could always go back to then, if you'd like?" she teases, though she could, if only for a few minutes.

"Anyway." He pulls her inside and into his workroom. "This is what I want to show you!" he exclaims.

Jasra shrugs. "What about it?" she asks, as if she didn't already know.

"I'm going to put the suit on. It's gonna be epically awesome!" he says, picking up the top half. She smirks, having seen this before.

"Question, it may be silly but… aren't those gonna hurt?" she asks knowingly, while pointing at the copper barbs lining the inside.

Simon's smirk drops again as he ponders. "Crap… they… they should auto-align, so hopefully it won't be that bad," he says reassuringly, though mainly to himself. Slipping his arms into the sleeves, he feels the little devices brushing against his skin. They line more than just the spine of the suit, connecting to meridians in the arms and chest as well. The pants, gloves, toe-boots, and headgear are also outfitted with similar connectors. Once suited up, he takes a deep breath and switches it on.

"Here goes nothi—aughh!" Simon barely finishes his sentence before the suit powers up. He grits his teeth as the meridian lines thread into him as if he were wearing a full-body corset.

Jasra grimaces, now living through a moment she had always stopped at.

The nanites inject next, flowing out from the meridian lines and into his system. At first, he jitters as they course through him.

"Simon!" Jasra calls out fearfully, as his skin turns pale. "Simon!" She grabs his shoulder as he collapses—gasping for air.

He holds up a hand, "I'm good, I'm ok!" he shouts. "That's normal, that's supposed to happen," he tells her.

"What?" she asks, "You're fucking gray—I thought you said you fixed that?"

"That's just them getting into the red blood cells," he says. "Phew." He catches his breath. "Yeah, binding with the cells kind of freaks the body out, but I'm good now. It looks like it's all working."

Jasra stares at him, incredulously. "You're still gray," she comments.

Simon shrugs, hopping out of his chair. He checks the computer's interface, comparing it to the display projection within his new and improved goggles.

"Lookin good." He grins when suddenly, his breathing grows staggard. "Oh, man…" He leans against the table, feeling nauseous before coughing up some fluid into his hand. "Uh… that's not good." He feels a gritty sensation with a metallic taste in his mouth.

The display on the monitor reads: "Warning Immuno-incompatibility," in flashing yellow letters.

"What?" she asks.

"My immune system is attacking this version of nanites. I should've expected that," he says, typing something into the computer. The body diagram on the display shows flashes of red where the microscopic bots are having trouble. He attaches an intravenous line to his wrist and recalls them.

"Looks like I'll have to work on that, but the suit feels great." He laughs as his color returns, though he can still taste metal in his mouth. Once his system is clear, he gets up.

"Do you wanna go for a little sparring?" he asks her, while playfully shadow boxing like an excited child.

Jasra takes a calming breath, while shaking her head. She smirks, thinking about it. "Well, since you're suited up…" She holds up a finger.

To Simon, Jasra appears to vibrate and shimmer for a second or two. Her casual outfit of a pink t-shirt, cut-off jean shorts, and turn-cuff socks, now lay on the coffee table with her now wearing her green body suit, complete with a green short skirt with burgundy pleats, green knee-high boots, burgundy knee-high socks, a wide leather belt with a gold hourglass buckle, fingerless leather gloves, and of course, a green cape with a burgundy lining. On the back of the cape is a golden hourglass.

Simon holds up a finger, looking at her and the coffee table for a second. "Wait, what?"

Jasra points to herself. "You like it?" She grabs the edges of her cape and turns her backside for him to check out.

Simon looks confused. "How did you?"

Jasra then realizes. "Oh, I stepped forward in time to when I was dressed," she says.

"You can do that?" he questions.

Jasra nods. "Baby steps," she says with a smile, and then gestures out the balcony toward Cedar Park and the whirling vortex of energy next to the basketball court, now more visible in the fading light. "After you, Guardian of Technology."

Simon grins, then runs with a hop into a summersault over the guardrail, landing gracefully below. He looks back up, waiting for her to follow, but Jasra smirks with a look down at him as she casually soars overhead.

"You're walking? How quaint," she teases, and Simon takes to the air after her.

"I was trying to be subtle," he rebuts.

"Since when?" she asks as they touch down on the basketball court and take their stances under the faint glow of the orange streetlamp.

Simon roots himself in a cat-stance with a seventy/thirty weight distribution. Jasra, on the other hand, stands casually, letting the wind blow around her as her flowing, reddish-brown hair trails to one side in the breeze.

"No stance?" Simon questions.

"This is my stance," she comments, and then rests her right arm across her midsection to grasp her wrist with her left hand.

The second Simon steps to pounce, there is a subtle beep of her watch. She appears to phase, blurring in his sight as if for a brief instant there were two of her. He throws a side kick off his right leg, and then without appearing to move, Jasra is to the outside of his attack. Taking him at the hip, she roots her stance inside his guard then trips him as she twists—beep!

With the ground rushing at him, Simon throws his hands out, bracing himself just inches away with a cushion of aether. He rests there for a second, lying with his upper half hovering before using energy to push himself back to his feet.

"Where'd you learn that hip toss?" he questions her technique.

"Sei," she replies.

Groaning, Simon retakes his stance. "I knew that wasn't yours," he says, while drawing aether from his surroundings. The whirling vortex bends and sways from his pull. There's a warming sensation as the aether moves through the lines of the suit to his devices—woosh—he dashes at blinding speed, dropping into a front sweep that catches the back of her heel.

Jasra tumbles and swings her arms out to carry her momentum into a cartwheel to avoid the ground. Beep, beep, beep! She sets all three watches, seeing the stream of possibilities in her mind's eye. Out of his attack, she sees him using the energy to launch himself, then strafe left throwing two punches before pooling energy into his hand for a third strike. His suit makes him faster than her and adds a bonus to his strength. Still, nothing is faster than knowing, and with that to her advantage, she looks a few plays ahead.

In the first option, she can dodge the initial two attacks, but she'll be out of position and likely get caught by his haymaker.

In the second option, she can block the first strike, deflecting his forward momentum enough to offset his footing. If she does that, he'll be too off balance for an energy strike.

While in option three, she can strafe to the right, where his guard is slightly open and jump into a round kick to his ribs. But his suit is likely to absorb the attack. The best action is to counter by catching his wrist and throwing him on his ass. However, she knows her boyfriend doesn't like to lose, and losing this early will likely bruise his pride, especially given his fancy new tech.

She opts to take the hit, initially rolling with the jab to the cheek and as she comes out, she projects a temporal bubble that forces Simon to move a few seconds forward, then backward through time. He becomes nauseous, not able to cope with the disorientation of time travel. Before he realizes it, she's behind him—kicking him swiftly, playfully, in the butt.

Simon "Grrs" in frustration, then powers up, circulating more aether through his core. Her strikes to him, though annoying, only serve to feed him more power. It's weird to absorb energy in this fashion because he's expecting a different result from being hit. It takes him a few tactical exchanges before he gets the feel of his equipment. The force of impact rocks his body, but he realizes he can simply step into the strikes to amplify the conversion factor.

With that in mind, he starts tanking hits—bam! Slap! Thwack! She delivers a left, right, and an elbow, but Simon doesn't even bother to block; instead, returns the favor with supercharged punches, whiffing them just inches past her as her image branches into shimmers and blurs. Their fight becomes an intricate dance of close calls and near misses.

"How many moves can you see ahead?" Simon asks her while taking a front kick to the chest and recycling the force into a telekinetic push, which she slips past, easily.

"Uh, I can see about five minutes ahead now, but for this, I'm keeping it to ten moves or less," she smirks, while teasing at the possibilities she sees.

"So, who's gonna win?" he asks.

"Don't worry, I'll let ya." She winks.

. . .

Seldin trained every day, practicing in symbiotic delight. The benefits of the malnar amplified his energy, making things possible that he once could only dream. Even unshrouded, he saw improvements. His control of the aether increased considerably in only a few short months. And by the end of that first year, Seldin found himself a new person.

With the day turning to dusk and the evening air beginning to cool, Seldin withdraws from his fun in the sun to seek cover for the night ahead. As he enters the mouth of the cavern, the malnar retracts its extrusions, unlatching from his back and spider-crawling to a perch on his shoulder just as he comes upon the home that he had made for himself. There, he scoops up the little flower and places it in a quiet corner where he had fashioned a soil-plot, and as he sets it there, it roots down into the dirt then closes its bulb for the night. Seldin then turns, fires a flawless stream of bluish-white energy to the large crystal in the middle of the room to shed light on the situation; the action comes naturally, as if he'd performed it hundreds of times before.

Shedding his clothes, he stands nude, bathing in the light as it sparkles, dancing amongst the crystals. Although his companion has hunkered down for the night, he is not tired one bit; in fact, he has never felt more alive. The power circulating in his aura plays with the structures that encircle him, teasing at the delicate pull that he feels all around. Outstretching his arms, he pushes the aether from his core, extending his aura to the edges of the walls. As the pull between his center and the center of the cave grows stronger, he begins to levitate, suspended by the energy as it courses all around.

Closing his eyes, Seldin then focuses his consciousness to the point of his mind's eye until he feels a swell of pressure building there. From that point, he moves the pulsating presence down into his center, just below his navel. It is there that he can feel the polar fluctuations of the Earth pushing back against him. Steadily, he oscillates the energy in his core, offsetting the polarity so that it causes him to roll as if he were cartwheeling in midair. This meditative dance is what he'll do tonight, what he did last night, and what he'll do tomorrow onward.

Grooaarr! He hears loudly from behind. The sound breaks his concentration, though not by much. He spins himself about, leaping with a push of energy, like two magnets opposing one another, then lands softly just past the edge of the pool. The bellowing roar echoes throughout the cave, growing louder and louder as he approaches. He can feel the presence of the beast, as well as the two weaker entities behind it. Coming from around the bend, he spots the bear in its entirety as it makes a ruckus and sniffs about the place—searching for the smell that is likely him.

"Ha, and where were you when I was starving?" he comments openly.

Hearing him, the animal responds with its own sounds. Through the roar Seldin can hear something… something else underneath.

"You weren't hibernating; it was summer. No matter. This is my dwelling; you can't stay here. There is a den a few miles south, just follow the river upstream," he says, and then begins to turn away.

It roars at him again, and he snaps back.

"Don't take that tone with me," he scowls.

The bear then stands, offering a ferocious growl as the two cubs tuck behind. Seldin takes a step forward, showing no sign of fear as he charges his body with the aether. The loose stones near him begin to rise, caught in the wake of his aura, which flares with faintly visible shimmers of energy that spark like static, arcing around him.

Backing away, the beast lowers itself to him, returning only a faint stare to make eye contact with a questioning look.

"I'm the Guardian of Life," Seldin answers. "You may call me, Sei."

With a gesture, the bear bobs its head, only slightly, as if to nod before turning away.

"It is late," Seldin says. "I will be kind enough to bring food and allow you to stay for the night. Come morning, you best be on your way," he offers, before returning to his den.

Within the cave yet undetected by Seldin, the Guardian of Dimension and the Guardian of Death observe as he brings fish for the bears.

"He seems more capable, now," Dean says.

"Yes." Tillman nods. "Confident and merciful, as life guardians are, but will he have nerve enough to do what is necessary?" he says, while watching Seldin laugh and play with the cubs.

Chapter 17

"Everyone Has Weaknesses"

Two years have passed since Seldin's quest of self-discovery began and as difficult as it was when he left his friends at the start of his journey, he can't help but feel he will miss the wilderness he is leaving behind. With the wind to his face, he takes to the sky before homing in on the aura of his best friend as he heads back to Florida.

"Whoa!" shouts a group of kids playing in the parking lot at Simon's apartment complex just as Seldin's feet hit the ground. "How do you do that?" one of the boys asks.

"Nice, Sei," Simon comments, while staring down at him from the third-story balcony.

Seldin shrugs at Simon then says to the kids, "It's magic." He waves to them before heading up the stairs the traditional way.

"Why didn't you just fly up?" Simon questions, catching him at the stairwell.

"Didn't want the kids trying to emulate me," he replies.

"Ah, well, it's good to see ya," Simon says, slapping his arm.

"Likewise. What's this?" Seldin points at the black skin-tight outfit Simon is wearing. "You going diving?"

Simon chuckles. "No, it's my bio-suit. These are meridian lines." He points at the round copper button-like nubs on his midline, arms, and legs.

Seldin touches copper strands linking each nub. "Interesting. Can you fly?" he asks.

Simon nods. "For about a year now."

"And you said it was impossible," Seldin says, and Simon shrugs. "Say, how'd you know I was coming?" Seldin asks.

"Jasra," Simon answers.

"Oh, she must be getting good then."

"Eh… she's been keeping an eye on you since you left," he comments.

"Oh…" Seldin pauses, "that's odd."

"Somebody had to make sure you weren't gonna die out there. You messed up your core the first week, am I right?" Simon asks with a chuckle.

"Yeah, that did happen. So, how goes business?" he asks as they head toward his suite.

"About the same; payin the bills. I had to move a lot of equipment out here, though, after the attack—"

"Attack?" Seldin stops.

"It's… a long story," Simon says dismissively, "So, why are you back? I honestly wasn't expecting ya for at least another year," he asks curiously of his friend, who quickly grows silent as if he has the weight of the world on his shoulders.

There's a moment of hesitation as Seldin lets out a deep sigh, and then turns to look over the guardrail. "A lot has happened, Simy, since I've been gone," his eyes scan the suburban landscape as he meanders in thought, thinking about what to say. "I considered staying out there a few more years, but there's just no time left. We have to prepare now." Seldin turns, staring directly into his eyes.

"Oooh, don't get all tense now," he says.

"Simon, this is serious," Seldin scoffs.

"And so am I." Simon turns a wrist to feign a look at his non-existent watch. "I haven't seen ya in two years. Take five minutes, relax. Besides, Jassie wants to see you, too." He turns to the door, guiding him inside. Simon's apartment is much nicer than Seldin remembers, surprisingly, for the presence of a busy mind seems to be absent.

Without hesitation, Jasra tackles him with a big hug as if she had set a trap of anticipation just inside the doorway.

"Sei!" She envelopes him.

"Oh… hey, Jassie," he greets her, awkwardly accepting her affection.

"I've been expecting you," she says.

"I can see that," he replies just as Simon cuts across to the kitchen to pick at the source of a delicious aroma.

"Are you hungry?" she asks Seldin.

"Um, no, not actually." He heads toward the dining table next to the kitchen. "In all honesty, I haven't eaten in over a year. But thank you, though," he says kindly as the two of them stare at him blankly.

"Bullshit," Simon says in disbelief.

"I didn't like killing things while I was out there," Seldin tells him. Simon shrugs, making a plate for himself.

"Well, that's amazing," Jasra comments, admirably-so. "How about something to drink?" she offers.

He shakes his head, "Hm-mm…" he mutters before looking to Simon. "Simy, can we talk?" he requests with a gesture of his head toward his workroom.

"Can I get my dinner first?" Simon glares.

In his office, Simon stuffs his face, while arguing with Seldin, who tells him of his experiences—the things he saw, and how the world is in danger. Simon simply cannot believe what he is hearing. He's likely to take Seldin's word over most, but this is too far into left field, even for him.

Throwing down his fork onto the plate of spaghetti, Simon kicks back in his chair. "Sei, I hate to say it, but you've been watching far too many movies. Nothing is going to happen." He attempts to console him.

"I saw things while I was there, Simon. I had visions of this—I fought alongside another race in some interstellar war, which we… they… lost. The suka called these beings the pulsari."

"Pulsari?" Simon shakes his head. "Hallucinations from being alone too long. It happened to Tom Hanks in Castaway," he says dismissively.

Seldin huffs, stepping back. "God damn it, why do you have to be so stubborn—after all we've seen?"

Speechless, Simon gapes. "I…" he gestures with upturned hands, "…I'm sorry. I've never seen an alien."

The epiphany hits Seldin and he tilts his head up slightly as it comes to him. He gestures to hold on for a moment as he turns for his bag, unveiling his keepsake.

"It's called a malnar—some plant species that inhabits Binax-Alpha. This type is known as beljusa—a sentient rose. It can create the others by dropping these." He fans the spores within its bud with the tip of his finger. "And there are a few subtypes: adori, boni, and cepella—to name a few. The suka taught me about them and the pulsari, who are on their way. I fought them, Simon, and they're strong. They have technology that we can't even touch. If we don't act now, we lose everything; just as they did."

"That's absurd," Simon says while looking over the rose.

"Oh, is it?" Seldin responds, holding out his hand. The rose springs into action, spidering up the length of his arm to the nape of his neck. Simon leaps like a frightened cat, jumping out of his chair as its leafy extrusions lace around his friend. Seldin's expression barely offers a wince at the pain that he has grown accustomed to.

"This, Simon, is a real bio-suit. At any given time, it triples my strength and amplifies my power. In the full light of the sun, it boosts me tenfold."

Clearly in shock and awe, Simon mutters, "T-that's incredible. How does it work?"

"It feeds on energy. That's how I learned to live without food. While in the suit, the beljusa nourishes me, gives me strength; I don't hunger, I don't fatigue or thirst—though now I've learned to sustain myself without it." He glances over his shoulder at the plant. "That's good, Lucy," he says. The limbs retract and the flower meanders down his arm to his backpack.

Simon's eyes just stay locked onto the critter, truly amazed. "It's uh, it's a girl?" he asks.

Seldin shrugs, "Honestly, I don't know. I figure since it reproduces asexually that it's more likely an it. I just prefer whatever is sucking on me to be female," he comments with what might be the first crack of humor he's made all day. Simon even offers a chuckle at it before the levity gets shoved aside and Seldin steps back into his worried persona.

"Simon," he says. "They all have these. I hope whatever you've made, your bio-suit, is even close to this."

Simon shrugs, "You don't have to worry about that. I'm currently running the suit with these." He pulls out a small clear glass case containing several vials of a mercury-looking solution. "They're my ultimate creation. So far, anyway." He smirks, handing one to Seldin.

He looks it over. "Nanites?" he asks.

Simon nods. "Third Generation. The fourth is cooking over there." He gestures with a nod.

Seldin turns, catching a glimpse of something shrouded behind a line of clothes in the corner before Simon continues.

"Between them and the suit, I should be virtually unstoppable. What do you think?" Simon asks.

Holding the container to the light, Seldin examines it further. "I don't know, honestly. I suspect this is more your territory than mine. So, what's the holdup?" Seldin asks, returning the item.

Simon shrugs. "Eh, I just finished them this afternoon before Jasra said you were on your way. I figured I'd wait for an extra set of hands. Second generation had some compatibility issues, so I designed this isolation chamber." He uncovers the device. "In the event of a catastrophic failure, I wanted a way to contain them," he says before activating the console.

"So, how long has that been there?" Seldin prompts, looking it over.

"About a month; the locking mechanism is mechanical instead of electronic and can only be accessed from the outside. It's a precaution against myself in case something goes wrong," he states.

"I understand," Seldin says, while examining the structure, feeling its make-up. It's a wonderful piece of equipment—three-inch-thick reinforced steel, and some sort of poly-resin for glass. It almost looks like it was made for deep-sea exploration the way it's put together.

"Alright, so this is the go button. Once started, it can't be aborted until the decontamination cycle is finished," Simon instructs him before stepping inside and closing the chamber door. There's a countdown accompanied by a subtle beeping sound as the door grinds shut, and a suctioning system fires off as the chamber pressurizes. Simon then hits the call button.

"Alright, Sei, whenever you are ready."

Trusting his friend, Seldin sets caution aside as he hesitantly extends a hand to the control panel and presses the button. There's a loud whoosh that spins up like a particle accelerator charging.

Simon notices Seldin's reaction, "That's just the energy grid powering on. It's what keeps them from getting out if they go rogue," he tells him before cracking the vial, releasing a cloud of metallic vapor, which engulfs him.

"Gah!" Simon grunts, leaning forward as bluish veins spread throughout his body just as his skin pales and turns gray.

"Simy, are you alright?" Seldin panics. He can feel his friend's power fluctuating. Simon's vison goes blurry, and he becomes nauseous and dizzy. For a moment, his skin burns and the room spins.

Not knowing what to do, Seldin presses button after button, not getting a result. "God damn it!" he yells, cupping his hands together, drawing in aether to blast through the chamber door. "Hani…" He focuses quickly.

"I'm good!" Simon yells back as the symptoms subside. "All done," he says. A green light flashes, and the chamber unlocks.

"Thank you for becoming one with Sim-Antics," a computerized feminine voice pleasantly chimes.

"Man, I'm so pumped!" Simon exclaims.

Seldin gives him an odd look. "Um, you're gray," he says.

"Oh, that's normal—you know what we should do?" He points at Seldin, while radiating confidence. "We should go check out Area 51!" Simon says, excitedly.

The idea strikes Seldin's own sense of curiosity, but then morality sets in. "Simy, we're supposed to be the good guys."

"Ugh, c'mon. I need a way to test out the new gear—it'll be fun. Besides, if you're serious about all of this *'ET-phone-home'* shit, then what better place to scout some grays?" he suggests.

"Even so, we can't just go around doing whatever the hell we want. That's the wrong message, Simon, and it'll draw too much attention," Seldin comments.

Simon waves him off, "Oh, pfft, two years ago, you wanted to reveal us to the world," he says.

"No," Seldin holds up a finger, "I said, *'one day, we'd be revealed to the world,'* it has to be done delicately—to go galivanting around—"

Simon groans with heavy breath. "Ugh, Sei, it's like you're trying to protect the coals from the fire; it's impossible. If these beings really exist, as you say, then it's our duty as guardians to investigate."

"What are you two going on about?" A sweet voice interrupts from the door, and they both turn a gaze toward Jasra.

"Raiding Area 51," Simon smirks.

"Sounds like fun, can I come?" she asks, adorably.

Seldin nods, outnumbered. "Ehh... of course." He smiles at her.

Simon furrows his brow, turning his face toward his friend. "Then it's settled. We leave tomorrow morning. But for now, let's do some sparring," he says with excitement.

...

Seldin watches from a bench in the park, observing his friends' techniques. Simon and Jasra are definitely opposites when it comes to the martial arts. He can tell by Simon's actions that he has become a much riskier fighter—willing to take hits for a quick advantage and far more reliant on his equipment than his instincts. While Jasra, on the other hand, is relaxed and very in tune with her gifts. She's patient, able to play the long game—waiting him out and bating his movements.

However, combat is a mental game and Seldin knows this as he watches intently for flaws in their strategies. Fighting, as silly as the notion is, is less about brutality and more about psychology, for it doesn't matter how good you are, if you doubt yourself, you will lose for sure. That's how he managed to keep up and ultimately stay ahead of Simon; growing up, he knew if he held on long enough that his friend would give up. It's rather disheartening when your opponent laughs in your face after you've delivered your most powerful attack—self defeat defeats us all.

That is the very thing that Jasra is doing to Simon; she's definitely not as fast as him nor anywhere near as strong, but mentally she is on par. Using her ability of time, she looks ahead five, ten, even fifteen moves—just enough to throw off his game. Seldin can feel it, the way the air frills and space twists every time she peers into the future, as if the action itself tickles the very energy needed to engage. It's amazing, simply amazing.

With his eyes closed, he takes in their actions, feeling their energy, watching and observing in a tranquil view of blue-green tones and yellow highlights. Their auras are prominent; their cores are fluctuating as they give off more and more power, and yet there is something else, something cold and sterile filling the air—those machines. They cloud the corona of Simon's aura as it radiates outward. Tiny little leeches they are, scooping up the free radicals that spiral off as he fights to his heart's content.

Seldin can tell that Simon can't see it, the way the aether behaves as Jasra peers ahead. Even with his tech, Simon is blind without the intuition he'd sacrificed. What started off as a game has now shifted into a losing sport, for Simon is showing signs of frustration. And very soon, it is apparent to even him, that he is not going to win this.

Jasra projects silent whispers of herself into the future to manipulate the outcome as Simon's present aligns with his misguided fate, subconsciously making the errors that she has planted. It's surprising to see him miss so blatantly, and it becomes obvious to Seldin that she's doing more than just seeing the future; she's presetting the outcome.

In the few short moments that follow, the fight is over. Simon rests on his pride, though trying to conceal his heatedness. He sits for a second on the hard surface of the basketball court while casting a gaze to the celestial body just past the orange hue of the streetlamp. Kipping up, he brushes Jasra's helping hand aside before moseying over to the bench to plop a seat down next to Seldin.

"Can't handle your girl, Simon?" Seldin teases childishly, reliving the days where taunts were prevalent.

"Shut up," Simon snaps.

Shaking his head, Seldin figures his friend's pettiness is only a matter of pride. He takes a deep breath as he offers a sighing nod to Simon before slowly moving out to center court.

"Are you sure you don't want to take a break?" he asks Jasra, who dances playfully.

"I'm good." She smirks and winks at him. Seldin then rests his weight casually, taking a rather nonchalant stance as he loosens up and evaluates his surroundings.

Perhaps it's unfair, watching and learning from Simon's mistakes, but this is a game of life; there are no rules, save for those self-imposed. Keenly observing, he feels out her energy, sensing for signs of fluctuation—changes in the flow of the air that casually wisps around them, blowing her beautiful reddish-brown hair in the August eve.

Then there it is, the flux he is looking for. Suddenly the air around her twists, leaving noticeable ripples in her wake. In the blink of an eye, the exchange happens: Jasra collides with a foot to her chest, nearly knocking her wind out.

Both Simon and Jasra are surprised at first, but the pause doesn't remain for long, for almost as soon as the hit connects, comes another. Seldin and Jasra seemingly disappear in their moment of combat. Simon can barely keep track. He rubs his eyes, looking on with a dumbfounded expression. Their actions are almost invisible to him, like broken timelapse photography that only snaps a few frames per second. Their images blend and blur in the crisscrossing light, occasionally casting the illusion of them being in multiple places at once.

Gawking in amazement, Simon simply cannot believe what he's seeing, the way they move. It's clear to him now, just how far she's come, and how much she's been holding back on him. According to his readings, Seldin's aura is holding steady at just over 15,000 joules, enough energy to power a small house. If the data from their experiments is correct, Simon figures his friend's potential output is likely in the neighborhood of 45,000 joules, which to his knowledge, is entirely unheard of in a living being. But even with him easily keeping at almost twice her strength level, she's giving him a run for his money. It's all in her gift.

She comes at him fiercely, making her way through a sea of possibilities. Seldin was right: her ripples are more than glimpses in time. She anticipates his actions by knowing what he'll do and influencing what he will not. Still, Jasra is finding him a difficult opponent. He's not like Simon. His actions are defensive, yet not reactionary. When it comes to the martial arts, he seems to have the answer before the question is asked. That baffles her—even with her foresight, he's challenging. However, it's those ripples that give her away, but it's not good enough.

A swift combination of kicks to his knee, abdomen, and head dazes him for a brief moment.

"Gah!" he stumbles, bouncing backward into a handspring to re-attain his balance. *'There's gotta be something else,'* Seldin contemplates, for he can feel the changes in the aether that occur whenever she alters time. Unfortunately, she can do so, so precisely that he has to be on his toes, keeping his power high enough to have the speed to respond. That puts his senses into overdrive.

Wham—bam—boom—smack—sounds each blow, and then—beep! He hears it—beep! And there again. *'Her watches!'* His mind races to a conclusion; his ears perk up at the sound. The beep acts like a signal, a momentary precursor priming the ripples and the events to come.

Setting up for a finishing blow, Jasra scans ahead. She plays with her visions, and the possible deviations that are open to her. Nudging him into dodging a kick, she sees that he'll likely block her upcoming attacks. Following the kick, if she jabs, he'll block with his left and return with a low uppercut to her sternum. Knowing that, she throws the kick; he dodges as expected, and then in comes the right jab out of her southpaw stance. Seldin's response can't be any more predictable, for the block with his left forearm happens immediately, as does his attempt at an uppercut. She cups his fist, taking his uppercut into her hand just as she swivels her wrist to take his, and then out of a sidestep, she twists. Lunging forward, Seldin hits the cement court and then bounces out of a rolling pushup to save his grace.

Shaking the soreness from her right wrist, Jasra readies herself. "You still haven't given up? I'm impressed," she taunts him.

"You know me," he says, while dusting himself off a bit, "I'll go until I can't."

Jasra nods with a snide smirk. As she goes to line up her next attack, she reaches a subtle hand to her wrist. Seldin's senses pick up the shift as the displacement of temporal energy ensues. Her fingers glide up her wrist, strumming to the control of the first watch—click.

"Huh?" She glances down at her wrist. Click, click—smack! Seldin strikes open-handed to her face, then closes in, folding his arm into an elbow that strikes in a downward motion to her collarbone. He then twists left, jumps, and thrusts a knee into her abdomen. Jasra's wind leaves her as she crashes breathlessly onto the hard surface of the basketball court.

Walking out to her, Seldin offers a hand to help her sit up. "I take it, that's game?" He smirks at her before glancing to the empty bench at the edge of the court. Simon is gone. He sighs, disappointed.

Jasra looks up at Seldin, while panting with her left hand to her chest. "Yeah… yeah… that's game," she huffs, winded, and surprised by the outcome. She rests back, still catching her breath. "Simon hasn't beaten me in over a year," she lets out a soft, breathy chuckle. "Yet you did it with ease."

Seldin shakes his head as he kneels beside her, feeling more fatigued than he has in a long time. "It wasn't easy, Jassie; I burned through so much energy just keeping up with you," he says with genuine amazement. "If I hadn't noticed your weakness…" He sighs, thinking.

Jasra looks at him with curious eyes. "My… weakness?"

Seldin nods with his gaze drifting out across the orange lit green court to the darkened field and the whirling vortex of turquoise energy just beyond the edge. Fight after fight replays in his mind.

"Everyone has weaknesses," he says, gathering his thoughts. "Simon's is ego; he doesn't let go easily. He often doubles down even when he's wrong. It can be hard to improve that way."

Jasra's eyes drift down with a nod. She then looks to him. "What about mine?"

"You have two big ones that I saw: you don't keep track of time in your head. You rely on your watches. That slows you down," he tells her, and she thinks on that for a moment while staring at the crumpled piece of jewelry on her left wrist. The other two are still ticking along.

"What else?" she asks.

"You seem to be able to predict my actions rather well, but not my intentions," he says.

"What do you mean? I looked into the future and saw your moves; I even countered them," she argues.

"Yes, that's true, but what you didn't realize was that I was baiting you—that I faked techniques to get you to expose your weakness. I used my blocks to damage your watches so you wouldn't know I was aiming for them," he says.

Jasra looks down. "I see..." She sighs, unhooking the watch bands, letting them fall to the court. Her eyes trail back up to him, "What about you, what are your weaknesses?" she asks.

Seldin lets out a sigh of his own as his eyes drift out of focus and he looks inward. "I..."

"Yo, Sei!" Simon calls out as he descends.

"Hey, where'd you go?" Seldin prompts.

Simon looks upward. "I like to meditate in front of the moon. It helps me think," he says in a calm voice then adds, "It's getting late, we should—"

Whoop-whoop—a squad car passes by.

"Simon, get down," Seldin says, pulling him to the ground just as a blinding light shines their way.

"Hey!" shouts the cop as he steps out of the car. "What are you three doing out here this time of night?"

Simon turns a shrewd gaze in the officer's direction, taking the lead. "Just shooting some hoops," he says.

The officer shrugs. "Yeah, well, the park closes at sundown. So, you're trespassing. Do you kids realize I could arrest you?" he states boldly.

Simon huffs, "Heh, you can try," he snaps.

"What?" the officer responds.

"Simon!" Seldin barks and then looks to the policeman. "Please excuse my friend; he has a habit of speaking before he thinks. We were actually just leaving."

An odd sense of calm comes over the cop, and he turns back toward his car. "Stay out of the park after dark and there'll be no issue," he says before driving off.

As the moment passes, Seldin turns to Simon with a disappointed look in his eyes. "What was that?" he asks.

"What? I could have taken him," Simon defends.

Seldin shakes his head. "Hostility sends the wrong message, Simon," he says.

"Yet you'll break into a government installation?" Simon rebuts.

"Let's be clear, that was your idea, but I'm willing to do what it takes to protect this planet."

"Whatever," Simon concedes, pushing off the ground.

"Where are you going?" Seldin asks.

"It's going to be a long trip!" Simon shouts.

Chapter 18

"The Mystic Gates"

The three of them fly through the night and well into the morning with Seldin and Simon almost neck and neck, while Jasra is just off Simon's left flank, completing the delta formation. None of them have spoken since they took to the sky from Cedar Park.

"Mm…" Jasra groans, squinting and wiping her watery eyes from the constant wind on her face. Sunup was hours ago, yet the frequent drooping of her head and the rumbling in her stomach make it hard to decide whether she wants food or sleep.

"Are you okay, Jassie?" Simon asks, looking back before slowing down to keep pace.

Jasra shakes her head while offering a long, slow blink of her tired eyes. "I'm starving," she says. Simon could use a rest too, yet he's amazed at how Seldin just keeps on trucking.

Taking her in midflight, Simon wraps an arm around her in what might be his first genuine sign of affection in weeks. He then nestles a kiss to her neck before facing ahead to Seldin, who is now several meters out.

"Hey!" Simon shouts and his friend looks back at them. "We've been flying all night, how about a break?" Simon prompts.

"We'll get there sooner if we keep moving; I think we're about halfway, now," Seldin replies.

"Yeah, well, we're hungry and tired!" Simon shouts.

The notion catches Seldin off guard. "Oh shit." He stops in midflight. "Sorry guys, I forgot."

"It's ok," Jasra replies. "It looks like we're over a small town."

"Yeah, might be a good place to take a break and recharge our batteries," Simon comments.

Seldin nods, "Alright," he says before leading the descent to a rest stop in the small dustbowl of a town near San Antonio, Texas. It's a little too obvious with its western theme—dusty roads, cacti, and tumbleweeds. With the energy he can detect, Seldin figures they're only about sixty miles or so from the major city.

There's a casual chime as they push through the door of the only restaurant in town. It alerts the staff while cueing the prying eyes and gawking faces of the nosy bodies filling the place.

"How many?" asks a rustic country gal.

"Three," answers Jasra, who takes the lead, eagerly awaiting a menu and hoping that breakfast is still being served despite the hour.

"So, where's the party?" prompts the waitress, awkwardly eyeing the trio as she guides them to a booth.

"What do you mean?" asks Jasra, sliding into the seat next to Simon. Seldin sits across from them on the other side.

The waitress' eyes shift between them as she points with the tip of her pen while offering a confused smile. "Karate outfit, scuba gear, and a green romper with a cape. You form the circus or something?"

"Oh!" Simon laughs falsely. "We're performance artists," he claims.

"Really?" the waitress asks, dumbfounded.

"Yes ma'am, we're up here rehearsing and scouting locations. We go live in a few weeks," he says as Jasra sits back and turns her face away to conceal her snicker.

"So, what do you guys do, exactly?"

Simon shrugs, "Magic tricks, sleight of hand." He kinetically pulls the saltshaker to himself. "Stuff like that." He smirks, showing off. Seldin just sighs, shaking his head, while glaring at him. Simon looks his way and shrugs as if asking *'what'* with his body language.

"And what do you do?" She turns to Seldin, who furrows his brow with eyes that peer beyond the window.

"Faith healing," he says in a dry monotone voice. "Uh, I'm not really hungry. I'll be outside when you're done," he says before heading outside to greet a balding little girl next to a charity van.

"Hello." He offers her a warm smile.

"Hi." She smiles, gazing up at him before returning her attention to the dolly in her hands.

He can feel it—the wrenching pain in her flesh and in her bones. "What's your name?" he asks, and her answer comes to him intuitively before she speaks it. *"Molly."* He's taken aback by how clear that was.

"Molly," she says.

"What a shame," he kneels to run a hand through her thinning hair, "to be so young and in so much pain." His heart goes out to the child.

"It doesn't hurt that bad," she claims modestly, unaware of her own pain tolerance.

"How old are you, sweetie?" he asks the little girl, though only for the sake of conversation, for that too, he seems to already know.

"I'm this many." She holds up her fingers.

"Six? That's a good age," he compliments. "How would you like it if it didn't hurt at all?" he asks.

"What in God's name do you think you're doing?" shouts a nun coming around the van with the rest of the children.

"Hello ma'am. I was just about to render my services to this young lady," he says.

"Molly come here, step away from him," she says to the girl before setting her sights on Seldin, once again. "You should be ashamed of yourself," she states firmly.

Rising to his feet, he angles himself to better face the nun. "The only remorse I feel is for the eight ill children in your care: one with sickle cell, two with aplastic anemia, four with brain tumors, and one with small cell cancer," he states with a powerful, penetrating stare.

"How do you know?" she questions, and for that Seldin doesn't have a good answer. He just knows.

"I can feel them—the cancers ravaging their bodies—their pain, and I can hear their internal cries for help. Just as… I can feel the life growing inside you," he says, astonished by his own clarity.

She grows deathly pale. "I'm sorry Lord, please forgive me," she pleads, kneeling with tearful eyes.

"I'm not your lord, nor am I here to absolve your sins. They don't exist anyway. I am here for them," he says, offering a hand to the girl.

Molly reaches out to him.

"Close your eyes." He places a hand to her chest. At first, he finds his confidence to be shaky, for he's never tried this on anyone else. Careful not to hurt her, he slowly peers into each cell, painstakingly reconstructing every molecule.

Molly giggles at the tingling sensation all over and the rush of warmth throughout her body. Soon, the lesions on her fair skin begin to fade as new follicles replenish her scalp. And much to the amazement of the gathering crowd, Molly opens her eyes to a new, healthy body.

For a moment, it seems too good to be true. Seldin carefully looks her over for any mistakes.

Then one by one he takes each child. By the time he is finished with the last one, little Timmy Martin, he finds himself surrounded by onlookers and two seemingly disappointed friends.

"It's a miracle, it's a bona fide miracle!" the nun shouts. "Who are you, how can we thank you?" she asks.

Seldin simply looks at her. He has to admit, the admiration, the praise, and the thankful eyes upon him feel amazing. There's just something about helping others that is so very satisfying. This, he feels, is the right moment.

"I am the Guardian of Life, and soon, other guardians and I will make an official statement to the world—we are here. Please, spread the word," he tells her before casually pushing off the ground, slowly lifting to a height above the crowd. His eyes fall to Simon and Jasra. "Let's go." He gestures with a tilt of his head northwestward.

Seldin's stunt angers Simon. About a mile away from the diner, he speeds up to catch his friend with full intent on giving him a piece of his mind.

"Hey, what the hell was all that back there?" he shouts over the wind.

"I don't know, it just kind of happened," Seldin replies.

"What ever happened to not galivanting?" Simon questions.

"I didn't misuse my power, Simon, I was helping people," he replies.

Simon pulls in front of him, coming to a dead stop that breaks the sound barrier. "Oh, I see, you self-righteous prick, the rules are different for Seldin Gardane!" Simon shouts.

"Simon, I was helping people, not showing up cops. There's a stark difference between what you tried to pull last night and what I did just now. It is vitally important that people trust us. You are more than welcome to use your power to benefit the world," Seldin says.

"Says who, you? Why are you trying to hold us back?" Simon questions.

"I'm not, I just think it's irresponsible for guardians to—"

"Christ, why are you treating us like we're special? We studied aether, we trained for this—anybody can be what we are! It's not my fault the rest of the world is so blind to the truth that they limit themselves," Simon rants.

"But that doesn't give us the right to abuse our power, we have a responsibility—"

"Guys, guys, wait!" Jasra positions herself in the middle, facing Simon with her back toward Seldin. "There's no reason to fight."

The air shifts with a fluctuating change, like a skipping pulse in Simon's power.

"Did you just take his side?" Simon questions, heatedly.

Jasra's face grows to confusion, "No—" she attempts to say before being telekinetically brushed aside as Simon decks Seldin across the jaw with a psionic punch that cracks the air in a brilliant burst of radiant energy and dislodges him from the sky.

Hurling to the Earth at the speed of sound, Seldin flares his aura, shakes off the hit, and then orients himself before blasting off in Simon's direction. Once again, they collide with the force of a sonic boom as does each subsequent blow. Each strike hits with a force that collapses the air around it, forming a super-heated pocket of densely packed energy, which ruptures immediately, releasing a pressure wave that breaks the sound barrier, and can be heard from several miles away.

Righting herself in the midst of freefall, Jasra turns about to face them. "Stop fighting!" she shouts, foreseeing the future of their turbulence—how the storm will brew, and the winds will churn in their fury, and they do, for one after another the blows keep coming. The sky darkens to the chaos of their calamity, swirling the air and billowing the clouds.

In the distance, the occupants of the neighboring cities gawk at the awesomeness of the whirling abyss that seemingly formed out of nowhere.

"Look at that!" shouts the nun, along with the other patrons of the dusty town, who stare on in terror at the ever-brewing funnel of madness, and the darkening sky of the immense electrical storm heading their way.

Back at the epicenter, Jasra watches helplessly in horror at both the present and the future. Not sure of what to do, she cups her mouth with her hand while frozen in fright. She's never seen them go at it like this. They were always playing before. It was always a game, but now it's real, and the town is paying for it.

The intensity of their energy warps the immediate atmosphere and blackens the land with hurricane-like clouds.

"You two have to stop this!" she shouts while rushing in to interrupt their skirmish, hoping to take advantage at the momentary distance between Simon and Seldin. She grabs Simon's shoulder in an attempt to pull him away, but he's in fighting mode. He doesn't think, and out of sheer reaction, Simon turns with an elbow to her head.

"Augh!" she cries out, falling to the ground.

"Shit!" Simon gasps, realizing what he's done. The action itself enrages Seldin, who, in that moment, loses the shield of his focused, calm exterior. He maxes out, catches Jasra, then charges at Simon in a blind fit of rage. They wrap up as if to grapple in mid-air as they spiral in all directions before aiming for the ground. They break away just before they hit, touching down forcefully on the desert road before charging at one another again.

The two go at it, trading blow for blow. With Seldin tanking damage as his body heals and Simon's suit feeding off the force of his enemy's strikes, they stand equal. An unstoppable force pitted against an immovable object—locked in a stalemate.

Seldin strafes, taking out Simon's left leg with a stomping hooked kick to the back of his calf. It drops him to his knees just as Seldin follows up by clasping his hands together, pooling aether. Before he can release the blast, however, Simon flicks his wrist, turning it upright while showering Seldin in a gray cloud of microscopic machines.

The nanites get to work, burrowing into his flesh. Seldin falls, exhaling from flared nostrils to expel the ones that rode his breath.

Hopping to his feet, Simon closes a fist to squeeze his enemy in the debilitating plume of artificial life that brings him to his knees.

Trying desperately to hold himself together, Seldin fights internally. Watching in his mind's eye, he can see them, the tiny little things ravaging his body. They meticulously invade his cells like a synthetic virus unraveling each molecule. But soon, Seldin's fear fades, for it doesn't hurt—the damage they're doing. And in turn, he reinserts the atoms they remove with the ease of his mind as if to tease them. His cells start rebuilding while his body is adapting—feeding off the aether.

Even with his heart stopped and his lungs frozen, Seldin finds himself fully conscious. It is in this moment that he realizes, given how benign his own flesh seems, that maybe, just maybe, he doesn't need his body at all. *'Am I immortal?'* he questions the epiphany before disregarding the presence of the nanites all together as he begins to rise to his feet.

Unfettered from his own demise, Seldin looks out beyond himself, feeling the desperation in the heart of his childhood friend while catching a glimpse of the need in his eyes. *'How do I gain from winning?'* Seldin asks himself then casts a glance to Jasra, who looks lost in her sight. She blinks, coming back from wherever she was in that glimmering moment to offer a shake of her head.

Seldin's eyes then fall center as he releases his own pride, dropping to his knees once again, letting them take him. His skin grows pale, then gray, and he gasps stiflingly before clutching his throat as he collapses.

"Simon, release him!" Jasra pleads, begging her boyfriend to come back to his senses, for his rage has deafened him. It takes several attempts to get through.

But then, as his fury starts to calm, the sight of his best friend crumpled before him frightens him. "Sei!" he yells anxiously, hurrying his best to undo the will of his machines.

"Jassie, help me!" he begs her while lifting Seldin up as he pulls the nanites out of him. "Dear God, what have I done?" he lets out in a genuine tone of concern.

"I told you two to knock it off!" she scolds while offering a helping hand.

"I'm alright!" Seldin gasps, while Simon eases him into a sitting position.

Simon sighs heavily. "I… I could have killed you," he says. His voice shaky.

Seldin nods, weakly. "But you didn't." He pats his shoulder.

"You guys, the storm. You have to stop the storm." Jasra points.

"Shit!" Simon looks eastward at the immense vortex heading in the direction of the town.

"I'm on it." Seldin leaps, taking off at blinding speed, then goes Simon, and then Jasra trailing behind.

With terror in the streets, the people of the dusty town frantically scurry about as the increasing speed of the wind begins to envelope their surroundings. Sand blows heavily in all directions, blasting the hell out of everything it hits while scouring the paint off buildings, cars, and street signs.

The intensity of the storm is just maddening. It's incredible, and still, it is picking up speed. What had spawned from their chaos has grown into a self-sustaining beast of insanity—like a hurricane on dry land, with no signs of subsiding. The storm's pull tugs at them. Seldin can hardly believe it himself, how quickly it has gained strength and the sheer magnitude of its power.

"Simy, are you seeing this?" he shouts back despite the wind.

"Yes. The storm seems to be thriving off the heat of the desert floor. Combined with the sheer winds, it's the perfect low-pressure system."

"But there's no water. I thought hurricanes needed water?" Jasra asks.

"It has sand," Seldin replies, then looks to Simon. "Simy, any ideas on how to stop this thing?" he shouts.

"Well, I can try destabilizing the air streams above the clouds, but we'll need something to disrupt the low-pressure system at its center. Can you throw another one of those beams?" Simon requests.

Seldin nods. "That's affirmative," he says, clasping his hands together as he powers up.

"Aim for the eye," Simon tells him.

Seldin nods. "I'm going to cause an explosion at the base, ready?" he asks.

"On three," Simon says.

"One," says Seldin.

"Two," says Simon.

"Three!" they yell in tandem. Simon releases a flood of nanites into the air. They move quickly over the canopy of the storm while circling in a clockwise direction to disturb the steadily flowing wind. At that same moment, Seldin unleashes an immense beam of raw energy that punches through the wall of the hurricane and erupts in a massive explosion at the storm's center. The disk-shaped mass of whirling clouds mushrooms upward as the counter twist of the air collapses the storm in on itself.

"Yes! Haha—take that you bubble of festering heat!" Simon gloats.

There's a sudden rush of wind around the collapsing vortex, which spirals rapidly in a counter-clockwise direction as the vacuum created by the explosion equalizes, drawing in everything around it—Seldin included, who is the closest to the storm.

"Oh, shit!" It rips him out of the sky and into the whirling funnel as the storm spirals outward, becoming even greater than before.

"Sei!" Jasra and Simon yell, barely escaping the pull of the vacuum.

Seldin can hardly see a thing within the hurricane. The clouds are densely packed with sand and other debris, including wooden shards, barbed wire, and cacti, which shred him as they hit.

Even at nearly full power, Seldin struggles to break free, but the adventure doesn't last for very long as all that is sucked in is just as quickly spat out. He hits the pavement within seconds of being pulled into the storm.

"Sei!" Simon howls, darting to the ground to aid him. "The storm is heading toward San Antonio," he says.

Seldin hops to his feet. "Damn it!" he shouts angrily while looking over himself to assess the wounds as they close. "I'm done with this—it's just a cyclone of energy. All I have to do—" He thrusts his hands forward, reaching out toward the storm.

"No!" Jasra grabs his shoulder. "You can't just rip it out of the sky, that's too much energy!" she yells.

"Then what the hell do you suggest?" he snaps.

"Wait, I've got an idea." Simon turns to them. "Jasra, how much time before it hits the city?" he asks.

"Uh, about five minutes," she says, and then Simon turns back toward the rumbling swell of dust. He readies himself then takes to the air. In a flash, it is over. The winds calm, and the storm ceases.

"Simy, what did you do?" Seldin asks, stunned.

"I didn't do anything," Simon replies, barely off the ground.

"Then who?" Jasra looks between them frantically when…

"Hey guys!" shouts Leon.

"Lee, what are you doing here?" they all ask simultaneously, taking in the sight of him and his friend.

"It was all over the news, *'Miraculous Savior Heals Kids.'* They're all saying it was the second coming," Leon says.

"But that was not even an hour ago," Seldin claims.

Leon shrugs, making a rather unsurprised face. "Apparently, news travels fast."

Simon then drops back to the ground, "Obviously not as fast as you. It took us nearly twelve hours to get here," he says.

"You gotta be like the wind, man—learn how to ride it," Leon claims.

"Speaking of… what's with the land-cane? You guys looked like you were having a hard time," Leon's cohort comments.

Jasra, Simon, and Seldin look between themselves before reasserting their attention to him—a slim young Hindu man with a clean, narrow beard, swept back black hair, a purple gi with long flowing angular sleeves, and a matching headband set with an amethyst gem worn like a bindi.

"Who are you?" Seldin asks with a tone.

"Oh, sorry, Sei. Uh, this is my apprentice, Almir," Leon introduces him.

"So, which one of you stopped the hurricane?" Seldin asks.

Leon bows with a gesture to himself. "Guardian of Earth, at your service," he says as they take in the sight of his gi. The top is thick, white, sleeveless and form-fitting, with "Guardian of Earth" written vertically in the Language of the Gods in large black symbols on the front left side. His sash is yellow, his pants a deep burgundy, and his shoes are black.

"So, how'd you do it?" Simon prompts.

"Like I said," Leon holds out a hand that turns to vapors then back again, "You've gotta be like the wind—oh, whoa!" He stumbles back, collapsing to the street. They all look to him.

"Are you ok?" Jasra extends a hand, and then her eyes grow wide at the sight of his cement-like legs melding into the street. She freaks out and backs away.

"It's ok, I'm alright," he starts to explain, "I can become one with any of Earth's elements, it seems. But sometimes my control is, well, flakey," Leon says, reshaping his feet before taking the assistance of Simon, who helps him up.

"You ok, Jassie?" Leon asks.

"Mm…" She nods, thinking she really should have looked ahead.

"So, what are you all doing way out here anyway?" Leon asks.

Simon swallows down a smug chuckle, "We're gonna raid Area 51," he says.

"Oh, no way." Leon looks at Almir for a second then back to the gang. "That sounds like fun, count us in." He grins.

Simon makes a face. "Uh, well, three's a company, five's a crowd—ya know?"

An elbow bumps Simon's ribs and he glances to Seldin, who steps past him.

"We should really get going, if we want to make good time," Seldin suggests and he, Simon, and Jasra prepare for takeoff.

"Wait," Leon stops them. "I know a shortcut."

. . .

The vantage into the canyon is vast with a vertical descent so far into the Earth that its depths become unseen, shrouded in darkness despite the afternoon sun and covered with a hazy fog from the crashing gulf below.

"Now that is a deep hole," Simon comments as he looks down into it. Jasra nudges him playfully as if to push him to the edge. "Hey!" he chuckles, clutching at the jump in his chest.

"C'mon, it's this way," Leon says before jumping from the ridge. Almir follows without hesitation, and as Leon's hand grazes the rocky mouth of a small cave, the others, too, follow suit.

As the gang enters, there's a rush of cool, albeit musty, air coming from the depths ahead. Leon holds steady, resting against the stony wall just beyond the entrance as he guides them through.

"This way," he says.

Simon and Jasra look around the cave in wonder, for it's new to them, the way the walls sparkle from the intrusion of the ambient light.

Leon smiles at the newness of their experience before catching the eyes of his mentor, who seems right at home.

"So, where are we, exactly?" Jasra prompts.

"They're called *'mystic gates,'* and they interconnect to junction points all over the world," Leon says.

"Let me guess," Simon interjects, "they're super-heated channels of subterranean air currents that follow the movement of the Earth's tectonic plates, right?"

Leon laughs. "You watch too many movies," he says as they make their way farther and farther into the belly of the Earth.

"Ooh… brrr, it's getting colder," Jasra notes with a shiver that drives her to push aether to her skin and attach to Simon for warmth. Seldin doesn't seem bothered at all by the cold, his body ever adapting, evolving against nature.

"That chill you feel is the result of the gate," Leon says with a gesture to a large polished overall surface on the flat cave wall ahead of them.

"Yes," Seldin remarks, his senses tingling from the gate's pull. "It's inverting matter and drawing energy from the air. Fascinating," he says.

Leon's eyes grow wide, for his teacher never ceases to amaze him. "How do you get it so easily? It took me months to figure this out."

"I love physics." Seldin shrugs.

"Alright, you two, get a room," Simon teases, drawing a chuckle from both Jasra and Almir. Though Almir is starting to see it too, the reason his teacher always spoke so highly of his own teacher.

"It's a wormhole," Seldin comments, peering into the gate's mirror-like surface, which partially reflects their side over what lies beyond.

"So how does it work?" Simon asks.

"Have you ever heard of quantum entanglement?" Seldin responds.

"Yes, of course, smartass. What I meant was, how do we use it?" he rebuts.

Leon looks to them. "That's easy, you just tell it where you want to go: China, Africa, Indonesia. If you pick a city or state, it'll get you as close as possible, usually within a few miles, though sometimes a few hundred. It all depends on where the junctions lie," he says.

Seldin smirks, offering a snide glare to Simon. "You wanna try it?" he asks.

Simon then scans the gate, unable to tell exactly where the energy comes from. "You first." He gestures to it.

Leon then nods to Almir, who turns to the portal and says, "Groom Lake, Nevada." The mirror finish ripples like water as the world beyond shapes to their destination. "Last one through is a rotten egg," Almir jokes before taking the plunge.

Seldin is up next. He takes his position before the veil while Simon ushers him on. A hand to the surface breaks the calm with tides that disrupt the tranquil scene. It's cold to the touch with a contradiction of warmth that travels the length of his arm as he eases himself through, purposely taking his time to examine the experience. His face then presses to the plane like peeking through a sheet of water. A flash of light then a field of darkness fills his view as if for a moment he was in space. Then a sudden pull draws him through from the other side. It's like diving, Seldin realizes as he crosses the threshold, though surprised by the gravitational whoosh that lands him on his knees.

Soon, Simon plops down beside him, and then comes Jasra, who gasps a shivering shrill as if doused with freezing water.

"Did you see it?" Seldin asks Simon with a smile on his face.

"The stars?" he responds then nods while warming his girlfriend's icy skin.

Whoosh! A rushing sound echoes with the emergence of Leon walking out of the void, seemingly unfazed. "How was the trip?" he asks the trio.

"I'm burning internally but I'm freezing all over," Jasra complains with chattering teeth.

"Oh, yeah, I'm sorry. I forgot to mention, you're supposed to pump your aura and shield yourself as you go through. It helps with that inside out feeling," he informs them.

Simon shakes his head. "Information we could have used yesterday," he retorts.

"Sorry, I'm used to it now," Leon says.

"You also forgot to mention the potential danger," Seldin comments.

"What danger?" Leon asks.

"When I passed through, the barrier drew energy from me; it's enough to kill a person without our training," he informs him.

Leon shakes his head. "No, you don't have to worry about that; the gates close when I'm not near them."

Simon stands. "Speaking of *'near them,'* what gives—the gate clearly showed an open field. Why are we still inside?" he gripes.

"Because that would be too easy. Like I said, they get you close."

"How did you find them?" Jasra asks.

Leon pauses for a second. "Well, this may sound strange, but not long after my power kicked on, they called to me," he says, playfully strumming at the fluidic surface. The others watch as he teases at its pull. "Ugh…" he lets out a grunt before dropping to the floor. Almir and Seldin rush to his aid, yet to their horror, his body is like stone.

"Lee, what's happening?" Seldin asks.

"It's happening again. Get me out of the cave," he pleads.

Out in the arid plains of Nevada, Simon and Seldin set him in a patchy field of rough grass and sand. Almir and Jasra also offer assistance.

"That's twice today," Jasra comments.

"Actually, it's been happening more and more," Almir confesses despite the glaring look of disapproval from his teacher.

"What is it, exactly?" Seldin inquires.

"Honestly, I'm not sure: power spikes or dizzy spells. They're momentary lapses in control. It's past now," Leon says.

"And how long has this been going on?" Jasra asks.

"Since Sei left," he replies.

Simon looks to Seldin. "I'm not detecting anything, Sei," he tells him.

"Me neither," he replies, "his energy feels normal. Lee, are you good?" Seldin asks, offering a hand up. Leon nods, grunting as he rises to his feet.

"Good. Simy, can you link to the satellite and tell us exactly where we are? Seldin turns to him, and Simon bobs his head.

"Yeah, the base is about seventy miles northwest of us, and by the looks of things, I'd say we're just outside of Las Vegas," he says with a sort of grin.

"Alright, it shouldn't take us long to get there. Why don't we—"

Right then Jasra speaks out. "I don't know about you boys, but I'd like to rest a bit."

"Oh, come on, we just got here," the others complain.

"Look, we've been flying all night, and the base isn't going anywhere, what's the harm in taking a nap?" she argues.

"She does have a point. Besides, we have yet to come up with a plan." Simon looks to them.

Seldin concedes. "You know, you're right. Okay, Jassie, you win. Let's get some rest. Then we can focus on a plan."

"But wait," Almir speaks up. "Where will we sleep?"

Seldin turns to him with a plain expression and a light shrug. "In the cave," he answers.

Chapter 19

"The Guardian of Death"

Nighttime in Nevada can be chilly, as with most arid climates. With the sun almost set and no other shelter in sight, the gang moves into the belly of the cave.

"Brrr…" Jasra shivers, taking a seat on a rocky stool to avoid the damp ground. "I'm not so sure about this," she complains while rubbing her sides to keep warm; she's too tired to use energy.

"It's not that bad," Seldin claims.

"You're not cold?" she seems surprised, but he shakes his head as he joins her on the rock, offering a warm arm, while Simon and the others commune at the entrance, catching up on the past year.

It's nice to have Seldin here, she thinks, hiding her smile from his piercing eyes, which shimmer like sapphires in the fading light. Likewise, Seldin stares into her emeralds—a lush green that matches her attire while contrasting the silky sheen of her auburn hair.

He's comfortable too, enjoying the pleasantness of their casual embrace, and there's a subtle shift in the aether as their auras overlap like two soap bubbles merging into one.

"Don't get too comfortable," Simon says in an abrupt tone. Seldin and Jasra snap their gaze to him in the urgency of the moment.

"She's cold," Seldin replies before quickly standing, casting a beam of energy to a hump of stalactite hanging from the ceiling. It glows orange, bestowing radiant hues throughout the cavern and a soothing field of heat for everyone in need. He then turns, breaking his locked eyes from Simon before heading outside.

The chilly air is soothing on his skin. Although he may have evolved beyond pain, he is not without sensation. It calms him in the moment, for he staggers inward, feeling that nagging tug on the strings of his heart.

Seldin had been callused all those years growing up as he trained and followed his nature, all the while watching his friends experience another, more foreign, way of life. For a moment, he feels the weight of his thoughts as they burden him with a hollow temptation. Had he missed out?

"No," he bellows a lofty sigh, "there is no room in my life for that," he tells himself, then glances up at the paleness of the moon. Another thought comes to him, one that brings a smile to his face. "I could…" He begins to crouch, as if cocking the springs of his legs.

"Hey Sei, what happened in there?" Leon shouts.

Righting himself, Seldin turns to face his younger friend, and his student, who trails behind.

"Nothing," he replies.

"Oh, well, those two are sucking face now anyway. Up for a match? I've been eager to test myself," Leon admits.

Turning his eyes back to the moon, Seldin ponders the idea. Does he really want to fight? He turns back, "Two on one, or free for all?" He looks to them.

A strange sort of smile hits Almir's face. "Do you really think you can take us both?" he asks with a sudden stroke of brashness.

Leon smirks at him and then glances to Seldin, who steps back, initiating the formation of a triangle with each combatant at the edge of their zone.

The cool air wisps around them as neither party wishes to give away a thing. The energies between them are calm with the moonlight overhead setting the stage.

"Are you going to make a move, Sei?" Almir looks to Seldin.

With his senses active, Seldin breaks his stare from Leon as he glances to Almir. "Your call."

Leon drops down, planting his hands to the dirt. The earth beneath Seldin erupts, smashing him with an angular pillar to the chest before he can react. If breath mattered, it would have knocked his wind out. Still, he's stunned in the moment as Leon moves to rush in, but Almir already has, strafing around the newly formed plateau to engage his foe from behind.

Seldin pushes off, jumping into a backflip to gain sight and the height advantage. From there, he thrusts himself downward, spearing his apprentice's apprentice in the back of the neck with an elbow that plants him face first into the dirt.

Leon then appears beside Seldin, coming out of a vaporous form, then shifting into a watery body that absorbs his mentor's punches like little splashes no more intrusive than fighting a wave.

To Seldin, it feels like he's hitting nothing; the force of his blows goes straight through. The leftover momentum sets him off balance, giving Leon the advantage as he strikes back, changing his fists to stone just as he makes contact, then shifts to water again. Leon's arm comes around as if to clothesline him, but as the arm strikes, the aquatic matter rapidly chills, freezing Seldin's arms as he blocks. Then quickly Leon follows up, transitioning from water to vapor before darting behind him and morphing into a body of flame to torch him with each strike.

Unable to block him, Seldin does what he can to avoid the attacks. It isn't that difficult really, for although Leon can shift quickly, his movements are slow, and worse, predictable. Soon Seldin is able to derive a pattern. He waits, knowing Leon will change to something solid just before impact. There it is—his mind detects the coalescing of aether within Leon's body as he readies to counter.

Out of the darkness, the heel of a boot catches Seldin's jaw, slamming him to the ground. "Agh!" he groans, coming up out of a rough landing that scraps him as he skids. "Welcome back," Seldin greets Almir, who charges in for a follow-up. "I thought you were down for the count," he says while dodging and countering Almir, effortlessly, until Leon catches up.

The battle becomes extremely dynamic with the way Almir and Leon play off each other's moves. It's like an intricate dance—a tango of two on one. Then all of a sudden, a streak of light comes from overhead.

"What hell is that?" Almir shouts, pointing at a soaring orb.

"It's a Foo Fighter!" Leon exclaims with wide eyes. Seldin looks too.

"What?" Almir gasps.

"You know, UFOs—alien spacecraft," Leon replies without a break in his gaze.

"Oh, dear God," Seldin groans loudly, "that is not what it means. Unidentified—in other words, we don't know what it is yet. Until then, we have to assume it is manmade," he scolds.

"You're the one out here looking for aliens," Almir retorts.

"True, but that doesn't mean we can jump to conclusions," he states.

"What do you think it is, Sei?" Leon asks.

"I don't know, but I'm going to find out." With that, Seldin is gone before the others can offer a reply. They stand there looking at the orb of light streaking across the sky and the subtle wake of energy that Seldin leaves behind.

"Wow, he is fast," Almir's jaw drops.

"Yup," Leon replies.

"Be honest." Almir turns to him. "Was he just toying with us?"

Leon glances at Almir then offers only a chuckle and a shake of his head in reply before turning toward the cave.

Seldin flies at high speed. His eyes are locked on to whatever is floating over the mountain range. Scanning the object with his senses, he attunes to it. It's not a plane, that's for sure; it's round, almost spherical. He can detect metal, some sort of alloy that seems oddly familiar, and traces of organic matter fused into the hull. The vehicle measures only a few meters in diameter—rather small, he thinks. Yet, the aura of the vessel is bright in his mind's eye, giving off a very powerful energy field that seemingly twists space, but he can't see beyond that, there's too much distortion.

Even though he can't sense any life aboard, the craft responds to his approach. It begins to rotate as if it had a discernible forward section before speeding off into the sky. The disruption of space between the object and its destination leaves a wake of emptiness—a pocket of nothing, and for a moment, Seldin finds himself caught adrift in it before hitting normal air, able to pursue again. The object makes abrupt stops and takes sharp turns at right angles—the classics of ufology. Yet, no matter where it goes or what maneuvers it tries, Seldin is there, taking turns and changing speed just as quickly, until it stops.

Like before, it orients itself as if to face him. Much closer now, Seldin can see the structural details: the egg-shaped hull, the perforations in the dark gray brushed-metal surface, and the organic— almost carapace-like features embedded in the material.

With no obvious signs of entry, Seldin wonders just how to access it. There are no doors or windows to speak of—at least, none that he can see. Easing up on the thing, he extends a hand.

Singe! It fries his palm on contact, and instinctively, he pulls away before attempting a second try. The vessel speeds off again, and in turn, Seldin takes flight. He follows it for a time before it stops once again. A fluctuation in the gravity field alerts his senses as the energy surrounding the craft quickly collects and is immediately discharged in his direction. Seldin swats, deflecting the blast with his right hand, and the ship zooms off.

Seldin stays on it, even as it weaves dangerously close to the mountain, until a military base enters his view. He stops, not wanting to trigger any alarms—there's no telling how they'd respond to his presence here, though he could venture a guess. Making a note of the aircraft's distinct energy signature, Seldin turns about and speeds back toward camp.

"Man, that was intense!" he says out loud. "I can't believe what I just saw. I can't wait to tell everyone," he rambles to himself. At his current pace, it takes only a few minutes to get back to the cave, and he hits the ground with hardly a thud then rushes in.

"Hey guys, guess what I…"

Jasra and Simon are curled up together while Leon and Almir sleep in opposite corners of the cave. He sighs, disappointed, and then heads back outside.

Out under the paleness of the celestial grace, he rests there taking in the moment with the light on his face while closing his eyes and watching the soft bluish-white hues pierce through. He then looks up, thinking back to an earlier idea.

"I don't need to breathe, right?" He ponders. Lowering himself into a crouching stance, he cocks his legs and—bam! He springs off, heading straight for the moon. He's sure he can do it, he's positive. Without the frailties of his human needs to hold him back, it should be a walk in the park.

Only sixty-two miles to space; at Mach two he should reach that mark in less than three minutes. The energy that expels from his being pushes him up like a rocket. Soon he hits the cloud banks, and shortly after that, he's above them. As his altitude increases, he begins to feel a swell in his body as the surrounding atmosphere grows thinner and thinner, applying less and less pressure on him.

With the darkness of space in his view, he begins to wobble, for at that height, he feels unsteady, unsure of what to root to. The Earth is so far away, yet the moon is farther still. His balance begins to falter, and he teeters back toward the Earth.

"Whoa, whoa!" he shouts. He's falling fast, descending rapidly as the ground rushes up at over a hundred miles an hour to meet him. Struggling to orient himself, he works quickly to straighten out his tumble before he and the ground become good friends. Seldin knows the math—even at terminal velocity, he's got a few minutes. Closing his eyes to calm his mind, he feels out the ley lines of the Earth's magnetic field, and like a compass, he aligns himself appropriately before soaring to the moon, once again.

Confident he doesn't need oxygen, he slows down for nothing, and punches through the atmosphere as he enters the innermost edges of outer space. "Yes!" he exclaims excitedly, though not hearing a sound in the void as he mouths the words. He pushes himself farther, feeling out the rim of the Van Allen radiation belt. At first, the cold touch of space slows his movement while the lack of pressure strains his body.

"Almost there," he says to himself. "Outer space, here I—ghah, ahhh, ahhh!" Seldin howls as the sun crests over the Earth, gradually heating him to over 250 degrees. Even at ninety-three million miles away, he is naked to its rays. Slowly, his body begins to cook; his skin reddens, then blisters, and then chars.

He must have overlooked how defenseless he'd be to it. Pain or not, he can't go on if he's destroyed. In a panic, he pushes himself back. Right then, the mother of all catch-22s hits him as he begins to burn on reentry. Pushing energy to his aura, he does what he can to deflect damage from all sides. Then, like a shooting star, a human-shaped ball of fire slams into the ground at full force.

Charred and broken, Seldin gasps as his bones crackle and pop under the blackness of his seared skin. Putting in the effort to sit up, he crumbles back to the ground. His body is just too damaged, and his power is gone from reentry. Physically, it doesn't hurt, not even a bit, he just can't move. There aren't enough muscles left to function, and hardly any energy remaining to stay conscious. For a while he drifts in and out, napping for a few minutes here and there. Seldin hasn't felt this weak since…

"Lucy!" He kicks himself awake and calls to her before blacking out once again.

Back in the cave, there's a rustling in a black bag. Her link to him is staggered, for his signal is low. Regardless, a sense of concern fills her stem. She kneads nervously at the bottom of the bag with her roots as she fiddles with the double zipper. Snaking a vine through, she opens the pouch just enough to get the rest of herself out. Once freed, she scurries, following the signal to him. He's close, she can tell, just outside the cave according to her senses, but why so weak—the nurturing instinct runs a gauntlet of curiosity.

Her roots punch into the soil as she crawls the nine meters from the opening of the cave to the outer hill of the crater and then to the center where she feels him most.

His skin is like leather, yet it peels like burnt chicken as she embeds her roots, burrowing into the center of his chest, plugging into his chakras. Although there isn't much light from the moon, she opens wide, fanning her petals to absorb what she can. The rest she pulls from the Earth, drawing the essence away from the surrounding foliage, which withers as she feeds him.

Seldin gasps as his heart begins to beat and his lungs begin to function. His organs, vestigial as they are, start to regrow as muscle and skin repopulate his body. Suddenly, his eyes open as he awakens, feeling the essence of himself filling out the suit of his flesh.

Clenching a fist before his eyes to test his strength, Seldin sits up and greets Lucy with a gentle caress that flaps her petals. She uproots herself then repositions to the back of his neck, where she prefers to be. He then looks himself over to make sure that everything is where it should be before standing up to brush the dirt and grit from the bareness of his newly formed exterior. He is of the proper height, proper weight, and his lineage seems appropriate. The only things lacking now are his clothes.

"It's a shame those don't grow back." He ponders the idea before glancing over his shoulder to Lucy. "Cover," he says, and like she's done so many times before, she wraps him in herself.

Scanning the concave crater as he looks upward, he affixes his attention to the moon. A deep inhale fills his lungs as he circulates the aether within his core. The Earth seems to shake beneath his feet as the energy of his aura pushes against the bowl-shaped depression, stirring up the loose soil.

"Let's do this." Boom! There's an immense bang that cracks the air from his sudden jump to hypersonic speed. In less than thirty seconds, he hits space, then outer space, several thousand miles above the Earth and beyond the sanctity of its magnetosphere. Supercharged by the malnar, Seldin pushes on as the flower enthusiastically drinks up the raw radiation from the sun—fueling his aura and protecting him from the harmful rays while boosting his speed to a whole new magnitude.

Determined to hit his mark, Seldin doesn't stop to admire the scenery; he trucks forward, aiming straight for the Sea of Tranquility. At a rate of over sixty-four thousand miles per hour, it takes him just under four hours to enter lunar gravity. Turning about, Seldin floors it hard to slow his descent as he makes a new, though small, crater. Touching down, he drops into a crouch to absorb some of the impact.

Able to rest for a moment, he relishes in the experience. With a hand, he scoops the fluffy dirt, admires it, and then stands to take in the awe and wonder. A black backdrop with a sparkling blue marble fills his eyes. It almost brings a tear that he manages to hold back while thinking upon those famous words: "One giant leap…" he utters with a wide smile, staring back at the Earth. A glance to the sun shows its brightness and then he looks over the lunar landscape. It is a different world entirely, with its own unique features: a topology so unlike Earth's, yet a familiar sense all around.

For a time, he investigates the landscape, particularly the landing site of Apollo 11. The footprints of Neil Armstrong and Buzz Aldrin are still present, forever imprinted in the moon's weather-free surface. Several pieces of survey equipment remain as well, including the infamous dune buggy. An idea swims in his head as a delighted chuckle escapes him, and he decides to trek over to it.

His first step is a doozy, throwing him horribly off balance in the weak gravity. He tumbles forward, then quickly rearward as he overcorrects himself, stumbling around for a moment or two before using energy to push himself down and keep his feet planted.

The vehicle leaves much to be desired, resembling a slightly more durable golf cart equipped with a T-shaped steering console and instrument panels that do whatnot. There are other devices too, yet what Seldin is most interested in is... "How do you make it go?" he questions curiously, examining the thing. The onboard batteries appear to be drained, and unfortunately, there are no solar panels in sight.

"Oh well." He hops on. "I'll just do this." He focuses, taking a page out of Simon's book and channeling aether directly into the electric motors. Zoom! It takes off, rolling over the unsteady terrain like an ATV on a muddy track.

Riding the buggy in the lack of wind, he gapes with a wide grin as he plays childishly in the weak gravity. Sharp turns round out, and donuts take a while, but neither twist nor turn goes un-savored. Hitting a dune at a harsh angle, the buggy rolls. Its momentum carries it through the air, and Seldin's head just clears the dirt as the wheels touch down and the rover skids to a halt.

"Awesome!" he expresses in the thrill. Fun like this is rare; in fact, he hasn't had this much of a good time in a long time. "Aw, man, if only Simon could..." Seldin stops to a thought that brings his mind to a halt.

"C'mon, Lucy. It's time to go." Getting off the rover, he stands and stares at the Earth. A glare from his right draws his attention to the sun beaming down upon him.

"Unveil," he says, but Lucy doesn't want to; she ignores his command.

"Unveil, I said. C'mon, unveil." The stubborn thing tightens up in protest. "Lucy, I have to learn how to defend myself out here. How else am I supposed to protect all life if I can't travel amongst the stars? There are worlds that need me. Now unveil, I'll be alright," he insists, and as he commands, his floral friend peels back the petal-like coverings of the helmet, exposing Seldin to the sun's mercy.

His eyes fill with blinding light, and instinctively, he throws his left hand up, turning his face away. "Gah!" he winces.

Lucy responds immediately, lacing her roots around him.

"No!" he urges. "Unveil. I'll be fine, unveil," Seldin insists. Lucy uncoils just as asked, taking her full retreat to the back of his neck, letting him stand nude in her absence.

The skin on his face, chest, and the front of his arms and legs redden. Seldin focuses with a grunt, pushing aether from his core and into his skin, trying to heal himself as blisters form in random spots before charring open; his exposed blood boils from both the heat and the lack of atmosphere.

On his backside, away from the sun, his skin grows cold, cracking as moisture leaves him and ice crystals begin to form. He drops to his knees, unable to keep up with the damage from all sides.

In that moment, Lucy's tendrils lace around him, once again.

"No!" Seldin shouts silently through gritted teeth—the sound going nowhere—but Lucy hears him just the same, as she always has. Hesitantly, she uncoils as he thrusts both hands out with charred fingers toward the sun, projecting an energy shield.

"I… need to… ugh! Figure this out!" he yells, feeling the strain of his own energy feeding back against him. Flying at supersonic speed is nothing compared to this; he can create air pockets and deflect the wind, but there's no wind here, just the full might of the star—no atmosphere, no magnetic field, no filter.

It's not just the heat that's tearing him apart but ultraviolet rays, gamma rays, alpha particles—everything the sun has to offer pierces straight through him and his shield. Even with his eyes closed and turned away, all he can see is white.

Seldin's mind races, searching for options, for answers. He doesn't understand why it's not enough power—why the sun's rays keep getting through even with his core crossing past threefold. His right hand draws back to his abdomen, feeling his meridians splitting to release the upsurge. How could he be so foolish to think he could match hundreds of trillions of tons of raw energy?

"Cover me!" he shouts, collapsing back on his rear, and Lucy obliges as Seldin drops his power down to base level. He gasps, breathing reflexively despite the lack of oxygen.

"I'm going about this wrong," he says, thinking. His mind then falls to the obvious: Earth's magnetic field. "Of course! It's only 0.3 gauss, maybe 0.6 at its strongest." He reaches out with his mind, trying to feel it. "It's so far, but I think that's right."

Seldin begins drawing equations in the regolith. "It's not exact, but if I'm right, I only need 0.001 joules to match that." He shakes his head. "That's nothing." He gets to his feet, facing the sun again. "Unveil," he says.

Once again, Lucy tightens in protest.

"Please?" he says.

Lucy uncoils from around his renewed body. A mixed flood of hot and cold hit him.

Seldin closes his eyes, turning his head away from the sun as his body warms on the front and cools on the back, burning and freezing at the same time. He focuses, moving more aether from his core to his aura, calibrating it as it shimmers and sparkles like a dancing aurora. The heat on his face grows comfortable; the cold at his back equalizes.

Slowly, Seldin gazes out toward the sun with his naked eyes. "Hah!" laughter escapes his lips, for he's done it. The field is solid; his wounds are healing. Seldin Gardane is standing on the Moon, ungarnished, unchained, in the full light of the sun.

He stares at himself, looking over and marveling at his own accomplishment.

"Congratulations!" a deep, accented voice chimes from behind, permeating his mind.

Turning quickly, Seldin's eyes lock onto the darkly dressed, hooded figure. "Who are you?' he asks.

Pulling down the hood of his coat to reveal his deathly pale face and bald head, the man answers. "I am Tillman, the Guardian of Death."

"There is no Guardian of Death," Seldin retorts and Tillman chuckles loudly.

"Such arrogance. There once was a guardian for every living world. You and I serve as balance; the cycle of life and death," he states.

Seldin's eyes trail downward as he rationalizes what has been said. "There are others?" he asks. Tillman nods. Then Seldin looks to him. "If what you say is true, then where are they? Why remain hidden all these years when we could have—"

Tillman shakes his head. "It's the trial of every guardian to ascend naturally—to evolve beyond the needs of the physical body and become one with the universe. It's what solidifies your role as a guardian. If I were to kick your soul from the flesh, it wouldn't fade into nothingness like so many others," he explains.

"So, we're immortal then?" Seldin inquires, curiously, thinking of the day's events: his fight with Simon, and his presence on the Moon.

Tillman nods. "In time, but we're not indestructible. The truth is, there are very few of us left. Our enemies have found ways to destroy us." He sighs while looking out into the blackness of space. His eyes then solidify onto Seldin. "Are you serious about your… current escapade?" he asks with a tone as if it's beneath him.

Seldin's eyes trail down, thinking. "You mean, Area 51?"

Tillman nods.

"You know about that?" Seldin asks.

"Of course, I do. We've been watching your lot for some time," Tillman says, and that fills Seldin with a strange sense of unease. Just how long have they been watching? He wonders—when he was in the woods? Or before that?

Seldin sighs, returning to the conversation at hand. "Should we not?" he asks.

Tillman shrugs. "It doesn't matter. Your friends have yet to ascend. Perhaps it'll be good for them," he raises a brow, "as long as they don't get themselves killed," he says.

Seldin crosses his arms. "Well, we have you, though, right?"

"They have you. I will not intervene. Just don't spend too much time goofing off. The universe is vast, and it does need us," Tillman says, sternly. With that, Seldin turns toward Earth as he pushes off.

"Oh, Sei," Tillman calls back and Seldin turns, touching down once again. "There are four guardians crucial to the system: Life, Death, Dimension, and Time. If you must save someone, make it one of them."

...

Jasra clenches her eyes shut, refusing the light of morning as it creeps its way into the cave. She makes a face and then stubbornly rolls over. A gentle kiss then nestles her forehead to ease the transition.

"Wake up, sweetie," Simon says softly with a nudge of his head to hers.

"Mm, is it morning already?" she asks.

"Indeed," he answers as she sits up to look about the cave. Everyone else is already outside.

"Come on." Simon tugs at her left arm.

Jasra grabs her boots, brushes the sand from her socks, and then buckles the straps before accompanying her escort. Her thoughts fixate on Seldin and the interesting dream she had, which might explain her... morning condition.

'How much of it was real?' she wonders, sorting through the images of space and the conversation with Death, but that notion quickly dissipates with the grumble in her stomach and the onset of hunger.

As they make their way to the surface, Simon's eyes grow wide, for he hasn't ventured out yet, either, nor seen the enormous hole in the ground. "Holy shit!" he exclaims, walking up to it.

Jasra isn't surprised, in fact, the knowing little snicker she lets out as her eyes deviate to Seldin, is more of an anecdotal expression. She blushes, clearing her throat. Of course, now he's fully clothed.

"Eat up." Seldin points to the bountiful assortment laid out on a blanket, like a picnic in the dried grassy field.

"It's good, too," Leon mutters, stuffing his face alongside his younger friend.

"Where'd all this come from, and what the hell happened?" Simon questions.

Seldin glances away, breaking from the eye contact that Jasra has been laying on. "Well, I needed a change of clothes, so I figured while I was out, I'd stop and pick up a few things in order to get the day moving. There aren't any restaurants nearby, so…"

"And the big-ass hole?" Simon points.

"Rough landing." Seldin clears his throat, and again Jasra snickers. Simon looks to her, slightly confused before he and she dig in.

"I've been surveying the land," Seldin says, "the base is seventy miles that way." He points northwest. "And it's guarded by frequent patrols that happen every—"

"Hey, did you tell them about the spaceship?" Leon blurts out.

Simon and Jasra look up. "Spaceship?"

"There was an unidentified object hovering over the valley last night. I followed it through those mountains, and it did land at Area 51, but as for it being extraterrestrial…" Seldin takes a breath. "The alloy isn't from around here, of that much I'm certain."

"Then it's definitely an alien!" Almir exclaims, but Seldin shakes his head.

"I don't think so," he comments.

"Then what was it?" Simon asks.

"I think it's a reproduction; some sort of experimental craft, but the energy was weird. I had a hard time sensing past the hull. I couldn't tell what was inside," Seldin says.

Jasra shakes her head. "Well, there had to be a pilot. How else—"

"Remote," Simon answers, his face blank and his eyes casting a downward gaze. "I'd like to see that craft."

"I second that," Seldin replies.

"Me too," Leon adds.

"Sei, you said you already had a look around, what's the best angle of attack?" Simon asks.

Chapter 20

"Area 52"

Eeerrr! Eeerrr! Eeerrr! The sirens blare as an emergency distress signal is triggered. Sergeant Di'Nau and Private Klater are the first to respond, deployed from Segal Army Base just a few clicks north of the adjacent, yet unmarked, research outpost hidden deep within the Peruvian jungle in an area known only as Secker 5-75.

Cutting around the embankment, Sergeant Di'Nau nearly rolls the jeep as he flies around the sharp bend, handling the slippery ground like a redneck out mudding. He's eager to get there, wanting to waste no time. The distress signal was received only four minutes ago, at zero-seven-hundred hours. The ten-minute drive is nearly complete, but the woods seem thicker today, which is holding up progress. Di'Nau flips a switch to ease their trek, and with the cutting rails now in place on the bumper, they manage to push through the unusually thick underbrush in relatively short time.

Coming up on the primary entrance, the jeep stalls as they hit a pocket of tall grass at the base of the valley where the facility lies buried deep within the mountain and extends some twenty-four floors beneath the surface. The grass tangles in the wheels, stalling the drivetrain, and rooting the vehicle in its tracks.

"Jesus, Sergeant, look at the grass!" exclaims the private as he stares bewilderedly at the overgrowth that covers the building's entrance embedded into the mountainside.

"What about it?" he questions, almost arrogantly, while hopping out of the jeep.

"Well, look at it—it's overgrown. Come to think of it, it's all overgrown—everything! It wasn't like this yesterday," Klater points out.

"Private, we're in a jungle. Everything grows fast around here," Di'Nau dismisses. "Now grab your gear and move your ass—we've got people in there!" he yells like a drill instructor.

Wading through the freakishly tall grass, they hack and slice at the bits that entangle them as they pass by.

"Man," Private Klater lets out, feeling a sense of eeriness creep in, "I don't like this, Sarge."

Di'Nau just shrugs before offering a rebuttal, "What's to like about it? We are here to do a job, and that's what we are gonna do," he states as they come up on the double-layered, four-inch thick steel compound doors, mired in rust and foliage.

Private Klater lets out a heavy breath while examining the corrosion levels on the door. "It's severely oxidized."

The sergeant shakes his head, letting out a lofty sigh of his own. "Klater, you have a keen eye for the obvious," he comments.

"Sir, I'm telling you, it wasn't like this yesterday—something's wrong here," he states.

"Well, no shit, that's why we're here," says Sergeant Di'Nau, who operates the key panel to the right of the door.

Ert-shriek! Sounds the metallic layers as they grind past one another before stopping halfway open. Klater and Di'Nau can see the second layer of doors through the parting of the first. Immediately, Klater grabs at the edge of the outer layer in an attempt to budge it.

"Shit!" he exclaims, jumping back and peeling his glove off. "It's hotter than a son of a bitch!"

Di'Nau shoves him. "Quick, step aside and grab your pry-bar," he instructs his subordinate.

Clink, clank! They force the wedge of the bars into the lip of the left door. Standing beside it as a shield, they heave hard left.

"Pull, pull, pull!" the sergeant grunts. It's hard, tight, and it hurts their hands as they strain, pulling against the friction, the heat, and the binding rust. Eerk! It budges a little, then err-kaboom!

Looking up from the dirt, Sergeant Di'Nau gasps, regaining his wind and catching the sight of a door that is planted into the ground, just inches beside him. Quickly, he snaps left then hops to his feet, rushing over to his downed subordinate.

"Private, Private, are you alive?" he tugs at him, rolling him over before slapping his face to rouse him.

Klater gasps, coming to. "What the hell happened?" he asks the sergeant.

"Backdraft," says the sergeant as he helps the man to his feet.

The private then snaps, hearing a loud rumble. "Look at that!" He points. The mouth of the cave begins to fold as part of the mountain crumbles inward.

Moving close, the soldiers watch their step, staying clear of falling debris.

"Sarge, what are you doing?" Klater questions.

"I'm going in," he replies.

"You can't, it's unsteady!" Klater shouts.

Immediately, Di'Nau grabs the soldier by the shoulder. "Look, we have men in there. Now if you follow my lead and stay frosty, you have nothing to worry about!" Di'Nau barks before stepping in and climbing over the rubble.

"How do you know anyone's still alive in here?' Klater questions.

"I don't, but if you were stuck in this hole, wouldn't you want someone to come dig your ass out? Now move it!"

It's hot in there. The air is dank with a musty smell, and the heat of the fire doesn't make it any more tolerable. All the computers have nearly been crushed from the collapse, while those that didn't get pummeled have been burned into puddles of melted plastic. Surprisingly, however, the plants are fine.

The innards of the tunnel, though crafted with concrete, tile, and other manmade materials, are lined with thick vines, flowers, and other forms of vegetation that appear to be thriving despite the heat. Klater glances upward at the natural skylight formed in the center of the ceiling where pipes and other debris have fallen through. Even with the power off, they can still see with the aid of the light cast from the few flames still roaming and the marginal bits of the sun that slip through the gap in the ceiling.

At the end of the tunnel lies a decontamination room and a single elevator shaft, which appears to be intact. Attempting to operate the console, Di'Nau shouts, "Shit, it's dead!"

"Well, why don't we just take the stairs?" Klater rebuts.

"Private, this is a biological research facility. It was designed to be self-contained in the event of a catastrophic failure to prevent possible outside contamination. In other words, there are no stairs leading in or out."

The private's eyes grow wide, "Then why the hell are you trying to get inside—the whole place could be toxic!"

"The signal we received was code yellow for help; code red is biological. Now, we need to get this elevator working," states the sergeant as he removes an access panel.

"What are you doing?" asks Private Klater.

"I may be able to tap into the emergency generators and get the elevators operational. Here, give me a hand," he instructs, and it isn't long before the lights kick on. Soon after, they step into the cylindrical-shaped conveyance and begin their descent.

"It's getting warmer," Klater says with his muffled voice resonating through the mask of his rebreather. The sergeant only nods, expecting the worst from what awaits them. His gut tells him the lack of communication likely means no survivors, but people could be buried alive with no way to call for help.

A little over a minute is all it takes to descend the two dozen floors to the heart of the research building. Private Klater and Sergeant Di'Nau double check their equipment before proceeding. As the door to the elevator slides open, the soldiers take in the eyeful of their subterranean surroundings. It's like a jungle down here, literally, with heat, humidity, and an abundance of local—or perhaps, not-so-local plant life. Though the power is on, the majority of the lights are out, with the hall being lit by patches of fire here and there.

"Move out," Di'Nau instructs, motioning with a hand before moving forward. Klater falls behind, staying back and watching the flanks.

The hall ahead is charred yet covered in the same creepy vines as above. Farther ahead is the storage room, while directly to their left and center of the hall are the researcher's barracks, which are the first on their list of places to check.

Easing the door to the women's quarters open, there's a thump at the floor—a shoe; it's a penny loafer wrapped in vines that trail outward from the white sock of the decaying scientist lying in the corner. Her expression is horrifying with wide eyes and a gaping mouth hidden behind clutched hands still poised in the death grip that grasps the leafy things that have encased her. Her flesh appears dry and leathery, shriveled like a mummy. What's worse is that she is not the only one. Like a scene from Aliens, there are corpses everywhere—pinned to the floor, ceiling, and walls. Some of them were taken while occupying the bathroom, while others never left their beds. The men's barracks are much the same, with no survivors in sight.

"What the hell happened here?" Di'Nau questions, but Klater has no answer to offer.

They back away cautiously, watching their steps. Their eyes track left and right for signs of movement as they turn about. The anxiety levels have risen now, after seeing humans turned into not-so-living scarecrows. Klater feels it the worst, for he's not as seasoned as his leader. The only combat he's seen has been in simulation, but that was with people—an enemy he can try to understand. Whatever is going on here is beyond him. Although in truth, Di'Nau isn't faring much better, but he works to suppress his angst and keep his lackey cool.

This underground jungle is thick, much like the outdoors, with foliage clinging to the walls, filling the halls, and hanging from the overhead piping, electrical, and ductwork. Across the hall is another decontamination chamber, which leads into the labs. According to the map on the wall, Laboratories A, B, and C lie just beyond the chamber.

Sergeant Di'Nau gestures with a hand, signaling to move forward, cautiously brushing the pothos and bromeliads aside as they make their way down the corridor and up the ramp of the corrugated floor to the chamber. Di'Nau takes note of the water running beneath the centrally-placed flood grates. He pauses, signaling his partner to wait. There's a sound of rushing water, like rain pouring from just ahead, and the chamber is cracked open.

Easing the door farther, Sergeant Di'Nau pushes with the barrel of his gun while peering through the narrow space between the door and the jam.

"Aahh—God, no! Di'Nau, it's got me!" cries Klater, who flails frantically, tugging against his captor.

The desperate howls of his partner chills Di'Nau's heart and he swings about, catching an eyeful of the unexpected. "Jesus, Klater were you born in the land of derr? You nearly gave me a heart attack; do you know that, private?" barks the sergeant, who is secretly relieved that it's nothing serious as he steps up to untangle him from the clingers.

"Come on Sarge, this shit's biting me!" he exclaims, pointing and pulling against the green bulbous leaflet folded like a clamshell clamped to his arm. "Get it off, will ya?" Klater whines.

"Hold your arm steady, Private," Di'Nau instructs as he slips his fingers just under the leafy lip to help pry the mouth of the thing open. It tears like Velcro from Klater's jacket as the thorny teeth peel away.

"Man, this thing's got a grip," says the sergeant, now prying from both the top and the bottom of the vice.

"Gaw!" grunts the private as his arm is freed. The sudden release causes him to stagger forward just a bit, and Di'Nau pulls him aside— snap, clap, clap! The mouth of the bulb opens and closes in a biting motion.

"What the hell is that thing?" Klater asks.

"Some sort of fly trap," Di'Nau states, "though I've never seen one that big before. How's your arm?"

"Sore," Klater replies, rubbing it.

"Come on, Private, and watch yourself. We're no good to anybody if we get ourselves killed," he tells him before easing his way through the door to the decontamination chamber.

The room is rather expansive for what it is, twelve meters long by eight meters wide, and ten meters deep from ceiling to floor with a centralized grated bridge that connects the two entrances. The ceiling is lined with scaffolding-like framework to support the lights and sprinkler system, while below the bridge is a processing station used for sterilizing large bits of equipment that come through.

Stairs on either side of the bridge, mirrored at both ends, run to the bottom level, which is flooded with water that narrowly reaches the base of the doors on the upper level. Aquatic plant life fills the basin while mold, algae, and mildew-like formations have accumulated on the walls, thanks to the humidity.

The overhead sprinklers are still going and have ruined the computers of the control station positioned at a circular junction point in the middle of the bridge, and much like everywhere else, the vast majority of the overhead lights are out. There isn't a trace of fire in here, it's simply too wet.

As the two soldiers slosh ahead, they examine the layout while thoroughly inspecting the equipment and the bodies of the two scientists who once operated the controls. The one is slumped over her console to the left with roots growing out of her face while the other is rooted in his chair to the right with a large flower-like thing protruding from his chest. The two men move on, for there is no one alive in here.

Coming down the ramp from the decontamination area, they stop at a T-junction when Klater catches a glimpse of something through the glass door of Laboratory B.

"Look at that!" He points at the fifteen-foot-tall rose, which stands firmly with its roots extending outward in all directions and some pressing through the very structure of the building. The bulb of it is closed, as if it were asleep. The two men can hardly believe their eyes. Could this be it, the source of all this madness? They wonder as they ease themselves closer to peer through the glass of the horribly wrecked laboratory.

Little white cotton ball-like things powder the floor surrounding the enormous plant.

"Careful," they both hear as images of danger pop into their minds.

"Did you hear that?" Di'Nau turns to him.

"Yes," he says before hearing something else. It's faint, gurgling, but definitely there.

"Help." There it is again. The two of them face to the right, seeing movement.

"Hold on, we'll be right there!" Klater rushes over before Di'Nau can say anything to stop him, for out of the corner of his eye the rose is budding, spewing spores.

"It's awake!" the voice echoes within their minds. Di'Nau readies his weapon, looking for where that voice had come from.

Klater shakes his head, pushing out the foreign presence as he kneels to the woman on the floor just outside of Laboratory C. He grabs her shoulder to rouse her, still hearing the pleas for help, and as she rolls over, her eyes open—lacking anything human.

"Klater watc—" Smash! A root crashes through the glass and latches onto Sergeant Di'Nau, who turns quickly and opens fire—ra-tat-tat! "Auh-Arrggh!" Di'Nau cries out as his life force is drained and he shrivels like the rest.

"Sarge!" Klater swings his rifle and fires at the greenish-brown, rope-like strand.

Chomp!

"Arg!"

The woman latches onto Klater's back. She bites into him as her fingers, which wrap around him, begin to split as vine-like things protrude through and tear into his flesh.

Thrashing harshly, he grabs back then turns, ramming her into the wall, knocking her free. She looks human, all the way down to her tan, lush, nipples, but she's not. The black things for her eyes, the spines for her teeth, and even the razor-sharp thorns of her claws give something away. Looking down at the piece of the blouse that he had torn from her in the scuffle, a sense of fear overtakes him when he sees it's nothing but leaves that dull in luster from the white of the fabric to a viny green. Klater then proceeds to do what any rational human would in that moment: he opens fire, blasting away bits of her, which de-camouflage as her leafy layers peel away.

The creature shrieks and shrills as it flails from the bullets ripping through, tearing her down to the vines that fashion her skeleton. She drops back, huddling in the corner. The onslaught continues furiously, blowing more and more of her away until—click!

"Shit!" Klater exclaims.

The creature stands, re-growing its leaves, and recoloring its disguise. Private Klater simply cannot believe his eyes, for it is back to a perfect human form. Daintily, she walks forward, popping her hips femininely as if to work off the laws of attraction. It even emits pheromones that are so cleverly deceiving. If he hadn't already seen the truth with his own eyes, he'd be convinced. As she gets closer, he works frantically to find another magazine.

"C'mon, where is it?" he shouts, searching himself when suddenly there's a loud crash, and from out of the corner of Laboratory C, rushes another beast. It's over eight feet tall, tan in color, and insect-like. It nabs the girl right away, and the two of them square off.

Klater turns back, running toward his fallen friend near the decontamination area—but wait! Before him is a large round compound door just up ahead and down the hall, outlined with caution stripes and labeled *'Emergency Escape Tunnel.'* Although barred by fire, it is just beyond

Laboratory A, and in his heart, he feels that it may be his only hope. As he reaches the junction of the decontamination room, he looks left, hearing the shuffling sound of bodies moving toward him— things he once thought were dead.

In a pinch of desperation, he drops down, grabbing Di'Nau's rifle then opens fire.

"Aaahhrrrr!" he howls fiercely as he mows them to the ground. In the heated moment, he glances back at the wasp-like beast shredding the girl. It stabs her in the chest with a spine from its wrist and as she falls dead, her human-like color fades to a dried leafy brown.

"No!" Klater shouts, his heart pounding as the beast turns toward him. He backs away fearfully, though unobservantly, tripping over the roots that entangle his legs. In a panic, he discharges his weapon in the fall. "Auhhh-aarrrgh!"

Chapter 21

"Area 51"

At about the same time Sergeant Di'Nau and Private Klater are arriving to make their unfortunate discovery, Seldin and the rest are preparing to make their move at good old Area 51. The six by ten mile rectangular-shaped base sits just southwest of the Nevada salt flats, otherwise known as Groom Lake. Known for its reputation, the facility is a powerhouse of rumors and frequently bombarded with suspicions of popular tripe. Even so, this relatively small detachment of Edwards Air Force Base is believed to be home to some of the most top-secret experimental aircraft in the United States. That being the case, it is kept under heavy guard.

"Colonel Mitchel?" the young female officer calls out, for there's a blip on one of her screens. Mitchel, the officer in charge, snaps his attention to her. With twelve people manning the control room, he has a lot to be focused on.

"What is it, Lieutenant?" he quickly asks of Second Lieutenant Andrews as he comes up behind her to review the three monitors of her section.

"Sir, I'm getting some unusual ground-level readings. Electromagnetic field levels just peaked, and our microwave sensors are going crazy," she says.

"Hm…" He causally strokes his beard, troubled by the readouts. "Anything on radar?"

"No, sir, nothing in the air, but the electron spectrometer is picking up five very high energy signatures approaching from the south. EMF readings are off the charts."

Colonel Mitchel turns about to address one of the changeover officers preparing to leave duty. "Major Peirce?" he calls out.

"Colonel?" Peirce looks over.

"What exactly was in Captain Deakins' report last night?" the colonel requests.

"One of our test drones encountered an unidentified entity," he replies.

"Unidentified?" Mitchel snaps. "Do any of these readings mean a thing to you?" he asks.

Major Peirce walks over. "That's impossible," he comments.

"What is?" his commander responds.

"Well, last night there was only one of these things—now it appears there are five. Lieutenant, switch to gamma emissions," he instructs her, and she quickly accesses the terminal to bring up the appropriate screen.

"Jeessuss," Mitchel lets out, "have you ever seen anything like this?"

Major Peirce nods, "Yes, last night—there, do you see this spike? The big one right there. The radiation levels match what Captain Deakins reported. Whatever it is, it stalked one of our spheres and defused its countermeasures," he states.

Mitchel turns his attention back to the lieutenant. "Do we have cameras on that grid?" he asks.

"Yes, sir," she nods.

"Bring it up; I want to see these entities," he instructs.

"You got it," she answers, flipping a switch. Right then, the lights dim as static shrieks over their radios and fills their monitors.

. . .

Simon slowly opens his eyes while withdrawing a hand, poised with his forefingers and thumb, from his temple. "It's done," he says, looking to his friends.

"Good, let's move," Seldin says with a nod toward the main gate.

The guards appear distracted, fiddling with their radios as the team approaches.

"Halt, this is a restricted area!" one shouts, catching sight of the quintet as the other guard readies his rifle.

"Do not come any closer or I am authorized to open—"

"Shh." Almir points: the two soldiers drop cold, and the group turns an odd gaze toward him. Almir shrugs, "I can influence people's minds," he admits.

"I like this guy." Seldin thumbs before glancing to Leon. "I thought you were training another Earth guardian; since when did we get a Guardian of the Mind?" he asks, though truly impressed by the feat.

Leon just shrugs as they continue onward, scanning the area just as he knows Seldin is doing.

Although the human body puts out about 100 joules of unfocused energy a day, or 1.16 millijoules per second, the aura can be misleading. Therefore, it is the core—the aether generating center of every being—that really matters.

Simon takes these values seriously, running the numbers to gauge the strength of his enemies and his crew. His friends seem to be getting stronger by the day—especially Seldin, whose aura appears to be giving off just over 170 kilojoules per second, nearly twice his own and ten times what he had calculated two nights ago.

'Is that his baseline?' Simon wonders before calling out, "Yo, Sei?"

"Yeah?" Seldin glances back at his friend, who moves up beside him.

"What do you think the odds are that we'll run into wielders like us out here?" he asks.

"Doubtful. I'm not sensing a single aligned core," Seldin replies.

"Hm… well the resting energy in a person's aura is what, a third of their core on average, right?" Simon confirms.

"Yeah, so?" Seldin questions curiously, for he should know this stuff—it's textbook.

"Well, that puts the average soldier here at a max of what—100, maybe 150 joules?" Simon inquires.

Sighing, Seldin upturns a hand. "Simy, that won't matter if their cores aren't—" He senses something. "I feel a large group gathering over there." He points to the west end of the compound. "Jasra, what's the best way inside?" Seldin turns to her.

Jasra shimmers, briefly blurring from view for just a second when a sudden sense of vertigo brings her back, causing her to teeter. "Oof..." She places a hand to her temple. "Something's wrong. I can't see past there." She points westward.

Seldin then focuses that way, picking up on the strange, yet familiar shift in the aether as well. "That's what I felt last night," he says.

"Then that's where we'll go," Simon says, scanning that way. Static flickers across his display. He taps at his goggles.

Jasra groans as she rubs her forehead. "They're gonna attempt to flank us; we should enter over there." She points to a set of reinforced compound doors on the west entrance.

Seldin then nods to Simon, who steps up before waving a hand over the keypad. It beeps as the red light on the panel switches to green. There's a shriek of a large lock unbolting, and the gang steps inside to a darkened corridor.

"Need more light?" Simon asks playfully, stimulating only what is needed to brighten their path.

"Simy, you didn't happen to pull up a map while you were in their computer, did you?" Seldin asks.

Simon lets out a soft chuckle. "This isn't a video game, Sei, nobody keeps blueprints of top-secret facilities on file," he rebuts.

"Corridor." Jasra points left.

"Leon," Seldin calls out when suddenly, a solid wall of earth rises to block the path of the incoming troops.

"Thank you," Seldin says.

"Hold it right there!" shouts another group of soldiers from up ahead.

"We should take the stairs," Jasra suggests while making a sharp right into the stairwell just as another stone wall moves into place, blocking the shots fired.

"How far down?" Seldin asks her.

"Two floors; the engineering section is just below, and from there is almost a clear path to— oof..." She wobbles.

. . .

Back in the control room, Colonel Mitchel's frustration is hitting its boiling point. The radios are still gurgling, while the monitors remain on the fritz.

"Edwards Air Force Base, this is Lt. Colonel Mitchel from Groom Lake. We are under siege—do you copy?" he shouts, only hearing static. Adjusting the frequency, he tries again.

"Edwards Air Force Base, this is Colonel Mitchel, do you copy—damn!" He throws the microphone before turning about.

"Alright, people! We're under attack and flying blind, let's move! Gorman!" shouts the colonel.

First Lieutenant Gorman snaps to attention. "Yes, sir?"

"Grab some men and get the generators back on. I want this base operational, pronto!"

"Yes, sir!"

"Major Peirce?" Mitchel yells.

"Colonel?" Peirce shouts back.

"Get down to the barracks and wake up Deakins, he's the only one who's seen these things up close," says the colonel.

"Yes, sir." Peirce steps away.

"Oh, and Major, ready the MECHs." Mitchel adds.

"What?" Peirce questions the order.

"Major, it's obvious that whatever is hitting us scouted us last night. It has disabled our power, our alerts systems, and our communications. We need tactics, and the MECHs may give us the advantage."

"But sir, deploying them in our own compound—" Peirce seems genuinely concerned, for the Mechanical Chassis and Harness System is essentially the ground unit designed to complement the spheres. Certainly, the colonel has overestimated the need, he believes.

"That's an order, Major. I want you on the ground and Deakins in the air. There's only one place they can be headed, and I want a nice surprise waiting for them."

"Understood, sir," Peirce replies.

…

Ding! The security panel chimes, granting access to the engineering section. Simon pushes the glass door open. "Wow!" he exclaims excitedly as the lights switch on before him. His gaze pans the room, taken in by the volume of the workspace and the voluptuous array of stations, tools, machinery, and the smell of freshly processed integrated circuits. "Look at this!" His excitement takes hold as he picks up a clear circuit board. "It's a crystalline composite with fiber-optic channels. Ohh, what an ingenious design."

"Simy, what are you doing?" Seldin asks as Simon's nanites swarm the component.

"Copying it," he replies, offering a subtle tap to his temple.

Seldin then takes up a piece of the solid semi-laminated material. "What for?"

"Guys," Leon interjects, "I hate to break this up, but we really should keep moving."

"Right." Seldin nods before looking over at Jasra, who isn't feeling well. "Are you alright?" he asks as she leans against a table, letting out a heavy breath.

"It's this place; time feels out of focus," she says, and Simon scans the area. Flashes of static fill his goggles again. His view ripples and blips with distortions. An orange caution symbol pulses on his heads-up-display.

"Oh, that's unusual," Simon comments, attempting to shake away the disturbance. "That weird energy is messing with my optics."

Seldin nods. "Your optics, our senses, and it's making her sick," he says.

"So, what do you think it is?" Leon asks.

"I don't know but I felt it last night when I chased that thing," Seldin replies and that piques Simon's curiosity.

"It could be radiation from an early-stage antimatter drive," Simon says.

Jasra rubs her head. "Sorry guys, I'm afraid I won't be much help," she says as her head begins to ache.

"Here, let me…" Seldin places a hand to her temple as he peers into her head, taking note of her enlarged pineal gland—the area chiefly responsible for psychic ability. "Hmm, there appears to be some swelling," he says.

Simon's face grows with concern. "Can you correct it?" he asks.

"I'm trying but there's nothing physically wrong. It's like there's a chemical imbalance, yet everything's in place," he replies.

Jasra giggles. "Mm… you're like, massaging my brain," she says childishly.

"What did you do?" Simon asks.

Seldin shrugs. "The same effect as laughing gas; it's all I could do, but it won't last," he answers before checking her. "Jasra, you good?"

"Super." She giggles some more.

"Alright then, which way?" Seldin asks.

"Um…" She takes a moment to focus. "These doors will take us to the research labs." She points, and the gang proceeds into the long hallway, which curves, branching off into various corridors.

Voom! There's a sudden whoosh as the generators kick back on.

"Simon?" Seldin looks to him.

"Sorry, they've switched over to nuclear power. Give me a sec to—"

An ear-shattering blast devastates the hall in regular quarter-second intervals, throwing the group off guard as hypersonic bullets whiz by— verrm! Verrm! Verrm!

Almir and Leon dive behind a wall of earth as the rest of the gang quickly follows.

"A little warning next time!" Leon shouts while cupping a profuse, bleeding hole in Almir's arm. The young man writhes in agony.

"I've got it," Seldin says, channeling aether to mend his wounded comrade.

"I'm sorry," Jasra pleads, "I, I didn't see them coming—augh! It's even worse now," she claims, grabbing her head.

"What the hell is that?" Leon shouts.

"Rail cannons!" Simon answers, shouting over the noise.

"What?" Leon looks to the Guardian of Technology.

"Specifically, in this case," Simon peers around the stone wall to analyze the machines. He taps his headgear, trying to get a clear picture through the rush of static, "tri-barreled, dual-mounted, electromagnetic weapons that accelerate a sixty-caliber projectile—"

Verrm! Verrm! The barrel swings his way.

"Shit!" Simon ducks back, holding the right side of his head. "Over seven times the speed of sound!" he shouts, then looks at the blood in his hand. He didn't even feel it. A diagram of his head appears in his HUD showing a digitized outline of the gash along the right side.

"Abrasion detected," reads the display as nanites are dispensed.

"Simon, are you good?' Seldin asks.

"Yeah," he answers.

"Then do something about that mechanized piece of shit," Seldin orders.

Simon lightly cracks his neck as the wound on his head closes. "You got it," he gladly replies. Edging his view out around the corner of the barricade again, Simon examines the eight-foot-tall bipedal mechanism, armed to its metallic teeth. Working to extend his mind to its circuits, he finds himself struggling to gain control.

Verrm! Kathunk! Verrm! Baboom! Verrm! Tathink! Shots continue to chip away at Leon's rock walls.

"Anytime would be great!" Seldin shouts.

"Ugh." Simon shakes the fog from his mind. "I'm getting interference," he says before flicking his wrist to project his infamous brood of microscopic machines.

They swarm the giant piece of hardware like killer bees. At first, the result is nothing. The unknown organic/metallic compound is too foreign. In time, however, the nanites begin to gouge the hull—eating away at it like acid. The first MECH in the wave of three staggers just as the buzzing cloud dissipates.

"Simon?" Seldin calls out, feeling his buddy's energy drop.

"The damn thing is leaking some sort of ionized radiation; it's killing my bots, and I can't sense past the hull," Simon pouts before casting another, much denser, swarm.

Seldin sighs. "That sounds familiar. Almir, any luck with the driver?" He looks to him.

Almir shakes his head. "Sorry, I can't sense past it either."

The readout on Simon's goggles flashes with frequent signal failures as he watches his greatest work fall like flies. It's infuriating, and he'll be damned to lose against inferior tech. He grits his teeth while working his few remaining bots deep into the hull. The mechanical nightmare starts to whine, and Simon grunts.

"Haahhh, ehhh-haahh!" He staggers, falling back behind the barricade as the closest MECH drops to the ground, revealing a hollow cockpit.

"It was remote!" Almir exclaims, looking back as Simon's gray skin returns to normal.

"That's it—that's all I've got." Simon pants heavily in exhaustion.

...

"Sir, I have a visual!" Second Lieutenant Andrews shouts, and everyone turns their eyes to her monitors.

"Good," Colonel Mitchel says, peering through the camera's three-quarter elevated view. He can clearly see an earthy structure at the far end of the hall and the remaining two MECHs firing at it.

"Can you get an angle behind that thing?" The colonel points.

"Yes, sir." Andrews accesses two more cameras: one over the MECHs and the other on the five members huddling behind Leon's wall.

"Do you see what I see, Lieutenant?" Mitchel asks. Andrews only nods, unable to believe her own eyes—they're children.

"Pull up sensors," the colonel commands.

"I guess it's my turn," Seldin says, his voice heard over the monitor. They watch as he stands. For a second there's a brownout; lights and screens flicker.

"Christ, do you see those emissions?" Andrews exclaims, slapping a finger to the monitor.

Stepping out from around the mound, Seldin's image suddenly blurs.

"My god…" Mitchel mutters, watching him casually sidestep the rail rounds, leaving fading afterimages trailing in his wake.

His movements rip the air, shattering it explosively in the narrow hall. Simon, Jasra, Leon, and Almir all huddle close together, tucked behind the dirt while clasping their ears—shielding themselves from the hypersonic pulses that occur each time Seldin stops abruptly or changes direction. It's just too much mass moving too quickly in such a small space. He's hurting them. Unfortunately for his friends, he doesn't realize it.

"Stop it!" Jasra cries out, her shrieks hitting him intuitively halfway down the hall through the well of noise. At first, he doesn't understand.

"Stop what?" Seldin halts at hypersonic speed, but it isn't until he looks back at the contorted hall left in his wake, that he realizes his error—there is nothing without consequence. He sighs, disappointed in himself for being such a child, and in anger, he clenches a fist. At once, the MECH nearest to him implodes then hits the floor in a crumpled heap.

"Are you guys alright?" He checks his friends, taking a knee behind the barricade before the third MECH can take aim.

Leon gestures with a thumbs-up, while Simon and Almir respond with casual nods despite wiping blood from their ears. Jasra doesn't say anything; her head simply hurts too much.

. . .

The onlookers from the control room are beyond speechless, having never seen such a feat. They stare, watching as Seldin retreats to offer miraculous aid to his friends.

"M-make sure you get all of this," Colonel Mitchel says to Second Lieutenant Andrews.

Andrews nods with an unbreaking stare at the monitor. Her mouth hangs open.

Colonel Mitchel then radios Major Peirce, who is remote piloting the MECHs. "Major, you've got them pinned down. Strike while you can," he commands.

. . .

Simon waves off Seldin's hand, electing to repair himself, but with his nanite supply less than one percent, he struggles to sustain his power. Frustrated, he sighs, shifting a reluctant gaze to his friend, who is busy soothing Jasra's headache.

The encroaching sound of mechanized feet clapping the floor grabs Simon's attention as warning flashes bombarding his HUD.

"Sei, look out!" Simon darts to cover, attempting to erect an energy barrier, but his power is too low. The MECH's arm punches through his field without effort and knocks him with a solid hit to his chest. Instantly, Simon's power suit converts the blow into useful energy, and he thrusts his hands forward, kinetically casting the MECH aside.

On that cue, Seldin fires a beam of aether through the wall into the next room. "Let's go!" He helps the others through before turning to Leon. "Seal it!" he shouts.

. . .

"Damn! Where'd they go?" Mitchel exclaims.

"Hold on," Andrews says as she quickly raps some keys, cycling through the surveillance grid until she finds the room in question. "There they are—laboratory nine, subsection two: MECH Assembly room." She points to the screen.

. . .

"Where are we?' Almir looks around the room filled with armatures suspending half-sections of beveled chassis and hydraulic limbs.

Taking up a segment of what appears to be a rail gun, Simon holds it for a moment, feeling the sheer weight—it's dense. Without the aid of his bio-suit, he's not even sure he could lift it.

"It's an assembly room," Simon replies to Almir before dropping the piece of equipment to the table—bam! There's a sudden thud from just beyond Leon's wall.

"It's coming for us," Leon says.

"Jasra, how are you doing?" Seldin asks.

She lightly shakes her head. "It's worse. The future is so distorted," she says with a groan.

"Lee," Seldin looks over to him. "You're up. When that thing comes through, I want you to hit it with everything you've got. Everyone else," Seldin pools aether into his hand and then chucks it toward the opposite wall, blasting another hole. "Follow me." He takes Jasra's hand.

"Wait!" Simon halts, grabbing several large chunks of hull from one of the assembly stations before hurrying behind. The four of them then dart down the long corridor, making their way to the advanced aeronautics block.

Trucking on, Simon does his best to work while in motion, releasing what few nanites he has left onto the metal.

"What are you doing?" Seldin questions.

"Upgrading. That thing's armor is made out of some pretty interesting stuff, I had a hard time cutting through it. I'm rewriting the nanobots' molecular structure based on the composition of the armor. Of course, this is only a prototype; I won't be able to fully synthesize—"

"Are you telling me you thought up a new design in under two minutes?" Seldin asks with surprise.

Simon looks at him sideways with a subtle smirk before graciously welcoming the new batch of nanites and the increase in power. Soon, his color fades, returning to that brilliant shade of pale gray everyone is so fond of.

"Sei?" he calls out.

"Yeah?"

"You're not going to believe this," he says, stopping to set down the remnants of what he had deconstructed.

Seldin stares at the vine-like framework of the chassis and the almost papier-mâché-like texture of the support mesh between the vines. His heart nearly skips beat. "Suka…" he lets out.

"What?" Simon questions.

Seldin shakes his head dismissively. "I knew I'd seen this before," he says, drifting into thought.

"Have you? What about this?" Simon accesses his wrist computer, which projects a three-dimensional holographic image of a funny little molecule.

"In the ship I chased." Seldin nods.

"Interesting… it's what they're using for metal, but it's not metal; it's some sort of organic compound with metallic properties. I've never seen anything like it before," Simon admits.

"Yes, we have." Seldin realizes, pulling Lucy from his pack, and Simon's mouth hangs open, seeing it present in the plant's cellular walls.

"Well, I guess that makes your quest for aliens all the more likely," he says.

"This isn't good, Simon, if they're experimenting with malnar, Earth could be in serious trouble," Seldin says, putting Lucy away.

"But wait, you said those polar-whatevers were using these…" He gestures, "…things as some sort of bio-weapon. Maybe this is a good thing—it could level the playing field," Simon rebuts.

Seldin's stomach twists into knots just thinking about it. He stares him down. "You've never seen how fast these things take over a world. We've gotta find that ship."

. . .

Hanging back, Leon faces the wall as it rumbles from the other side. Bam! Bang! The MECH beats against it, testing for weaknesses. At first, it tries knocking through the mound of earth filling the gap but it's as solid as granite.

With a tablet-like device in hand, Major Peirce deactivates the machine.

"Peirce, what are you doing?" the colonel shouts over the radio.

"Sir, they've managed to defeat two MECHs on remote. Let's see how they handle the real thing," Peirce replies while climbing aboard.

"Good luck, soldier," Mitchel says.

Once inside, Peirce reactivates the device, checks his controls to ensure everything is in order, and then analyzes the wall. According to his scans, the newly formed material filling the gap is much denser than the concrete around it. Piece sidesteps it and aims at the section of wall to the slab's right—wham! He rams the MECH's fist into it. The steel-reinforced concrete immediately buckles.

"Ohh…" Leon readies himself, seeing the wall ahead of him, crack. There's a panicked swirl in his stomach and a sense of tension all over—an odd mix of anxiety and anticipation. He swallows hard, for he's never tested his abilities—not for real, but he won't let his mentor down.

"Don't fail me." He focuses, closing his eyes as he culls the aether around him.

Wham! Bam! Thud! The wall gives way, crumbling to the sight of the MECH behind it.

"Peirce, do you see him?" the colonel asks.

"Yes, sir. Thermal scans indicate that he's not quite as strong as the other one," he says, feeling gung-ho. Cranking up the MECH, Major Peirce readies his mechanical fist then moves in with a powerful step that launches him and the two-ton piece of machinery toward Leon.

Leon's eyes widen as it barrels toward him. He tries to dodge when that first strike hits its mark, right to the side of his head. There's a flash of sparkles and darkness, and then another flash, and another. Pain rings throughout his body and with a forceful uppercut to under his jaw, the MECH lifts him from the ground, driving him up into the drop ceiling.

Falling from the body-shaped hole, Leon hits the floor hard. He wasn't expecting such fluid motion from this clumsy-looking automaton. It takes him a few seconds to shake the stars from his head.

"Puthewa!" Leon spits blood on the floor, grimacing from the immense pain all over. *'Maybe this was a mistake,'* he thinks, his body shaking.

Thud, thud, thud, Peirce gets closer, staring down at the well-built young man resting on all fours. Readying the rail gun, he takes aim.

"I… will not…" Leon pants, shakily.

Bang—whoosh! The air fills with a cloud of vapor that reconstitutes behind the bionic menace as the Guardian of Earth reforms.

Strike, strike, whoosh! Leon delivers two good blows then billows around Peirce, only to solidify and hit him again. He Thai-kicks at the structure's leg above the knee joint, and then throws a left jab and a right hook to the armored chassis—ting, ding, dong!

"Gawh!" Leon shouts, turning away to cradle his right hand and rub the sting from his knuckles. The special alloy is tough as nails with a durability he's never tested. Hardly nudging the thing, his hands and shin ring out in soreness.

Seeing a moment of weakness, the soldier capitalizes and lands a kick to his back, causing the kid to stumble forward.

Leon then turns about, rolling with the momentum—clink, clank! He connects again before Peirce lines him up for a shot.

That loud, inescapable noise punishes Leon's ears as the sixty-caliber rounds punch through his left arm, shoulder, and chest like a series of dies activating in sequence. The first shot severs his hand below the wrist.

"Aaaaargh!" Leon howls. As the second shot tears through his shoulder, his body begins to phase. There's a splash and then a spray of water as the third hits his chest. By then, the Guardian of Earth is full hydro, with his injuries spilling together like holes in the ocean. In mere seconds, Leon is whole again.

'Did I just get my arm back?' He looks himself over for a second, dumbfounded by his own ability, for all those times he's turned to sand, air, or water, it never occurred to him that he could heal like that.

With renewed confidence, Leon counter attacks, cooling his liquid body to hit as solid ice.

Peirce stands firm against the tide of Leon's onslaught, shaking his head as the hull of the MECH chimes like a gong. It's dizzying, but tolerable. His armor holds steady, chipping away at the young man's frozen fists.

Realizing that it's not working, the Guardian of Earth changes up, morphing into a body of dense rock—ding! He rattles Peirce, causing him to stumble. At last, he's getting somewhere.

Major Peirce maneuvers to regain balance before swinging a backhanded strike to Leon's head—whoosh! The kid poofs to the ground, planting his hands as he reconstitutes. There's an immense rumble from above when a sudden column of earth crashes down, dropping the major to his mechanized chest.

"Major, come in! Major Peirce?" calls the colonel over the com, getting no response.

With the MECH cracked open, Leon peers inside. "Well, that explains things." He rubs his jaw. Knowing he can't rightfully leave him there, he pulls the unconscious major from the cockpit before running to catch up with the others.

. . .

The long hall appears to stretch and twist in Jasra's view. "Augh!" She staggers before giving in to the nauseating throb in her head.

Simon turns to catch her. "Are you alright?" he asks, easing her into a sitting position against the wall.

Seldin looks to Almir, gesturing for him to keep an eye on the hall before kneeling to check on her.

"It's too much," she cries.

"She's getting worse, Sei. Is there anything you can do?" Simon asks, and unfortunately, Seldin shakes his head with a lofty sigh.

"All I can do is dull the pain, I can't stop what's causing it," he laments.

"Well, do something, fast," Simon huffs and much like before, Seldin reaches a hand to her temple. Soon, Jasra's labored breaths ease, growing steady and deep.

Seldin glances to Simon. "The swelling in her brain is worse," he says.

"Caused by that weird energy source?" Simon asks with a puzzled face.

"Well, that doesn't make sense, why is she the only one sick?" Almir chimes in, looking back.

Simon points to Seldin. "You said something before about a chemical imbalance," he says.

"Yeah," Seldin throws a hand up in frustration, "but everything's there," he retorts before looking into her again, seeing no difference.

"Wait, you're basing that off the needs of a normal person, right? What do we need—more specifically, what does she need that we don't?" Simon proposes.

Seldin looks up in thought; he's right. He tunes his senses to the environment. "The aether is a little stale but why would that matter?" he comments.

Almir gestures with an open hand. "Well, maybe it's not just aether. She can see through time, right? Isn't there a particle for that?"

"Tachyons!" Simon and Seldin exclaim.

Simon then scans the compound. "Shit, Sei, he's right, there's hardly any in here." He stands, looking around.

"She's going through withdrawal," Seldin realizes.

Simon eyes wander in their sockets, looking without direction as he thinks about the situation. "The weird radiation?" he asks.

"Possibly. If they are experimenting with matter/antimatter reactions then it's conceivable the natural flow of tachyon particles is being disrupted," Seldin speculates just as the sound of hasty footsteps echoes down the hall.

"Hey guys!" Leon calls out.

"You made it." Almir smiles at his mentor.

"Yeah, that guy was… everything alright?" Leon asks, catching sight of the situation.

"For now," Seldin says as he and Simon help Jasra to her feet.

"Alright, Jasra, can you see?" Seldin asks.

Jasra shakes her head. "No, the future is still very fuzzy," she says.

But then Simon has an idea, "Wait, your sight gets worse the closer we get, right?" he asks, and she nods. "Then why not use her as a detector?"

Seldin's eyes shift to Simon with intrigue, and then Jasra puts in her two cents.

"Wow, you guys are really caring," she scoffs sarcastically.

"No, he's right. We can use your disadvantage to our advantage. Try to focus on where we need to go and aim us in the direction that hurts the most," Seldin says.

"Oh, no, I'm not liking…" she complains, already starting to feel uncomfortable again.

Stepping in front of her, Seldin looks into her eyes. "I'll do my best to alleviate the bulk of the pain, alright? Just feel it enough to guide us," he insists.

"Ok," she replies as he takes her hand.

Leon leads while Almir covers the rear. Simon, Jasra, and Seldin stay centered with Simon holding her up and Seldin easing the pain.

"Ohhh… mmmm," she moans, closing her achy eyes.

"Hun?" Simon seems concerned.

"We're close," she says, and they continue, crossing another hundred yards or so of the subterranean maze. "Turn left." She winces, and they take the corner.

"Fire!" an officer commands—ting-tink-ping-tink—bullets spray their way.

"It's an ambush!" Leon turns from the squad, pushing his friends back against the wall.

"Move." Seldin scoots around Leon before asking, "Jasra, are you alright?"

She nods. "Yes, there's a hangar around that corner—augh—but I can't see any farther," she says.

The strange energy emanating from within the hangar distorts Seldin's senses. He struggles in his mind's eye to make out the obscured signals of the soldiers guarding a large circular door.

"There's... s-six," he counts with clenched eyes before looking back. "Almir—"

"No, wait." Simon takes the lead. "There's something I want to try," he says while cracking his knuckles and back, as if the warmup is necessary, before casting a cloud of nanites, which soon grows darker and denser. The others watch as a familiar, frightening form takes shape.

Dumbfounded, Seldin steps up to the eight-foot-tall piece of machinery. "Heh, you eh... couldn't have done this sooner?" he questions, examining the MECH.

Simon lightly scratches his head. "I only recently acquired materials," he retorts and Seldin gestures for him to proceed.

Simon then turns his gaze toward his creation, and in his mind, he can see what it sees: connected through his machines. The automaton moves forward then takes that left, listening to Simon's intuitive instructions.

. . .

"Colonel, are you seeing this?" Andrews points out, stunned by what's on the monitor.

"Deakins, they have a MECH!" the colonel shouts.

"I'm on it," he replies, loading a grenade round into the launcher mounted under his tactical rifle before ordering his squad to lay down suppressing fire. Captain Deakins then takes position, sighting in on the monstrous machine as their rounds bounce off the hull. Floomp—boom! The grenade hits center mass with the explosion wrapping around the corner.

"Ahh—ugh!" Jasra and the others yell out as Seldin deflects the enveloping force away from them.

Clank-thud-clank—the MECH marches out from the smoke, bearing only minor damage. Brrrrrrrrph! It opens fire and immediately, Deakins and his squad divide.

"That doesn't sound like a rail cannon," Seldin comments.

Simon chuckles, hearing the screams of the soldiers. "Twin BB machine guns. I figured you didn't want casualties," he remarks.

Kaboom! Another grenade hits, blowing out the MECH's right hip.

"Yes!" Deakins shouts.

"Damn, it's down," Simon says.

"Can you fix it?" Seldin asks.

"Working on it," he replies, tapping the static from his goggles. The right lens blips and then the left. "Come on…"

Watching the fiasco over the monitor, Colonel Mitchel offers Deakins some praise. "Good work, soldier. Now finish them!" he orders.

"You got it," he readies his rifle.

Taking over the bot's automated systems, Simon brings it back to its feet then takes aim, firing on the troops.

"I'm hit!" they shout out, being pelted with BBs. Unaware of the lack of danger, they gather their fallen and huddle toward the center of the large circular door.

Launching a smoke grenade, Deakins takes advantage of the cover, and then accesses the control panel for the door.

Without a clear shot, Simon sprays and prays until a sudden change in pressure causes the smoke to billow, spilling into the next room. A rush comes over him and his eyes widen. "Shit, they're getting away!" He and the others dart around the corner, coming up on the rapidly closing door. There's a suctioning sound and a clank as it seals shut.

"Damn!" Leon shouts, smacking the face of its solid surface.

"I've got it," Seldin says while channeling aether into the door; the metal whines in protest.

Simon steps up behind him, resting a hand on his shoulder, and Seldin stops, looking at him. "Aren't you forgetting something?" Simon asks.

Seldin shrugs with a halfway glance.

"Guardian of Technology, remember?" Simon winks and Seldin concedes, stepping away to check on Jasra.

"How are you holding up?" he asks.

"Not so hot," she replies, resting her head against his chest.

...

On the other side of the door is the holy grail—the sphere, centered on a landing platform in the middle of a circular room and overlooking a long launch tunnel lined with yellow and white caution stripes.

Captain Deakins knows he has little time before they come through that door. Assessing the situation, he checks his men.

"Are you hit?" he asks Private Winters and Corporal La'Fae, who are down and cradling wounds.

The corporal lifts a hand, revealing a relatively small though bleeding hole in his right bicep. "I'm not sure how bad," he replies, and Winters has similar injuries to her thigh.

"Can you walk?" asks the major.

"It hurts to put pressure on it," she replies.

"Alright, you and you," Deakins points to Ortiz and Mathews, who are among the four still able to stand. "I need you two to take flanking positions on the catwalks above the door." He then looks to Privates Brody and O'Brien. "Help La'Fae and Winters to a safe spot and then cover me long enough to launch the sphere," he orders before manning the computer station to the right of the launch pad.

...

"Hey," Leon whispers to Almir, "get ready." He gestures with a tilt of his head toward the door as it begins to open. Almir gets into position just as Seldin and Jasra separate.

Retaking control of the MECH, Simon moves it forward just in front of Seldin, who scans the newly available area just beyond the door, searching through the radiation for the faint auras of the soldiers.

Using Simon's toy as a shield, the group lets it take the brunt of the assault. Seldin then steps around it, firing a stream of white energy at the man on the upper left catwalk, while Almir focuses on the guard to the right, whose eyes roll back as he collapses.

As the bot moves forward, the rest step inside the room, behind it. Leon then channels aether into the ground, shaking the floor. As the other two soldiers lose their footing, Simon jumps, taking out the first with a flying kick to the chest before dropping down to sweep the other, causing him to land flat on his back, out cold.

"You'll never get your hands on it!" Deakins yells at the top of his lungs and the group snaps their gaze to him as he hits the launch button. The bay doors rumble loudly as they open.

"Shit, there it goes!" Simon points as the sphere zooms off, up and out of the tunnel. Immediately, Seldin hurries after it, his expedited takeoff shatters the air—boom!

The others flinch in that instant, and then Simon gazes up the tunnel. Boom! There he goes. Boom, boom, boom! Leon, Almir, and Jasra take flight after them, zipping out into the dry desert sky as quickly as they can muster—or as quickly as she can muster, for Jasra isn't nearly as fast as them.

Leon soon realizes that even he can't catch up. He stops in midair, panting with labored breaths while watching the remnants of their trails in the distance. "Jesus, they're fast," he says.

"Yep." Jasra nods tiredly though feeling much better now in the open air. "Don't worry, they'll be back," she assures him.

. . .

At over three thousand miles per hour, Simon is having a difficult time keeping up. He's not even close to riding his friend's coattails. To make matters worse, the ship can take corners on a dime, changing direction almost instantly without losing speed—creating G-forces that would crush any ordinary pilot. He wonders then how it can do it, or moreover, how he can do it. Seldin must be flying close to Mach seven, he figures. That blows Simon's mind, for overcoming the frictional forces alone is challenging enough. If it weren't for his nanites and specialized suit, he would have burned up a while ago.

Gutting it out, Simon directs his brood to collect to just under his skin to act as a heat shield for areas that are unprotected by his bio-suit, namely his face. He then pushes forward, doing his best to catch up to Seldin's speed without being torn apart.

'Maybe I can convert friction into energy?' he considers, given the design parameters of the suit—sharp left! "Oh shit!" Simon exclaims, barely making the course change and nearly crashing as Seldin and the sphere alter their heading without hesitation.

Through his mind's eye, Seldin focuses intently on the craft, wondering what's inside, but like before, he's unable to get past the interference. It doesn't matter, he shakes the effort, ready to grab it when a sudden presence from behind gets his attention. It's Simon, he realizes with a glance over his shoulder. "Damn." He eases up, sandbagging, for he almost had it.

"Simon, can you sense anything?" he yells

"Eh… it's not completely solid," Simon remarks, pulling up beside him.

"Obviously, but I can't see inside, can you?" Seldin yells.

"No, but I think I can gain access Jedi-style," he answers. Seldin makes a face.

"Exhaust port!" Simon shouts, while concentrating a stream of nanites toward the craft.

The little robots trace over the surface of the sphere, working their way along the peaks and valleys of the textured hull until coming to a small fissure only a few microns across.

Error messages fill Simon's vision. "Mmmother…" he huffs, and Seldin looks over.

"What's the matter?" he asks.

"It's the radiation—whatever's spilling out is depolarizing their circuits," Simon explains.

"Are you saying you can't do it?" he asks.

Simon's head snaps his way. "I've got a few ideas left. I'm gonna use the nanites to construct an antenna through the exhaust port. That should give me a direct link," he says, instructing the bots to gather, forming a tight cylinder of nanite layers wrapped around a nanite core. As the outer layers die and become inert, they provide insulation, protecting the center line from decay.

Flash after flash, Simon watches in hope as thousands of signals fade with each new length being added to the chain.

"Come on, come on." He focuses, telling them to move deeper into the ship. The signals they send back are distorted, but it's a picture, nonetheless.

"I'm in," Simon says with excitement. "No pilot, but there is a cockpit and a touchscreen console—"

"Enough on the details, just shut it down!" Seldin exclaims. Simon clamps shut, tilts his head just a little as he focuses and then...

Eeerrrnnnnnmnuumm—the engines power down, leaving the craft at gravity's mercy. Tink, clank! It scrapes a mountainside before plunging into the dry desert sand.

"Nice." Seldin grins as he and Simon touch down through the plume of dust and smoke.

Simon offers a smirk. "Thanks. Say, how do you fly so fast without burning up?" he asks, looking down into the shallow crater as they approach the ship. With the engines off, the radiation has decreased, but there's still the matter of getting through the hull.

"It's simple," Seldin says as he slams a high-powered fist into the skin of the sphere. "I push the air ahead of me out of the way—I learned it from you, actually." He works his hands into the hull. "You used to..." Seldin grunts while gradually adding more and more energy to his muscles as he pries, "...do that back when you drag-raced, to make your car faster. An ingenious, no-drag, no-friction technique."

Simon shakes his head, having forgotten about all those years ago. "I can't believe you remembered that," he says while offering a hand as they tear the vessel open, revealing an empty cockpit.

The craft is just as round inside as out, with a seat designed to conform to the shape of the pilot, and a single console positioned in front. The inner walls are smooth, acting like a screen with a $360°$ view. Simon couldn't be happier, having access to all this new tech, but soon his delight grows to extreme discomfort as the core of the ship is exposed. The two of them back away almost immediately.

"Ohh," Simon groans, feeling nauseous.

"Yeah, no kidding," Seldin agrees, feeling strangely disoriented as well.

"That's one hell of a drive system, Sei; I'm pretty sure that's antimatter," Simon says despite his distorted scans of the unit beneath the seat.

"Antimatter is necessary for antigravity propulsion, but look at that energy." Seldin tries to maintain focus on the weird wispy strings dancing around the core. "That's not aether," he says with a cautious approach, reaching for the handle of the container. It's hot and getting hotter; his fingers start to burn with a tingling sensation trailing up his arm as he gets closer.

"Ahh." He jumps back, cradling his arm and feeling real pain for the first time in days.

"You alright?" Simon rushes over.

Although confused by the experience, Seldin nods. "Apparently, whatever that is disrupts flow of aether," he responds, his hand still shaking.

"But isn't antimatter made of aether?" Simon questions as he scans again, and Seldin's eyes wander with his thoughts.

"It's not the antimatter, it's what it's giving off—a biproduct of the reaction," Seldin replies.

Simon's jaw hangs open. "Anti-aether?"

"We've gotta tell the others." Seldin turns, but Simon's eye catches a flicker.

"Wait!" There's a blinking icon on the ship's monitor. "It's a distress signal," Simon says.

"From Groom Lake?" Seldin asks.

"No." Simon shakes his head. "It's coming from some place in the southern hemisphere," he replies, reading the coordinates.

"I think it's time we ask a direct question," Seldin states.

...

Away from the debilitating effects of the radiation, Jasra is able to see much clearer. She rests, hovering calmly with her eyes closed despite the echoing cadence of a hundred or so soldiers marching on the ground below.

Almir's eyes shift to his mentor, looking for guidance as the troops form up in a semicircle with weapons trained to the sky. Leon then glances to Jasra with equal concern. He doesn't want to show his hand, but he can't help but feel nervous with so many barrels pointing their way.

"You, uh… wouldn't wanna perhaps, open your eyes?" Leon asks. She doesn't, for her gift works better this way.

"Don't worry, they won't fire without a reason," Jasra assures him.

Almir quickly looks over. "Toppling their base isn't—"

"Sei's back," she interrupts.

"Is he?" Leon scans about, and then hears a roaring sound like a fighter jet approaching.

"You in the sky, you are surrounded!" the voice babbles on.

Almir looks past Leon to Jasra. "Should I put them out?" he asks, bringing a finger to his temple just as Seldin and Simon whiz by. The voice of the Guardian of Life enters them all and they follow just as quickly.

Simon and Seldin hit the ground hard, touching down at the heart of the formation while taking their landing a little too seriously. The suddenness of their actions startles the men, causing them to open fire.

At first, they all flinch—except for Seldin and Jasra—as the rifles discharge, spewing wave after wave of bullets in their direction. But as those projectiles grow nearer and nearer, they begin to move slower and slower. Simon, Almir, and Leon look on with amazement while coming out of their cringing postures.

Seldin, on the other hand, merely offers a smiling gaze back toward Jasra. "Is this you?" he asks, astonished by her precision.

Everything beyond the forward wall of unnecessarily-slow-moving bullets appears to be in normal time while the guardians seem to be in a small pocket of accelerated time with Jasra at the epicenter.

She nods at Seldin's question while holding back a playful smile.

"Can you stop them indefinitely?" Simon asks curiously.

"Eh… that depends." Jasra gestures. "Everything takes energy. It's easier to affect relative time than actual time," she answers.

"What's the difference?" Leon asks.

"Well, relative to us, those bullets are frozen, but from the bullet's frame of reference, we're moving really fast. However, if I were to move them to a point where they rust to dust, that would be a permanent change," she explains.

"And more costly," Seldin comments, and Jasra nods.

"What about time travel?" Almir asks.

"I'm still experime—don't!" she tries to warn Seldin as he playfully plucks a round from the air. Though frozen to him, it still retains all its force, and the moment his fingers wrap the copper jacket he jumps back, flinging the bullet, which drifts to a halt.

"Fascinating," he comments with intrigue while repairing the split in his fingertips.

As the battalion's rifles click to empty, Seldin snaps back to attention. "I am the Guardian of Life," he begins, but the soldiers offer no response. He then pauses with a glance back to Jasra. "Can they hear me?" he asks.

"Oh, sorry." Jasra laughs. "If they can, you probably sound like a chipmunk on acid," she answers, adjusting the temporal field before nodding to him.

Seldin starts again. "We are the Guardians. Who's in charge?" he asks in a commanding voice to the astonished faces gawking at the feat before them. Then, from behind the crowd comes an answer.

"I am," Colonel Mitchel responds in an equally commanding tone as he approaches, "and you have just committed an act of war on this country."

"Colonel." Seldin moves forward, telekinetically dividing the wall of bullets to clear himself a path. "This facility is experimenting with a technology not of this world, and I would like to know the source," he demands.

Mitchel laughs. "I'm under no obligation to answer you, boy," he says.

Holding his confidence, Seldin steps closer to the military officer. "Colonel, the materials you possess come from a system nine lightyears away. Not long ago, it was conquered by a militant race known as the pulsari, who are on their way here," he says.

Averting his eyes, Colonel Mitchel thinks for a moment before looking at Seldin. "I don't trust you," he says.

"Fair," Seldin begins, "but consider this: not much remains of the world I tried to save. I lost against the pulsari."

Almir whispers to Leon, "What's he talking about?" But Leon just shrugs in uncertainty.

"And if this test here today is any measure of Earth's defenses," Seldin pauses, "are you willing to stand alone?" He glances to his friends. "Because I'm not."

Right then Jasra gets a mental flash, "Sei, watch out!" she warns just before—

"Gaaahh!" A piercing screech enters Seldin's mind like needles stabbing his brain. He drops to his knees as images of a subterranean labyrinth overtake his vision.

Seizing the opportunity, Colonel Mitchel gives the order. "Arrest them!" He points when unexpectedly, all weapons train on him.

"Almir!" Seldin shouts as Jasra, Simon, and Leon help Seldin to his feet. "Release the—arrgh!" He drops down again, seeing phantom flashes of a leafy woman while hearing the muddled screams of a dying soldier.

"Boni… here?" Seldin shudders at the possibility of spore drones. Boom! He launches, knocking everyone near him to the ground. It doesn't take long, however, for the other guardians to give chase.

"Sei, what the hell is going on?" Simon's call reaches him intuitively despite the distance and the speed, but Seldin's focus is elsewhere. The very idea his suka friend could be on Earth—and worse, fighting malnar, sends chills down his spine. He must go faster, he thinks as Lucy moves from his backpack and takes root.

"Follow through the gates," Seldin projects the location to Simon before zooming out of sight.

Chapter 22

"The End of Youthful Games"

Dean hovers over Area 51, groaning at the sight below. Between the billowing veils of sand and smoke and the chatter of the scurrying soldiers, he is not very pleased.

"I can't believe Tillman allowed this," he gripes with a literal snarl. "Then again..." His senses pull focus, detecting the faint presence of unrefined elter—or anti-aether—throughout the compound. The idea that humans stumbled have upon it, even if they don't know what it is, gives him pause.

"Now where the hell are those kids?" he asks himself before applying those keen senses of his, like a bloodhound tracking a scent, and Dean does take a whiff. "Snnhhhhhh." He inhales, for his nose knows; the skin of his nostrils shifts briefly to reptilian-like scales before morphing back to the freckled Irishman they'll be expecting.

...

With Jasra in his arms, Simon leads the pack, setting the pace with a Mach number they all can adhere to.

"Jesus, do you feel that?" Almir blurts out, for it's the strongest thing he's ever felt.

Leon nods. "Yeah, it's coming from up ahead," he comments.

"It's Dean," Jasra says.

"It can't be Dean," Simon rebuts, "he's not that stro—whoa!" He stops, unable to believe his own eyes as the figure he's grown so familiar with comes into view. Jasra just smirks, rolling her eyes as they approach their bearded friend, who holds himself steady at the edge of the clouds with his auburn cloak flapping in the wind.

As the young guardians gather, they find themselves a little intimidated by Dean's stoic appearance and how well he carries it. His back to the sun, he hovers, arms crossed with the light dancing along the ribbed surface of his reddish-brown armor, formed of a strange alloy and held together by leather straps that lock into a medallion in the center of his chest. Inscribed with markings from the Language of the Gods, the emblem boldly represents the guardian's rank and position.

"Where is the Guardian of Life?" Dean demands with a gaze like an angered parent, staring in disappointment.

. . .

Soaring over a remote part of the South American jungle, Seldin finds himself frantically searching for signs of life—its life, for the signal has gone cold, and that worries him. Taking to the ground, the force of his landing blows the trees and grass like a tsunami.

"Where are you?" he calls desperately, hoping for anything: a spike in power, a painful vision—anything.

Whoosh! There is a sudden rushing electrical hum from directly behind him with a shimmering circular dispersal of violet light.

"Sei!" Simon shouts as he and the others step out of the portal.

"Glad to see the gates have better accuracy this time around," Seldin says, but the distraction is brief, however, and he turns away to realign his senses to a more pressing matter.

"Actually, it was Dean," Leon says, and that name strikes an immediate chord with Seldin—answering the question of just how long they'd been watching, for he's known him since he was a kid, maybe ten… or eleven. His stomach twists as Dean steps out of the portal, which closes behind him. But it's not curiosity Seldin feels in this moment with the suka's life in the balance, it's betrayal.

"Simon tells me you're responsible for that mess back at Groom Lake," Dean scolds.

Seldin straightens up with a quick glare at Simon. "Did he?" he asks, not caring much for Dean's tone.

"The Guardianship is not a game!" Dean states with a reverence.

Simon then steps up, his voice shaky. "Sei, this is the Guardian of Dimension, he's—"

Seldin cuts him off. "We don't have time for that right now; we're looking for a suka warrior. He's an insectoid about eight feet tall with tan skin. I lost his signal a few minutes ago, but he might still be alive."

"Seldin! You need to take this seriously," Dean states, and Seldin snaps his gaze his way.

"I don't care about Area 51, Dean!" Seldin shouts with real rage in his voice. "I care about the suka! I care about malnar on this planet! Now, if you're not part of the solution, you're a part of the problem!" Seldin turns away, continuing his scan of the area.

Dean is taken aback. This is not calm, focused boy who left for the woods two years ago. He sighs with disappointment. "You know, I had high hopes for your ascension; I thought it would bring maturity, but what you all did—exposing us!"

"Are you still here?" Seldin retorts before turning away to regain focus. "Just let it come to you," he whispers to himself, closing his eyes.

"Over here, I see something!" Leon exclaims, pointing straight out about a hundred yards and thirty feet below at the bottom of the shallow ridge. They all look. It's a military jeep.

Simon leaps, swooping down to it. "It's withered!" he shouts back. Creeping vines have managed to weave into the metal, making it brittle and flakey to the touch. Snapping off a piece, he examines it further.

"Report," Tillman's message reaches Dean's mind and he steps to the back of the group.

"It appears you were right, there was elter at the base," Dean replies.

"Any risk of exposure?" he asks.

Dean shrugs, *"I don't think so; it's too unrefined to be dangerous at our level,"* he says.

"Then what's the hold up?" he questions.

"They've stumbled upon some stray malnar," Dean replies, and he can hear Tillman sighing through the telepathy.

"Solve it and make sure you're near Jasra when she ascends," Tillman orders just as Simon finishes his scan.

"It's only been here a few hours, yet it's completely stripped of all vital compounds," Simon says, baffled.

Right then, Jasra reaches a hand to Seldin's shoulder, stopping him from stepping forward.

"Sei," she says with a trembling voice, and he turns to look at her pale face and watery eyes. "He's over there." She points left with a shaky hand, having already seen what's to come.

The sight of the suka slumped over in the bushes, paralyzes Seldin like a bolt of lightning into his heart. "No!" he rushes over.

Almir and Leon stand frozen at the reality of it, and Simon too, pauses the moment he makes it back up the hill. But soon, the sorrow in Seldin's voice draws them near as he tries to rouse it.

"Come on!" Seldin pleads, He can feel its energy; it's not all gone—not dead yet. Giving up a portion of his own life force, he offers it to the creature, but the suka rejects it, pushing him away with a gurgling groan as it opens its enormous eyes.

With no time for a greeting, it fills the young guardian's mind with all that has happened—the base, his imprisonment, and the experiments. Seldin watches through the suka's eyes as it fights its way to the surface.

"Gah—enough! Let me help you!" Seldin pleads, but the suka knows its time is limited—it must bring him up to speed. Taking his mind again, it shows him a vast array of ships—a fleet—no, an armada—and all the planets in its path. Seldin realizes then, it is not just the Earth that's in danger.

"Two worlds before Earth." Seldin gasps, shaking his head, but then another image pops in— one that couldn't be more clear—the destruction of Earth or the destruction of the pulsari.

"No!" Seldin shouts, desperately. "Let me help you. Together we can—"

The suka pushes him away, letting out a sorrowful moan before closing its eyes. Its body then jerks and twitches convulsively before settling into a cross-legged pose.

"No!" Seldin screams, feeling its life slipping away. He focuses on its core, delivering pulse after pulse of aether. The energy rocks the suka, but it doesn't wake. "Come on! Don't go!"

Jasra covers her ears, doing her damndest to block it out. The others hold still, casting sympathetic gazes. Even Simon's face shows a hint of pity for his friend's loss.

Dean's heart sinks. He steps up, placing a hand on the young guardian's shoulder. "I'm sorry," he says genuinely.

Composing himself, Seldin stands, his eyes fixated on the suka's remains. "How long have you been a guardian, Dean?" he asks, then looks over his shoulder at him. "And don't insult me by saying it's a recent development."

Dean lowers his eyes as Seldin turns to face him. "Four centuries," he answers.

"You should have told us—" Seldin starts.

"I couldn't—" Dean tries.

"—from the beginning what we were."

"I couldn't risk that!" Dean shouts.

"How many lives might have been saved had we known—had we prepared?" Seldin's fury builds.

"It's our highest law!" Dean states, backing up as Seldin steps closer. The air around them picks up in small gusts, at first, then heavier.

Seldin clenches a fist. "You scolded us for being childish while concealing the most profound truth from us!" He throws a punch that rips the air, but he hits nothing; instead, he finds himself relocated several feet away. It takes him a second to realize before turning around.

"And what if we'd been wrong, huh? Only one guardian of a type, Sei!" Dean points to Seldin. "One Guardian of Life!" He points to Leon. "One Guardian of Earth!" He then points to himself. "One Guardian of Dimension! There can't be two kings—if another tried to ascend in your place, they would die!"

"That's no excuse for keeping us in the dark when so many lives could have been saved!" Seldin shakes a fist.

Dean gestures openly with both arms. "And risk everything?" He points to Seldin. "You have no idea how rare knowledge of aether is in the universe—the ability to control it—the potential for ascension—the lengths we went through to keep you hidden from—" He stops, abruptly.

"From what?" Seldin asks.

Dean shakes his head with a dreadful look in his eyes. He turns his back to Seldin. "Ascension has to be natural; otherwise, we might be sending some poor bastard to his death." He sighs.

Seldin turns back toward the suka. "As if you cared about life," he scoffs, kneeling beside his fallen friend. He closes his eyes and places a hand on its chest.

"You can't bring it back," Dean says as Seldin channels aether into the corpse; its surface withers to ash and billows away in the wind like glowing embers.

Sighing, Seldin then stands. "I wasn't trying to," he says before turning toward his friends. "In less than two days the pulsari will be arriving at Oqu IX; that's what the suka said, but we need to fortify Earth first."

Simon looks to him. "And how do you propose we do that?" he asks.

"We use the malnar; I've done it before," Seldin replies.

"What?" Simon questions.

"But then how do we get to the other planet?" Leon asks.

Dean then chimes in. "Well, I can—"

"We don't want your help, Dean," Seldin says sternly, and Dean gestures with a shrug before stepping away.

Simon's face contorts. "You want to use those… those things—weren't you the one who said they were dangerous?" he asks.

Seldin nods. "But they're only dangerous when weaponized, otherwise they become part of the ecosystem," he says.

"Are you sure?" Jasra asks.

"Yes, the suka taught me about them. He brought six with him, including Lucy, so he could defend against the pulsari wherever he went. But when he crashed here, the government seized everything," he explains.

"I don't believe this." Simon turns away.

A curious thought comes to Leon. "So, how did it know to contact you?" he asks.

Dean's eyes flick to Leon, then carefully to the others.

Seldin shrugs. "Maybe it had something to do with Lucy, I'm not sure. It's odd though, he seemed like he already knew me," he replies.

"Don't be so surprised," Dean interjects despite the immediate cold stare from Seldin. "We're known throughout the universe, and the Guardian of Life has a unique gift that enables him to communicate with any lifeform regardless of language; it's an intuitive sense."

"You're suggesting it knew I was a guardian before I did?" he asks.

"Maybe, but I agree with Simon," Dean changes the subject, "it's a fool's errand to go chasing these malnar."

Seldin then straightens up. "Well, I didn't ask for your opinion in this matter, Dean." He looks amongst his friends. "Any objections that I might care about?" They all hold silent, looking between themselves. "Good, then I say we fortify this planet. This is what we're looking for…" Seldin passes the suka's memories onto them.

Leon gasps as the terrifying images pour into his mind. "What the hell is this?"

Flashes of shifty foliates in various forms meander in and out of everyone's view as their eyes seem to stare blankly into the space between them and Seldin—except for Dean, who seems unfazed by the incoming knowledge.

"Ahh!" Jasra screams, frightened by the true appearance of the spore drones with their vine-like framework, their leafy exterior, and their creepy eyeless faces with vestigial stares that mock their prey.

"Those are the mean ones. The ones we need are like Lucy," Seldin tells them as they shake off the horrible visions.

"Be aware: what was supposed to be our salvation may now be our destruction," Seldin sighs, "the military has been modifying them, much in the way the pulsari have. The one he showed me was violent and uncooperative. We can only pray that the others weren't affected. Now listen." He looks to his friends. "These organisms are protean and may not always take a common shape. Scan for their energy signatures. If they attack you, go for the spore—that's where they are vulnerable," he informs them.

"What else did it tell you?" Dean asks with his eyes locked to Seldin, but Seldin steps away.

"Alright, split up into groups. Jasra, you're with me," Seldin instructs. "According to the suka, the entrance is over there." He points when...

"Hey, wait a second!" Simon stops him. "Why don't you pair with Dean, and—"

"Seriously?" Seldin questions him with a glare to Dean. "Besides, couples don't work well together," he says before turning toward the facility entrance.

Simon makes a gesture of frustration. "Who the hell does he think he is?" he complains loudly, looking to Dean.

Dean shrugs. "Our boss," he answers before complying.

Simon then chases after him. "What? You're stronger than he is," he questions.

"That doesn't matter; there's a pecking order—four guardians crucial to the balance of the universe: Life, Death, Dimension, and Time, and you'd do right to follow it," he says.

Simon's shoulders sink. "Oh, I'm not liking this—you mean, we actually have to listen to him?" he gripes.

"You are free to make your own choices, Simon, but know this: at its core, the universe values the cycle of life and death above all things," Dean explains.

…

The entrance of the now abandoned base lay open, overrun by vegetation and shrouded in smoke from the few remaining smolders hidden beneath the rubble. An echo of a moment plays like a memory scarred through time as Jasra and Seldin pass where Sergeant Di'Nau and Private Klater once had.

To Jasra, it's clear as a bell with ghosted figures reliving their last few minutes like a movie rewinding just for her. Seldin, on the other hand, sees only the energy as he sifts the area with his senses.

"You seem tense," Jasra comments, while listening to his heavy breaths.

Seldin glances her way. "Is it that obvious?" he asks.

She nods subtly. "Maybe you should take a break, rest for a minute?" she suggests, casually shifting her gaze between him and the ground as she walks.

They have been at it all day, he considers, then shakes the thought from his mind. "I don't need rest, but you can if you like," he says.

"Damn it, Sei, you just lost a mentor and had a fight with a close friend. Are you honestly going to stand there and tell me you're not hurting? Because aether doesn't heal the heart," she says, staring into the blueness of his eyes and the pain he holds behind them.

He nods, conceding to her wisdom before taking a seat on a broken slab of concrete by the door. Wiping a single tear from his cheek, Seldin looks off, allowing the day to catch up with him. His body shakes and he buries his face in his arms.

An arm slips around his shoulder when Jasra moves to join him, resting her head against him in a show of solidarity. His watery eyes shift to her in the moment as he realizes.

He sniffles, wiping his face. "Heh." He smiles softly. "How many times did it take you to get me here?" he asks curiously.

Jasra tries to hold back a smirk as she blushes. "A few," she admits, "but I could tell, you needed to clear your head."

Taking a deep breath, he nods. "There's something I didn't tell the others," he says and Jasra looks at him despite his outward gaze.

"The suka said the pulsari won't listen to reason—they won't negotiate. They want only one thing: to be the dominant force in the universe. He said the only way…" Seldin wipes another tear. "Is to destroy them."

Jasra sits up, her eyes looking back into a half-forgotten memory—a future—a ship—and her friend. "Sei…" she hesitates.

"As the Guardian of Life, I cannot allow an act of genocide," he says with a heavy exhale. "There has to be another way." He stands.

Jasra looks up at him, holding his hand. Her heart shakes her chest. "W-what if there isn't?"

Seldin sighs, looking into the crumpled hall before them. "There has to be." He then points into the building. "How far can you see?" he asks, closing his eyes to feel out the energy ahead.

Closing her eyes as well, Jasra responds. "About fifteen minutes before I am forced back here. That takes us down the shaft to either the decontamination room or a storage room adjacent to an escape hatch," she groans, attempting to push beyond the edge of her range. "That's it, that's as far as I can go," she says.

"Any opposition?" he asks.

"Hmm-mm." She shakes her head as they step inside. "This way," she says, pressing the appropriate buttons on the keypad to the elevator, as if she's done it before, and soon that sinking feeling kicks in with their descent.

With the chime of the elevator door, they prepare to step out when—whoosh—bursts a gust of flame, getting a fresh dose of oxygen. Seldin acts quickly, projecting a field of energy to divert the raging fire.

"You alright?" he asks, hearing her cough and gasp through the smoke before realizing she can't breathe.

In his haste, he grabs her, takes a deep breath, and places his mouth over hers while using his lungs to filter the air. Jasra's eyes widen in his action as he breathes for her.

'How selfish of me,' he thinks, for not considering her needs first. She holds on tightly and he can feel the shake of her panicked heart.

Expanding his aura to encompass them both, he expels the smoke to create a pocket of breathable air. He then pulls back to unseal their lips, but Jasra's grip tightens.

"It's alright, you can let go now," he projects into her mind before insistently easing her back. Jasra gasps for a second or two as she catches her breath.

"Next time, you should give me a heads up about the smoke," he comments, clearing his throat as they continue forward.

With a hint of red in her cheeks, Jasra returns his stare. "I… um… I will, next time."

...

"Listen, I'm not saying Sei would make a bad leader, but the guy can be preachy as all hell, ya know? Besides, I don't buy into this preordained crap," Simon comments.

Dean chuckles. "So, you don't believe your innate understanding of technology was intended?" he rebuts.

Simon shakes his head. "Of course not. I'm only good at it because I put in the effort; it was a choice," he argues.

"What if I told you the game was rigged, that you chose it because you were programmed by circumstance to love it," Dean says, and Simon pauses in thought.

"Could you even tell the difference?" Dean adds, watching Simon sort it out.

"Programmed by what—God?" Simon questions the notion.

Dean shrugs. "Maybe. All I know is the universe has a way of creating what it needs," he says, and Simon makes a disagreeable face.

"I just can't stand the idea that we're meant to be," he scoffs.

"Not at all." Dean shakes his head. "You got here because of hard work, but situations in your life shaped your desire—the stronger your affinity for technology grew, the more attuned you became with your guardian role," he says.

"You're saying, I was nudged?" Simon comments, and Dean nods.

"I know I was. Growing up, I was the outcast; all I wanted was to be someplace else, until one day, it happened. But the hard truth is, we got lucky: wielders are very rare in the universe, and even the, only one or two ascend per millennium." he says as Simon turns off the beaten path to examine some unusual plant life.

"Is that…" Simon's eyes widen at the sight of long thorny fingers attached to an even stranger body, shriveled on the ground beside them.

"Yeah," Dean says in a quiet voice.

"Uh, Dean…" Simon utters, tapping the man's shoulder.

Dean then looks up, following Simon's captive gaze. "Oooh, shit."

Chapter 23

"A Malnar Problem"

Above the ridge that hides the base, Leon and Almir are busy putting their aether sensitive skills to work.

"I don't feel anything," Almir says in frustration.

"You have to relax," Leon instructs, thinking back to just a couple years ago when he was first learning the ropes. "If you force it, it won't work. Just let the energy come to you."

"Ugh, sensing people is so much easier."

"Yeah, Sei used to have me feel for lizards. He'd catch one, paint a colored line on its back, and then let it go." Leon reminisces.

"Did you ever find them?" Almir asks while fanning the frons of various plants as he searches for signs of malnar.

Leon nods. "It took a few months to get their signals down; I think by the time I learned to distinguish one lizard from another, there must have been at least a hundred flamboyant reptiles roaming the woods," he says and that gets a chuckle out of Almir.

"Well, what do you feel now?" Almir asks.

"No cheating," Leon says. "Use your ow—whoa, that's a big hole!"

Almir whistles, staring down into the enormous chasm seemingly cut out of the ground and leading straight down into a dimly lit bottom.

It's hard to tell just how deep it is from the ridge, but the circular opening has a radius of about four meters. The outer rim is jagged with rocks of various sizes strewn about the perimeter, while the hole itself appears to have been created with extreme heat. Some rocks on the inner walls are scorched while others are melted.

"What do you think made it?" Almir asks, taking in the faint musty smell of smoke mixed with a hint of ozone. Leon just shakes his head, for he hasn't the faintest idea.

...

Within the base, Jasra and Seldin are just now crossing the bridge of the decontamination area. The lower levels are flooded, with various things swimming about.

"It happened fast, whatever it was," Jasra notes observantly, keeping a close distance to Seldin, who is just a step ahead.

"Yeah, that's how they do it—hit and run," he comments, feeling things out.

The environment has changed dramatically since Klater and Di'Nau passed through some time earlier. Their shadows are all that remain as Jasra watches them run to an inevitable end. There's nothing alive in here now except the malnar, which have transformed the interior into a jungle. She sighs, taking a moment.

"Now you sound like the one who's stressed," Seldin teases with a glance her way.

"It's just the past." Jasra looks around. "Hindsight is easier than foresight." A faint laugh escapes her lips. "Though ironically, it's easier to move forward than back," she comments.

"Maybe time is like a river, always—hey look." Seldin points at the fish-shaped plants swimming below.

Leaning over the rail to see what he sees, Jasra fakes a smile. "Neat," she says, not wanting to break his spirit, for it's nice to see him smile at something, even if she lacks his curiosity in this moment. Maybe it's the grumble in her stomach or the horrid screams of the ghosted figures passing her by. "I'm starting to peter out," she admits.

And that takes Seldin back. "I'm sorry, I keep forgetting about—"

"It's alright," she dismisses.

"No, it's not. I shouldn't make you guys push so hard. As soon as we get topside, we'll take a break," he says.

She nods agreeably. "I'm not so sure you're going to find what you're looking for here, Sei," she says, peering ahead.

His own senses confirm it, not detecting the mind he thinks he should, but he has to see. "The suka said it was this way." He leads down the ramp and through the set of broken glass doors.

"Watch your right," she warns, and sure enough, at the bottom of the ramp, a soldier jumps out, clawing and swiping at them.

"Huaarr!" the man lets out an inhuman shrill.

Right away, Seldin grabs him by the neck and slams him into the nearest wall. The texture of the monster's skin feels real with warmth and even a pulse under his grip, but he knows better, seeing through its disguise.

The drone flails, slashing, biting, and snapping at him. Bringing his other hand ready, Seldin takes an uneasy breath before punching through its chest to the soft fragile spore. And like so many before, the malnar drone—the boni— shrivels to a withered heap of vines.

"Thanks," Seldin says to her.

"Don't mention it," she replies with a soft smile, finding joy in their collaboration.

Seldin's eyes then trail right. "God no," he lets out, feeling a stutter in his chest as he crosses the short hall to the open door of Laboratory B. He had hoped their senses were wrong.

"It's gone," he laments, staring into an empty room with light pouring in from above. His gaze then shifts upward. Shielding the sun from his eyes, he peers through the enormous hole in the ceiling.

Tapping his arm, Jasra then points upward, seeing shifty shadows. "There's movement," she says when…

"Hey!" Leon's voice echoes. "What are you doing down there?"

"What are you doing up there?" Seldin rebuts before he and Jasra rise out of the pit.

"I thought you guys were in the base," Leon comments.

"We were." Seldin glances down into the hole. "This is right over Lab B."

"Lab B?" Leon questions.

"Well, did you find any of those creepy plant things?" Almir asks.

Seldin looks to him. "None like Lucy, but the base is infested," he answers.

"It's about the same up here," Leon says.

Seldin scans the area. "Well, there has to be a beljusa around here somewhere," he says.

"Why do you say that?" Leon asks.

"Because all these little ones didn't grow themselves," he replies.

Whoosh, swoosh! Simon rushes out of a flash of violet with Dean casually following behind. The young Guardian of Technology pants heavily, catching his breath.

"There…" Simon stammers, "…there's another base a few miles that way." He points past the jeep. "Covered in malnar," he says in a panic.

"The whole thing looks like a giant flower," Dean remarks, and that catches Seldin's ears immediately.

"Show me," Seldin says, and Dean waves a hand, opening a portal for him to look through.

The entire facility is like a giant hedge maze with a fence fashioned from layers of creepers, three feet thick. Thorns like daggers cover them while tiny little blossoms wink in all directions. The main gate itself appears to have an organic double arch with eloquent streamers and other twisted vines defensively strewn like barbed wire.

"There are soldiers there, Sei," Simon begins, "but they're not—"

"Not people? I know," Seldin responds, "I told you they can change their shape. The beljusa—or rose queen—releases spores that can mimic anything they touch. They can also assume a number of default forms, but they're not sentient, only the queen is." He looks to the others.

Simon paces. "This is bad, right?"

"I don't think so." Seldin shakes his head.

"Don't think so? Look for yourself!" Simon shouts, pointing through the portal.

"Didn't your alien friend say they were aggressive?" Leon asks.

"Yeah, but I think he was mistaken."

"Why do you think that?" Dean asks.

"Because we're still alive," he replies.

"Tell it to those soldiers," Simon rebuts and Seldin turns to him.

"She may have acted in self-defense—"

"That's bullshit!" Simon exclaims.

"I need to speak to her!" Seldin insists.

Simon throws his hands up in anger. "All you do is talk!"

"There may be a chance to salvage the situation!" Seldin shouts back.

"You're insane." Simon turns away.

"And you're a fool if you think you can take them in broad daylight," Seldin replies.

"Then I'll wait for dusk," he retorts before turning about. "Who's with me?"

"Simon, listen, she's only taken the compound. There has to be a reason," Seldin tries.

Dean steps away. "I'm sorry, Sei, I agree with Simon," he says, and Almir joins them.

"Don't do this—wait," Seldin pleads. "Just give me a chance to speak with her. If I'm right, we gain an ally. If I'm wrong…" he sighs, "…then we'll do it your way."

Simon's eyes shift to Dean for a moment before looking back to Seldin. "You have five minutes," he says, and with that, Seldin turns toward the base.

Wasting no time, he calls out to her, *"This is the Guardian of Life,"* he says, but the beljusa does not answer. Moving down the ridge to a clearer vantage point, he then tries again.

Perhaps he acted too hastily when he killed the boni a few minutes ago—the thought comes to him with worry not far behind, for he dreads to think of Simon's actions if he fails.

Dropping down, he takes a seat while focusing intently on the base. Even Lucy comes out to help, fanning her petals like a little antenna. As the seconds turn to minutes, the beats of Seldin's benign heart begin to shake his body.

"Please," he begs, hearing only the wind. With time up, Seldin stands, disappointed in his defeat. As he turns to head back, something enters his mind: a vision of him—and only him—surrounded by malnar within the queen's chamber. The message is simple but clear: *"Come alone."*

Ecstatic, he hurries back, for there isn't a second to spare. *"Guys!"* he projects the message. *"The beljusa has*—where is everyone?" He stops, his eyes falling to Dean, who stands alone.

"They went to Simon's to rest; there's still a few hours before nightfall," he answers.

"Nightfall? Dean, the beljusa has agreed to see me," he says.

Dean shrugs. "That is not a ceasefire, you've accomplished noth—where are you going?" he demands as Seldin turns away.

"To handle this diplomatically," Seldin answers, and as Dean watches him storm off in anger, he smiles with a subtle nod.

"Very good," he whispers to himself.

...

Seldin feels hot and flushed as he marches over the unlevel terrain, smacking the foliage out of his way. It's not so much a sense of anger that is coursing through him right now, more like anguish.

How could his friends take such a radial position? It's lunacy, he thinks, even for Simon.

Overlooking the valley from the hilltop, Seldin continues to meander in thought as he stares off at the small outpost engrossed with foliage. Suddenly there's a hand to his back and he jumps with a startled huff as he turns to see her.

"Jasra?" he gasps.

"Just wanted to let you know, Leon and I voted for you," she says with a sort of playful smile that catches him off guard.

"Well, that's a relief. At least the mutiny wasn't unanimous," he chuckles falsely.

"You're the one making decisions for the good of the group. Simon…" she sighs, "…only cares about himself. That's what makes you the better leader," she says and Seldin turns about with a huff.

"I don't care to lead; I care about preventing an unnecessary war," he states.

"My point exactly," she reiterates.

"So, you think this is all about his pride?" he asks, turning to face her.

"What else? There's always been a power struggle between you two—and you heard the way he threw you under the bus with Dean," she says.

Seldin rubs his face as he sighs. "Uhh, what am I gonna do?" he laments.

"Kick his ass, of course," she retorts.

"No, I'm serious—what happens when I get down there, sort things out, and he still wants a fight? It'll undo everything—and worse, make an enemy out of a potential ally," he says with genuine concern.

"Tell the beljusa what's going on; Leon and I will stand with you," Jasra says encouragingly.

Seldin frowns, shaking his head. "She's requested that we meet alone."

"What?" Jasra exclaims.

"Those are her terms, and I won't break them. No, your place right now is with Simon—"

"But I don't want to be with Simon, I want to be with you!" Jasra immediately looks down, covering her mouth. "I mean, he's shown such little regard for... what's important," she says.

"Dean believes in him," Seldin comments.

Jasra nods before looking off as she wipes her eyes. Seldin moves close, rubbing her shoulders in a gentle embrace.

"Jassie," he takes a breath, "if this thing goes badly... you supporting me can only make it worse. How do you think Simon would react?" he asks, and she nods.

"How did you get out here anyway?" Seldin asks, and she looks to him.

"Dean, he uh... let me out," she replies.

"You should get back before Simon notices," he says and she rolls her eyes. "And... I need to meet with the beljusa. Thanks for checking on me." He smiles softly before stepping backward off the hilltop. He leans back with his arms open, allowing gravity to take him toward the valley floor.

Rotating as he nears the ground, he then directs the aether beneath his body to carry himself forward while the grass below seemingly reaches for him as he passes over. With the main gate ahead steadily approaching, he lets himself touch down, hardly making a sound.

Unaware of what awaits him, Seldin stands patiently, calming his heart as he stares at the vine-covered, chain-linked gate.

"I'm here," he says. A few minutes of silence pass with no reply from the queen, but then, from behind, two hands reach his back. Looking, of course, he takes a startled breath as his gaze passes left then right to the standard-shaped drones he is so familiar with.

Forward they guide him as the gate opens and he is brought inside. From there, he looks about, but the creatures to his left and right force him to look forward. Still, he manages to sneak peripheral glimpses where he can.

What he sees surprises him, for every structure is completely green except for the few floral arrangements that dress the various vines. These things are more than a mere bouquet, however, for the roots that anchor them, burrow effortlessly into the materials beneath as they absorb and mimic what they touch—save for other malnar, which appear immune to the effects.

Drawing him down farther and farther into the lair, his escorts guide him along with subtle tugs and pushes to keep him moving forward. Their assistance, although initially unsettling, enables him to close his eyes and capture what is not obviously visible. With his mind open to the energies around him, he begins to realize that this hive, despite being formed of individual plants, acts more like a single organism composed of thousands of members working collectively to serve one mind—her mind—much like what he felt when he peered into the first drone he encountered on the suka home world.

It simply blows his mind that in spite of all the beljusa's control over this place, her presence is barely noticeable. In fact, it isn't until they reach the queen's chamber that her energy becomes obvious.

With his eyes closed, her aura is bright, illuminated by wispy whirls of golden light set on a canvas of blue subtones, yet it is in plain view that her magnificence truly shines. She's even bigger than the ones he planted on the surface of Binax-Beta. Her roots touch everything and form the oval-shaped den they're in.

As the boni bring him before her, they shove him to his knees, and he complies without resistance.

"Brilliant, you're using their energy to mask your own," he comments observantly before a rush of meaning enters him, forming a question within his mind: *"What do you want?"*

...

Unable to nap, Jasra lies in bed, staring up at the ceiling while streaming the paths of the immediate future. She just can't seem to get beyond that fifteen-minute hurdle, for her sight distorts each time. Sitting up, she kicks off the blankets in her apparent frustration. Her eyes then fall to the lack of Simon.

"Typical," she gripes before taking a few breaths to calm herself. "If I can't master the future…" she mumbles to herself as she takes a different time-worthy angle. Yet, unlike the future, the past has only one possibility.

Lying back down, she takes advantage of hindsight, for it's easier to see what's already happened than it is to sift through an endless web of branching paths. The moments of the day rush past her—her and Seldin on the cliff—the argument with Simon—and the kiss she stole—then suddenly, she finds herself back in the forest with Seldin weeping over his insectoid friend.

She's never gone this far back before; this was over an hour ago. It takes her a second or two to regain her bearings, but the tide of time is against her, and as the seconds tick on in the present, she's gradually ushered forward as if tethered to some invisible force.

The more she resists the pull of time, the more nightmarish her experience becomes. She finds it impossible to move—save for the actions already taken—and her words seem inaudible, except for those already spoken. The moments behind her grow more and more distorted, drifting farther out of focus, while what's ahead of her gradually grows all the more clear.

Whoosh! Jasra is flung forward, colliding with the present. "Dang it!" She thrusts a fist against her mattress as she sits up.

"If only I could change it," she expresses with exhaustion before rolling out of bed for a well-needed snack.

Bzzt-bzzt-pop! An electrical noise gets her attention as she passes Simon's workroom, seeing him zapping a small, faceted sphere with his micro-welder—pop-pop!

"Now what are you working on?" she asks with a subtle tone. The sound of her voice irks Simon, for he was enjoying the peace and quiet. He glances to her, though barely making eye contact as she wispily creeps beside him.

"Just one last upgrade before tonight." He holds up the round device resembling a metal golf ball. "I've already added armor plates to the bio-suit, and the latest batch of nanites are synthesizing," he answers as he works.

"Par for the course?" she questions, though Simon doesn't care for her snooty inflection.

"Sei thinks this can be handled peacefully; I don't. Even if that queen-thing cooperates, how do we know it can be trusted?" he asks openly.

"You should trust Sei; he is the Guardian of Life after all—"

"Pff!" Simon scoffs, turning his back to her.

Jasra cocks her head, looking down at him as he works. "Unless… that's not what this is really about," she says.

Simon doesn't look at her. "I won't follow bad decisions," he says.

With disappointment in her heart, Jasra moves to the door. She then pauses, looking back at him. "What if I told you, you don't win tonight?" she presents.

"Do you know that for sure?" Simon asks without a glance her way.

"No," she replies.

"Then don't bother me with it," he snaps, "and shut the door."

Complying, Jasra then heads down the hall toward the kitchen. She forces out a smile as she crosses the living room, catching glimpses of Dean and the boys looking rather silly in their battle gear while watching anime on the television.

"Anyone hungry?" she asks while making herself a sandwich.

"Always," they unanimously reply before crowding in to pilfer the various delights in the refrigerator.

"Ham?" she offers.

"Please," Dean promptly replies while moving his short, stocky frame around her to get to the cabinet in search of a plate.

"So, what's it like living forever?" she asks. The question gets a smile out of Dean.

"I'm only four hundred and forty-nine," he says plainly, "but you get to see a lot of transitions—it's amazing watching the world evolve around you. I was actually born in a small country town in Ireland, July 15th, 1570. It was mid-summer and like every newborn child, I was totally oblivious to the world I had just arrived in."

Leon and Almir join them as they move to the kitchen table. Dean continues.

"The renaissance was on its way out and the modern age was on its way in with art, music, money, and war. My mother was a traditional Irish woman, raised Catholic, and my father was an egotistical asshole who vanished when I turned ten," Dean states.

Jasra nods with interest. "Tell me about when you became a guardian," she says.

A soft sigh escapes his lips. "You guys can't really be interested in this," he comments.

"Sure we are," Almir begins, "it's one thing to believe in something." His eyes shift to Leon then back to Dean. "It's another to have proof," he says.

"Well." Dean nods. "I was about eighteen when I learned who I really was; prior to that, it was a horrifying experience. See, back then, they were still burning people at the stake for being witches or werewolves, and at a young age, much like you all, I discovered I had these powers. I could use telekinesis, sense auras, and I possessed great physical strength and speed.

When I was about fifteen, I was burned after trying to impress a girl with my power. She told her father and naturally, it didn't go well. But when I didn't die, I was exiled.

For a while, I moved from place to place, never quite able to fit in anywhere—especially since my powers were growing. It was becoming harder and harder to hide my true self, so I decided to join the military, where I could be more useful than feared.

I spent most of my time at sea, and my shipmates seemed to appreciate me. But it was at a pub in Bristol that I transformed for the first time."

"Transformed?" Almir exclaims.

"Yeah, after getting into the middle of it with an Englishman and a Spaniard. The two were arguing over a trivial matter—something about a tab. Sabers were drawn, I tried to intervene, and got stabbed for my troubles. I don't remember the sensation being all that bad, but the sight of my own blood sent me into a blind rage. I woke up on a vessel with my father standing over me. It was then that he told me the truth," Dean says, remembering the argument as if it were yesterday.

"The truth—that you were a guardian?" Leon asks, and Dean shakes his head.

"No," he makes a face, "that I'm half uzadden. My father came from Tara, a planet in the Draco Dwarf galaxy; he fell in love with an Earth woman, and here I am," Dean states.

Jasra's eyes shift for a second. "Wait, if you're—he's an alien, then how—"

"Oh—we uzaddens have an extraordinary gift that enables us to become whomever we consume. If I drink your blood, for example, I could transform into your spitting image, complete with your current knowledge, experiences, and even your power, but the effects are temporary unless I take your life. That's why my father left: not wanting to kill the man who gave him his form, he was only able to change so many times. He saved the last for me when he came back," Dean explains.

"Does that mean you'll eventually be stuck in your alien form?" Jasra asks.

"No, since I'm a half-breed, I can change from human to uzadden as long as I have the energy. Many of my other forms, however, are limited, and I use them sparingly," he says.

"So, you're like… a vampire?" Leon asks.

"Yes," Dean sighs distastefully, "I am a dragon-vampire," he replies.

"Do you sparkle?" Almir asks.

"Go fuck yourself," Dean laughs.

Chapter 24

"A Stitch in Time"

Dusk arrives and with it, an army. Not a conventional battalion by any stretch of the imagination, but rather a small squad of five guardians staring down the slope of the hill leading to Segal Army Base.

"It looks normal," Jasra says with surprise in her voice as she gives a partial glance to her left, where Simon is standing.

"Perhaps they moved," Dean says to his right at Simon before gazing down the line past Leon and Almir, who stand just right of Jasra.

Not liking that idea, Simon scans the facility. It does appear completely normal: concrete buildings, reinforced perimeter fencing, and asphalt roads—even the lights seem to function. Yet, there is one thing he is not sensing: a true electric circuit. The energies he is picking up are hybridized bio-electrical, and the signal, despite how faint it is, is malnar.

"Come on out, Sei!" Simon shouts.

Dean leans casually toward Simon. "Any plans for fighting in the dark?" he questions, given the nearly set sun.

Simon cants his head with a cocky expression. "Of course." He then aims his right arm just over the base. Tilting his fist down as a gun-like device pops up from his mechanized gauntlet, he then fires four small metallic balls.

Each unit takes a position, hovering over the corners of the compound before opening their tiny, faceted doors to reveal high-intensity diodes, which cast light brighter than the day.

Seeing this fancy display, Jasra looks over to Simon with a displeased expression. "So, that's what you were working on," she comments.

"Mm-hmm, dispersal spheres. They have multiple purposes, which range from creating light to carrying nanite payloads, and a few other nifty tricks." He smirks, though Jasra is not amused.

"Oh," Simon adds, just as Seldin steps out from the main gate, "and no UVs. The light is specifically meant for our benefit." His eyes then fall to his friend, who takes a position front and center of the compound.

Seldin's heart is racing, seeing his friends lined up as if ready to take him on. It's hard for him to believe that anyone would follow Simon's lead so blindly to a cause he knows nothing about. His eyes shift between them as he does what he can to feel them out. It's moments like this that he wishes he was a better telepath, for he can only get the unguarded, surface-level thoughts.

Leon and Jasra are on his side, that much he knows, but Almir, Simon, and Dean are proving harder to read. Even so, he worries Almir's allegiance has shifted to Simon—of how much, he can't be sure.

"Lucy." He glances to the rose at his back. "Get ready. Simon! I've spoken to the queen. She's here to help us! We don't have to fight!" he shouts.

"Look around you! They've already made the first move!" Simon shouts back, making a gesture toward the infested military base.

"No, they were defending themselves! But with the malnar reinforcing the ground, the pulsari won't be able to land here—forcing an aerial battle, which may give the Earth a fighting chance! Once the malnar spread out, they'll lie dormant until the pulsari arrive!" he explains, and the group looks amongst themselves, but Simon is not convinced. The very idea seems ludicrous to him.

"Let them spread out? Clearly, you've spent way too much time with the enemy, Sei! They've poisoned your mind! If they engulf the Earth, we'll be defenseless!" Simon shouts back.

"Simon, the suka brought these to help us, they are not our enemy! Please listen to reason!" Seldin pleads with him.

Simon shakes his head, for what his friend is spouting makes no sense to him—not after the terrible things he'd shown them all. "I'm sorry Sei, but you give me no choice! If you won't help me defeat the malnar, step aside or I'll have to consider you a loss!" he shouts, and then Jasra looks to Simon with a frightful face.

Seldin looks down for a moment. "If this is the only way." He sighs, swallowing down the lump in his throat. Dean then reaches out toward him with a glance to Simon.

"Shall I remove him from the battlefield?" he asks with a sense of eagerness.

Simon shakes his head. "Let's see how strong his will is, first. Almir." He looks down the line and Almir nods as he brings a hand to his temple to aid his focus.

"Mm…" Seldin grunts, closing his eyes to the sudden swimmy sensation in his head. The moment he tries to resist, it grows to a piercing throb of pins and needles. "Ugh… get out!" He grits his teeth, staggering while fighting against the will of the Guardian of the Mind, but soon, Seldin finds himself down on all fours when a swell of peacefulness washes over him. He relaxes and bows his head.

Jasra and Leon turn fearful gazes to Almir, and then back to Seldin.

"That's it," Almir says softly.

Simon nods, satisfied. "We got him," he says when all of a sudden, Lucy digs her roots into Seldin's flesh, encapsulating his body. As the petal helmet closes around his head, the foreign presence in his mind weakens.

"Stop that thing!" Simon commands Almir, while pointing at Lucy.

"I'm trying." Almir concentrates, but he's never dealt with the mind of a plant before—extraterrestrial or otherwise. It's nothing like a human's: there's no brain, at least, not one he's familiar with, but there is a will, a strong one, and it's in the way.

Seldin abruptly shakes his head, feeling himself settle back into the driver's seat. "No!" He clenches his mind. "Get… out of my… head," he grunts, casting his gaze up the hill to Almir.

"Ahh!" Almir winces, staggering back. "He… they… they pushed me out!" he exclaims with astonishment.

Simon snaps his eyes down the line at Almir with a stunned look on his face and then anger. He sighs, cracks his neck, and then looks back at Seldin standing there at the bottom of the valley in his foliate suit. A cocky smirk stretches across Simon's lips. "So, he wants to play?" he says, his voice fiery. "Dean." Simon says to the Guardian of Dimension.

Dean nods. "Gladly," he says, reaching a hand out toward Seldin.

Right then, the fence around the base comes to life when a hundred spore drones step out as if they were there all along and form up behind Seldin just as he steps back, blending into the ranks.

"Shit! Jasra!" Simon glances to her. "Tell me his moves!" he insists, but Jasra doesn't answer him. Instead, she turns her nose up in protest while closing her fists behind her back.

"Jasra?" Simon seems confused.

"I will not help you hurt our friend," she says without a look to him.

Simon then looks past her to the Guardian of Earth. "Lee, earthquake—now!" he orders, but

Leon follows Jasra's lead, refusing Simon's command.

"Follow my orders or I will have you removed from the battlefield!" Simon scowls in a threatening tone. Getting no response, an idea comes to him as he looks down the line. "Almir," he says simply.

Almir nods. "You got it."

Suddenly, Leon and Jasra drop to their knees while grabbing their heads. The process doesn't take long, and before the boni horde reaches the top of the hill, the earth beneath the ensuing wave begins to buckle. Many of them fall into the cracks while others simply climb over their kin in relentless effort.

Dean does what he's good at, forming pockets and portals of bent space to reposition the troops as they get near while Simon fires several dispersal spheres into the crowd. The devices detonate on impact, spewing clouds of nanites that work quickly to find a way into the leafy skin of the creatures. The drones that are hit, slowly grow gray and turn around to attack the opposing forces.

"Dean, this would be a wonderful time for you to remove some of these things from the battlefield," Simon says.

"Behind you!" Jasra shouts—now under Almir's control—as one of the creatures intercepts Dean's position.

Dean works hard to combat this lone malnar, whose fighting techniques appear so familiar. Dean parries, strafes left, and then ducks right before going for the money shot, but this drone has no spore, he discovers when his fist strikes something solid beneath the leaves.

Seldin clasps Dean's arm and twists hard to launch him off balance.

Simon turns about as more and more boni push through his protective wall of gray spawn. He casts another dispersal sphere, quickly taking control of several more drones, but it's not enough, he soon realizes then turns to Almir.

"Almir, can you control those things?" Simon shouts, but Almir isn't sure.

Refocusing his will, Almir concentrates on a single drone. Unlike Lucy, it doesn't have a mind of its own; it's an empty vessel receiving a signal from somewhere else. That emptiness, that lack of resistance, allows him to trace the path of this other mind as it imposes its will upon the creature.

The signal enters the spore and runs down through the boni's extremities. It's a literal puppet, Almir realizes as he slips his mind in, causing the creature to give a simple gesture of a thumbs up.

'Heh, it worked.' Almir thinks to himself before expanding his will to the rest of it. The boni stops moving immediately and turns around, following his command. "I got one—whoa!" he shouts right as another boni takes a swing at him. He dodges, and then quickly takes that one as well.

"Any time, Almir!" Simon yells.

One by one, Almir grabs another, and then another, expanding his mind to a handful of drones, then to more, and more. Soon, the edge of his mental limit is reached with those within his grasp turn to attack the main gate, while facing opposition from those outside his control.

"Argh!" Almir grunts, trying his damndest to get more than thirty, but it's a strain, and he can feel the presence of this other will starting to fight against him, while the two strongest minds under his control begin to slip away.

"I'm losing my grip!" Almir shouts as several boni drop from his grasp. Fighting to keep them, he struggles, losing a few more, along with Leon and Jasra, who stagger and stumble for a second or two before regaining themselves.

"Shit, take them!" Simon commands.

Immediately, Almir lets go of the horde to follow Simon's order—imposing his will on Jasra, once again, before she can fully recover. He then turns to seize Leon, who is just now getting back to his feet.

"Damn it, Almir, get them!" Simon gestures to the malnar, but his wishes are easier said than done, for his friends are strong willed and fighting against Almir's control.

For every drone Almir retakes, he can feel his grasp loosening with the beljusa's lingering presence creeping back in to regain her foothold. This tug of war is futile, he realizes, and Almir decides to rethink his strategy.

Following her signal, Almir feels out a path back to her. It's hidden well, buried beneath the dense wall of malnar lining the base—their collective energies forming a one-way telepathic shield.

"I can't hold them all; it's either a few strong minds or a bunch of weak ones. However, if you can clear out the bio-static interference, I may be able to get the queen!" Almir shouts back.

Seldin then lunges from a jumping kick off Dean's chest to clock Simon across his face.

"Simy!" Dean shouts to alert him as he opens a portal just before Seldin lands the strike, dropping him right behind Dean, who turns in anticipation to blast the Guardian of Life with a wave of energy.

Ducking out of it, Seldin turns, throwing Dean through his own rift before casting a ball of aether toward Simon, catches him in the shoulder, knocking him back.

Simon's suit, however, does what it was designed for and absorbs the bulk of the impact, converting it to useful energy, giving him a power boost on contact.

Seldin's barrage doesn't stop there. Taking advantage of Simon's momentary loss of balance, he continues to drill him with one attack after another—unwittingly feeding him with each strike. Simon then counters with a setup that gives his friend the ground.

Feeling the need to turn it up a notch, Dean draws in the aether; loose debris pulls his way as his body sucks in the energy. His muscles pump, his bones harden, and his red hair and freckled tone grows more reptilian as he shifts into his uzadden form—a semi-translucent dragon-like man with purple and green patches of iridescent scales.

Almir's eyes widen. "You do sparkle!"

Bam! Dean swings his massive forearm, launching a boni right into Almir before turning to plunge his taloned hand through the chest of another, which withers.

Almir lands on his back in the grass, while wrestling with the creature's thorny claws and snapping jaws. He focuses, releasing his control of a boni further up the ranks to take over this one.

"That wasn't cool, man!" he shouts at Dean, who snorts with dragon-like chuckles.

"Huuarrgh!" Seldin dashes, pouncing Simon as the two of them roll along the sloped ground. Avoiding his previous mistake, Seldin readies a fist aimed for Simon's face when Dean's giant hands grab Seldin's shoulders and fling him like a ragdoll, tumbling skyward.

Reorienting himself, Seldin turns in the air then flies back toward Simon and Dean while zigzagging his position to throw off their game.

"Left, right, he's gonna kick!" Jasra instructs them on where he's going to be, and what he's going to do, but even with that, he's quick and her verbal instructions are more distracting than helpful.

"Just give us a distortion field!" Simon screams at the top of his angered lungs, and suddenly, Seldin's position slows to a tenth of his speed. The temporal dome does more than halt him; it also stalls the invasive plant things that creep to crawl the moment they cross the threshold.

Simon pants heavily with a look to Dean. "Get his ass off my field!" he scoffs, turning away as Seldin disappears in a flash of purple light.

…

Slamming to the asphalt, there's an abrupt sound of screeching tires accompanied by the blaring noise of a horn, and before Seldin can stand, he's down again—clobbered from behind. It takes him a few seconds to realize where he is with the mid-morning sun shining through the smog.

Onlookers gather, chattering in a foreign tongue while gawking at his alien-clad figure lying in the street. Although he can't understand their slurs directly, the meaning of their words comes through.

"What is that?" many of them question as he slowly gets up and looks about. Pictographic symbols label shop windows and street signs. His eyes then fall to the people—he's in Japan.

"Daaaaammmmmnn!" he exclaims in the middle of stalled traffic before turning to the crumpled car that hit him.

The young driver looks bad, holding his bleeding forehead—and he screams, terrified by the living incarnation of Swamp Thing approaching.

"Don't worry, I'm going to help you," Seldin says, and despite his English, the frightened Japanese man appears to understand. Seldin puts one hand on the man's head and the other on the car, working to restore them in tandem, and for the first time, he finds himself appreciating his father's mechanical knowledge.

Sirens then fill the air as police gather around and take aim on him. As the Japanese man's head wound closes and his car returns to normal, Seldin looks around again.

"Everything's alright," he says, allowing Lucy to reveal his very human face. "I'm… uh… an American doing a movie—just signing an autograph."

The policemen lower their weapons and then look amongst themselves in confusion.

Turning back to the driver, Seldin asks, "What's your name?"

The Japanese man looks up at him. "David," he answers, and Seldin smiles with a soft chuckle.

"Not quite what I was expecting. Take care of yourself, David," he says before leaping into the sky.

…

Even with Seldin out of the way, the battle is a stalemate. Simon's infected malnar are equally matched against their counterparts. Even Dean appears to struggle with the incurring forces despite Jasra's barrier of slowed time, Almir's force of will, and Leon's rather effective ice technique—the only other thing that seems to kill them.

"Leon, make it snow, freeze the base, do something!" Simon orders.

"Alright!" Leon, still under Almir's control, changes to the element of water to create an icy rain that turns to hail, then to snow, but the effect isn't the same as freezing them directly—for they just keep on coming.

Simon then looks to the Guardian of Dimension. "Dean, get these fucking things off my battlefield!" he commands.

But Dean can't just drop them into a random city. Unwilling to think for his new commander, he looks over. "And just where—"

"Hurl them into space, for all I care!" Simon exclaims when—poof, poof, poof—nearly half the field clears. "Good, now we can—"

Ffffshhhewww! A yellow beam of light punches through the night's sky, hitting the temporal distortion field. The energy slows, gradually coalescing into a massive glowing orb. More beams follow, one after another, until the field is overloaded and kaboom! It collapses in a spectacular explosion.

Jasra screams as the surge of energy overwhelms her. She drops to the ground in a daze.

Simon snaps his gaze to her. "Jasra!" He rushes over when another beam cuts across his path—he dodge the first one and then gets hit by the second as another beam strikes Dean, knocking him face down in the snowy dirt.

"Ugh!" Dean grunts, spitting icy mud.

"What is that?" Almir looks up in a panic, momentarily losing control of his puppets. Leon shakes the fog from his mind before turning to deck his apprentice.

"Gah!" Almir falls back on his pride just as another beam rips from the sky and hits Leon.

"It's the sun!" Simon exclaims, dodging the pulses of light. "Up there they have the sun!" He realizes. "Dean!" he yells at the top of his lungs— whoosh! "Shit!" He dodges again. "Rip them out of the sky!"

Hearing the order, Dean hoists his hands upward to open a series of drone-sized portals. The boni, however, take advantage of these new windows, and with a direct line of sight to the Guardian of Dimension, they open fire—knocking him down again and again.

"To hell with this!" Simon grunts, casting more nanites into the horde. This time, he doesn't focus on controlling the drones; instead, he works to tear them apart, stripping them to the vine. Still, they keep on coming.

The boni—or spore drones—are just that: drones. Like worker ants, they care only to serve the queen without regard for themselves, injured or not.

"You gotta hit the spore!" Dean yells as he gets swarmed by boni on his left and struck by beams on his right. For each drone he kills, another two latch on.

"Who needs the spore when there's nothing left?" Simon rebuts, instructing his constructs to finish the job. Three boni in front of him fall to dust as he strips them of everything, leaving a nanite cloud in their place.

"Free material," Simon laughs, then turns, hearing Dean grunt as he flings the creatures from his scaly hide.

"Huuraarrr!" Dean roars.

"Nice moves, cool armor!" Simon compliments with a supportive smack to his shoulder, just now noticing how well it retains its shape to Dean's much larger form.

"Thanks." Dean clobbers another drone. "It's called fleryl. My people gave it to the Greeks several millennia ago."

Regaining his control of Jasra, Almir then uses her to help recapture Leon, freezing him in place as he works on his mind.

"Sei's coming back!" Jasra warns just as Seldin hits the dirt and fires off a steady beam of aether to Simon's head.

In that same moment, Simon shoots a dispersal sphere at Seldin. The stream of aether catches Simon's face, putting him down right as the device explodes, releasing nanites all around Seldin, who swats at the cloud as if fending off a swarm of biting gnats.

Dean phases out of this dimensional plane to escape the energy blasts still drilling him from space. He then reappears beside Seldin and thrusts a shin kick to his gut. It folds him down, setting him up for an elbow to the spine. As soon as Seldin hits the snow, Simon is on him.

Much like their previous battle, Seldin pushes out the nanites with relative ease, but Lucy is having a harder time. Normally, their symbiosis would be enough to protect her; however, she is vulnerable without the benefit of the sun and is unwilling to leech Seldin's energy during battle.

Seldin can feel their bond slipping. He fights harder, drawing more aether from his surroundings, intentionally bringing his core past threefold.

"Aaauuugh!" he grunts then—boom! He releases the energy all at once in a powerful shockwave that destroys the nanite cloud and floors everyone near him, including the encroaching boni, which gain nothing from the concussive force, unlike Simon, who hits the ground with a charge.

Seldin quickly gets up with a bounding leap and aims himself right for his best friend.

Seeing Seldin coming at him, Simon prepares a defense from his grounded position when all of a sudden, a pillar of earth extrudes diagonally into Seldin's path, knocking him sideways. He stumbles, staggering a bit before being hit again from the other side. Leon then rushes in, taking a solid rocky form as he attacks his former mentor.

"He's going to jump kick!" Jasra warns and Leon dodges gracefully as Seldin leaps, twisting into a thwarted technique.

"Jasra, Leon, stop! We need to work together!" he pleads, but it's no use; they're not themselves. Their emotionless faces and awkward movements tell him something's wrong.

Getting to their feet, Simon and Dean look over the battlefield as showers of light continue to rain from above, but they are no longer targeting them. Instead, they're aiming straight for the other boni on the ground. As the light hits, it supercharges them.

Using the accumulated photonic energy, the drones begin to melt away the snow while focus firing on the nanite infected malnar. The intense solar beams do nothing to the plants themselves, but the radiant heat severely damages the micro machines that are controlling them. Soon the gray drones fall only to rise up green and ready to return to battle. This change in events leaves Simon frozen in place, for the number of malnar on the ground has remained consistent despite all the ones killed, thrown into space, or taken over. The queen just keeps making more—and now they have a way to defeat his bots.

"Tell them to hit me!" Seldin projects a message to the queen, who promptly complies as nearly a hundred malnar concentrate their energies on a single, solitary target. The nanites in Lucy die off, restoring the bond between her and her companion as she feeds him the upsurge in energy.

With Seldin's strength heightened, he plays defensively, making it difficult for Jasra to choreograph Leon's moves.

"What's with you guys?" Seldin asks. Then it hits him—the only one not fighting is Almir. Seeing him standing off at a safe distance, Seldin grabs Leon then hurls him toward Almir just as Simon and Dean rejoin the fight.

Using telekinesis, Simon does his damndest to hold Seldin in place, but his friend's strength is beyond fathomable—over five hundred thousand joules with the beljusa joined with him. To Seldin, Simon's attempt isn't even noticeable.

"Jasra!" Simon calls for assistance then looks to Dean. "Remove him!" he orders as they all grab Seldin, telekinetically.

Projecting a distortion field, Jasra coordinates with Dean to twist time and space. Ahead of Seldin, closest to Jasra, time is slowed, while behind him and farther from her, time is accelerated. The dissident forces work on him unevenly while Dean places a rift just in front of him, easing it closer as Simon telekinetically holds on to Lucy's leafy exterior.

"Aaaaaaghhhh!" Seldin screams, fighting against the spaghettification as he and Lucy are pulled apart the very moment Leon collides with Almir, knocking him out cold.

"Where the hell am I now?" Seldin exclaims, feeling around in total darkness. Everything he touches is solid with a polished, yet coarse, sandy texture. Without any visible light, Seldin attunes to his other senses to make out his surroundings. It's stone, he realizes; there are other things here as well: some of wood, others of clay. Not having the luxury of time to explore, he searches for an opening then follows it through one maze-like junction to another until he sees a sliver of light.

With light comes heat—dry overwhelming heat mixed in a deceiving breeze of dusty wind as he reaches the surface. Panning his view across endless golden dunes, he screams out furiously.

"Ah, you've gotta be shitting me—fucking Egypt? Goooddddd-daaaamnnn-iiittt!" He takes to the air—boom!

"Sei!" He hears Jasra's voice.

"Where are you?" Seldin looks around.

"I'm home; Leon is here too. After you knocked out Almir, Simon had Dean send us back. Where are you?" she asks.

"You're not gonna believe this but I'm way the hell out in BFE—literally," he replies.

"Listen, you have to get back now. Simon has control of Lucy, and she's huge—like a tree; he's going to use her to crack open the base," she tells him.

"It won't work, I mean unless he's using her as a battering ram; malnar are immune to their own abilities. That's why the fight has been a stalemate," he says.

"Hold up, those things just circled Lucy, they're burning out Simon's controls," she says.

"Good, they're coming to her aid," he says.

"Oh no, she's turning around—she's gonna fire on Simon!"

Hearing that, Seldin kicks it up a notch, but even at this rate it'll take him ten minutes to get there. "Ugh!" He grunts, feeling an electrifying tingle coursing through as his core reaches its max. The energy feeds back, cascading all around him—kaboom! Seldin slams into a mountain.

Rocks and other debris crumble around as he pushes himself up out of the rubble.

"What the hell?" He looks about before getting back on course.

"Lucy!" he calls out to her telepathically *"Don't!"* he pleads, but she sends back images of Simon fighting her. *"Simy! Stop!"* Seldin projects to him, while accelerating faster and faster.

Soon, that strange sensation reemerges; energy arcs and pops as he gains more speed.

There's an explosion, a sudden flash of light, and he finds himself spitting dirt in the middle of the Great Plains.

Getting up again, he dusts himself off then looks around. "How the hell did I get here?" he gasps. Feeling out his location, he shakes his head, for he overshot his destination by an entire continent. "God damn it!" his voice echoes over the land.

…

Moving quickly, Dean casts a rift between Simon and Lucy just as she fires. The beam of energy passes through the whirling gate of bent space and she shoots herself instead; there's no damage, but the force rocks her. Right then, Dean leaps across her path to pull Simon out of the way as more drones reach the hilltop.

One after another, Dean smashes them into piles of leaves, but the ones he doesn't kill don't stay down for long, and more boni gather around. Dean turns to engage, but Simon grabs his arm with a petrified look.

Satisfied by the fear on Simon's face, Dean pulls away with a subtle smirk, and then makes a terrible blunder.

"Dragon's breath!" Dean chants, pitching forward with a belch of fiery plasma. The malnar he burns simply stare back, charged by his fire, before returning his token gesture with beams of their own.

"Arrgghh!" Dean drops to his knees as they encircle him and latch on with their vine-like roots. He tries to phase out, but it's too late: they've already drawn too much of his energy while pummeling him with blasts of aether from all sides.

By the time Simon can intervene, Dean is down for the count. Shifting back to his much weaker human form, he lies unconscious and charred to the bone.

From above the valley floor, Seldin soars at blinding speed. The ground beneath him appears swarmed by ants—leafy-green, energy-spitting ants. He lands just as Simon's new drones turn to stall the field again.

"Lucy!" Seldin calls to her enormity, but Simon doesn't take kindly to his friend's arrival and tackles him immediately. They struggle against one another, exchanging fist and foot while Simon's armor absorbs the force so that he can move more quickly. In turn, Seldin moves even faster until that tingling sensation returns just as he dodges Simon's punch—bam!

Seldin's sudden change in position is jarring at first, for he's moved a few meters away. "Did I just teleport?" he questions the feat.

Simon is stunned, knocked flat by the force of whatever just happened. Performing a kip-up, he then looks around rather frantically.

"Where the hell—so you think you're fast?" Simon taunts while dashing toward him. The very idea of being toyed with fuels his anger.

Seldin readies himself then darts toward Simon. The two of them collide and exchange strikes once again.

"Simy, you have to end this!" he shouts.

Simon fights back. "I'm not stopping until they're gone!" he argues, grabbing his buddy by the throat.

Utilizing his strength, Seldin bridges Simon's right arm and twists him to his knees. "I'm not playing with you!" he shouts.

Simon glares up at him. "Neither am I," he retorts while releasing three dispersal spheres. Each trails with strings of nanites dangling like the tendrils of a jellyfish. These delicate strands tease at the aether in the air as the spheres move in synchronicity, creating a calculated matrix of entangled particles between the span of a triangular formation.

"I studied Dean's technique; he isn't the only one who can fold space. You should let go, Sei, before I send you to the other side of the galaxy," Simon threatens as the spheres draw the field of energy closer and closer to him.

"You're bluffing," Seldin says while tightening his grip.

"You're right; I'll probably just drop your ass on Titan. I'm sure it won't kill you, but it'll take you a hundred years to... get... back!" Simon grunts, intentionally rolling against Seldin's grasp, breaking his own arm.

Seldin pounces to regain control, tearing the upper half of the neoprene material from his friend's back.

"Gahhhh!" Simon cries out as the meridian probes are ripped out of his spine, spilling both blood and nanites. The moment the two guardians separate, Lucy prepares to fire.

"Stop!" Seldin orders while placing himself between her and Simon.

Right then, the center of Segal Army Base opens, and the mother of all malnar sprouts up from the depths.

"Shit, the queen—get up!" Seldin tries to help him up.

"Get your hands off me!" Simon shouts, pushing back with his left hand, while his right arm dangles, twisted within the torn half of his bio-suit.

"Simy, the game is over! The beljusa is done! She doesn't think this can be resolved, and now she's coming to put an end to it! If you leave now, she'll stop!" Seldin says.

Simon sighs stubbornly, then takes Seldin's hand as he gets up.

"I'm not going anywhere," Simon says, closing his grip on Seldin's wrist, "but you are." He turns, thrusting him into the rift.

"Whoooooaaaa!" Seldin shouts before losing his breath to the impact of a desolate, icy surface. His hands sink into the thin layer of snow and grit as he stands up in the relatively weak gravity. The air is cold and densely packed with nitrogen, methane, and hydrogen, which give rise to the thick opaque blankets of orange smog blocking the light of the sun. He can barely see more than a few feet in any direction, let alone the stars, through the heavy atmosphere.

At this point, Seldin's heart is pounding, for he dreads the truth in Simon's words regarding where he's been placed. Pushing aether beneath himself, he rises slowly through the foggy banks with more light becoming visible the closer he gets to space. But where he'd hoped to see a shining star, he instead finds the massive rings of Saturn and the enormous body that governs them.

"I guess this is Titan," he says with a frog in his nervous throat as he swallows down with a hard gulp, for the sun is only a spec from here and Earth is infinitely smaller.

Jupiter, on the other hand, he can see quite clearly; after all, it's only about a hundred million miles away as opposed to the sun at almost eight hundred and ninety million miles away.

Sadly, that puts Earth at nearly a billion miles from him. Even at his fastest, it would take approximately five years—five years, two months, and fourteen days to be exact, to reach Earth if he were to go all out. And that is assuming he could match the trajectory while avoiding the pull of the sun.

"God damn you, Simon," he mutters, for by then, this war would most certainly be over, and worse, the pulsari would be there to start up a new one.

"Dean!" Seldin calls out, but silence—either because he's still unconscious or it's true what they say about space.

Back on Earth, however, Simon isn't faring very well. With his right arm still broken and his suit still torn, he is having to rely on more basic skills—such as flight—but the larger beljusa has no intentions in letting him get away. The moment he lifts off, vine-like tendrils latch on and slam him down.

"Sei!" Jasra calls out.

Lucy runs to intercept the queen, and there's a colossal clash as the two square off—unable to hurt the other.

"Jasra?" Seldin hears her plea as his mind fills with her vision.

"It's the queen! She's gonna kill Simon!" Jasra shouts.

Boni sink their roots into Simon's flesh, draining him of his precious energy while heating themselves to burn off his nanites.

"You gotta stop time!" Seldin orders.

"I can't, I'm out of range!" Jasra replies, flying as fast as she can with Leon.

Ordering her brood to hold Lucy down, the queen marches toward Simon.

"I'm sorry." Seldin hears the faint weak voice of his best friend. Fear fills them both as they share in the moment, watching the beljusa's petals

fan open with visible specks of energy charging into her enormous parabolic bulb.

Seldin's mind runs through his options. *'Maybe I can do it again.'* He powers up, pushing his core to the edge of that fatal three-fold limit. "Think fast thoughts," he tells himself. There's a rush of scattered light spidering in all directions when out of nowhere, he is standing in the middle of the field, staring up the hill from the bottom of the valley.

Bewildered, Seldin looks around rather confused, as if he has awoken from a bad dream.

"Look around you! They've already made the first move!" Simon shouts back, making a gesture toward the infested military base.

Jasra then looks to Simon, who seems to carry on without a miss, and then to Seldin. There is a feeling of rapidness in her chest, a sense of anxiety governing the tempo of her heart as she stares down at a seemingly disoriented friend.

"Come on, remember," she whispers in hopes that he will—that his puzzled expression is the product of her tampering.

He looks around for a moment, taking pause before setting his eyes on the line of frenemies atop the hill.

"No, they were defending themselves! But with the malnar reinforcing the ground, the pulsari won't be able to land here—"

Unfortunately, like everybody else, Seldin's apparent bout of déjá vu gets shrugged off as he continues to follow the path already inscribed. Dismayed by that, Jasra sighs, suddenly feeling her consciousness slipping out of sync.

"Uh…" She takes a hindered breath as she focuses every ounce of will, drawing upon the aether and her gift so that she might not act as a puppet of fate. The boys are already sniveling, settling into their roles unhindered. If this plays out, she knows how it is going to end.

The ghosted forms around her start to solidify as her essence aligns with the vessel she once wore—though still tethered to a present whose future is still in the making.

Right then, the fence comes to life when a hundred spore drones step out as if they had been there all along and form up behind Seldin just as he steps back, blending into the ranks.

"Shit! Jasra." Simon glances to her. "Tell me his moves," he insists.

Stepping out of line, Jasra gets in front of Simon and stares directly into his eyes. "S-stop t-this," she says with a noticeably weak voice.

'What does she want now?' Simon thinks, for she's obviously upset about something. "If this is about earlier—"

"Ugh!" She gasps, almost losing her balance. "If t-this w-warr haappenns, we aall lose… you—argh!" She fights to keep ahold of herself, but fate is persistent. "Truusst… Sseii…" Her voice trails with exhaustion. She then collapses as Simon catches her. "You need to trust Sei!" she exclaims.

Looking into those wonderful green eyes of hers, Simon sighs. "Sei made his choice when he chose them over us."

What he says leaves a deep well in her chest and she stares at him with desperate eyes just as he scoots her aside, ready to take on the army of malnar rushing toward them like a green tsunami.

"Now tell me how to win," he orders while stepping forward in anticipation.

"Yyouu d-don't wiinn!" she shouts at him, trying to get the fact through his thick skull.

Simon glares back at her from over his shoulder; his eyes then shift to Dean. "Get her off my battlefield!" he orders.

"No, no, you stubborn aa—" A haze of purple light zaps her away.

Dean then steps up, prepared to take the initiative. Without the Guardian of Time to stifle the incursion, he sets up pockets of randomized space that keep the boni at bay while Simon gives Leon the order to freeze them.

Strafing around the drones, Seldin uses their energy to mask his signature while Lucy takes care of his appearance. Watching closely as the drones ahead vanish, he feels out the variances in the aether surrounding the group. Seeing an opening, he darts for it to take on Simon.

"Sei!" Jasra calls to him.

"What?" He tunes in, though startled by her randomness.

"Youu… have t-to… listen to me," she says just as he collides with Simon.

"Ugh!" Simon grunts, hitting his back on the ground. A cushion of nanites brings him to his feet, and he quickly engages.

"Dean, push forward, use the portals to move them back!" Simon says while exchanging strikes with Seldin.

"Sei, you have to listen to me!" Jasra persists. "T-this isn't the p-present, it's the past!"

But her facts distract him, causing him to lose focus and leave his guard open enough for Simon to kick through to his face. Stumbling back, he spins about, keeping his momentum to prepare a counterattack when a dispersal sphere hits his chest.

Seeing his mentor fall, Leon moves in; opening the ground directly beneath Simon, he sinks him to his hips then closes the earth around him while Seldin rolls and swats at the buzzing bots.

"Almir!" Simon shouts for help, and like a good dog, Leon's would-be apprentice acts against him.

"No!" Seldin exclaims, flicking his left hand toward Almir, blasting him back with a telekinetic push before altering his own kinetic aura to impart an intense electrical shock to the nanites.

Leon glances behind as he sees Almir drop, and then he turns to intercept him.

"Going to take my mind, huh?" Leon scoffs angrily, melting the ground to a muddy slush before freezing Almir within it.

While those two are working against each other, Simon digs himself free with the aid of his machines, then intentionally drops his guard to counter Seldin, who is speeding his way.

Seldin strikes center mass with a blow to Simon's chest, and then sweeps his calf with a low kick. Simon takes each hit willingly, smiling the entire time. Each blow imparts a force, which transfers vital energies that are absorbed by the awesomeness of his technology, and like his counterpart, he too can manipulate and cultivate the aether around him; it's high time he used some.

The specialized machines fill his blood and storm his cells. Simon's gray skin tone streaks with darkening veins as his entire body becomes electrified. The energy arcs like lightning as it is cast from his hands to strike his enemy down, yet the beljusa Seldin wears drinks in the surge.

"Jasra, tell me what to do!" Seldin shouts.

"I can't!" she exclaims, for there are too many ripples. The changes made are already reshaping the present as she knows it, making her visions unclear and her presence in the past even more unsteady.

Leon turns from Almir, ready to blast Simon with a chilling experience. Thrusting his hands forward, he focuses to create a stream of ice. It doesn't work—it won't go. He stares at his hands as they turn blue and that frosty coating creeps up his arms and then to the rest of his body. His legs shatter, and he falls back. "Gaaawwhh!" he cries out.

"Leon!" Seldin's heart races as he tries to push past Simon to give aid when—poof! In an instant, he's in central Japan.

"Dean!" Seldin shouts in anger.

His spontaneous appearance causes a ten-car pile-up. He should stay to help them but his friend… he shakes his head, making the decision. Seldin focuses hard, supercharging his body.

"I need to get there. I need to be there now!" he tells himself. The sense of urgency overtakes him when all of a sudden there's a deafening explosion as his molecules are flung apart.

Reassembling, he collides into a building a mile away. Seldin gets up, looks around, dusts himself off and tries again. The onlookers gawk at the vegetable man as sparks dance all over his body and he remarkably disappears in a flash of blinding light.

"Aaahhh!" Boom! He crashes into a mountainous white crater, lifting a plume of fluffy, powdery dirt into the sky. As the dust quickly settles without even a trace of billowing, Seldin screams furiously, realizing where he's at. He turns about looking at the blue marble that is Earth, filling the sky.

Back on the battlefield, Simon steps over Leon, whose powers continue to fluctuate out of control. He then projects some nanites to cut Almir from the frozen ground before stepping up to Dean.

"To hell with this, I want you to create a passage into the heart of that base; we'll get the queen," Simon orders as Almir joins his side.

"You ready?" Simon looks to the Guardian of the Mind, who tries to scan for her the moment she comes into view. The queen makes a heavy bellowing rumble in protest as she fights against Almir's domineering mind.

In a brilliant flash of light, Seldin appears, slamming into the ground just as the rose queen steps out from the portal.

"Jasra!" Seldin exclaims.

"Look around you! They've already made the first move!" Simon shouts back making a gesture toward the infested military base.

Trial after trial, Jasra arrives at this moment hoping to fix it, but the battle goes forward anyway. The ripples she makes with each minor change cause the stream of time to snap back like a river washing away her efforts.

She's tried warning Simon, fighting with Seldin, fighting against him, and even taking the battle completely into her own hands. Yet all of the results have been the same. Each time she goes back, it gets harder with the pressure forcing her forward, growing stronger and stronger. Every transition requires more and more energy for her to make the simplest of actions until even breathing feels impossible.

Dropping to her knees, she nearly faints. Her head is ringing inside, and she almost loses her lunch from the nausea. This causes everyone to turn her way, even Simon this time, who is in the middle of making his epic speech.

"Y-you guys—evveryyonne, lisstten t-to me!" she cries as the temporal stress works to force her back into her own timeline. "T-this is…" She gasps. "Th-e s-sixth time we've—been here. Plea-ase don't… fight the mal-al-nar. You haavve to t-t-rust Seeii!" her voice skews as she bellows.

"Wait here," Seldin tells his army as he eases up the hill to see what's going on.

Simon just stares down at her for a moment, and then glances over to the approaching enemy. "Hold it!" He steps forward, but Dean grabs at the back of Simon's collar and pulls him rearward.

"Stop," Dean orders, reasserting his command before checking on Jasra. Leon and Almir gather around as well.

"What are you doing?" Simon questions.

"Game over, Simon. If the Guardian of Time says it's bad, it's bad. This ends here," Dean says as Seldin kneels to take Jasra. But there's nothing he can do, she's simply been in the past far too long. The more time she spends here, the farther she is from the present.

Simon, however, is not convinced. "Get away from her!" He pushes Seldin, who looks up at him with a dreadful face along with the stares of the others.

"I see what this is." Simon steps back, pointing at them. "Fine, if you're not with me, then you're against me!" he snarls, ready to take them all. But Jasra loses cohesion and faints from exhaustion. As the timeline snaps her forward, the others live out the effects of the change.

Simon, now angered by this mutiny, fires a dispersal sphere into the line. The blast showers them in a cloud of nanites that envelopes them all. Dean, Leon, and Almir choke and gasp as their bodies are raided with these technological parasites.

Chuckling manically, Simon's laughter builds as his visor's indicator shows a display of each person under his command, but then from the ominous wisps of nanite-filled smoke, Seldin leaps out, grabbing him by the throat as they roll down the hill.

The boni swarm in as Seldin mounts him and smashes Simon's face over and over—the one spot that doesn't give him energy. As the plants grab hold of the Guardian of Technology, the Guardian of Earth steps in to freeze them off like a bad case of warts.

Seldin, of course, guards against the shower of ice with a shield of energy, but that distraction gives Simon the opportunity to kick him off.

"Dean!" Simon orders, and just like that, Seldin is hurled to the other side of the planet.

"Goooooodddaaaaammmnnn it!" Seldin roars as he is again set in the middle of Japan. Kinetically he stops the cars coming for him as if having a moment of déjá vu.

The battlefield, on the other hand, is falling apart. Without the sun, the plants stand little chance against Leon's ice and Dean's dimensional rifts. The horde of malnar outside the base is falling fast.

"Almir," Simon says with a cocky voice while pointing to the wall of the base. "Get ready, we're gonna crack this thing open." He snaps his fingers to cue Dean, who quickly produces a vortex leading to the heart of the facility.

Almir goes for it right away, fighting with the monster's impeccable mental fortitude.

Shrilling in agony, the beljusa falls then rises at the implicit instructions of her new master, who waves with a rather cocky gesture for her to come to him.

Kaboom—explodes a pulse of brilliance as Seldin appears between the queen and the group.

"Dean!" Simon snaps his fingers again, "Kindly remove him fro—"

Flash! Seldin's form appears in two places at once as he simultaneously disintegrates and reintegrates in another location—Simon's location, to be specific.

The sheer release of energy from his act of teleportation knocks Simon back—boom, boom!

Seldin teleports again, adding a punching fist to his posture as he rematerializes to knock Simon's teeth in. He misses, appearing just behind him, then staggers a bit, still not fully acclimated to this new ability.

Phasing out of this plane of existence, Dean materializes behind Seldin to grab him just as he teleports away. Although the grab is successful, it does nothing to stop the transition from happening. The concussive force as Seldin vanishes, renders Dean on his ass.

Seldin's attempt to spawn behind Almir lands him inside the old research base instead. "Gah!" he grunts, frustrated at his obvious lack of aim. Calming himself, Seldin focuses, envisioning the grassy area just outside the main entrance of the facility. The energy builds up and then in a pulse of light, he teleports to the surface then takes flight, aiming dead for the battlefield.

Phhhrreww! Seldin fires an energy beam to Almir's back and one to Leon before teleporting between the two of them—using the shockwave to his advantage. By this point, Simon is back on his feet, rallying the spore drones to go after Seldin.

With Leon out cold, Seldin takes a breath as he quickly darts over to Almir, who stares up at him with weakness in his eyes.

"Goodnight, my friend," Seldin wishes before blasting him in the face.

At the moment of Almir's fall into unconsciousness, the rose queen snaps back into action, regaining control of her brood, which she then uses to corral her foes. The spore drones latch onto Simon and Dean, holding them in place as she sinks her roots down into the soil beneath her while reaching out for the two of them.

As both guardians succumb to the queen's debilitating grasp, they collapse from the loss of energy.

Seldin takes pause, relieved that it's over. "Thank you for helping me," he tells the beljusa as he makes his way up the hill to tend to Jasra. But the queen isn't finished. She moves over to Simon—the cause of it all—and aims her bulbous bell of petals at him.

Even in this debilitated posture, Simon can feel her approaching as the strength of her aura becomes more prominent. He can see the faint shadow of her giant body creeping over him as he lies helplessly on his side, facing away from her.

Simon feels himself slipping, barely able to lift a finger or turn his eyes to see her lingering just within his reachable corners. In this moment, he is afraid; a sense of panic and urgency works its way in as his lungs freeze with the cessation of his diaphragm. His heart would throb at a million miles a second if it could, yet even its rhythm eases to a halt as the life energy that sustains his body is culled out.

For all intents and purposes, Simon should be unconscious, although somehow, he isn't. His mind fills with dread, awaiting that moment when he will be no more, yet those tiny little creations of his work tirelessly to keep his mind active and his cells alive.

In a whimpering tired projection from within, a petrified Simon calls out to his best buddy. *"Sei!"*

Immediately, Seldin turns around, feeling Simon's core drop dangerously low.

"No, stop!" he yells at the queen but the beljusa ignores his order, even if it is a plea. She can't trust this menace to be anyone's salvation. Reaching her roots deeper into the Earth, she pulls the life energy from the surrounding forest, preparing to burn out the mechanical wonders keeping his body alive.

Seldin's heart jumps as everything that is not malnar begins to shrivel while she charges her bloom. The energy begins to pool in the center as her parabolic bell of petals starts to glow.

"No!" Seldin exclaims, getting in the way of her beam as she fires.

The air crackles with superheated oxygen and the smell of ozone from the laser-like protuberance scorching everything it touches— save for the malnar encasing Seldin's body, which eclipses the majority of Simon as the pulse of fiery light rushes over them.

Capturing some of this energy, Seldin concentrates, feeding it back against its source.

"I won't let you do this!" Seldin exclaims, but as altruistic as his actions against her may be, she takes it as a sign of betrayal and sics her brood on him as well.

The drones surround him, latching on with their vine-like tendrils to drain his life away, yet his beljusa protects him from their energy-sapping techniques.

This angers the larger queen, who sees no other choice but to use physical attacks to break down the defenses of her own kind. The order goes through with little hesitation, for the drones are just that. They move closer, forge their finger-like extensions into thorny talons, and proceed to cut into Lucy's leafy hide to gouge at the person underneath.

As they slice into and expose his flesh, he burns in the focused cone of the queen's attack—hot enough to melt steel. Luckily for Seldin, his body doesn't feel pain. He continues to resist while Lucy gladly drinks in the energy, passing it to him as he furiously repairs the chunks they futilely tear away.

Their stubborn exchange, however, causes the queen to change up her tactics. Ordering her brood to join in, she weaves her vines through Seldin's open wounds, rooting firmly into this new battery, which she intends to drain quickly.

Losing energy, Seldin grunts, dropping to his knees. Lucy does her best to feed him the power she absorbs from the photonic blast—recycling the aether between them. However, this exchange can't possibly last forever, which means sooner or later, one of them will fail. In this case, Lucy who is taking the most damage. Seldin knows that his window to act is closing; he needs to do something while he still has the strength.

"Don't make me do this," he pleads to the rose queen once more, but her response is the same.

"Lucy!" Seldin's heart flutters with what he's about to ask: "How do I stop her?"

The answer appears in his mind, showing him the organism's anatomy.

With little time left, Seldin cultivates what aether he can—pulling from his surroundings and drawing from his core. His body heats up, accelerating his molecules as his matter converts to energy, and he grabs hold of the beljusa's base like a bear hugging a tree.

The queen screeches, digging her powerful roots farther in to hold Seldin at bay as he willfully imparts an uneven force on her body.

"Argh!" he screams, holding on with all his might. Everything in his view seems to stretch away as his essence reaches the speed of light. In an instant, his image appears in three places: where he is, where she is, and where they are to be. As those avenues merge in a brilliant explosion, every drone linked to the queen drops.

In his weakened state, Simon can only watch through the haze of falling dust while his friend lies huddled over the flaccid half of the beljusa still rooted to the ground. Its upper half is missing—left scattered into the infinite.

"Ugh." Seldin stands, bearing a remorseful grimace to the dead creature and the sight of his own chlorophyll-stained hands still clasping the tubule organ he had removed. His eyes then pan over the state of the battlefield, and then to Simon.

"I hope you are satisfied," Seldin's voice is coarse as he walks over to his bestie.

"Sei…" Simon tries, too drained to speak.

"I should take your power; you don't deserve to be a guardian," Seldin scolds harshly. His pain is obvious, even for Simon to see.

"I'm… sorry…" Simon manages weakly.

"Sorry—is that all you have to say for yourself? You put everyone in jeopardy for the sake of your own selfish pride and forced my hand against our only known ally. Now the pulsari are still on their way and we have even less of a chance to fortify Earth before they arrive!" Seldin walks past him, hiking up the hill to check on Jasra and the others.

Simon just lies there, internalizing the situation while working to regain his strength. It should be him up there with Jasra now. He wrestles with himself while recalling the nanites he used against them all. He feels terrible—a rare thing for him. Maybe he did let his pride get the best of him, he thinks, for in all of their disagreements over the years, this is by far the worst. An unpleasant sensation creeps in whenever he feels the eyes of his best friend upon him.

As the others get to their feet and gather around, Seldin takes a rest, cradling Jasra, who is still unconscious from her battle with time.

"Sei," Simon utters, his senses pulling him northward. "I'm picking up helicopters headed this way."

"It sure took them long enough," Leon comments as Seldin reluctantly hands Jasra to Simon with a long stare into his eyes before turning toward the base.

"Dean, get them home. I'm gonna look for the other malnar before the military shows up," Seldin says.

"Would you like some help?" Dean offers.

"Not from you," Seldin replies as his flowery companion unveils.

Chapter 25

"A Glimmer of Truth"

The night grows cold as Seldin searches through the rubble of Segal Army Base for the beljusas he'd seen huddled in the queen's nest just hours before. Clingers that once draped the walls have shriveled and died, much like the other malnar in, on, and around the compound, leaving scars in the structures they had fused with.

He sighs, dismayed with a heavy heart, for his eyes are not seeing and his senses are not detecting anything of use within the debris. With the battle still so fresh in his mind, it bothers him that things had to come to this.

Taking a knee, he sinks a hand into a heap of dried soil cluttered with crispy, brittle bits of plant matter.

"Where are you?" Seldin asks in a sad, quiet voice as he scans the area to no avail. Then, a faint tug at his shoulder pulls a glance to the companion at his back. Lucy's petals are in full bloom with her budding bulb aimed off to his right.

"What is it, girl?" he asks as her grip tightens and he moves to follow her captive gaze to a pocket of woven vines. Although dead, the butterfly-looking drones that lie there have taken on an all-too familiar shape.

"Find something interesting?" The sudden voice of Dean startles him, and he looks on with a scornful gaze over his shoulder.

"Cepella," Seldin replies returning his attention to the fallen malnar. "Was I not clear?"

"You were," Dean replies. "So, you've found cepella. What does that mean?"

Seldin stands. "It means they can fly the old-fashioned way without expending aether," he replies.

"Then they're intentionally hiding their signals from us," Dean comments.

"Thanks to you," Seldin snaps, angrily.

Dean slowly approaches from behind with a subtle downward stare. "You'll have to forgive me: Simon would have mutinied anyway; it's his nature to oppose authority. I merely sided with him to mitigate the fallout. At least it's out of his system," he explains.

Hearing that, Seldin turns to him. "And now one beljusas is dead and the others are missing," he retorts.

"It's better than the alternative; he could have rallied against you during a real battle. Trust me, you don't want that. Still, I hope this hasn't damaged our friendship," Dean says.

"Fifteen years of dishonesty damaged our friendship, Dean," Seldin steps away, hearing the chopping sound of helicopters approaching.

"In spite of what you think, Arius and I spent that time nurturing you all from a distance so that you could find your way naturally," Dean says, and Seldin's ears perk up.

"So, he's a guardian as well?"

"He used to be." Dean looks away. "Arius stepped down a long time ago." He pauses. "After we went into hiding," he adds.

"From what?" Seldin looks to him.

"War." Dean sighs then shakes his head. "I'm not supposed to be telling you this, Sei. It's on a need to know, but to my knowledge, there are only four of us left—not including you or your friends," he says with glassy eyes that stare off into some infinite distance.

"Tillman said there was once a guardian for every planet," Seldin comments.

Dean can remember it like yesterday, looking back at all the carnage—the screams and the paralyzing sensation of his own terror. A utopian city of great wonders toppled in ruins with scattered bits of immortals fading away into nothingness. It boggles his mind how easily guardians were destroyed as if their meager existence was insubstantial to the figure blurred by his fear yet known by his heart.

"Dean, Dean?" Seldin calls out, jogging him from his sudden lapse.

The Guardian of Dimension looks to him. "Hmm?" he mutters.

"What happened?" Seldin asks.

"A demigod was born," Dean answers, recalling the moment. "It destroyed thousands of guardians with ease. If it learns we're alive, it'll come for us."

"Where is this thing now?" Seldin asks.

Dean shakes his head with a pale, anxious face. "Nobody knows, and to be honest, I pray we never do."

…

There's a glorious sizzling sound followed by tap, tap—pop as an egg or two splats into the pan. The smell of bacon—the sweet succulent fragrance of butter…

'Oh, that's the right stuff,' Jasra thinks with a smile as her eyes crack to the two gents roaming the space between the kitchen and the living room. Almir is manning the stove while Leon is dancing his martial arts in front of the television, mimicking the moves of some silly Kung Fu movie.

Moving to the table, Almir catches Jasra's freshly awakened eyes upon him—or rather, his plate.

"Want some?" he asks of her tiredness, strewn out on the couch.

Leon looks over to her immediately, catching the direction of Almir's gaze. "Jassie!" He rushes to her with a warm smile as she sits up. "Everything's fine," he tells her.

Not feeling or seeing Seldin's presence, she then looks ahead.

"No, it's not," she huffs when suddenly Dean appears from a flicker of purple light.

"Where's Sei?" Leon asks.

"He said he needed some time alone," Dean replies. "Where's Simon?" he asks.

"In his room, I guess," Almir answers with a tilt of his head toward the door halfway down the hall to the right.

"That's his office." Jasra corrects.

"So, what happened?" Leon prompts while getting himself something to eat.

"All of the beljusas are missing," Dean says, and the others look to him in shock.

"What?" Leon and Almir exclaim.

"Then it's as I feared," Jasra sighs.

"What is?" Dean asks as he grabs a plate.

"The alliance with the malnar was a failure; my efforts to change the past…" she trails off sadly.

Leon looks to her. "Then why not just go back and try again?" he prompts her.

Jasra's face sours. "It's too late now. I can only go back so far, and it takes so much energy." She sighs. "I… I guess this outcome was inevitable."

"You shouldn't change the past…" Dean begins when Almir hops into the recliner, "…it's dangerous."

"Well, I've had enough role playing for one day. Let's see what's on." Almir steals the remote with a little psychokinetic action before flipping through the channels.

"Will you grow up?" Leon scowls as he, Jasra, and Dean glare at Almir for a moment.

"Ladies and gentlemen what you are seeing is not a hoax. Taken from hundreds of cellular phones and security cameras, the footage is now streaking across the internet like lightning. At just 8:30 a.m. Japanese Standard Time in Tokyo, a mysterious being appeared out of nowhere and vanished just as quickly, causing a riot in the streets and over a hundred-thousand dollars in damage. While the intentions of the creature are unknown, many speculate it to be malevolent. One eyewitness account describes the details of the apparent attack," the announcer says just as the scene changes to a three-quarter close up of a young Japanese man with the name 'David Wong' appearing at the bottom of the screen.

"I didn't know what happened at first," the translated voice dubs over, "it felt like I had been hit from behind. When I looked up from the floor, I saw it: the bank entrance had been blown away as if by a bomb, and this monster was standing in the middle of it all. Before I could rationalize what I was seeing, it let out a beastly yell like a yeti. Suddenly there was this blinding light, and I was thrust into the teller counter. Then the creature was gone," he says.

"Oh…" Dean sucks air through his teeth. "That's my bad. I sent him there—well, technically Simon… never mind."

The others glance to him and then back at the television, which goes on to recap about the miraculous healing event witnessed in Texas the day before.

...

Practice make perfect, they say, but it also helps alleviate some frustration. Simon's actions earlier and the missing malnar are at the forefront of Seldin's thoughts. How can he trust him again? They've been friends forever, yet a rift seems to be forming between them. Then again, he thought the same of Dean not too long ago.

"Ugh," Seldin sighs, trying to clear his overly worked mind, but then the thought of a demigod creeps in.

"Aarrghh!" Boom! Seldin lands hard, dropping into a crouch while coming out of a teleport with the trailing momentum sinking him a few inches into the lunar soil. He quickly jumps to the air again, throwing a jab, a right cross, and then an aerial spinning kick. As he twists, his body begins to dematerialize and boom-boom! He vanishes and then reappears just feet away.

Carrying his momentum, he keeps to the air while teleporting just after each strike. Seldin's antics leave small craters across the already-blemished surface of the moon. The dents he makes grow smaller with each attempt as he tirelessly works to master this new technique.

Pausing, Seldin looks around; his eyes fill with the vastness of space and the terrestrial bodies of the celeste. The sun is out and bright, yet it's the miniscule twinkle before the star that catches his sight.

"Why not?" He chuckles at the very thought. Gathering energy, that stretched view occupies his field of vision, once again, as the small planet, twice out, grows closer—flash!

"Oh shit! Hot, hot, hot, hot!" he shouts into the vacuum the very moment he materializes onto the smoldering surface of Mercury. It's not that bad, actually, only about six hundred degrees where he's at on the northern far side with the sun just cresting over the horizon. Much like on the moon, the thin, almost nonexistent atmosphere makes for a slow, fireless burn that leaves uneven, ashy patches in his gi, while his boots start to melt from contact with the ground.

Seldin focuses, quickly adjusting his aura to shield himself from the rampant temperatures and the proximity to the sun before healing his body and repairing his clothes.

"That's better." He looks himself over, then takes in the moment as he marvels at the tiny planet while squinting from the light. It's simply amazing how moonlike it is, he thinks, for the craters really sell it.

The unfamiliar world fills him with a calming sense that quiets his raging soul. Exploring, he takes the time to experience everything he can about this new place, where no mortal as ever walked. Mercury's gravity is weak against his steps while its crystalized sand feels like hot granules of pulverized charcoal in his hands.

Lucy is enjoying herself too, soaking up the wonderful abundance of solar energy as she dances freely upon his back. There's a lot to take in, for the sun occupies so much of the sky. The Earth by comparison looks like a small blue moon barely visible in the daylight.

"Where should we go next?" Seldin asks Lucy, who shrugs in foliate fashion at the question.

"Well, there's Venus or Jupiter," he considers. "No, they're in opposition; I'd have to teleport through the sun—and that could take eons." Seldin's eyes then trail the sky, catching a faint glimpse of red just beyond Earth.

"That'll do." He smiles, culling the aether. The ground beneath him vibrates, pulling the glassy soil toward him as he dematerializes. Even in this state of light, Seldin remains conscious—fully aware. Although sight and sound are non-existent, he can feel the gravity like an inverted sphere as he approaches the planet.

The nine-minute trip is over in an instant as the Guardian of Life materializes onto the surface of a red, dusty world.

"Woo!" his voice echoes loudly and he inhales the Martian air, taking in strong metallic, sulfuric odors. Unlike the other rocky bodies he has been on thus far, this one reminds him the most of Earth. The sky is a surprising mix of blue and gray, and he can feel the wind blowing across his face; the temperature is comfortable, if just a little chilly.

Lucy isn't exactly happy about the drastic change, however. She shrivels up, closing her bud, like drawing the strings of a hoodie. She'd rather have the infernal surface of Mercury than the temperate climate of Mars.

Seldin smiles over his shoulder. "You're welcome to come out; I'm considerably warmer than the air," he invites her envelopment when—

"No way." He sees a dusty old lander some distance out. Laughing like a kid on Christmas morning, he glides over to it.

The conically-shaped vessel stands a little over two meters tall with three triangular petals locked open. Brushing away the layers of dust, Seldin gapes for a moment at the yellow sickle and hammer insignia.

"This must be Mars 3," he says aloud before inspecting the unit further. Although history isn't his strong suit, science is, and Seldin knows the lore quite well. The Mars 3 probe, launched by the Soviets in 1971, mysteriously went quiet after touching down.

"Hmm..." Seldin kneels beside the unit. "The battery appears to be assisted by a set of crude solar panels, but it still works."

Seldin makes a face of confusion. "Then why won't it..." He fiddles with it, unsure of the malfunction. The lunar buggy was an easy fix, it only needed power, but that's not the issue here. He sighs before catching sight of the broken antenna.

"That's it, they lost transmission." He realizes. Envisioning the antenna in his mind, he extends his awareness into the metal, reconstructing it one atom at a time. He then smiles, opening his eyes to the refurbished device. "It's probably not up to Simy's standards, but it should work," he comments to himself.

"What are you doing?" Seldin hears a voice just ahead of him and he looks straight at Tillman and some other guy standing on the opposite side of the craft.

"I was—"

"Goofing off," the other figure answers. He's young-looking: dressed like a punk with an unorthodox mix of jeans, Keds, spikey bracelets, and tunneled earrings in his pointy ears. At least his pants are up, the thought crossing Seldin's mind while taking in the shaved sides of his head and tatted skin.

"And you are?" Seldin inquires before the man turns obtusely while popping a zippo to light a cigarette in an environment with low oxygen and high concentrations of carbon dioxide.

"You do realize that's not going to work?" Seldin claims, knowing the laws of chemistry, but it lights just the same. The man snaps the lighter shut as he exhales a puff of smoke.

"Who says it won't?" he questions, gesturing a tilt of his wrist to show the cherry before taking the cancer-stick to his lips and presenting a hand to Seldin.

"Name's Welic, I was trained by Khy—"

Tillman glares at him and then Welic raises his hands defensively.

"Oooh-kaaay… you two talk. I'll just be over there checking out those lovely—ah-haha!" he blurts out, directing his attention to the rover inside the capsule. "This is beautiful, so retro!"

"I thought guardians couldn't be trained." Seldin turns to Tillman.

"Mentored," Tillman smooths over, "He had already ascended."

Shkk—pop! The tab of a soda can opens, and they look to Welic, who makes a cocky face.

"What?" he questions before slurping from his can of Monster. "You guys can do that aether thing to get your energy, but I prefer all-naturraal," he emphasizes before taking another sip.

"Welic, here, is the Guardian of Vice," Tillman says.

"So, another guardian from Earth? Where'd you find this guy?" Seldin asks.

Right away Welic chuckles. "Pffft, no! I'm not even human," he claims. "Just look at these ears." He traces the stretched lobes and pointed tips with his finger.

"Right, like you can't do that with a little cosmetic surgery," Seldin quips.

"Welic comes from Ensantiel like your friend Arius; it's a floating city in the mid—"

Tillman tries to explain when the Ensantiellian seemingly shimmers then appears on the other side of the capsule. The transition is immediate without any stirring of dust. In fact, it was just a flicker.

"You can teleport?" Seldin looks to Welic with a surprised expression.

"Yeah, can't you?" Slurp.

Seldin turns back to Tillman. "Dean told me a demigod killed Arius' people," he says.

"Not just his people," Tillman sighs with a genuine look of sadness behind his eyes.

Seldin sort of bobs his head. "He said all the guardians too. I assume his teacher as well?" he asks with a nod toward Welic.

Tillman shakes his head. "Khyrah is the God of Chaos." His eyes shift to Seldin. "A demigod," he says.

Seldin's mouth hangs open. "Khyrah? I've heard that name before." He turns away as flashes of memories flood in. His mind works back, sifting through his time with Theresa and Watcher's Keep. "The sorcerers…" he mutters.

"Yes," Tillman nods, "Khyrah is the god they worship." He sighs. "She used to be an ally before the war," he says.

"But why did she—"

"Sei, I need you to focus on now. The pulsari have reached Oqu IX. As the Guardian of Life—"

"I'm responsible for them," Seldin finishes his sentence before asking: "How should I get there, teleport with Welic?"

"Oh, God no. You'd never get there in time traveling at light. Have Dean grant you passage," Tillman replies.

"Wait, you don't understand. A lot has happened since—" Seldin tries.

"Oh, please—a petty squabble with the Guardian of Technology has you miffed?" Tillman dismisses.

Seldin's face contorts angrily in defense, "There are malnar on Earth, and thanks to him—"

"Let the Guardian of Earth handle it; that's what he's there for. You need to be on Oqu IX—and tell Jasra to stop messing with the timeline!" he commands sternly and Seldin cocks his head.

"You know about that?" he asks, surprised.

Tillman scoffs at the absurdity of his question. "Do I know about it?"

Welic interjects. "Everyone feels the ripples of a temporal shift. It's like déjà vu." He takes a drag of his cigarette.

"Including the demigod trying to kill us, son," Tillman adds with a tone.

Seldin's eyes lock to his. "Information I could have used yesterday, Tillman. Now, would you mind filling me in or are you going to hold back like Dean for fifteen years?" he retorts.

Tillman's eyes shift downward. "You're right, Sei, we haven't told you everything. Here is the truth: within the infinite dimensions of our universe, there are demigods—beings so powerful, the only thing greater is a true god. Some universes have a malevolent god. Others have a god of good. Our universe doesn't have one. So, when Khyrah turned on us, there was nothing we could do. No one to call upon. She slaughtered nearly every guardian that day. Only Dean, Arius, Welic, and myself remain."

"A multiverse?" Seldin's eyes meander.

"Yes," Tillman says.

"I assume she hates us because we're in her way of conquering it all?" Seldin asks.

"Guardians are the product of a universe without a true god. We are… a way of balancing the scales. But do they hate us? No, they consume us," Tillman answers.

Seldin's face contorts. "Consume us?"

Tillman nods. "Demigods have an insatiable hunger. They feed on everything—stars, planets, all the material, all the life, until there's nothing left," he says.

"And because of that, the Guardian of Time can't exercise her power?" Seldin asks.

"Not if she wants to live," Tillman says.

Seldin sighs. "If Jasra's benched, then we need you. Help us fight the pulsari."

Tillman shakes his head. "You wouldn't like my methods," he says, his words send a chill down Seldin's spine.

"You're talking about genocide." Seldin shudders at the idea.

"Yes," Tillman says.

Seldin's heart trembles. "I can't do that."

Tillman sighs. "Then more innocent lives will be lost."

Seldin lets out a heavy breath. "How can you... expect me to even consider it?"

Tillman looks out at Earth in the sky. "In my thousand years as a guardian, I have learned one universal truth." He turns to Seldin. "Only two things ensure peace: force and the threat of force."

Chapter 26

"Simon's Confession"

The cold water running down Jasra's face is soothing after all that; it helps to ease the mental strain and the ringing inside her head. She looks up into the stream of water raining down upon her from the showerhead as she leans slightly forward to place her hands on the slick tiled wall. She takes a deep breath before running her head under the water again. Her visions are still blurry, fogged up from her meddling—or so she thinks. At this point, she can't tell if it's her or the future that's cloudy.

Standing straight, she watches as the droplets crash and explode upon her bare chest before falling to the drain at her feet. Bringing a hand up, she examines the process more closely: how the beads of water compress from impact, the force separating them into multiple pellets as the energy divides almost evenly amongst them.

Going forward a few seconds, she then stalls the motion before taking the flow in reverse an equal amount of time. The droplets that splash down rewind into larger spheres, which race up along a predetermined arc, governed by gravity and time to the lip of the showerhead above. She rinses and repeats several times, playfully knocking drops out of sync to test her strength and readiness. A few minutes one way or the other doesn't seem to bother her, yet larger distances leave her feeling disoriented.

Wiping her face, Jasra realigns herself with the present. Finished with this, she chooses a path with her already dried and dressed in the robe that draped the hook on the bathroom door before stepping out. She then pauses, tapping a knuckle on Simon's workroom door to see if there's any change.

"Feeling better?" Leon asks, stepping past her to get to the now unoccupied bathroom.

"Mm-hmm." She nods, though internally she's saddened by Simon's lack of response. *'What could he possibly be doing in there?'* she wonders, and then lets out a breath before proceeding down the hall to join the others in the living room just as a phone rings.

"Yo," Almir answers his cellular device. There is an angry voice attacking from the other side. Jasra just smirks at his expression, happy that she doesn't have to deal with that mess.

"Yeah, M-Mom, no I told you I would be crashing with Lee for a few—yeah, well I left you a note, didn't I?" Almir then makes a sour face, hearing a click, and he pulls the phone away from his ear. "I gotta go—Jesus, I'm the Guardian of the Mind and I still have to answer to my parents," he complains.

"That reminds me," Leon says as he plops on the couch, "I need to call my mom, too." He reaches for his phone.

Dean just shakes his head. "Lee, aren't you eighteen? When are you gonna tell her to cut the apron strings?" he chuckles.

Leon sighs, shaking his head. "One more year, and she's being more of a bitch than usual now that Ryan spends most of his time at Watcher's Keep," he stresses.

"Ohh man, haha!" chuckles Dean when suddenly, there's a burst of white energy. Everyone covers their ears and shields their eyes. Then from out of the boom comes a voice.

"I think you cracked the walls, haha. You need to work on that entry," Welic says, patting Seldin on the back.

"Jesus freaking Christ, man!" Almir shouts at them, making a face.

"Sorry, guys. I've been practicing getting the compression field down," he says, his eyes falling to Jasra, who is reclining on the couch in her bathrobe beside Leon. She looks up at him in the moment, pleased that he's back; a hint of a smile touches her lips.

"It looks like you need more practice, and who the hell is this?" Almir gripes.

"Name's Welic. Hey, Dean." He offers a nod his way.

"Where's Simon?" Seldin asks them.

"Still hiding in his workroom; he hasn't been out all day," Jasra says.

"I need to speak with him." Seldin heads down the hall.

"Well, I think we should be going," Leon says as he and Almir move to the front door. Jasra then makes her way to the kitchen to prowl around for something to fill the void in her stomach.

With her just out of earshot, Dean looks to Welic, scooting him a little farther out of eavesdropping range.

"So, what do you think of the new life guardian?" he asks.

Welic just shrugs, not really knowing the man, but he offers his opinion anyway. "There aren't too many people who have my confidence, but I'd follow him," he says.

"Good," Dean replies.

"He asks a lot of questions though, and I didn't realize Tillman hadn't mentioned Khyrah," Welic comments.

"You didn't—" Dean whispers.

"No, Tillman cut me off before I could, but why not just tell him?" Welic asks.

Dean shakes his head. "I already told him about the demigod and what it did to us."

"But he should know about Khyrah and what really happens when you try to wield more aether than the body can handle; otherwise, they're all bound to make the same mistake."

"That's not what happened, and you know it. Khyrah made a choice, plain and simple. Don't go putting the idea in their heads," Dean says.

...

Down the hall, Seldin knocks on Simon's door. There's no answer, but he can feel him inside.

"Simy?" he calls through the door. Hearing no reply, he knocks again.

"Go away," a muffled voice pierces the door. Seldin then tries the knob; it's locked. Dropping his awareness into it, he moves the aether through the tumblers and then tries the knob again. Simon turns toward the door as it opens.

"I said go away!" he telekinetically slams it shut, then relocks it.

Pop—Seldin materializes into the room, the force knocking a few loose things around.

Simon isn't happy about the intrusion, not one bit. Using telekinesis, he pushes Seldin up against the door.

"Why doesn't anyone listen to me?" he questions but his strength is still weak from the battle and Seldin flares his aura, breaking his kinetic grip easily then slaps his face.

"Knock it off, what are you hiding from?"

"I'm not hiding!" Simon shouts, and then stumbles back into his chair, his breath growing heavy and staggered. "I'm... fixing..." He looks away, shaking and rubbing his eyes.

"Fixing what?" Seldin asks softly, feeling his friend's anger, his embarrassment, his shame.

"I made a lot of mistakes on that battlefield, mistakes that I wouldn't have made if I… h-hadn't been so… emotionally stupid," Simon says.

Seldin shakes his head. "Simon, it was not entirely your fault. Dean—"

"No, I'm not talking about Dean—Jasra loves you." What he says causes a shock in Seldin's chest; he was hoping to keep that quiet. "A part of me always knew." Simon's eyes wander. "Mix that with… everything else…" He cants his head with a false laugh.

"Simon…" Seldin begins.

"No, it's alright." He waves Seldin off. "Let's face it, I've never been a good boyfriend," he scoffs, "I'm even worse with emotions."

Simon stands, pacing. "To be honest, what burns me the most is how much farther ahead you two are," he says.

Seldin shakes his head. "That's not true."

"It is," Simon rebuts. "And I have to be honest with myself. I can't keep up with her at half my level, and you're three times stronger than me, last I scanned."

"But you are getting stronger—you created new materials that I would have never thought of and developed new tech way faster than I ever could."

"It's not just that." Simon shakes his head. "It's this whole fated nonsense. Dean said you're supposed to be our leader. How am I supposed to compete with what's meant to be?"

It isn't easy for Seldin to hear such pain coming from his best friend. The last thing he'd ever want is to hurt him, which is why he held back in Texas. As for Jasra, it's true they've always had chemistry, but he doesn't have time for that.

"Simy—"

"Don't. I don't want sympathy. If I had been using my gifts properly, this wouldn't have even happened. My mind wouldn't have been clouded. I would have known exactly what to do and how to do it. With a brain faster than a supercomputer and nanites flowing through my veins, I should have been able to weigh the options, take the most logical path, and if that path was to fight, I would have been concise in that action! Yet I was reckless, emotional, and in the end, I laid there petrified of my own mortality and consumed by my envy." He sighs shamefully. "And now this world may suffer for it." Simon drops into his chair, brooding.

"Simon, we haven't lost yet. There should still be four other beljusas out there. We just have to find them before the pulsari arrive," Seldin says, and Simon sits back, thinking about it.

"As soon as I fix myself, we'll go find them together," Simon says, extending a hand to his best friend. Seldin accepts with a sturdy grasp.

Getting up from the desk's edge, Simon moves around the room to the centrifuge still spinning on the table beside the chamber.

"And how do you intend to fix yourself?" Seldin asks.

Taking up a vial from the centrifuge, Simon presents it. "With this: version four. It'll eliminate the emotions that limited my potential, and I'll be able to realize energy levels that were simply unobtainable with version three," he says.

"Are you sure you want to do that?"

"Absolutely," Simon replies, walking over to the isolation chamber.

"I'm going to need you to man the console when they're ready," Simon looks to him.

Sighing, Seldin shakes his head. "I, I don't think this is the way, Simy," he says with sincerity.

"I'm the Guardian of Technology, and technology has to advance. Then… then we can chase after those flowers," Simon insists.

"Actually, we're on a much different assignment," Seldin presents, and Simon looks to him curiously.

"Oh, I thought—"

"I spoke with the Guardian of Death; he said that the pulsari are attacking another world as we speak. That stupid scuffle of ours wasted so much time, we have to move now," Seldin says.

"But what about the malnar?"

"Leon is the Guardian of Earth. Right now, they fall under that jurisdiction," he replies.

Simon thinks for a moment. "I see. When do we leave?" he asks, for the idea of going off world intrigues him.

"Now," Seldin tells him before stepping toward the door.

On the way back to the living room, Seldin calls to the Guardian of Dimension, not feeling the immediate presences of the Guardians of Earth and Mind. "Dean, get them back here," he instructs.

"What's going on?" Dean asks just as he opens a portal to Leon and Almir hovering in the afternoon sky.

"You two." Seldin gestures for them to come through the gate. "You can't go home just yet. Leon, I need you to lead a search party. You're looking for the beljusas; take Lucy with you. Normally, you need six to make the array, but five will have to do." He hands her off to him.

"What's going on?" Jasra questions.

Seldin then looks to her. "Us four…" He gestures a circling motion of his hand to her, Simon, and Dean, "…are going to Oqu IX to stop the pulsari. Leon, Almir, and Welic are going to track down the missing malnar." Seldin then turns his focus to Leon.

"Start back in South America and work your way from there. Now listen, I know I'm giving you a lot of information, but the placement of the flowers is important. When I set this up on Binax-Beta, the suka had me plant them in natural conduits opposing each other on the equator and the poles, just like a compass. Do you understand?" he asks of his former student.

Leon glances away in thought trying to grasp it all. "I think so." He pauses. "Each flower in a conduit on its own corner of the world, right?" he double checks.

"Correct. Also, the others may not be in the most cooperative mood. You'll probably have to gain their trust, but Lucy can help you with that. Okay?" Seldin asks.

Nodding, Leon glances to Almir, and then to Welic, who feigns a salute to Seldin before stepping up beside the Guardian of Earth.

"Dean?' Leon looks to him and then a portal opens in the jungle near Segal Army Base.

Chapter 27

"St-Oqu-ed"

"Where did you say we are going?" Dean asks of Seldin, who looks amongst them.

"Oqu IX," he replies.

"Are you sure you're ready for space travel?" Dean questions him and Seldin nods.

"I've already been to the Moon, Mercury, and Mars," he answers.

"Okay, then, haha!" Dean chuckles.

"Wait a minute, when the hell were you on the Moon?" Simon seems baffled.

"Uh… hmm, well I've been there a few times," Seldin replies.

"What about everyone else?" Dean looks to Simon and Jasra who return his stare.

"I'm up to try," she says, and Simon nods in agreement.

"Me too," he replies, hardly able to contain his excitement at the idea of experiencing another planet. *'What will it be like?'* he wonders with his super brain computing the possibilities just as a ring of purple flames spirals open. The air hits them like jet-wash flooding the living room. The other side of the gate is darkened in the twilight of a setting sun and the twinkling lights of a busy city with skyscraper-like buildings eclipsing the light.

One by one they step through and as the gate closes behind them, it becomes apparent they're no longer in Kansas. The gravity on Oqu IX is twice as strong as it is on Earth while the oxygen levels are only about one percent of the air—a drastic change from what they're all used to.

It's vastly different than Binax-Beta, Seldin realizes, as the world is hardly nourishing to him; he can feel the intense pull of gravity and the crushing, ear-popping weight of the atmosphere bearing down upon him.

Simon, too, notes the differences; the nanites in his blood compensate for the lack of oxygen while employing their due diligence to strengthen his muscles and improve the benefits of the bio-mechanical suit. The icons on his display flash as he watches the performance of his internal machines.

The bizarre climate isn't really all that foreign to Dean. In fact, it reminds him of some parts of his home. His eyes slit more reptilian, adjusting to the dimming skyline as his scales grow as black as shimmering charcoal. His physical appearance morphs, gaining three feet in height before his hips and legs reshape into something more beast-like. He drops forward, bracing himself on all fours as sleek, slender wings sprout from his back, below his scapulae. The scales that cover him grow more ridged, forming striations all throughout his form while the scaly hairs on his face harden and sharpen to make a beard of spines that conforms to the contours of his head, chin, and jawline.

This form should serve his needs well, as the dragons of the swamps from the Kingdom of Banne are used to high concentrations of nitrogen and methane. Dean then looks over himself before checking the integrity of his fleryl—his special armor—which holds its shape snugly to his much larger, more rigid body.

As the harshness of the new world settles over them, Seldin's concern grows for his friends. *'Can they—?'* his mind jumps as he quickly pans his gaze about to Simon, Dean, and then to Jasra.

"Are you okay?" he asks of her, thinking back to the research labs and the suffocating smoke, and she stares almost blankly into his eyes.

"I'm fine. The gravity is a little—"

"You can breathe?" Seldin's question comes with surprise as Jasra's cheeks redden and she lowers her eyes, innocently.

"Oh—ooh…" He sighs, remembering his best friend's words to him. 'How awkward, but it makes sense. His thoughts wander, putting the pieces together before passively shifting his gaze in hopes that Simon isn't paying attention.

"So, this is Oqu IX?" Simon looks about the mirror-like sheen of the planet's salt-flat landscapes, which seemingly stretch over the vast majority of the world, reflecting the sky almost perfectly with the sun moving out of position to set behind them.

The architecture of the city they stand in is fashioned of great columns of sodium enriched compounds that further aid to the reflective qualities of the planet's surface. Natural lights line the edges of the roadways in intricately connecting bands of luminosity that shine upward from the streets themselves. The lighting of the buildings is similar, as if built directly into the structure.

Simon is simply beside himself with the awe factor; his instruments are going full throttle to take in everything of wonder. Jasra too, is excited about it, hardly feeling the drag of the gravity as they move toward the heart of town.

It's a different place for the new guardians, full of unknowns. The animals and plants are anything but carbon-based. Their high salinity combined with other properties suggests silicon, or maybe something in between. Their bodies seem to glow with various hues in startlingly patterns like similar to a cuttlefish.

Although most of this part of the city remains untouched, the buildings farther uptown are riddled with malnar. Explosions, weapon fire, and indiscernible grunting can be heard from up ahead as flames ravage the buildings in the distance and a horde of what might be people scamper in fright.

The beings are shortly statured with colorful, slender bodies and smooth skin. Though adorned with feather-like apparel, the creatures, much like the plants and other panicked stricken animals, emit radiant pulses of bio-luminescence.

A solitary eye stretches like a thin membrane from the top of their heads to the upper ridge of a beaked face. They flail a set of bilateral arms attached to a single pivot in the middle of their narrow torsos. A similar aperture forms a single leg with a wide foot. They run with a hobble or a hopping motion that is aided by the springing action of their curved spines. As they scurry about or ride by on some sort of treaded vehicles resembling snowmobiles, the natives split around the group, avoiding them with equal haste as the danger they're fleeing.

"Are these the Oqus?" Simon asks as he tries to examine them and their technology.

"They're called Spriis, but yes. They're about as tech-savvy as the people of Earth, give or take a century. Though they've already managed to colonize their solar system, hence, Oqu IX," Dean explains.

Seldin can hear their cries within his mind, begging for the help of their god to save them.

"The colors are so pretty," Jasra notes.

"It's how they communicate." Seldin replies, and Simon looks to him.

"You can understand them?" he asks.

"Yes," Seldin answers as images of their horror work into his mind, and a thunderous roar draws his attention as he looks above the towering skyscrapers.

The sky comes to life with airships of a sort, sleek and serpent-like with single inline fission drives that propel them forward as they swim through the air to swarm a much larger form.

The quartet stops their march as soon as the enormous hovering craft, steadily moving toward them, comes into view. It has three large petals that fan out and curve upward while a stamen, of a sort, drapes down with three equally spaced appendages surrounding a central stem that daintily drops an almost endless supply of spores that snow over the city and become whatever they touch.

Farther out are more of the zeppelin-shaped carriers waiting to unfold like the ship before them, likely loaded with an equally dreadful spawn. It's a very familiar sight for Seldin. The memories that pour into him flood his mind as his heart fills with the beat of anger.

"I've seen this before," Jasra lets out a stunned breath. Seldin quickly looks to her.

"When?" he asks.

"It was in a vision I had, a—a dream."

"Tell us what happens," Simon says. Dean's ears perk up as well.

"It's not… I don't think it was here. I'm pretty sure what I saw was on Earth," she replies, her eyes then meet Seldin's.

"Well, that's not happening," Seldin says before launching himself toward the ship.

"Wait!" Jasra shouts after him when a clawed hand takes her left arm.

"Come on!" Dean's voice carries like a low growl as he thrusts his wings to take to the sky.

In mere moments, Seldin's altitude centers with the craft, several thousand feet from the ground. The Oqu planes swoop around him with focus on a much greater, mutual target. He then powers up, following the formation of the pilots as they circle about the ship and fire upon it. Seldin expands his senses to feel out the familiar essence of the vessel, determining the strength of its aura before releasing a powerful surge of aether that explodes as it hits its surface.

"Hardly a dent!" Simon shouts, watching the readings on his HUD.

Seldin then circles around and tries again. Fffsssreeww—boom! The explosion rattles the sky, complementing Oqu's mortar-like weapons from the ground and their volley in the air. The raw energy of his attack offers no harm; instead, it feeds the large flower-like construct.

"What the hell are you doing?" Dean asks.

"I was hoping the solid structure of the hull was vulnerable. Simon, can you control it?" Seldin asks.

Simon nods. "You got it!" His view advances as he extends his awareness to envelope the enormous mass. His goggles flash various characters of an unknown language. A portion of his mind separates, breaking down the syntax as he looks deeper into the system in search of the machine code that controls it. Simon has never sensed anything like this except for maybe what he felt in South America. There are no consoles, no computer screens, or manual input devices of any kind that he can detect.

Within the ship, suspended from the umbrella of a jellyfish-shaped ceiling, drape locks of opaque organic matter, which cling to thousands of gray-skinned beings embedded therein. These dangling strands surround in circular fashion a quartet positioned back to back, facing outward as if to look in all directions. In this way, the pulsari are at one with the craft and universally connected to those aboard as if each member were a cluster of sensory neurons plugged into a much larger collective brain, governed by the four who command at its center. They feel everything the ship can and see all that it is able with its sensitive, energy-sensing mind. And they know they're here.

Following the path of the fading light, the vessel continues to move in a sun-worthy heading. Without a discernable front, the ship is able to navigate freely in any lateral direction while maintaining its vertical orientation relative to the topology of the planet and its magnetic field.

Looking to Simon, Seldin notes the expressions of strain on his face. "Everything alright?" he asks.

"Mm," Simon groans. "It's not the easiest thing to sync with; they have safeguards everywhere," he says.

"Well, can't you just upload a virus or something?" Seldin prompts, but Simon just shakes his head at the absurdity of such an idea.

"With what, a Trojan Horse and an Apple computer? That ship is the perfect definition of biological and technological harmony. It may be out of my scope. I'm not even certain there's enough physical technology available to be fruitful and I can't directly interface with a biological system. You have a better shot at that than I do," he says, frustrated, though admiring its traits.

"Are you saying you can't do it?" Dean asks him, and Simon snaps his eyes to him.

"I'm saying, if I can, it'll take time." Simon then glances to Jasra with a hopeful expression.

"What about the nanites?" Seldin asks.

"Yes, of course!" Dean looks to Simon.

"Puppeteering a handful of boni is one thing, overwhelming something the size of a city..." He shakes his head before doing an internal scan of just how many nanites he has available. Gathering as many as he can, he runs the numbers. The human body has roughly a trillion cells; by comparison, the boni only had about nine billion and it took a quarter of that to control one plant.

'What if I only go for the nervous system? What is a plant's nervous system?' Simon wonders before presenting a dispersal sphere to Seldin.

"Let's do it," Simon says.

Seldin then nods before facing the ship. Opening his mind, he feels out the organisms then projects a message: *"Pulsari, we are the guardians, and I am the Guardian of Life. We demand that you cease your attack and remove your invasion party at once."* Seldin's heart then drops. "Dear god, I can see them," he whispers as all those within the vessel turn their collective gaze to him and the rest of the guardians. Seldin's mind fills with places they've destroyed, and those who have tried to stop them.

The four members of what might be the ship's bridge focus as they scan the group's collective energy. Connected to the malnar vessel, the pulsari can clearly see their auras—how they glow with wonderful gold hues around their bodies. The so-called Guardian of Life is only rated at 289 kilojoules, while the cyborg and the girl are almost tied at a shoulder-shrugging 190 kilojoules. The dragon is the strongest, they determine, with a core reaching 777 kilojoules. With the cresting sun still at their side, the aliens are not worried. The equivalent of a voice then enters Seldin's mind.

"Glrah banaschi cha."

Seldin makes an incredulous face.

"What is it?" Simon asks, seeing Seldin's stunned look.

Seldin turns a slow gaze to him. "They just told us to go to hell."

Continuing forward, the ship makes no effort to stop while the malnar on the ground redirect their attention and start firing beams into the sky. The Oqus, on the other hand, look on with confusion, for these new beings hovering above seem to have come out of nowhere.

Slesk, the commanding officer in charge of the ground troops, gives the order to use artillery.

Beams of energy and explosive shells begin to ravage the air.

"Damn it," Simon scowls. "Now they're shooting at us. Just throw it!" he urges, fearing the planes to be the next to strike. Seldin does just as ordered—he hurls the sphere directly toward the giant ship.

"Look out!" Jasra shouts, warning them to the barrage of weapon fire and the Oqu fighter jets that are turning about. The others move to dodge, but out of instinct she claps her hands together in a motion to gather energy then thrusts them forward. The aether projecting from her core ripples the air as the distortion field envelops them. The pulses of energy slow to a standstill as does the bizarre looking artillery shells as they enter the outer edges of the temporal bubble.

Moments later the sphere hits—bam! That blast is miniscule in comparison to the scope of the ship. Simon's nanites then come online, visible in his HUD. Like a cancer, the little bots spread out—replicating as they go. At that distance, the car-sized wound appears to them the size of a baseball.

"I think it is working, I'm in!" Simon says.

"Good," Seldin replies when Jasra throws in her two cents.

"Guys, I can't hold this forever," she says with a gesture of her head to the ever-growing buildup of energy and shells at the edge of her horizon.

"I've got an idea," Seldin says, wrapping his arms around her waist.

"What are you doing?" Jasra gripes.

"Just trust me. Alright, Dean, Simon, let's all move together," he says, pushing her along as she maintains the time field, which moves with her. The dangers trapped in her bubble fly off as they're freed.

"Good thinking." Dean looks to Seldin, but right then the pulsari ship begins to glow.

"This isn't good," Simon comments.

"What?" Seldin turns to him.

"They're using their energy to burn off the nanites," he says.

Time and space shift in Jasra's view as the last few moments rewind. She shakes her head, rubbing her eyes as her vision returns to the present.

"Damn it," Simon scowls. "Now they're shooting at us. Just throw it!" he urges Seldin.

"No, don't! It's a waste," Jasra interrupts just as she envelops the group in a temporal bubble to shield them from the incoming attacks. She then ushers them to slowly move clockwise around the vessel.

"Is this the past?" Dean asks immediately.

"No, it's the present; I just looked ahead. The nanites will fail, we need another strategy," she informs them.

"Aw, heck with it." Simon thrusts his hands forward, grabbing the ship telekinetically. He's instantly forced back as the ship's forward motion pushes against him.

Seldin joins in, as does Jasra, with the same result. It's like trying to hold back a train, they realize as they slide through the air.

Dean takes pause, watching their attempt before slowly adding to the effort. There's a noticeable difference in resistance, and the others look to the dragon-man as he is forced along with them.

"Dean, how strong are you?" Seldin asks.

"In this form?" Dean thinks. "My core is about a million joules," he replies.

Seldin shakes his head. "It's not enough, even together," he states the obvious, running the math in his head, figuring the thing's mass to be sixteen thousand metric tons. If only he had Lucy.

"Sei, the energy doesn't have to be exact, does it?" Simon questions him as they ease up to regroup.

Seldin sighs in frustration. "To push an object in normal gravity you need a force roughly ten percent its mass. Here, we need twice that—and it's moving," he states.

"You're forgetting about overload," Simon comments with a glance his way. "If I triple my core and you triple yours, we'll have more than—"

"No, that's suicide," Dean interjects.

"What?" Simon scoffs. "You know damn well we can push it."

"At these levels?" Dean barks in a deep dragon voice. "Breach your core and you're done."

"Well, what about you?" Seldin looks to Dean. "Can you take a stronger form?" he asks.

"No." Dean's eyes shift away.

"Well, that settles it. We can't use energy blasts it," Seldin says.

"We can't use telekinesis to stop it either." Simon says, looking to his friends.

"And the nanites were a bust," Jasra adds.

"Wait, what about freezing it in time?" Simon throws out an idea. Jasra shakes her head,

"A temporal field that big?" she questions the possibility.

"I got it!" Dean snaps his fingers.

"What?" The others look to him.

"I can create a rift the size of the ship—drop it off at their home planet."

"What's the catch?" Seldin asks.

"I need time to get the energy," he replies with his eyes to Jasra.

"How long will that take?" Simon asks.

"A few minutes," Dean answers.

"We'll give you two," Seldin says while cracking his knuckles. He and Simon then head toward the battlefield. They hit the ground with tremendous force, creating a shockwave that levels fifty yards of enemies as well as a few fleeing Oqus.

Rushing in headfirst, Seldin lets his fury fly as he crushes the spores of Oqu-shaped boni.

Simon follows Seldin's pattern, working his hands past their viny leaves to the soft, cotton-like orbs beneath. The creatures drop immediately, but then something unexpected happens as tiny fluffs sprinkle down from above. They root in, stealing his energy.

"Ugh!" Simon shouts.

Hearing his cries, Seldin turns about and darts over to grab hold of the little bastards—squeezing them with his thumb and forefinger like popping a flea. One of them begins to grow into a Simon-like construct.

Simon stares at his doppelganger with a bewildered look on his face—for its face, its eyes are artificial and empty. It reaches for him, and he defends when Seldin punches through its back and crushes the spore. It drops dead.

"Huuuarrr—don't let them touch you!" he tells Simon before diving back into the mass of malnar.

Back in the sky, Jasra is working to keep Dean and herself out of sync with the rest of the battlefield in hopes of expediting his process. Similar to what she did at Groom Lake, as far as the universe is concerned, they are moving at an accelerated rate while all other things are in normal time. This distortion draws the attention of the pulsari, whose combined minds analyze the situation, and even through the veil of twisted space-time, they can tell that the core of the dragon-man is growing denser as his aura excitedly ignites. At this rate, Dean will be ready in two minutes of normal time.

Being more than aware of the guardians' abilities, the pulsari prepare a response. The three appendages of the ship's stamen angle forward as the petals fold around and the body of the craft closes into the cigar-shaped zeppelin form—charging a pulse. The energy that accumulates wisps, culminating into a virtually lightless mass save for the few strands of violet and ultraviolet that spill outward in what might be seen as a glow, or rather the inverse of a glow.

Despite being temporally displaced, Jasra's head becomes swimmy and her forward vision askew. Although unaware of the consequences before them, she doesn't need to see the future to take a guess at what's to come.

"Dean, we have to move!" Jasra shouts while squinting past the pain in order to maintain focus.

"Just a few more seconds," he begs.

"But I can't see!" she yells.

"I'm almos—"

On the battlefield, Simon comes out of a dodging motion to scoot from a boni's path before disintegrating it with a plume of nanites. He then freezes, looking up and back over his shoulder toward the ship.

"Shit, Sei, do you feel that?" he calls out.

Seldin stops immediately. With his attention to this new thing, he takes a staggered breath. "That's not aether," he says, staring in shock. Cupping his hands together, he packs as much aether as he can before releasing the beam of bluish-white energy to intercept the pulsari's weapon aimed toward his friends.

Chapter 28

"Another Earth Guardian"

Once home to an ancient civilization, the ruined temple of Chavin, north of Lima, Peru, is now an archeological site frequented by explorers and tourists alike. The wide-open lands feature vibrant green mountains encircling the stone marvels that everyone—including Leon, Almir, and Welic—are all so curious about.

Arriving at the site at about the same time Seldin and the others make their giant leap into space, the trio holds back while hiding a few yards from the enormous crowd surveying the ruins. It was Lucy who led them to this place. With her petals affixed like a satellite dish, she attunes to the energies that flow here—and it's a good thing too, for Leon isn't at the top of his game.

"Just look at all those people." Welic comments while taking a drag from his cigarette.

"What are we going to do?" Leon asks, feeling overwhelmed. The job that his mentor laid upon him may simply be too great. It's bad enough they don't know where the beljusas are, but what if someone else finds them first? His thoughts dwell on the unknown.

"Yeah, I didn't realize there was going to be this many people. How'd those flowers get so far out anyway?" Almir questions, and Welic shrugs.

"Maybe they flew here? Heck if I know. All I know is, we've gotta go get them," Welic says.

"But how?" Leon points. "Look, there's even a camera crew over there."

"Maybe they're making a documentary film about giant alien roses stalking the good people of Peru?" Welic jokes while performing monstrous marionette gestures with his hands and making roaring sounds.

"This isn't funny," Leon scolds.

"You're right, it's hilarious." Welic smarts.

"Well, how are we gonna get past all them, huh?" he gripes.

Almir then shrugs. "This may sound crazy but… why don't we just walk on in?" he suggests.

"What?" Welic and Leon both look to him.

"I mean, it is a tourist site. So, unless those things are twenty feet tall, everything should be fine, right?"

Welic considers it, as does Leon.

"At any rate," Almir continues, "you can control the elements of Earth, I can control minds, and Welic… is just—"

Welic slurps from his can of Monster.

"Never mind." Almir shrugs. "What I'm trying to say is, it shouldn't be that difficult."

The group then steps out from a pile of ancient rubble. Leon keeps pace with Welic, who seems to have the desire to lead. Almir then questions his own judgment after taking a moment to examine their outfits.

"Ya know, maybe we should have dressed more casually," he comments.

"Nah, we'll just say we're Americans." Welic smirks.

"Technically, so are they," Leon retorts before noticing a strange pull in the air coming from just ahead of them. Perhaps it's been there this whole time or maybe it just started. He isn't sure. His eyes then fall to the flowerpot in his hands and Lucy's point of focus.

"Guys, I think that temple was built on a conduit," Leon remarks.

"Well, that's convenient; Sei said you'd need to locate them anyway," Welic says.

"A what?" asks Almir.

"A natural convergence point of energy; they correspond with the intersection of ley lines," Welic tells him.

"Ok, I'm missing something." Almir sighs.

"Did I teach you anything?" Leon asks, and then Welic takes over.

"Much like your body, a planet has chakras and pathways for energy to flow through. Civilizations that are in tune with aether often build their cities around them," he says.

"Why is that important?" Almir asks.

"The flowers feed on energy. I bet we'll find them at the temple's center," Leon states, now with confidence.

The trio continues marching across the grassy and rocky field while avoiding the odd stares and the occasional near collisions of the tourists who snap photos of the ruins. Up a bit farther and leading into one of the main structures, is a lavishly long line corralled off like a ride at an amusement park with a hostess at the end.

"Siguiente en la fila. Por aquí, por favor. El recorrido comienza en un momento," the hostess says as two or three guests from the larger line step up to a smaller group of five.

"What's she saying?" Welic looks to Leon.

"She's saying something about a tour through the temple," Almir answers.

"Well, let's take it," Welic suggests.

Almir makes a face. "Why not just teleport us inside?" he asks.

"Because someone might see it," he says.

"I don't get it, Dean said plenty of races know of us already, why hide?" Almir questions.

"Humans are funny," Welic remarks.

"I don't like this," Leon says while glancing around to the handful of armed military personnel. Two of the uniformed men gather, talking quietly amongst themselves before seeming to glance in the trio's direction.

"I'm not sensing anything unusual in their auras," Welic says as he looks around. Still, Leon feels uneasy as they get in line.

"We need to pay for the tour, I think." Welic puffs on his cigarette while gesturing to the hostess.

"No, we don't," says Almir, walking up to her with a finger to his temple.

The woman then unhooks the rope at the corral post and lets them in. Leon and Welic glance to him, making equally surprised faces, for he seems to have no reservations about using his gifts in such a fashion.

"Hmm," Welic mutters as they walk by a partially tented group of tables set up with televisions, computers, and recording equipment. "I wonder what they're filming," he says, looking everything over as does several other passersby.

"I don't know. Do any of you speak Spanish?" Almir asks. Leon looks to him.

"I thought you did," he replies.

Almir shakes his head. "No, I can control their thoughts; I don't know what the hell they're saying," he rebuts right as Welic adjusts the volume on one of the TVs.

"Hey, here's something in English." Welic chuckles—slurp!

"This just in! Good morning, I'm Robert Wiskell bringing you this breathtaking report. Since the day man first looked to the sky, he has asked the question: 'Are we alone?' Kraivich Volksee—a technician for the Russian Space Association—believes to have startling evidence that may finally give us that answer. Three decades ago, the RSA lost contact with the Mars 3 lander, just minutes after touchdown. Well, ladies and gentlemen, after thirty years, the lander is transmitting. The signal came in at about 3:00 p.m. yesterday afternoon in Krasnoyarsk Krai,

Russia, and while the majority of the images show a desolate rocky landscape, the first one hundred pictures clearly show something different: two men, apparently human, and one plantlike figure matching the description of a creature witnessed by hundreds in Tokyo just hours before. They appear to be casually conversing. None of them are wearing any noticeable forms of protection, breathing apparatus, or space suits—suggesting an oxygen-rich environment contrary to what officials originally believed. The younger man is even smoking a cigarette." The camera zooms in.

"Hey, that's me," Welic laughs with a gaping smile before taking a drag, but his grin quickly drops as other viewers gather around.

"When were you on Mars?" Almir asks.

"Just a few hours ago. Sei was out there exploring when Death and I caught up with him, and then we did some teleport practice" he says.

"You should probably hide your face," Leon notes just as fingers point and indiscriminate jibber starts to jabber amongst the gawking crowd.

The program continues: "Who are they? What do they want? What were they doing on Earth not long before these pictures were taken?" the newsman asks.

...

"My God," bellows the president of the United States, "how many are seeing this?" He looks over to the vice president.

"I… I don't know, sir, the whole country—maybe the world," he replies.

"Get it off the air now!" he orders.

"Yes, sir." The man picks up the phone on the president's desk.

"Mr. President, as you can see, our situation is serious," says a military general sitting across from him on one of the two semi-circle couches in the center of the room. The secretary of defense looks to the general and then to the president, who stands and paces around the Oval Office.

"General Scott, I'll admit, if I hadn't seen the footage you showed me this morning, I would have thought you were crazy," he states, facing out the window.

"That's understandable, Mr. President. The circumstances are bizarre," replies the general.

"To be honest, I was hoping it was a hoax—or at worst, an isolated incident." The president sighs.

"I assure you, sir, that up until now, there was no way of knowing these beings had appeared in other parts of the world," the general says. The secretary of defense then looks to him.

"We should bring in Colonel Mitchel," he suggests to the general, who nods and then stands to address his commander in chief.

"Mr. President, if we could continue with the briefing, I'd like to introduce the man who encountered these anomalies firsthand."

The president nods and General Scott proceeds, opening the door of the Oval Office. Colonel Mitchel promptly steps in, greeting the president in pristine fashion before introducing himself.

"Mr. President, I am Colonel Glenn Mitchel of the United States Air Force."

The president gives the man a nod to be at ease. "Colonel, General Scott here tells me that you're the expert on these phenomena."

"An expert? No sir. To say otherwise would lead you into a false sense of security. However, they made their presence known when they attacked my installation a day ago, and we were able to gather some intelligence on them, sir," Mitchel says.

"What do you know about them, where do they come from?" asks the president.

The colonel pauses. "May I?" he asks, gesturing to the large view screen. The president nods in reply before Mitchel connects his laptop, bringing up the footage of the guardians infiltrating Area 51.

"Although we lost power when they attacked, we were able to get some data. From all accounts, they appear to be human," he says.

"That's impossible." The president shakes his head in disbelief.

"I thought so too, at first, sir. Granted, given what we've seen, that could merely be a clever form of camouflage. However, blood samples taken at the site—"

"Wait, wait," the president interrupts. "Blood? You mean, we can hurt them?"

The colonel nods. "Yes, one of our MECHs landed a successful hit." He switches to the footage of Seldin in the hallway of the facility with Leon, Jasra, Almir, and Simon huddled in safety behind a wall of earth. "Unfortunately, this one…" He points to Seldin on the screen, "…possesses some sort of healing power, but that's not the half of it." He skips the video a few moments ahead. The screen flickers, Seldin clenches a fist and the one MECH crumbles.

The president's mouth hangs in shock.

"He calls himself the Guardian of Life; he crushed a two-ton piece of military-grade hardware by thought," the colonel says in frustration. "What's worse…" He skips to the fight with Leon and Major Peirce. "Everything you're watching right now… has been play."

"A game?" the president asks.

"Yes, sir. They were testing their abilities; the Guardian of Life admitted it," Mitchel says.

"For what purpose?" he asks.

"I don't know, but our sister facility in South America was destroyed yesterday. If I had to guess, it was the guardians, sir," Mitchel says.

The president cocks his head. "Just what was in that facility, Colonel?" the president asks, and Mitchel looks to General Scott, who nods.

"Research," Mitchel responds, "we were experimenting with extraterrestrial plant life—"

"Extraterrestrial? You mean that thing in Japan?" The president scowls before turning away. "This is a disaster." He sighs.

"Mr. President, if the guardians did attack that facility—"

The president turns around. "I want a lid on this. Take as many men as you need and lock that area down," he orders.

Mitchel nods. "We're already on it, sir."

"Sam?" The president looks to the vice president. "Were you able to pull that broadcast?" he asks.

The vice president shakes his head. "I'm sorry, sir, but the Peruvian government is outside FCC jurisdiction," he answers with his sincerest apologies.

A voice then comes from the television. "Ladies and gentlemen, an unprecedented event is streaming live from Lima, Peru."

...

"What do we do?" Almir looks to Leon as the crowd encircles them. Cameras focus in, and soldiers train their guns. Acting quickly, Almir brings a hand to his temple.

"No." Leon places a hand on his friend's shoulder. "Let's handle this diplomatically."

"Friends!" Welic exclaims excitedly, raising his hands as he steps forward. His sudden movements startle the crowd, and those with weapons, open fire, delivering a fear-filled greeting of their own. Tourists scurry in panic as the Peruvian soldiers unload into what they can only perceive as a cloud of dust.

The wall of stone seems to have come out of nowhere to absorb the attack, but it's not as solid as Leon's usual work. Instead of granite, it's more like gravel. Chunks of rock and other debris chip off from the shots.

Leon drops to his knees, his body straining. Something isn't right: it shouldn't take this much focus to forge such a simple construct. The wall loses integrity and crumbles as he collapses.

"Argh!"

"Leon!" Almir shouts, coming to his aid. Immediately the gunfire ceases; the soldiers seem frozen. Seizing the opportunity, Welic grabs his friends and then in a flash, the trio is gone.

…

The president and his cabinet members watch in horror.

"You see, Mr. President. It's just as I feared," Mitchel states with a gesture toward the television.

With a glance to his right, the president nods to Colonel Mitchel. "Do what needs to be done," he permits.

. . .

Inside the temple there is a flicker of light when Almir, Leon, and Welic appear in a secluded spot. Leon's body surges in pain. He falls back, slapping the wall as he does, which causes random spires of rock to sprout, nearly crushing Almir, who ducks out of the way.

"Jesus!" Almir dives to the floor just as the spires hit the opposite wall. The chamber shakes and rattles with several tunnels collapsing around them.

Welic projects an energy field to shield them all from the falling debris.

"Aarrgh!" Leon cries out, pulling his rocky hand away from the wall; his right arm is encrusted with bits of warped flesh, bone, and stone from his fingers to his elbow.

"Leon, what's happening?" Almir asks.

"Ah—gaw, I don't know!" Leon shouts, for it's never been this bad before. Welic has no clue either; it's nothing he's ever seen.

"Alright, Lee, calm down man; take it easy. Just rest here," Welic says.

"Where are we?" Almir looks to Welic.

"Inside the temple," he answers, glancing at the stone walls lit by faint yellow overhead lamps and supported by wooden framework.

"But where are the people?" Almir asks, looking around.

"I feel human auras over there." Welic gestures with a nod eastward before noticing Lucy, who is in full bloom in her broken flowerpot on the ground. "Lee, we need to look for the malnar. Do you think you can stand?"

Leon shakes his head as he writhes; the trouble is slowly spreading up his arm.

"Alright, Almir, you're telepathic, right?" Welic asks. Almir nods in response.

"Good. I'm gonna take Lucy and look around. They've gotta be here somewhere. Call if you need anything," Welic says as he scoops up the little flower.

…

Seldin's beam cuts at a hard forty-five degrees through the air as he pours out the aether to fuel his counterattack. Simon stands frozen in the moment, calculating the trajectory as he looks skyward toward his airborne friends and the incoming pulsari strike.

"Dean!" Jasra shouts, her body shaking with fatigue.

"I know!" he shouts back.

"I don't… think I… can hold it any… long—ah!" she moans as the field slips, dropping them back into normal time just as Dean reaches his desired strength.

Looking up, Seldin's eyes widen. "Oh shit!" His heart races as the pulse of absent light narrowly skirts his beam. "No!" he shouts.

Right then, Dean catches a glimpse of the dark orb—an energy he knows to be elter—closing in. Swooping around Jasra, he creates a field of his own, warping the space between them and the ship. The gate can't open any sooner, for the danger is right there—the point of collision is imminent.

"Dean!" Jasra cries out as his body shields her from an unforeseeable future and she tucks her head before attempting to assist by bending time once again. Her heart pounds with fear, for she's never felt death so close.

The Guardian of Dimension, on the other hand, is confident in his strength and the speed of his defense. The portal opens with milliseconds to spare, showing a clear path to the bridge of the pulsari ship when out of nowhere, there's a flash of light and Seldin appears.

"Gotcha!" he exclaims, grabbing them in the heat of the moment as he begins to teleport.

"Sei, no!" Dean shouts at the top of his lungs, attempting to pull away as he and Jasra are dematerializing.

The rift implodes immediately, collapsing space in on itself and destabilizing the approaching mass of elter. The sky is ripped black as anti-aether cancels out the light.

In an instant, the three sky-bound guardians are thrust apart. The explosion tears Jasra and Dean from Seldin's grasp and casts them in opposite directions, forcing them to rematerialize out of sync as they hit the ground.

The whole ordeal is over in fractions of a second, with Simon unable to do more than watch the carnage as his friends and the pulsari are engulfed. The sound is louder than anything he or the Oqus have ever heard; it rattles his chest. Making haste, he dodges the confused fire of the Oqus to reach his friends.

Dean howls and flails wildly, flopping about on the ground like a fish as he thrashes, tears, and slashes at the ever-growing ulcers in his hide, in an effort to cut away the affected parts. The negative radiation sticks to the normal matter of his body, cutting through his scales and lacerating the tender flesh beneath as the elter exsanguinates his system of the very aether that drives it.

Jasra and Seldin's injuries are only marginally better with minimal burns, but elter reacts quickly and violently to aether, causing a cascading effect until one of the reagents is gone. The damage is small, but only by comparison. Most of the flesh on Seldin's back and sides has been eaten away while Jasra's left arm and thigh are riddled with quarter-sized burns an inch deep. As the elter/aether reaction ceases, the ulcers left behind poison them with radioactive decay that is almost as dangerous as the elter itself.

Simon does his best to aid his friends; believing Seldin can heal himself, he treats Jasra first. She's in tears; it hurts so much. The flesh of her arm and leg continues to break down while nanites rush into her system to combat any further disintegration and repair the damaged tissue. It's a battle in and of itself to be sure, for the tiny machines are just as vulnerable to the radiation as her cells are. Many of them crumble in the effort, and Simon's hands begin to tremble as he sees error messages flood his goggles.

Seldin pushes himself from the dirt. He can feel the drain of aether the injuries have caused. He gasps in agony—pain. He hasn't felt it in so long. Everything aches and burns with such intensity. Focusing his effort, he strains to control the fleeting energy that vanishes on contact with its counterpart. His injuries aren't healing, but it's not the damage to his body that stifles him now. Getting to his feet, he staggers before collapsing again, for there isn't enough muscle left in his back to keep him upright.

"Jasra! Dean!" Seldin calls out to his friends. He has to know if they're ok.

"I've got her!" He hears Simon shout back, and Dean growls.

"What of the pulsari—their ship?" Seldin tries to look—click, click—he hears all around him as several Oqus close in.

Dean isn't in any condition to deal in a cordial manner. He swings violently, knocking one of the Oqus to the ground. The others back away as he flails and growls. "Groaarrr!"

Taking no further chances, the Oqus ready their ion rifles and fire on him.

"Dean!" Seldin shouts, watching from the corners of his eyes. Focusing what energy he can, he uses telekinesis to hold himself upright as he moves his unstable body to intercept. Getting between Dean and an Oqu, he swats the rifle as it discharges past his left ear. The other Oqus turn and shoot him as well.

Thrusting his hands to cast a defensive barrier, Seldin consumes the telekinetic energy needed to stand. Feeling himself teeter rearward, he instinctively redirects the aether to steady himself again, inadvertently dropping his shield. Shots pelt his body, knocking him into Dean.

Powering up, Simon rushes in.

"We're not your enemy!" Seldin tries to reason, but the Oqus turn toward the Guardian of Technology, who dodges the first two shots coming his way. Taking the third to the shoulder, he rolls with the impact as his suit absorbs the force. Sweeping one of the little bastards off his feet, Simon then releases the storage of energy, causing a shockwave to knock the others back.

"I'm so fucking done of this shit!" Simon shouts. Kicking his system into overdrive, he reaches out left then right—grabbing two of the Oqu tanks. His miraculous mind delves into their circuitry. Everything slows down for him in this state of heightened awareness as he works that super brain of his to unlock the secrets of their technology.

Vsshoom, vsshoom! The engines kick on and the vehicles take readied positions. Jumping out for dear life, the Oqu drivers scurry to their weird feet before aiming their rifles at Simon.

This isn't what Seldin wanted; they're supposed to be helping these people, not combating them. He has to do something, but his pain is high, his energy is low, and his body is too far gone.

The tank's weapons power on; the ion chambers begin to fill. It's a showdown between Simon and the Oqu warriors. Through his goggles, he rates his opponent's energy levels, calculating just how much is needed as he sets his sights. Each Oqu, or sprii as they're called, has an unfocused core of around 300 joules.

"Stop!" Seldin shouts, his arms held wide, dividing the two factions. He stumbles in the effort. "We're here to hel—"

Phrew, phrew, phrew! It's an ambush; beljusa squads attack from all sides. Having a full surround, they get the drop. The Oqus turn to fight, but several fall immediately from rifles that fire pulses of inverted light that disintegrate them on contact.

Simon strikes back and Seldin takes up one of the fallen Oqu rifles. Photonic based weapons or not, he hasn't a choice; he's too weak for anything else and there's no time for hesitation. He opens fire. It doesn't matter at this point if his attacks are like candy to them; he aims for obvious weak points: knees, groin, shoulders, face—anything to knock them off balance. If they're anything like what he remembers from Binax-Beta, there'll be a pulsari underneath.

"Where the hell did they come from?" Simon exclaims, flabbergasted, but then looks to the sky. The malnar ship is open, in full bloom, and dropping the spores along with the horde. Simon feels a loss of hope, for only one petal shows any sign of damage.

Responding quickly to these new enemies, Dean pushes Seldin out of the way before rolling to his good side. With his aether severely drained, he resorts to the physical, plunging a fist deep into a leafy body—going straight for the kill. Yet, the soft, tender thing he grabs is not the spore he was expecting.

The blue blood and pale face of the scary gray thing beneath the leaves, startles Dean. There's a ghastly shrill and he looks down at the still-beating heart in his clawed hand as the creature falls back. The thought of his next action sends him back to the days when he fought for the form of Gruba—the dragon of the forest—and he bites into the heart. The blood he tastes courses through him like a miracle elixir filling his mind with knowledge.

"Simon!" Dean shouts, getting the young guardian's attention before looking with a nod aimed beyond the sky. "There's a ship up there!"

Simon smiles, feeling the wonderful sensation of actual, physical technology, not like the malnar ship—which is composed of so much living material—but metal and circuits—things he can understand. As his mind reaches out for it, he opens himself, excited for what he'll find.

"Aaaaaaaaaahhh!" Jasra screams, and immediately, Simon, Seldin, and Dean turnabout.

"Oh, no!" Simon runs to her aid, delivering a jumping kick to the side of a pulsari's face and driving his heel through the reddish bulb of its floral headdress.

"Jasra!" Seldin attempts to run as well when a violet light-sucking blast blows away his right shoulder. "Gahh!" he drops, shielding his face as best he can from the explosion.

Jasra screams, her eyes breaking into tears at the sight of him being ripped apart like that. She rushes to him.

Simon's eyes lock to his fallen friend, and then to the pulsari standing a few feet behind, wielding a sleek-looking metallic weapon.

Dean turns, following Simon's line of sight to the alien just as another bullet-sized pulse of elter is fired. It flies through the air and slows to a creeping halt just inches before Dean's face. His heart literally skips a beat before he glances just off to his left, over his shoulder.

"I can't hold this forever, Dean," Jasra's voice trembles. "Get us the fuck out of here," she pleads tearfully while cradling Seldin—or what's left of him; the right side of his face is scorched, and his right shoulder is missing. The canyon left in his body exposes bone, blood, and organs she's never seen firsthand as they spill out. The very sight of it turns her stomach.

Dean nods, and for a moment, the air between them crackles and wisps before fizzling out. "I…" he stammers, feeling real fear, "…I can't, I can't get any power!" he exclaims.

"What?" Simon looks to him in fright before kneeling to help Seldin, whose energy is nearly gone; he can feel his friend slipping in and out of consciousness.

The pulsari soldiers, however, are relentless in their attack and continue firing into the distorted bubble of time with each shot stopping like the first.

"They have elter weapons; I should have warned you," Dean laments.

Jasra wishes she had the strength to go back just ten minutes, but her power is weak as well. Believing their only option is to flee, she then looks to them. "We have to get out of here now!" she exclaims.

Dean nods with a painful grimace, reverting to his human form while holding the charred hole in his side. "We can't travel like this; we'll need transport. Simon, can you get that ship?" he asks with a skyward gesture.

"I've got a better idea." The epiphany hits Simon as he reveals three dispersal spheres.

"What are you doing?" Dean asks as they lift from Simon's hand.

"I was going to use this on Sei when we were fighting in South America. If my calculations are right, you're not the only one who can fold space," he says. The spheres then form a triangular arc of energy among themselves as they orbit each other in a counterclockwise fashion.

"Simon, hurry, my power is slipping," Jasra pleads, feeling her grip loosening, and they all watch as the things caught in her temporal field slowly start to move.

"I've almost got it!" he shouts back; the energy among the spheres builds.

"Are you sure you can do this?" Dean asks while staring desperately at the pinnacle of the potential gate.

"To be honest, I haven't tested it yet!" Simon replies loudly, trying not to break his focus.

Elter bullets inch closer, closing around them like needles of an iron maiden with each approaching faster every second.

Dean grunts, darting over to help carry Seldin. "Simon, we're out of time!" he yells.

"I'm sorry!" Jasra cries as the field drops.

…

Outside the temple of Chavin, the military presence is growing, with soldiers pushing civilians to the outer rim of the compound. Several men take point, examining the mysterious stone wall that has sealed the entrance.

The first in line, Corporal Ronny Martin, casually places a hand to the rigid surface riddled with various imperfections as if it had sprouted from the ground.

"Whatcha got, Corporal?" asks Sergeant Norel Bascur.

Ronny looks his way before offering a reply. "It's solid." He then taps the butt of his rifle against it. "About a meter thick," he says.

Sergeant Bascur sucks his teeth. "Any way through?" he asks.

Ronny then looks to the man at his right, gesturing with a snap of his fingers. "A shaped charge will minimize the damage to the temple, but

I'm worried we've got civilians in there," he says as his subordinate steps up to prime the entrance.

Norel nods. "Do it," he says when a sudden loud chopping sound slices through the wind rolling in from the north, carrying a strong gust along with it. The men halt, turning with gaping mouths at the squad of Apache helicopters and the single spherical craft to the center of their formation.

"You've gotta be shitting me!" Ronny exclaims, watching as they land.

Meanwhile, inside the temple, Welic has stumbled upon a lower chamber with an entryway barred by a spiraling web of spine-covered vines, laced together as if to form a dilating door.

"Ahh! Awrgg!" Leon writhes in pain.

"It's ok, man. You'll be ok," Almir whispers to him. He's never seen his mentor—his best friend—in such a condition before. He's always been strong and fearless in his eyes, but Almir can hear his friend's panicked thoughts.

Leon's power is betraying him; the flow of aether is beyond his control. Each of his transitions depends on the output of his core and as the aether builds within, his body begins to morph. A rocky texture creeps up from his arms while the rest of him starts to heat up. He's burning inside.

"Gaww!" Leon screams, fighting against the change with every ounce of his willpower. His skin blackens like the crust of lava, which fractures, spilling the molten contents underneath.

Almir jumps back, for fear of being scorched alive. *"Come on, Welic, he's getting worse,"* he says telepathically.

"But I'm close, I can feel it," he replies with Lucy guiding his hand.

"Abort! Leon needs help!" Almir insists.

…

Whoosh—a portal opens into Simon's living room.

"Ugh!"

"Ahh!"

"Ooof!"

"Graurr!"

The four of them collide as they fall through—pew—pew—boom! Elter shots rain in, devastating the apartment.

"Close it!" Jasra shouts as a pulsari soldier reaches through.

Simon pushes her out of the way right as it fires. The blast knocks out the living room wall to the outside, shaking the building. Dean jumps up, his injured side buckles when he twists about and kicks the alien in the face.

Right then, Simon disconnects his link to the dispersal spheres. Another soldier lunges through just as the portal snaps shut, severing the creature at the torso, spilling its blue blood and innards everywhere.

It screams, flopping next to Seldin, who turns a half-conscious gaze before grabbing its back with his left—and only hand. Mustering what strength he can, he works his fingers into the flowery headgear and tugs.

"Help... me before... it regenerates!" he tries to shout.

The roots of the beljusa have already begun mapping out a new lower half of the wearer and its extremities.

Jasra jumps at the monster's gun hand while Simon, Dean, and Seldin grapple to free the scary looking gray thing from the foliage. The pulsari screeches then makes some sort of vocal utterance.

"What is that?" Simon asks.

"It's calling... the others," Seldin pants, understanding its language as fluently as his own.

The pulsari struggles and thrashes to break free. Its body is almost completely healed, but the beljusa's roots in its spine begin to tear as a result of the group's combined effort to remove the living suit.

"Schuree!" the creature howls as it squirms and fights back. Seldin's hand slips, dropping a section of the beljusa—giving it a chance to reattach. It's in that moment Jasra manages the gun from its hand and takes aim.

"Shoot it!" Simon yells, but she's afraid. What if she misses? What if the blast gets them too? She hesitates in the action.

"Shoot him, shoot him!" Simon commands once again. Frightened of her next move, Jasra closes her eyes and squeezes the trigger just as the monster breaks free of their grip. The pulse hits center mass and the pulsari is violently ripped apart, letting out a blood-curdling shrill.

Jasra has never killed before, not even in self-defense. She stares down at the charred mess she made while the action settles into the recesses of her mind. She drops to her knees, bawling.

"Hun?" Simon tries to comfort her. He moves the alien weapon to a safe place.

"I... d-didn't... want to," she mutters.

Seldin knows all too well how she feels, for he has never liked killing, either—and yet, it has become such a part of their lives.

"It was him or us," Simon says softly with a supportive arm around her shoulder.

Jasra nods; she understands, but that doesn't mean she has to like it.

"Simon... I need... your nanites," Seldin stammers while holding in the bulk of his organs. He can see in his mind's eye the poisonous elter coursing through and annihilating his aether.

Simon acts quickly. The tiny machines work their magic, going into both Seldin and Dean to eliminate the contaminated cells.

"It's a good thing I'm home," Simon notes, for the nanites he's losing can be resynthesized in his workroom.

"Ugh," huffs Seldin, getting a hand up from his best friend.

"You feel better?" Simon asks.

Seldin shakes his head. "My energy feels off," he answers with a glance to Dean, who appears equally lethargic as he gets to his feet.

"Simon." Dean gestures, redirecting his attention to the prying eyes of the neighbors peering through the gaping holes in the walls.

Simon turns about, before casting nanites to reconstruct the place. "It's... alright, I own the building—nothing to see here!" he shouts, and Dean takes a well-needed seat.

"What the hell was that back there?" Seldin questions the Guardian of Dimension.

"Elter," Dean answers while averting his eyes. "It's the inverse of aether—the two cancel each other out."

"You mean like antimatter?" Simon turns, and Dean shakes his head.

"The reaction is similar, but antimatter isn't harmful to us; however, it can be used to make unrefined quantities of elter," Dean replies.

"That must be what we found at Area 51," Simon looks to Seldin, and Dean nods knowingly.

"Dean, that's the second time you've held back important information, and it almost got us killed," Seldin scolds.

Dean stands immediately with an angry gesture. "Everything was fine until you pulled me from the sky!" he shouts.

Jasra shakes her head. "I don't get it!" she huffs, and they look to her. "How can that stuff hurt us so badly?"

Sighing, Dean retakes his seat as he tries to explain. "Every universe is made up of some form of energy. In ours, it's called aether; it vibrates at a certain frequency."

Seldin looks to him. "And elter vibrates at the exact opposite?" he asks.

"Right." Dean nods.

"But that doesn't—" Jasra begins.

"It does," Seldin interrupts, thinking upon it, "as we ascend, our essence becomes one with the universe—we become aether. The absence of it would mean—"

"The absence of life," Simon says with his mental gears turning.

Jasra seems confused. "But aren't we already made of aether?" she asks.

Simon shakes his head. "Look, we can discuss philosophy another time; right now, we have a planet to save. Sei, grab the rifle. Maybe we can use the new batch of nanites to formulate a counteragent," he says, heading toward his office.

The indicator light on the centrifuge and the icon flashing in his goggles alert him to the finished product. Picking up a vial, he swirls the solution while holding it to the light before placing it into the appropriate slot of the large isolation chamber.

"I'm gonna need you to operate the console. Do you remember how?" he asks. Seldin nods just as Simon opens the hatch.

"Ooohhh my God, Sei!" Simon and Seldin turnabout immediately, hearing Jasra's cry. The two of them dart out to the living room where she, Dean, Welic, and Almir are all crowding around Leon, who is lying on the floor. Dean and Welic are patting out the flames, which have ignited the carpet. The heat that radiates from Leon's lava-like form suddenly cools to a chilling body of ice, and then hardens to stone before falling into a cloud of vapor then back to fiery flame.

"He's out of control!" Welic shouts, projecting a field of energy to contain the heat.

"What's happening?" Seldin inquires, trying to get closer when Lucy scurries over to him, happy to be reunited.

"I don't know." Almir looks up at Seldin in panic. "We were tracking down the first of those flower things when it started," he says.

"Lee, Leon?" Simon moves in, peering through the energy field along with Seldin.

"He's unresponsive," Seldin says.

"Do you see anything?" Simon asks.

"His power is fluctuating rapidly. I can't make out any discernible pathways for the aether to flow—everything is jumbled," he answers.

"Can you heal him?" Simon asks. Seldin shakes his head, trying his best to shift Leon's energy back to a normal phase.

"I don't know what's causing it," Seldin states at a loss before shifting his gaze to Almir.

"Don't look at me, it's never been this bad before. I mean, you've seen it. Sometimes he loses control," Almir says.

Simon then extends a probe from his wrist, spraying nanites over Leon. The tiny bots surround him while analyzing the constant changes in energy before entering his body. Once inside, they disperse, with each robot penetrating a single cell.

"His mitochondria are supercharged with aether, but I can't—"

Suddenly, Leon's body shifts into flames, his internal temperature quickly rises to well over three thousand degrees Fahrenheit, melting the nanites.

"Gah!" Simon backs away.

"Don't worry, I've got him," Welic says, containing the intense heat within an energy field.

"Dean, have you ever seen anything like this before?" Seldin asks, but Dean hesitates.

"Don't hold out on us again," Simon says.

Dean sighs, looking into their eyes. "Remember what I said about two kings?"

Simon turns around immediately to look back at Leon. "Shit, you mean… there's another Guardian of Earth—are you sure?" he asks.

"But I thought Leon was the Guardian of Earth," Jasra says.

"There can't be two," Seldin follows up, remembering Dean's words to him.

"Madeline must still be alive," Dean comments, "though I've never seen a reaction like this before."

"How do we stop it?" Seldin asks.

Dean shakes his head. "You can't, he's reached the level of ascension. Once it happens, he'll die—absorbed by the stronger guardian," he answers.

Simon then slaps Seldin's arm. "Come on," he says, rushing to his lab.

"Where are you going?" He follows.

"I need you to run the console," Simon says, heading toward the chamber.

Seldin grabs his arm. "Simon, wait! You said this new batch will take away your emotions. Are you sure you want that?"

"A small price to pay." Simon opens the chamber door. "I mean, look at yourself: your emotions are clouding your judgement right now when we could be saving Leon. Version four will not only make me more powerful, but I'll never hesitate again," he says, stepping into the chamber.

There's a suctioning seal as the unit pressurizes, and Seldin stares through the glass at him. As much as he cares for Leon, he worries for what Simon is willing to lose. Extending a hesitant finger, Seldin presses the start button.

The huge generator kicks on. Voom, voom, voom, sounds the coils powering up. As the old nanites rush out, the new nanites flood in. Simon begins to choke and gag; his body is not liking the transition. He goes from gray to pink to gray again as the new bots start to integrate.

Simon's eyes widen; it's like a high. Suddenly his mind starts to race with the rapidness of his own beating heart. The sound of the machine working around him becomes muffled as his brain starts to process information at a rate so high and so fast that everything around him feels like it's standing still. Even the sound that hits him takes its time. He can feel his own sense of excitement drawing away as the little devices interface with the systems that control emotion, granting him the wish he so desires. His face grows plain and expressionless. Things are becoming clear, as if he were hovering above a sea of answers just flowing beneath his feet.

Bringing a hand up before his eyes, Simon watches as his cells begin to flake off. His motion is so fast it's like a blur to Seldin, who perceives his friend as vibrating.

"Something's wrong," Seldin says, seeing Simon's atoms trail away like dust. "Simon!" he shouts, thrusting a fist against the glass—cracking it—before frantically hitting the abort button.

"Warning, nanite infusion failure!" a computerized voice exclaims in repetition.

Seldin grabs the handle, but the chamber is locked; the decontamination cycle has to run first. The process can't be halted, can't be stopped. That was the contingency Simon had put in place, but

Seldin has to do something; he strikes the glass again, trying to free his friend.

Without emotion to govern him, Simon has no fear, even now. With his mind syncing up with the devices all around him, knowledge pours in abundance, and he knows then what he must do. Shaking his head, he holds out a hand for his friend to stop, lest he break down the chamber door and expose the others to his creation.

"Simon!" Seldin's voice seems to warp, distorted by Simon's mental speed.

Seldin's heart breaks in the moment; he can't let this happen. He's not willing to lose his best friend. Cupping his hands together, he draws in as much aether as he can with Lucy rushing in to envelop him. His palms heat up as he focuses.

"Hanih spiiihaaa!" Seldin blasts the door. The heat of his beam melts the steel to the ground, but it's too late. Simon is already gone.

"No, no, no, no—Tiiillllmmaaan!" Seldin shouts his lungs out, bellowing in agony at the base of the chamber. The space inside is empty. There is nothing left. He can't even feel a trace of him now.

The tiled floor cracks at the force of Seldin's angered strikes, which come one after another until the pain he feels can no longer be contained. He trembles. The energy emanating from him warps the air in the room as the building rattles from his attempts to latch onto every strand of energy within his range.

Hearing their friend's howls, Jasra and Dean run to the workroom. Jasra's heart sinks as her eyes fall to the empty chamber and Seldin there on the floor before the melted door. She too then cries out at the tremendous loss.

Dean, however, sees no time to mourn. He can feel Seldin's core rising rapidly—two-fold, approaching three. "Seldin stop!" he shouts. The building starts to shake.

Grabbing Jasra, Dean quickly pulls her out of the room, enveloping her and the others in a shield of energy to protect them from the dangers of Seldin's over-powered core.

'Damn it...' his mind races in panic—he should have warned them.

Welic looks up at Dean, catching the terrified look in his eyes; this is what he feared—it's just like before. The young guardian's core is growing denser by the second.

"We need to stop him!" he shouts to Dean.

Despite her pain, Jasra's tearful eyes open to Welic's plea before peering into the room of blinding white light. With her forward sight showing the consequences of inaction, she makes her next move.

"What are you doing?" Dean latches onto her arm, yet she tugs away against his strength even with the force of Seldin's energy ahead of her pushing back.

"Sei!" she calls out through the squall of his madness. Ever-so careful with her approach, Jasra cautiously watches each failing outcome of Seldin's furious though fruitless attempts to reconstruct his best friend from energy that no longer exists.

Slowing time to weather the storm, she eases closer, bringing her arms around him in a gentle embrace. And as he feels her touch with the shift in time realigning to a moment of stability, the rage that fuels him begins to temper.

At once, he begins to feel. His emotions no longer shrouded by anger, he sobs, turning his face to her chest just as Lucy unveils so they might weep together.

Suddenly there's a pop of light as the Guardian of Death appears.

"Where were you? What took you so long?" Seldin bellows heavily while wiping his face.

"On the other side of the universe, trying to assess the damage she did," he answers, pointing rudely to Jasra.

"Simon is dead. Tell me you can—" Seldin begins before being cut off.

"Sei…" Tillman lowers himself, "…this won't be easy for you to hear, but it is the truth: there is no heaven—no mystical place to retrieve a soul. When the spirit cannot hold its form, it dissolves. To reconstruct it from nothing…" His eyes fall to Seldin's attempts—the disfigured heaps of biomatter in the chamber. "…would be an impossible task."

"But I have to try," Seldin mutters.

"Damn it, Sei, we're not gods. Even if you could manage, it would be a mere imitation," he says and Seldin looks away, not wanting to listen.

"Jasra." Seldin looks to her, desperately. "How far can you go back?"

"No!" Tillman shouts. "How many times must I say it? Do not tamper with the timeline. What's done is done! Trying to bring him back will only make things worse for us!"

"Worse?" Jasra's voice quivers just as Seldin rises to his feet.

"Tillman, I'm getting really sick of you telling us what we can and can't do!" he yells.

The Guardian of Death asserts himself. "Everyone feels the changes she makes, including Khyrah!" he exclaims. They all look to him before hearing the voice of Welic from the hall.

"Hey guys, he's getting worse!" he yells.

Without hesitation, Seldin runs out then kneels beside Leon.

"We've gotta figure out something fast," Welic says just as the others catch up.

Tillman's eyes fall to Leon, recognizing his condition immediately. "So, Madeline is still alive," he comments with eyes to Dean, who nods.

"There's gotta be something we can do," Almir says.

"Not as long as there are two guardians fighting for the same position," Tillman says, and his words resonate in Seldin's mind.

Moving closer to Leon, Seldin scans his friend, waiting for his energy to shift to a less hostile state. "Welic, get ready to drop the field," he says.

"What are you going to do?" Almir asks.

"I'm going to push his core out of alignment," Seldin replies.

"He'll lose his connection to the aether," Tillman states.

"That'll make him mortal," Dean adds.

"I know." Seldin sighs.

Almir grabs Seldin's wrist. "You can't—it took us years to get here," he states.

"What would you have me do? If we leave him like this, he dies. At least this way…" he says, looking amongst his friends, "…he has a chance at life."

Conceding, Almir lowers his eyes before backing away.

Welic then looks to Seldin. "Ready when you are," he says.

Seldin nods. "On my count: three… two… one." And on that mark, Leon transitions from molten rock to a frozen form. Welic drops the barrier, releasing a chilling breeze that hits everybody just as Seldin reaches in. Placing a palm at Leon's center, he takes hold of the energetic mass just below the navel. In his mind's eye, he can see the unsteady flow of his friend's core, and as he pushes aether against the current, Leon lets out a hellish cry before dropping limp with his body returning to a state of normalcy.

"Bravo," Tillman whispers out of earshot.

Taking to his feet, Seldin looks to Death. "Tillman, where is Madeline?" he demands but Dean interjects.

"Nobody's seen her since—"

"Since Khyrah?" Seldin questions, looking to Tillman, Dean, and then to Welic, who nods.

"She went into hiding. Most of us did," Welic says, lowering his eyes.

"Hiding, seriously? Madeline has been hiding for four hundred years and Leon is dying on the floor? She's supposed to be the Guardian of Earth—where the hell is she?" Seldin shouts, then Jasra cautiously raises a hand.

"Who's Khyrah?" she asks.

"Some demigod they're all afraid of," Seldin snaps with a gesture toward them.

"You should be too," Dean says heatedly.

"Even if I were, I can't imagine showing such cowardice. Madeline doesn't deserve to be a guardian," Seldin says before looking to Leon and then to Welic.

"Welic," Seldin says softly, "take Leon home. His stepdad is an asshole, but he should be safe there. Don't forget that we still need to find the missing malnar. The rest of us will work out a plan for Oqu IX."

Chapter 29

"Getting Back Up"

Out on the rear balcony of the apartment, Seldin stares without focus; his mind is filled with visions of youthful play, moments of fondness, and memories of their worst fights. The tragedy of Simon's death is far more than any of them ever expected to bear. With Tillman gone, leaving them to their own devices, they mourn. Jasra tearfully cradles her knees on the couch while Dean sulks with a blank expression, seated at the kitchen table. It almost seems unreal.

Seldin sighs despite his stoic expression before wiping away a tear. "What could I have done differently?" he exhales, placing his forehead to the railing when the rolling sound of the glass door behind him steals his attention with a glance over his left shoulder to Jasra as she steps out.

"Almir left with Welic," she remarks; her voice is sad and dry from over-crying.

Nodding, Seldin then looks out over the balcony while resting his chin on the rail in his slumped posture. "I thought he might."

"Thinking about Simon?" she asks the obvious question.

"Tillman said Simon wasn't ready to ascend; his soul simply couldn't exist outside the body." He sighs. "And now... there's Leon."

"There's nothing else you could have done," Jasra says with a comforting hand to his shoulder.

"But I am the Guardian of Life, I should have done more," he rebuts painfully.

Shaking her head, Jasra disagrees. "No, I should have gone back in time—there are other possibilities—I could, maybe I still can," she says before choking up, and Seldin turns to hold her as she cries.

"You can't. You heard Tillm—"

"I don't care! I don't care! Why can we do these things yet not change the world? It's not fair!" she drops down, pulling him to his knees on the balcony floor with her.

Gently drying her tears with a caress of his hand, Seldin then holds her close. "You're right, it's not fair. I want more than anything for you to go back, believe me. But if there's any truth to what they've said then we can't risk it," he says.

"I saw you," she says abruptly with a gaze into his eyes.

"What?" Seldin responds with a confused expression as Jasra speaks.

"The future; it was in a dream while you were away. Simon wouldn't believe me but the pulsari came and you were so different…" Her voice trails off.

"Different how?" Seldin asks but Jasra shakes her head.

"I forgive you," is all she says just before Dean walks out.

"For wha—" he tries to ask, confused.

"I just received word from Tillman. Oqu IX… the… there's nothing left," he states sorrowfully.

…

"C'mon, Chad! C'mon, you got him!" Ryan chants, rooting for his younger stepson.

"Come on, Chad!" his mother joins in.

Chad dives for it, rolling under Neil's swing of a staff before coming around and driving the heel of his crouching-kick into the back of Neil's knee, causing him to fall back onto the uneven pavers.

"C'mon, Neil!" Elma shouts.

Kipping up from the ground, Neil makes a circular scooping gesture with his right hand, while chanting before pushing a blast of air forward, knocking Chad on his backside.

"Bah, Chad, use what I taught you!" his stepfather shouts.

Slamming an angered fist to the dirt, Chad then aims a watchful eye to Neil's position, while internally chanting his mantra. He then takes to his feet, dropping into a horse stance as he gestures, drawing runic symbols through the air. The wind picks up, blowing around him as the power circulates. Neil too, takes to the action, conjuring his own magic.

The sounds of the drums around them, played by Sarah and Elma, fill the backyard with a rhythmic cadence to match the tempo of their motions as Chad and Neil draw from the ancient powers around them.

Ryan rests back in his lawn chair watching the evening spectacle before passing his rather fragrant cigarette to Sarah. She puffs as she plays—bonk—buda—bonk.

"See, this is how it should be, family together with friends. Why can't your other son be more like his brother?" he asks of his girlfriend, who just shrugs, taking another drag when suddenly, a flicker of light takes form between the combatants.

The unexpected arrival of the stranger and his friends cause everyone to take a defensive posture. Welic takes a knee, placing his fallen comrade on the ground.

"Leon!" Sarah exclaims, rushing over to him. Chad follows suit. Ryan steps forward hesitantly, for the newcomer is unfamiliar, though his eyes catch Almir.

"Who is this?" Ryan asks, he asks him.

"The name's Welic, I am the Guardian of Vice," he says before telekinetically stealing the joint from Ryan.

"Hey!" Ryan shouts.

Welic takes in a deep puff. "Not bad." He exhales, while casually turning and looking up and down the backyard training area, scanning the auras of the sorcerers. "So, you're all worshipers of Khyrah, huh?" he says with a keen smile.

"Worshipers?" Sarah makes a face.

Welic takes another drag. "Interesting." He thinks aloud. "Is it the whole planet?" He asks, his mental gears turn as he hands the joint to her.

"Um…" Sarah looks confused.

Welic then gestures to Almir. "I presume you already know the Guardian of the Mind?"

Neil looks to Welic before shifting his gaze amongst his friends. "Guardians? Real guardians?" he questions the very notion. "You've gotta be kidding."

"I thought the priestess—" Elma utters before Ryan interjects.

"She said there were a few left, but I never thought I'd see one in the flesh."

"Three, actually," Welic states, pointing between himself, Almir, and Leon when Ryan quickly rebuts.

"Are you saying that Leon is a guardian?" he asks in a questioning tone.

"The Guardian of Earth—or… he was. His power was taken," Welic replies.

Ryan looks down at Leon. He never would have guessed the boy could be capable of such a title. It's hard for him to believe.

"By who?" Sarah asks.

"Seldin, he—" Almir starts to say.

Ryan steps in immediately. "Are you telling me that Sei guy did this?" he spouts angrily before looking to Sarah. "I told you that guy was a bad influence!" he says.

"You don't understand. Sei is the Guardian of Life, and his actions saved your son," Welic states.

"Oh, that's horse shit!" Ryan exclaims.

"It's true," Almir interjects, "Leon ascended to replace the former Guardian of Earth, but she's still alive."

"Since only one can exist, Leon was forced into an early retirement. It's a shame, too. We could really use him; we've already lost one today, and no one has seen the other in centuries. I trust we can leave Lee here with you? Without his connection to the aether, he can't help us," Welic says.

There's a subtle groan as Leon's eyes open. Everyone moves closer.

"Ugh…" he grunts, trying to sit up, getting a hand from his mom and brother. Things feel different, he realizes as he looks himself over. That internal flow he's so used to is missing. "What happened?"

…

Seldin's breath is heavy as he stands, turning toward the balcony. His eyes, though glassy, drift aimlessly while his hands rest on the rail with an ever-firming grip.

'*All those lives,*' his mind fills, drawing no comfort from Jasra's hand to his back. "Take me there," he says in a soft dry voice.

"Sei…" Jasra tries.

"To what gain?" Dean asks.

Seldin then turns to face him, looking past Jasra. "I said, take me there," he reaffirms.

Dean's eyes lower in a sort of nod before a whirling vortex of violet light emerges, and without hesitation or even a word, Seldin steps through.

Despite his experience on the suka home world, his heart sinks at the very sight, yet nothing could have prepared Jasra, who immediately covers her sobs just as her knees hit the desolate land. Dean, however, is no stranger to this level of destruction. His heart hardened from centuries of the like, he can only take it in.

The high sodium landscapes have been reduced to silica dust. Where once stood vibrant roads and beautiful columns of iridescent magnificence, now lay barren, beige wastelands. Just like Binax-Beta, there is no evidence—no remnant of even the smallest form of life.

"In the wrong hands, the malnar are truly devastating," Seldin lets out, feeling the air around him rapidly cool from the lack of atmosphere.

Dean nods. "Yes."

"The pulsari must be stopped before—"

"Sei—" Dean attempts.

"According to the suka, the next planet should be—" Seldin talks over him.

"Seldin! The pulsari are not hitting just one planet—do you think this is the only world that fell today? They have fleets stretched halfway across the galaxy."

"Are you saying we should give up?" Seldin looks to him.

"What I'm saying is, you need a better strategy if you want to stop them all," Dean replies.

"He's right, Sei," Jasra speaks up, "and we need to move fast. I fear our encounter here has shortened our timeline."

"Are you certain?" Dean looks to her with an odd sense of concern.

"At best, we have a few months," she responds with a hand to her temple.

"Months?" Dean questions.

"You can see that far out?" Seldin asks.

Jasra shakes her head. "Only fragments, but the pieces are much clearer," she says.

Dean rubs his face then steps away. "How far can you see?" he asks curiously.

"Clearly? Mmm…" She looks ahead, gauging her range. "A, uh, about a day," she replies, her eyes shifting from side to side as she watches the future unfold.

"Anything useful?" Seldin asks.

"Yeah, we'll have the most success there." Jasra points northward beyond the sky. "I… I don't know what it's called." She pauses.

"Aphéd!" she and Dean then say in unison before looking at each other.

"We can't hold back," she adds.

Seldin closes his eyes as he faces in that direction. A sense of pressure and warmth flood in. "I can feel them," he says, "two ships. One's entering the planet now."

"Alright." Dean faces his young friends. "Aphéd is home to the veilon, and it has a very dense atmosphere for a habitable world. It's mostly methane and a few other hydrocarbons, with very little oxygen. Even so, you need to be careful using beams. We don't want to accidentally ignite the air," he informs them.

Chapter 30

"The Battle of Aphéd"

It's midday on the veilon planet known as Aphéd. The amber glow of their yellow sun diffuses in the sky as the light scatters through the dense atmosphere. The relatively weak gravity and thick air grants the veilon the ability to swim like little black squids gliding effortlessly just a few feet off the ground. A race of farmers, the veilon grow eed grass—a brown seaweed-like plant favored by all—and raise sbesu—a strong working animal similar to a bison in both size and stature with a single hinged limb centered in its underbelly as a means of locomotion.

As the natives carry on with their day, the sky becomes alive with a loud clatter and tremendous rolling clouds that spill over like an avalanche cascading down a mountain. All veilon in the area stop, captivated by the spectacle. Hardly past the Bronze Age, many of them look on in fear, unable to explain the rapid change in the weather while others flee in search of shelter from the cigar-shaped object emerging.

A sudden electrical arc of whirling purple light erupts a few meters behind a stunned veilon, who turns a cautious gaze to the three foreign figures stepping out. Their movements appear effortless as they march through the grassy plain despite the thick air and low gravity.

The big one looks ferocious to the farmer—a dark four-legged beast with iridescent scales, while the other two stand upright and are much smaller by comparison. They have pale skin, something the veilon are not used to, and bizarre, thin tendrils from their scalps: one's is long and red, with the other's being short and brown. That one shows its teeth before making a strange gesture from stubby digits on its forelimb.

Seldin's smile fades as he lowers his peace sign; his eyes track forward toward the rumbling sound ahead.

"It's already starting," Dean says, pointing skyward as the ship unfolds and flowers out.

"This planet's atmosphere blocks most of the sun; it should give us an advantage. Now remember, we're up against malnar," Seldin says.

"Right, physical attacks only," Jasra nods.

"Or energy without light," Dean adds.

"And don't let them touch you," Seldin says just as the spores start to snow over the land and sap the life from Aphéd. The tan grass withers then regrows in a near instant, replaced by something new, while veilon-shaped boni rise from the fallen natives.

"Jasra," Seldin begins, "keep me updated on the future, and I'll pass it to Dean. You're our ticket to victory," he says while casually brushing off the spores he crushes.

The clustered mind of the pulsari within the heart of the destroyer ship pull focus, transmitting to the mothership the presence of the guardians. Right then and without hesitation, thirty beljusa-clad pulsari soldiers land forcefully, surrounding them with elter rifles in hand.

"Looks like they're not holding back," Dean comments.

Seldin shakes his head. "And neither will we—oh, and Jasra, one more thing." He looks to her, "Fuck Tillman."

The pulsari troops open fire, laying down a barrage of aether-canceling pulses from every angle, but Jasra is ready. Keeping her mind in the here and now, she stops time immediately before reversing each blast back to its caster. The explosions are devastating—disintegrating the first line instantly.

Seldin and Dean spread out, each taking half of the second line, with Jasra maintaining control from the center. Her temporal field gives them ample time to react to the incoming firepower.

The foreknowledge that trickles down from Jasra to Seldin to Dean is invaluable. Dean evades by shifting planes while twisting space to return fire. Seldin, on the other hand, weaves casually between the bolts of elter that creep by—a little too closely at times.

In spite of the obvious advantages the Guardian of Time provides, this shared view is awkward, with layers of reality superimposed upon another. It isn't the easiest thing to work with, Seldin discovers when he strafes, turning face-first into a blast of elter—pap—boom!

"Nnnoooo!" Jasra screams and reaches outward with both hands as if to grab the very fabric of time, she pulls. Stepping backward through the seconds, the event unwinds.

Seldin's eyes widen with him narrowly slipping past the elter as time moves forward once again. He then releases a spread of kinetic force to knock down half the wave on his side. For the other, he leaps, landing behind a soldier before punching through the beljusa it wears, ripping out the stem. Without their bio-suits, he knows the pulsari can't regenerate, and with that thought in mind, he teleports from one to the next, using the concussive force of his reintegration to his advantage. To his enemies, it seems instant.

Dean snaps his gaze to Jasra, feeling the unexpected rush of déjá vu. "What did you just do?" he beckons.

"Not on my watch, Dean," she states boldly, then points to redirect his attention to the incoming shots.

"Whoa!" He dodges with a look across the field to the soldier making a rude gesture toward him and bearing a scarred chest. Dean then smiles. "I remember you," he says.

The pulsari warrior retakes his aim but the distance between them is meaningless to the Guardian of Dimension, whose large, black dragon fist appears as if from an acme hole with a bone-crushing force that peels the floral hood from its face. The alien never saw it coming. Dean then latches onto its head and pulls it through.

...

"Yes, Mr. President, two of the specimens have been secured, but we're having some trouble with the big one," says Colonel Mitchel over his radio as he surveys the area. A razed temple and downed spheres marred with scorched cutaways from high energy blasts show his apparent level of success while the rat-tat-tat of machine-gun fire rocks Lima, Peru's evening sky.

Boom! Bang! Pew! The few remaining MECHs fire at the rather large and disgruntled beljusa. Once discovered at the heart of the temple, it made quick work of the soldiers that got near, consuming their life and releasing spores. However, their weaker human shapes proved less useful in an open battle than the drone's default forms.

Cepella—butterfly-shaped spore drones with a two-meter wingspan, swoop over the battlefield, raining beams from the sky. Soldiers duck and dive with some returning fire, but the bullets that tear through their leaves cause only negligible damage by comparison.

"Ehherrr—ahherr!" screeches the beljusa as the MECHs march forward to pelt her leafy hide, but she doesn't stumble. With the cresting sun at her back, she returns fire—phrewm! The beam melts through one of the hulls as boni latch onto the other machines with their viny tendrils before blasting them as well.

Making his way to the half-opened sphere, Mitchel checks the pilot's pulse. "Deakins?" He tries to rouse him with no success. Unhooking him from the cockpit, the colonel lifts him out and then turns around.

"Ahhh!" Mitchel screams at the giant rose rushing toward him with vines thrashing and whipping around. Out of nowhere, there's a faint sparkle of light.

"I got it!" Almir shouts, taking the malnar's mind. She shrills in protest, backing and slinking away.

The sudden appearance of the guardians, however, causes Colonel Mitchel to draw his sidearm. "You," he points to Welic, "were the one on Mars," he says.

Welic smiles. "Wow, you must have seen that on TV. Good memory. Say," he eases closer, "you wouldn't happen to have a beverage, would ya?" he asks, taking one final sip from his can of Monster before tipping it over in his hand and shaking it with a disappointed look on his face.

Mitchel stares at him bewildered with a subtle shake of his head.

…

"Piece of cake," Dean mutters at the apparent ease of their success and Seldin nods.

"It's the atmosphere; the malnar can't get enough sun to match us. Even the veilon clones are struggling. Look." He casually grabs a fluttery cepella, which hardly puts up a fight as he reaches for its soft, fragile spore. It squeals then shrivels to a viny brown pulp.

Dean then taps Seldin on the shoulder as he gestures with his chin upward. "Hey, they're making a break for it," he says and Seldin's eyes follow his friend's line of sight. The destroyer is closing up, retaking its cigar-shaped form as it heads toward the mothership high in orbit.

"No, they're not," he replies. Peeling off the top of his gi, he centers himself under the craft. Knowing he can't let them escape, the Guardian of Life opens his core, drawing in the surrounding aether. The air around him billows off into vapors as his body heats up and he grunts, feeling the strain of internal pressure building within his meridians. Though the increase pads his physique, gouges and gashes soon sprout as his meridians tear, rupturing as he redlines his core.

"Sei!" Dean shouts with wide eyes, feeling the young guardian's power spike into dangerous territory—well past that threefold limit.

"Get ready, Dean," he says, thrusting his hands to the sky while anchoring his energy into the planet beneath his feet. Seldin can feel the mass of the ship tugging against him as he telekinetically latches on with all his might, and with one fell swoop, he pulls hard, slamming his hands to the dirt. Without warning, the pulsari aboard the destroyer meet the ceiling as the vessel rushes toward the surface of Aphéd.

On that cue, Dean powers up, breaking into a ferocious roar while forming a rift overhead. Sparks fly with purple lightning arcing across the void that opens within the heart of the mothership in orbit above.

Those at the helm scatter in panic, but there's nowhere to flee from the impending collision. The elongated destroyer falls through the portal, smashing into the mothership with a brilliant explosion silenced by the vacuum of space.

With the vortex sealed, the sky becomes alive as the light from the blast bombards the thick atmosphere like a huge projector screen.

Exhausted from overloading, Seldin drops down, panting heavily.

Dean morphs back to his human form then looks over his young friend's tattered body; his condition reminds him of centuries ago. "What the hell were you thinking?" he scolds.

Seldin glances up at him, still catching his breath. "I got the job done," he remarks.

"At the cost of us all?" Dean questions angrily. "Look at yourself," he gestures, "had your core ruptured, you'd have taken us with you. You don't wield more power than the body can handle—ever!"

Their argument is cut short, however, for in Seldin's weakened state, he loses the link to Jasra, who runs up to them. Her eyes shift from side to side as she surveys the land.

"Hey, guys…" The active malnar draw her concern. "We're not done," she says.

"Yeah, what?" Seldin looks to her with confusion, as does Dean.

"But we took out both ships," Dean says.

"Ah, shit!" Seldin's gaze snaps to the sky. Immediately the three of them dive in all directions as an enormous, thorny tendril slams into the ground between them. As soon as it hits, another one sweeps horizontally—knocking down anything standing.

Suddenly an angry shrill enters Seldin's mind as images of a horrifying creature fills his vision. It's larger than a beljusa and shaped like an amoeba with a round floral body set in the middle of its many vines.

As Dean pushes himself from the dirt, he sees it—a malnar the size of a building meshed with bits of mechanical debris, which falls away from its leafy flesh as it moves about.

"Sei, get up!" he rushes over, ducking back and sliding on his knees as another large vine cuts across at their height. He shifts, phasing between dimensions. Arriving at Seldin's location, he grabs him and then moves to Jasra, who is working to slow the creature, for it's not only big, it's fast.

"What the hell is it?" she asks.

Seldin shrugs, having no idea. "Whatever it is, it was part of their ship. I've never seen one like that. Its power is incredible, and we just gave it a boost," he states, parrying another swipe.

"It's too big, I can't envelop it," Jasra complains, only able to restrain the limbs caught in her field.

"Well, it can't keep this up forever—not with all that cloud cover. So, let's give it hell," Seldin says.

"I'll take the left!" Dean roars, morphing mid-step and charging onward with a thrust of his enormous black wings.

Seldin then veers right, but his little stunt from earlier has taken a toll. It feels like he's run a marathon. His draw on the aether is weak and his wounds are slow to close—swoosh!

"Ugh!" he takes a direct hit across the chest as the creature flings him into the air. Tumbling and twirling as he rushes upward, he brings his mind into focus, working to stabilize his rapid ascent. However, the energy he pushes out does little to affect his velocity and soon the orange-beige skyline fades to starry black.

Back on the surface of Aphéd, Jasra catches another tendril in her temporal web as she circles around in the opposite direction of Dean's motion.

"Jasra, keep your distance!" he orders before taking a hit, himself. The swipe of the vine launches him rearward. Much like Seldin, Dean finds it difficult to decelerate even with his wings flared open, but he has a plan.

Opening a portal, Dean slams, shoulder-ready, into the body of the beast—rocking it just a bit on impact. Immediately, he pushes off, dodging around its whipping vines to fly underneath the monster, looking for a soft spot. Dean soon realizes—that's not a belly.

"Oh shit!" he lets out as a thorny mouth chomps down, taking all of him in one bite. "Raargh—" his roaring scream cuts off with the crunch of its powerful jaws.

Jasra screams. "No! Give... him... back!" she howls; the moment ceases to a halt as she steps the seconds back, but as the past reshapes to the present, it eats him again. And then again. Until finally he portals out of the way.

Coming about, he swings an arm outward to deflect a vine when another catches him off guard with a punch clean through his chest—spearing him to the ground.

"Gruaarh!" Dean roars, coughing up blood. He grabs onto the vine with his large, black dragon hands, but he can't budge it. The malnar begins draining his energy. He grows weak, shifting back to his human form. Not having the energy to transform again, he goes for broke, biting into the vine.

The malnar, however, is not having it, and soon, the Guardian of Dimension feels faint as his life force is drawn out of him. His vision begins to fade, his grip loosens. Then as his hands drop to his side, the fabric of time unwinds again.

The moment backs up to just before the second strike, which flies toward Dean just as he opens a rift, allowing the creature to punch itself in the mouth. Immediately, he closes the gate, severing its limb. There's a ferocious howl as the monster rears back, flinging its nub and spraying chlorophyll everywhere.

Angered, it rallies the other malnar, calling upon the shifty boni and fluttery cepella to come to its aid, but Dean makes swift work of those that get caught in Jasra's outer radius.

Suddenly, a soaring sound from above comes rocketing through the sky. Within an instant, the beast hits the ground as Seldin makes his entrance—landing full tilt on its back.

"Yeah!" Dean cheers, albeit prematurely, for the monster wastes no time bucking the Guardian of Life as it gets back up.

Right then, the unexpected happens as a mob of dark squid-like figures swim slowly through the thick gaseous air, toting a variety of farming tools. Though primitive by Earth's standards, the veilon's bronze-like equipment may just prove sharp enough. Taking flanking positions, they form up, surrounding the enormous plant-creature.

"Heh." Seldin pauses, unable to believe it. Even Dean and Jasra turn and watch as they gather around. Their bravery is refreshing, and it stirs something within the guardians' spirit.

"Let's not disappoint," Seldin says to his friends before gathering aether, accelerating his molecules.

Dean readies as well, pooling energy into the palm of his hand, forming a tear in space while Jasra tightens her temporal grip on the malnar's trapped limbs.

In a brilliant flash, Seldin appears with a thud—ramming against the side of the creature as he materializes. On that mark, Dean casts the rift ahead of the monster. As it stumbles toward the vortex, the Guardian of Dimension prepares to seal it. Closing his fist, the portal cinches around the body of the beast, but unexpectedly, its trapped legs reach their length, snagging against the time field— resulting in only a small portion of its main body being cleaved.

There's a deafening screech from the creature as it staggers, flailing around. The veilon take that opportunity to attack but the malnar is desperate for survival. Rooting into the ground, it pulls energy from the planet into its upside-down bell, inverting the aether. There's an eerie shift in the air as the guardians take notice.

Jasra can feel it already. "Ugh!" She grabs her head, losing her grasp of time.

"No..." Dean manages to get out just as Seldin yells. "Move!"

Kaboom! An arc of darkness showers the landscape as the mass of elter explodes. A near miss, though close enough.

As the dust clears, Seldin opens his eyes, shifting his gaze across the land to Dean, who appears to be dazed and in his human form but alright. Seldin then looks to Jasra. Her lack of movement and weakened aura fuels his resolve. Getting up—clink! His hand brushes something solid. It's an elter rifle in the hand of a dead pulsari. Immediately, he grabs it, turning about.

"Dean, check her!" He points to their fallen friend before opening fire on the malnar.

The Guardian of Dimension does as instructed; phasing over to Jasra's location, he lifts her. "She's alive!" he shouts, though he can't say the same for some of the others. Bits and pieces of veilon are everywhere.

The creature roars, shimmying, swaying, and dodging frantically—not liking the taste of anti-aether any more than they do.

"Shhhrrrlll!" it screams from the pulses that strike its limbs. The decay happens fast, creeping up the infected vines like a virus. Without hesitation, the malnar swipes at its own leafy flesh, severing the irradiated parts to stop the destruction before taking to the air.

"Dean, get her off the battlefield!" Seldin shouts, going after it. Knowing there isn't much time left before it bathes in the sun, he powers up, pouring his energy into the capacitance chamber of the rifle. Fearing there are only seconds left, he pushes himself to the brink of another overload just as they breech the atmosphere. He can feel the malnar ahead of him, gathering energy and readying another blast.

Not risking the chance of it regaining strength, he teleports. Appearing at the mouth of its bulb, he fires point blank.

From the ground, Dean watches as the sky shimmers with darkness. "Sei…"

…

The eyes of Colonel Mitchel stay steady at their corners, locked on the odd-looking figure crouched beside him. Uncertain of his next move, his thoughts dwell on the happenings of Area 51, the destruction of their research lab, and the responsibility laid upon him by the president. Is he a captive? He wonders, debating how to respond. With the short-stocky one dealing with the monster, this may be his only chance. Immediately, he draws his weapon, but Welic is quick to act, stopping the bullet with his palm before it even leaves the barrel. To Mitchel, the guardian's actions were instantaneous and the resulting blow-back stings the colonel's hand. "Gah!"

"Whoa, gratitude. Maybe next time we'll let it eat you," Welic remarks.

Cradling the soreness of his hand, Mitchel looks to him with hostile eyes. "What is it you want?" he asks.

Welic shrugs, gesturing with a look just as the angered beljusa reverts to a more docile state along with her horde. "To save this planet," he replies plainly when suddenly the Guardian of Dimension steps out from a swirling flash of purple with a petrified look on his face.

"We just lost the Guardian of Life," he states. Welic stands just as Almir closes the distance, packing the beljusa into his backpack with Lucy.

"Hey guys, I got her. What's going on?" Almir asks, catching their grim expressions.

"Sei's dead," Welic tells him.

Almir shakes his head in disbelief. "Impossible—wha—what of Jasra, what about the Guardian of Time?" he demands.

Immediately, Dean shakes his head, knowing what's to be asked. "She can't go back, she's injured," he says.

"First Simon, then Leon, and now Sei? Soon there won't be enough of us to defend Earth!" shouts Almir. The voices of the trio grow into an indiscernible chorus.

Colonel Mitchel then stands. "Hey, hey, gentleman—guys—at ease!" he bellows his command voice. "Now, what's this about Earth?" he demands as his few remaining soldiers gather around. "Stand down!" he shouts to them, his arms out.

The unpleasant stares from the Guardian of Dimension's reptilian eyes chills the encroaching men before he asserts his gaze to the man in charge.

"This planet is about to be under siege, and we've lost three of our best warriors. That includes the Guardians of Earth and Life. What faction do you fight for, soldier?"

Surprised, the colonel stammers. "I-ugh-th—the United States," he replies.

"Then contact your president. We have to prepare the world," Dean says.

Chapter 31

"Guardians Revealed"

There's a soft hum and a gentle metallic scraping sound from the coin machine's reciprocal motion, which fills Leon's senses as he stares somewhat brokenly through the glass and metal case. The occasional pop of a quarter falling used to rile him, yet today all he can do is stare.

He can no longer detect the magnetic field of the metal in, on, and around the machine, or feel the faint amount of resistance the glass used to offer toward his intentions, seemingly so long ago. Leon sighs heavily at the lack of aether flowing through his meridians despite the focus of his mind.

Just a day ago he was the Guardian of Earth and could will matter to his desire. To go from that to nothing… Leon shakes his head, finding it difficult to set aside his feelings of animosity toward his mentor, even in knowing his good intentions. To be left like this is hard to forgive.

A sudden chime of the door echoes throughout the store as does the sound of footsteps approaching from behind.

"So, this is where you've been all day," comes the voice of his stepfather.

Leon offers him no response, hoping he'll get the message. Today is just not the day. But Ryan is not going anywhere.

"Are you going to play the game or just stare at it?" he asks with a tone.

"Go away," Leon says, his voice coming off rather coarse and dry as he turns from the machine. Seeing his stepdad barring his path, he hesitates before stepping past him toward the door when a few words from the clerk's TV catch his ear.

"A radical group calling themselves 'The Guardians' has emerged. Although officials have yet to comment on their origin, it has been released that they are in fact real and are expected to speak publicly before the world leaders later this afternoon."

"So, it's true?" Ryan asks before Leon forces the door open on his way out.

Ryan turns, following him outside. "Hey, where are you going?" he demands, grabbing onto his stepson's shoulder. Leon turns immediately, locking Ryan's wrist, dropping him to a knee before shoving him.

"Oaf!" Ryan falls back on his pride.

Leon turns back toward his walk.

"I'm not the one who took your power, Leon. That was your so-called friend!" Ryan shouts, getting up from the ground.

Stopping mid-stride. He fights with himself to tame his rage. *'If Sei hadn't done it, I would have died.'* He rationalizes, turning back. "Sei is the Guardian of Life! He… deserves some respect!" he shouts with a disgruntled tone in his voice as he stares Ryan down.

"Hmph…" Ryan scoffs. "So, what does that make you?" he asks, and Leon sighs, looking down without an answer.

"You know there are other ways, Leon. You should listen to your father," he says.

"You are not my father!" Leon shouts and Ryan sort of bobs his head.

"Fine, I am not your father, but I'm a part of this family, whether you like it or not," he rebuts.

Leon's face sours. "Yeah, well, I don't want to be a part of this family. All you all do is kick me when I'm down—and Chad can do no wrong. I was literally the guardian of this planet—where the hell is my respect? You know what? I don't need it. It's time I went on my own." He turns and starts walking.

"Leon!" Ryan shouts.

Leon stops with his fist clenched.

"You know, there was a time when you and I got along. We were nearly inseparable before Seldin came around and filled your head with grand ideals about aether," Ryan says.

Leon faces him. "Sei taught me energy without sorcery—without sacrificing my soul!"

"Now look at you, cast aside. And where is this Guardian of Life?" He gestures openly.

Leon straightens up. "As the former Guardian of Earth, I will not stand for your bullshit, Ryan," he says.

"That's right, you're not the Guardian of Earth—your mentor saw to that!"

Wham! Ryan eats pavement; his jaw hangs open, sore from the back of a hand he never saw. He turns about, seeing red. Taking to a bow stance, he lunges, throwing a punch off his right toward his stepson's face. There's a sudden clap as his fist stops in Leon's hand.

"I may not have a connection to the aether anymore," Leon clenches, causing a pop in Ryan's trapped knuckles.

"Gahhh!" Ryan drops to his knees, unable to free his hand.

"But years of exposure has honed my body," Leon says, watching his stepdad tug flutily at the fingers clamped over his fist.

Ryan grunts as he fights against his grip. "All I'm saying is… there's… always… another way!" he manages before tumbling back as Leon lets go.

"My time as a guardian has ended," Leon says, turning away from him once again.

"So that's it?" Ryan stands, cradling his hand, "You're just gonna sulk and give up?"

Leon looks to him with anger. "There can only be one Earth guardian."

Ryan responds simply. "Then fight for it."

Leon's eyes lower, the thought had never occurred to him. "Nobody has even seen the other one in hundreds of years," he replies.

"Like I said, Leon, there's always another way," Ryan replies.

. . .

Elsewhere in the cosmos, the heights of the northern mountains located in the small continent of Nichele are breathtaking this time of year, with a full celestial backdrop of the much larger gas giant, which the moon, Faur-162, orbits. Although the planet Faur is uninhabitable, at least three of its moons are suitable for life.

Faur-162 is home to the garlamites, a humanoid species with gray, rock-like skin, called schale, and hair that grows in spiky veins of colored minerals called karton.

Cali, the daughter of the town blacksmith, Odel, takes in the spectacle of the reddish-blue sky as her father mills about on their trek. Her short, copper karton shimmers in the strange mix of light.

Tink-tink, tink-tink. Odel taps at the sturdy ground with a small, hand-sized pickaxe. Chipping at the rocks beneath the soil, he grins with a mouth framed of stubby pebbles before holding an oil-soaked canvas over his find. Faint yellow sparkles dance on the cloth.

"Cali, come here!" he calls out.

"Oh, fantastic, this will bring a great harvest," she says, placing a small flake of the glittering rock upon her tongue. Cali barely manages to delight in the flavor when suddenly, a deafening crack draws their attention to the sky.

Odel and Cali embrace each other. Frozen in fear, they watch as the fiery mass rumbles through the upper atmosphere, leaving a trail of smoke behind as it plummets, rocketing toward the ground. It's all over in a matter of seconds—bam!

It hits the ground with a tremendous force, sending tremors through the land beneath them, and as the smoke clears, Odel's feelings of dread are replaced by an overwhelming sense of curiosity. Shaking his daughter, he can barely form a sentence.

"I-i-it lan-landed just over the ridge!" he manages before running after it.

"Wait!" Cali calls out as her father slips from her grasp. She pursues, following along the hiking trail a few hundred yards before stopping breathlessly at her father's back.

His trembling finger points as he casts an unblinking gaze into a wide crater and at the badly charred remains of a being unlike anything he's ever seen before.

...

The crowd outside the United Nations building in New York City is flooding with reporters, religious fanatics, and citizens gathering around as the designated time of 4:00 p.m. approaches while the world's finest are brought in under heavy guard. Despite the ample amount of patrolmen cordoning off the area, it is the military presence that draws the most concern.

Watching from a window, the president sighs as the crowd builds. "This is why we don't televise. Where are the guardians?" he asks, looking to the secretary-general.

"They assured us that they would be here," the secretary-general replies.

Checking the time, the president turns. "And the world leaders?" he asks.

"Well, sir, given the short notice, only a handful could physically be here. The rest will be tuning in over the network," he says as they move into the conference room.

A brief echo of feedback rings from the speakers as the secretary-general taps the microphone.

"I've got it," the president says, pushing him aside before addressing the nations.

"Good afternoon. Today," he hesitates as he speaks off the cuff when an arc of violet electricity pops, forming a vortex behind him, and out steps Dean, Jasra, Almir, and Welic, causing gasps and awe to fill the room. Looking back to the crowd, the president continues. "Today an extraordinary page in our history turns as these remarkable beings come forward, bringing news that I hope will unite our world," he says before nodding to Dean and then stepping away.

"Where is everybody?" Dean whispers to the president.

"I'm sorry, some international flights can take up to fifteen hours or longer. It's a big planet."

Dean shakes his head. "It's not," he replies, opening portals at the seats of the missing personnel. "Please, join us, for this concerns you too," he says to the leaders of Australia, Singapore, Qatar, Africa, and Dubai, who eventually, though reluctantly, step through. As the portals close, Dean continues.

"My name is Dean, I am the Guardian of Dimension. To my right is Jasra, the Guardian of Time. To my left are Almir, the Guardian of the Mind, and Welic, the Guardian of Vice. We are here because some time ago, Seldin, the Guardian of Life received word that an extraterrestrial race of planetary conquerors known as the pulsari are on their way to Earth. When we moved to intercept, there were two other planets standing in their path. Oqu IX was destroyed just days ago, and although we were successful in saving Aphéd, it took the sacrifice of the Guardian of Life to do so. According to the Guardian of Time, we now have less than two months. We must act now if we're to prepare," he says and the peaceful order of the chamber stirs into an uproar. Heads begin to turn as the room fills with indiscriminate chatter while members from around the world debate in open forum.

Dean sighs as his gaze meanders, watching the likes of angered fists pumping and stern faces scowling throughout the room. *'Maybe this was a mistake,'* he wonders, but it isn't long before rants from the crowd address the stage.

"Are we to take you seriously?" asks the Queen of England when suddenly comes the voice of the Australian Governor-General.

"Are you questioning their power? He just bent space to bring us here!"

"How do we know it wasn't a trick?" calls out another.

"That was no hoax," chimes in the Singapore Prime Minister followed by the Prime Minister of Japan.

"What about that thing in Tokyo?"

…

Busting through the entrance of a stone and grass hut, Odel and two other villagers move into the main living space with Cali not far behind. The burden of the wooden stretcher they carry shows as fatigue upon their faces and heavy panting breaths.

"You see! You see!" Odel shouts openly to the occupants of the large, round interior, who make a path, moving furniture and other knickknacks out of the way.

"Ugh," Odel falls from exhaustion, losing his grip on the stretcher and dropping the charred remains of Seldin to the floor.

"Father!" Cali rushes over to assist.

"Get him up, quickly!" Odel commands before turning his eyes to the village elder, Keen, and their leader, Marta. They rest the stretcher on the floor and help him onto it.

"You were telling the truth," Marta says.

Odel nods with a gesture toward the stretcher, his hands shaking. "Yes, it's as I said; a being from the sky."

Keen then speaks out. "Odel, that's superstitious nonsense. No one lives beyond the clouds."

Marta's eyes shift to him. "Elder, how can you deny what's before your very eyes?"

"I'm not denying that we have a very unusual garlamite here, but to say he's a god from the heavens is preposterous," Keen replies.

"Well, what do you think he is?" casts a voice from the crowd.

"And how could mere schale and orres survive such a fall?" Cali says.

The elder's face contorts from his thoughts as he gestures with a hand toward Seldin. "He hardly made it intact. First, all his schale has come off." He takes up Seldin's remaining hand, squeezing the soft pink flesh in demonstration, which contrasts the rather hard and rocky exterior of his own. "And furthermore, his entire right side from shoulder to hip looks to have been burned away," he says, looking over the man's nude remnants down to the nub at his right knee.

Odel kneels beside Seldin on the floor. "But that proves it, doesn't it? No schale…" he touches the side of Seldin's face and then runs a hand through what's left of his hair. "And I've never seen karton so frail and brittle—and look—" he raises a hand stained with blood. "His orres is red, not green like ours. Clearly, he's not garlamite." Odel stares down at him in wonder. "What else could he be?"

…

Pushing through the large wooden double doors of Watcher's Keep, Ryan enters with Leon at his side. Ahead of them is the great hall, which opens to a wide room of pews lined in rows, like any other church, and facing a ceremonial altar atop a raised floor with stairs leading to it.

Leon looks around, gazing at the enormous stone statue of a beautiful god-like figure standing with her hands out and low in a welcoming posture.

"Khyrah?" Leon asks, and Ryan nods.

"Good memory," he says.

"I only remembered because I overheard the Guardian of Death before I blacked out—"

"You've got some nerve coming here," says a stern voice from behind and above, and Leon and Ryan turn to see the disappointed face of Theresa staring down at them from the second-story balcony. A soft giggle follows.

"Heh-heh," the little one in her arms points, "strangers," she says.

"Yes, sweetie," Theresa says to her two-year old daughter, Emily.

Ryan nudges his stepson with an elbow, "Go on," he says, and Leon snaps a with face back to him before sighing and looking up at Theresa, once again.

"Uh, forgive t-the intrusion, Theresa—"

"Priestess Theresa," Ryan corrects.

Leon scoffs for a second. "Priestess… Theresa… may we have a few minutes of your time?" he asks. The words seem to come at great strain. He then lowers his eyes in a respectful bow.

Theresa turns her nose up and with a motion of her head, signals for them to join her as she walks toward her quarters.

…

"And that's the whole story," Leon finishes.

Theresa gives a knowing nod, while tending to her daughter. She lifts Emily into a highchair at the kitchen table. "There you go," she says then looks to Leon. "Sounds like you're in quite the pickle," she chuckles when then tea kettle on the stove starts to whistle. Theresa gets up. "Would you like some tea?"

Leon shakes his head. "No."

"Mommy, cans I has a sammich?" Emily asks.

"Sure thing, sweetie," she replies with a smile before looking to Leon. "Are you sure you don't want any tea?" she offers.

Leon scoffs. "Theresa, c'mon, this is serious. Ryan said you could help me."

"It's funny, you coming to me after all that naysaying," she teases with a smirk to Ryan, and Ryan grins smugly.

"Theresa!" he grunts.

"Lee!" she grunts back. "Fine." She sets her cup down, "I'll help you on one condition," she presents to him.

"What?" he asks.

"That you apologize," she says.

Leon's groans are muffled by the giggles of childish laughter.

"You gotsta says you sowwy," Emily teases.

"You're kidding?" he questions Theresa, but she shakes her head.

"All I want are a few words about how good sorcery is," she smirks.

Looking down, Leon hesitates.

"Really?" Theresa rolls her eyes. "You came all this way to restore your power and yet you're stuck on pride?"

"I..." He doesn't want to say it, but she's right—this isn't the time for pride. "I am... sorry, sorcery is..." His eyes flick to Ryan and then to Theresa. "Okay," he manages, hearing more giggles.

"Good enough, I guess." Theresa smiles at him then presents a teacup. "So, this other Earth guardian, no one has seen or heard from her in centuries?" she asks.

Leon nods. "That's what the Guardian of Vice said: Madeline went into hiding after several guardians were destroyed."

"And only one of you can be…" she shrugs, "…active at a time?" she asks.

A sigh escapes Leon's lips. "All I know is when I was starting to peak, I lost control. They told me my power was being consumed by the other one."

Theresa nods in acknowledgement, "The reason your power is being taken is you and this other guardian are inexplicably bound by your cosmic duties, but we can use this connection to our advantage," she says.

"How so?" Leon prompts.

"Your tea is getting cold," she reminds him. Leon's eyes shift down to the cup before making a confused face.

"I told you I'm not—"

Ryan then groans. "Lee, when the Priestess offers you a cup of tea, you drink it," he scoffs as she slides the cup closer.

His eyes follow the motion of it, then to her gaze, and then back to the steaming brew.

'What's the big deal?' he wonders—smack! She pops him upside the head with an open hand.

"Just drink it."

Taking it up from around its stout exterior, Leon can feel the intense heat through the cup. If his hands were anyone else's they'd have burned already. The tea smells of orange and chocolate with a hint of other spices throughout. As the cup touches his lips, he tips it back, taking that first sip. Without hesitation, Theresa places her hand at the base of the teacup and tilts it farther.

"I thought you said you were in a hurry," she comments, making him chug the scalding liquid. He then exhales a steamy breath with a cough.

Leon grabs his head. "Argh!" Immense pressure builds from within. Pain hits him like a train driving up his nose. It's intense and nauseating like a migraine.

"It'll pass," Theresa says, and as if attracted to a light shining in his eyes, Leon looks up, casting a gaze into apparent nothingness.

"What is this?" Leon gasps, seeing a soft golden haze of light extending from his core and out into the world.

"The potion you drank will serve as contrast, making visible what is usually not. Be careful, Leon. It's obvious this Madeline doesn't want to be found."

Chapter 32

"The Sky Being"

Time passes quickly on Faur-162 with its shorter, eighteen-hour days. Although the arrival of the mysterious stranger has made some of the villagers anxious, most of the townsfolk have continued on with their lives, much like Odel, who hammers away at the bits of ore brought in from the previous day's harvest while his daughter works inside, tending to their guest.

"Good morning, Odel!" greets his nearest neighbors, Pama and her husband Ruso.

Looking up with a grin, Odel smiles. "Good morning, Pama. What can I do for you today?" he asks.

Ruso and his wife gesture with baskets in hand. "Oh, nothing, we just brought along some provisions for our mutual friend. It's not every day we get to meet a sky being," he replies.

"Has he awoken?" Pama asks.

Odel shakes his head. "I'm afraid not, but Cali's inside with him now," he says, waving them along with the casual line of other guests.

Careful to not tug too hard at Seldin's oddly soft skin, Cali dabs with a cloth at the sores covering most of his body, but the scraping sensation against his cheek draws his eyes open to the strange-looking creature prodding at him with a finger pressed into a material akin to burlap. The roughness of it is like sandpaper, and slowly he moves an unsteady hand to hers.

Cali gasps, yelping loudly as he takes her hand. "Father!" she screams, dropping the rag to the bowl of solution beside his cot and moving away, slamming into those behind her.

Hearing his daughter's screams from outside his hut, Odel quickly runs in. "Cali, what's wrong?" he asks, and she points.

"He's awake," she replies and Odel's gaze snaps to their guest. Taking a moment to compose himself, he slowly steps up to him when suddenly, Seldin lurches, vomiting over the side of the cot.

Odel and the others jump back. "What do we do?" calls out a random villager when Pama offers her two cents.

"We should get the elder!" she shouts.

Turning about, Odel waves his hands. "No!" he shouts. Cali then steps around the mess, wiping Seldin's mouth and face with a damp cloth. To him, the room feels as though it's spinning as nausea and vertigo set in.

"Odel, it's obvious he's sick. We should get the elder right away," Ruso comments.

"No, he's our guest. We should comfort him. He's had a great journey. Let's just try to communicate first," Odel says before turning back toward him. "I'm Odel, and this is my daughter, Cali." He gestures to himself and then to his child, but Seldin's eyes are barely open and the sounds they make aren't discernable. The dry, parched sensation of his mouth, however, causes him to open up.

"Water," he asks.

Odel then looks to Cali. "What did he say?" he asks her. Shaking her head, she shrugs.

"I don't know, Father," she replies, for his words are like grunts to them and theirs are guttural to him.

Stepping away, Odel wipes his forehead. Dismayed by their apparent lack of communication, he decides to pour himself a drink.

"Maybe," he hesitates, "you're right, we should get elder and the chief," he says softly before taking a sip. The obvious action gets Seldin's attention, and he reaches out desperately with a shaky hand.

"I think he wants some, Father," Cali notices and Odel hands it over right away.

Seldin promptly takes a healthy gulp—cough! The others jump back again as he gags, spits, and heaves, as if he wasn't already in enough pain.

Those around him come to his aid immediately, but the gesture is pushed off as he works to compose himself.

"Acetone?" Seldin gasps questioningly. "Don't you have water?" he asks again before taking a good look at his attendants. The reddish light coming through the open ports of the hut serves only to accentuate their hard, rocky exteriors.

. . .

"You've been awfully quiet since we left Theresa's," Ryan comments, his hands on the wheel as he offers casual glances toward his stepson, who is resting with his head back against the front passenger seat.

Watching the yellowish stream of connective energy between himself and his counterpart, Leon replies. "Just thinking."

"About?" Ryan asks.

"What I'm going to say when I find her," he says, but in truth he doesn't know how to approach it. After all, Madeline has been the Guardian of Earth for centuries. Who is he to just waltz on in and lay claim? He wonders.

"Are you sure this transport of yours is gonna be there?"

Leon looks to his stepfather. "It'll be there. The question is: can I use it? When I was still a guardian, the gates responded to my presence. I have no idea if that still works," he replies.

Ryan shrugs. "So, what, these gates have just been there since the beginning of time?' he asks.

"I assume they were created by the other guardian so she could get around easier," Leon replies.

"And how do you get to them?" Ryan glances over briefly.

"They're hidden in caves. The one we're headed to," Leon points down the long stretch of highway with no end in sight, "is in a small cave near Crystal Beach. The cave itself is off limits to explorers, but inside the main tunnel is an offshoot that leads to it. Unfortunately, it's covered by a layer of rock," he says.

"I guess she didn't want anyone to find it," Ryan comments.

"No," Leon sighs, "I sealed the entrance when Almir and I hopped to Texas to find Sei."

. . .

"Alright, yes sir," the president says over the phone, "thank you. We'll be in touch." He hangs up. "Russia has agreed to give you access if needed," he says to Dean, who crosses his arms.

"I'm glad to hear it," Dean says.

"And how long will it take you to place these?" General Scott gestures to the five beljusas sitting in planters on the Oval Office coffee table.

"Minutes, once we have the final word of the world that they can be safely looked after," he answers, glancing to Jasra, Almir, and Welic before looking at the general again.

"Are you sure about this, John?" General Scott addresses the president.

Dean speaks up, "General, we don't… typically work directly with the governments of worlds—it takes too long. Believe me when I say that we're doing this for your benefit, not ours."

...

All around Odel's hut, the villagers gather hoping to get a chance to greet the newly awoken being from the sky. The village leader and the elder have already gone in, offering their own attempts to communicate with him, but their efforts have been all for naught.

Seldin, too, is having an equally difficult time. The swimmy sensation of his head, and the other problems besides, are taking their toll. He's not even sure how he hasn't bled out yet. He looks at the blood-soaked bandages wrapping his torso, right shoulder, and right stub of a leg. He closes his eyes, trying to push out the pain.

Holding his left hand before his eyes, he tries to focus, attempting to feel the power cycling from his core and flowing to his palm. Yet nothing.

Sighing, Seldin takes a heavy slow breath in frustration, trying not to upset himself. "My core must be out of alignment," he rationalizes his inability to connect—not just to the aether—but to them. To make matters worse, he's starting to understand his sickness. The clumps of fallen hair and the looseness of his nails are obvious signs.

Looking to the group, he motions for them to step back.

"Go." He staggers in breath. "Go! You shouldn't be near me!" he tries desperately.

"My name is Keen." The elder gestures to himself.

Setting down his left and only hand, Seldin huffs with a shaking of his head. "It's no use," he laments before looking to him as the man tries again.

"Keen, Keen," Keen tries.

Marta then places a hand on Keen's shoulder. "Let me try," she insists before engaging with Seldin. "Marta," she taps at her chest, "I am Marta."

If this were any other time, their display might almost be laughable, like watching a human trying to speak to a chimpanzee, for the bizarre syllables coming from her mouth seem almost impossible for the human tongue.

'This is getting us nowhere,' he thinks to himself while listening to the unbearable rumble in his stomach. Although the very thought of food turns the churning to something awful, if he's to fight this without aether, he'll need to try.

Bringing his hand to his mouth, Seldin then gestures a biting action.

Marta then looks to the others. "What do you think?" she asks.

"He tried drinking earlier. Maybe he's hungry," Cali suggests but Marta shakes her head.

"That doesn't sound right, you said he was ill. Sick people don't eat," she says.

"It won't hurt to try," Pama says, then picks up a basket. She selects a tasty morsel the size of a potato and passes it to him.

Seldin gladly reaches out for the offering before the weight and the solidity of it becomes apparent. A laugh almost escapes his lips as he realizes.

"Of course," he sighs, setting the rock down. Without aether to sustain him, the reality of starvation seems all the more likely if dehydration—or worse, radiation poisoning, doesn't kill him first. He then taps at his chest.

"Seldin, Seldin," he tries to no avail before looking away.

"What do you think he's saying?" Marta asks.

"Maybe he's saying he can't eat it," replies the elder.

...

"Here we are, Crystal Beach," Ryan says, bringing the car to a stop. Leon looks out before grabbing his single duffle bag.

Ryan then looks to his stepson, a hint of pride behind his eyes. "Are you sure you don't want me to come with you?" he asks.

Shaking his head, Leon then slings his bag over his shoulder. "This is something I have to do myself. Thank you, Ryan," he says, offering a hand and his stepfather grasps it firmly.

"Good luck," Ryan says.

"Ryan, I think you should know: Khyrah, according to Welic, is the demigod responsible for killing all the guardians over four hundred years ago. This magic you practice, drawing power from her, can only bring about our destruction."

"Says the man using it to get his own power back," Ryan replies before waving goodbye and stepping on the gas.

Leon sighs at the futility of his attempt to get through to him as he drives off. Without the ability to fly, he looks around then takes to his long journey on foot, heading toward the cave.

...

Seldin rests back, taking a break from the frustration as he watches the others indulge in their bizarre cuisine. Rocks, rocks, and more rocks he notices as those who come to visit him take slivers, shards, and flakes of various minerals from the trays and baskets on the table as if eating hors d'oeuvres at a party.

"Are you sure you don't want some?" Cali offers a Ritz-cracker-sized portion of a rather lustrous black and silver mineral. Reaching out, Seldin takes it with a curious expression upon his face.

"This is uraninite," he says with surprise in his voice. "I suppose… I don't have to worry then, at least about you." He then shakes his head as he returns the fragment to her.

Laying back again, Seldin finds himself a little bored of watching others eat, and he taps at the baseboard of his cot with his fingers—thump, tha-thump, thump. The material drums with familiarity.

"Wood?" He turns, looking at the structure. "If they have wood, then they have plants," he realizes before taking a closer look at the woven structure of the baskets placed around the hut. "Grass…" he thinks aloud, "…it's not exactly nutritious, but… I could eat grass." He then gestures with a thrusting motion of his hand toward the open doorway.

"What do you think?" Marta looks to Odel, who steps closer before following the action with his eyes.

"I… think we're starting to communicate. Grab a chair." He points.

On the outside, Seldin is surprised by how Earthlike the planet is, with the exception of the red tint covering everything. Their proximity to the gas giant and the prominent red star in the sky explains that, but where's the food? He looks around with desperate eyes.

The arid, rocky landscape bears very little vegetation with only a few sparse trees dressing the mountains. A few meters farther out, however, Seldin raises a hand to halt the group carrying him along like a mighty pharaoh when he spots a greenish patch. Motioning to ease forward and down, Seldin then pushes himself from the chair—plop! He hits the ground.

"Ugh!" Seldin grunts with a wince from the shock of the impact that sends a rush of pain throughout his tattered body.

Odel and the elder rush over but Seldin waves them off before sitting on his stub and taking up a handful of the grass-like blades. They're coarse to the touch, almost like sawgrass but thick like a reed crossed with a stalk of celery. A gentle squeeze between his thumb and forefinger separates the pulpy fibers, releasing the potential nutrients beneath—and more importantly, a possible source of water. But first he has to test it.

Checking for reactions to his skin, he waits a few minutes before hesitantly licking his thumb. It's bitter with an earthy taste but not unlike what he'd expect. Negative calories or not, he goes for it. Biting in and breaking the stalks off in his teeth, he chews at the tough fibers before taking in another bite.

A bit of nervous laughter and an abundance of sighs come from behind as the group gathers around.

"Who knew he liked grass?" chuckles a delighted Cali.

...

Crunch, crackle, and clank are the sounds that echo throughout the cave as Leon's fists hammer at the rocky barricade blocking his path. The force of each punch is like a sledgehammer, chipping off bits of the much larger slabs with each blow. Years of aether coursing through his meridians has strengthened his body, for the average person would crumble at the task like the wall he is striking. Even so, it isn't going down without effort and the occasional bloody knuckle.

"Mm-mother!" he winces, taking pause to examine the gash before angrily throwing a basketball-sized chunk of rock at the wall. Crash-crackle! It hits with a hollow pop as it busts through to the other side. Leon huffs with satisfaction before peering through the hole, adjusting his headlamp to compensate.

"It's not big enough to climb through." He sighs, reaching across to feel for weaknesses before grabbing at the edge and pulling.

"Mmmm—auughh!" he grunts—clunk! "Oaf!" Thud! Leon falls back, taking a small section of the lower wall with him.

"Ugh!" He gasps, rolling it off him. The light of his helmet sparkles against the walls past the opening and he moves closer, checking the size before squeezing through the crevice like a soldier crawling under barbed wire. He tucks a bit, then rolls, accommodating the dip just beyond the wall to the cave floor.

Leon then brings himself about as he stands, panning his eyes across as he looks around.

"It was right here," he says softly while pressing his hands to the sheer polished surface that is the far wall. Although there's no swirling or shimmering effects, the perfectly smooth circular rockface is evidence that it was, in fact, once here.

An uncertain pressure builds inside him as he speaks. "Take me to Madeline," he says with a desperate rasp in his voice. Nothing happens.

"Take me to Madeline!" he shouts, thrusting the heel of his fist against the wall, cracking the surface. "Come on! Open!" But again, nothing happens.

Dropping to his knees, Leon rests back. The sense of defeat is overwhelming as his eyes follow the glowing trail from his core to where the portal once was, deadening into the wall. Taking a furious inhale, he exclaims at the top of his lungs, "Maadeeliiinnneee!"

"I challenge you! I challenge you for the right to be the Guardian of Earth—face me, you coward!" he rants while furiously beating a fist against the wall. The sensation of it crumbling beneath his hands causes him to back off, and he stands there staring into the fractured rock with heavy huffs.

With his hands shaky and his heart full of anger, Leon can feel something within him beginning to take over. Slowly his lips move, mouthing inaudible syllables at first, and as the sounds grow louder with the rhythm of the rhyme, he takes ownership of the choice.

"What's hidden shall shine, what's mine shall be, open the path, for I can see. What's hidden shall shine, what's mine shall be, open the path, for I can see."—Crack! The wall splits as the cave rattles, and again he chants.

"What's hidden shall shine, what's mine shall be, open the path, for I can see!" Another crack forms, following another quake that knocks Leon down.

"What's hidden shall shine, what's mine shall be, open the path, for I can see!" he shouts with intent. The shaking of the cave intensifies as a luminous green glow fills the space. The effects grow with each iteration of the rhyme. Again and again he chants.

"What's hidden shall shine, what's mine shall be, open the path, for I can see!"

Poof! Boom! Sparks fly as arcs of lightning crackle and flash about the cave. Leon can feel the pull as the chill of air rushes in with the violent formation of the gate.

Staring at its shimmering surface, Leon commands: "Take me to Madeline!"

Chapter 33

"The Hollow Earth"

It's been two days since Leon entered the realm of darkness. With his headlamp burned out and his provisions gone, he has had to resort to the likes of magic just to keep going. All around him are great pillars of black crystals, intense, unrelenting heat, and pressure he's never felt before. He could be at the center of the Earth for all he knows, but wherever he is, it's obvious that intruders are not welcome.

The spells he casts for magical light only last a few seconds before the energy culled gets violently sucked into the crystals. Perhaps it's fate that he's without aether, for he suspects such a being would not last long in here. His line, too, is having problems maintaining a consistent heading without the golden glow being pulled one way or another.

...

"Ah, that's good," Seldin says with a smile, despite Cali's inability to understand him. The wood fibers she is tying to his stump might just do the trick, he thinks. She returns his smile before standing and offering a hand. Her father, Odel, joins in, taking Seldin's impaired side as they work together.

Placing his peg and his good leg to the floor, Seldin pushes as they lift, helping him to stand. He winces with pain shooting up his stump.

"Oh…" Cali mutters, easing up, but Seldin insists with a nodding gesture to keep going. It's awkward at first, and he teeters before stumbling. Yet, his companions are quick to catch him as he works to find his balance.

"Thank you," he says to them. One step at a time, he eases about the hut. It's the first time in days that he's been mobile, and it feels good despite the pain.

"And how's our guest doing?" asks Marta, who peers in with a gentle knock at the entrance.

"See for yourself." Odel gestures.

"May I come in?" she asks and Odel nods.

"Of course, Chief. You know you're always welcome."

Marta then proceeds, observing Seldin as he walks. "Ah, Sky Man, how are you?" she greets with an adopted gesture, waving her hand. Seldin waves back in response.

"It's almost time for his breakfast," Cali says to Marta before offering Seldin a bowl of roots, berries, and seeds.

"So, his appetite is strong? That's good. I take it he's no longer sick?" she asks, while staring at the strange food.

Odel then shakes his head. "Not that I can tell," he says as his daughter pours a cup of rainwater and then offers it to Seldin, who tilts his head, noticing a dark blemish on the back of Cali's hand. Gently taking hold for a better look, a sense of dread reaches his face and he immediately steps back.

"What is it?" Odel asks. Cali shakes her head dismissively while hiding her hand.

"It… it's nothing, Father," she says, but Seldin motions at his own sores on his chest and face before pointing back to her hand.

…

The sweat rolling off his brow only adds to Leon's discomfort, for the farther he travels, the tougher, and the hotter, it gets. With nearly half the day behind him, he pants from exhaustion while crystals from all around poke and prod at him. Hardly able to go on, he collapses just as his surroundings grow dark once again.

"Huhh." He exhales. "C'mon, Madeline. Where are you?" he asks openly with a huff before drinking the few remaining drops from his canteen. Leaning his head back, he shakes the container.

"Uuh."

One drop, then two—thud! He tosses it then plops flat on the harsh, hot ground. Leon can barely keep his eyes open. As his heavy lids slide closed, he catches a faint sparkle in the distance.

"Mmm," comes a groan as he forces his head up for a better look. "What is that?"

...

"How can this be?" Seldin questions it, for they eat radioactive ore as a delicacy. "It has to be elter—residual from—" He looks up, hearing commotion from outside. The chief, elder, and some others have gathered, along with Odel and Cali.

"It's worse than we thought, this illness is spreading. Gattiel, his two children, and about a dozen others have spots as well," Ruso says.

Marta then turns to Cali. "How long have you had that?" she asks.

"I..." she hesitates, "I noticed them yesterday morning. There's more on my arms and chest," she replies before looking to her father, who shakes his head.

"It's my fault. I should never have brought him in. But what do we do now? We can't just turn him out," he says shamefully, lowering his eyes.

The elder bobs his head in thought. "I'm afraid we'll have to. Whatever he has is spreading. He could infect the entire village," he says.

"No, don't say that!" Cali exclaims, tucking her head into her father's chest.

Feeling for his daughter, Odel then looks to his chief. "I brought him here, he's my responsibility, and only those who have been close to him have been affected. We'll just keep everyone away," he says.

Ruso and Pama scowl at the idea. "That's not enough. We have to get rid of him!" Pama shouts.

...

Steadily growing brighter, the light ahead slowly fills Leon's view the closer he gets. Soon, the walls of the crystal tunnel begin to fade with the white glow eclipsing his view until the haziness of it all becomes clear, leaving him breathless where he stands.

Leon can't believe it: it's a world—an ecosystem existing entirely underground, complete with flora and fauna. There are fields, forests, and mountains, with a sky raining light from charged crystals overhead. The warmth of the light is complemented by the cool breeze on his face. He can hear birds chirping and bees buzzing, but most importantly, the rushing sound of running water. To his left is a lake churning by a waterfall.

Wasting no time, Leon bolts for it, making a beeline across the field.

"Water!" He gasps deeply before plunging his head in—splash! It's cold but good. "Ah!" he rears his head back, flinging water from his wet hair while taking a glorious breath.

But something's terribly wrong. From out of nowhere, the grass comes alive, wrapping his hands and feet before lifting him upside down as a feminine figure slowly comes into view. At first, all he can see is the sway of her long brown dress brushing over the grass and the walking stick in her hand. It isn't long, however, before the cold stare of her eyes pierces through him.

…

The growing commotion outside Odel's hut intensifies the already unsettled feelings within Seldin's chest, for although he can't understand a word they say, he can certainly get the gist. If only they hadn't brought him in, or if he had followed his instincts when he first arrived, none of this would have happened.

It's obvious to him now, the long-term effects of elter on living tissue. And while the reaction in him appears to have slowed, once started, it's like a burning ember. Given enough time and without something to stop it… that's why that malnar cut off its own limbs, he realizes, for even it knew the value of severance.

"Open your doors, Odel!" Ruso shouts with a pickaxe in hand and a mob of angry villagers behind him.

Standing firm in front of his home, Odel puffs out his chest. "I will do no such thing," he states, while gently coaxing Cali behind him.

But then Gattiel steps up, ushering his eldest son in front. Odel averts his eyes from the shale cracking on the boy's arms and face as the ulcers slowly grow.

"Don't you look away. You brought this plague upon us. Now, give us the sky man so we might end this!" Gattiel demands.

"Hurting him won't stop this, Gattiel," shouts the chief from behind, and the crowd parts to let her and the elder through.

Gattiel, Ruso, Pama, and the others turn to face them as they approach. "How do you know?" a random voice questions as the argument ensues.

With them distracted, Odel whispers to Cali. "Get inside."

Taking his advice, Cali eases back while slowly creeping into the hut and closing the door before looking around to an open, empty space.

"Sky Man?" she calls out. His bed is empty, and his food is gone. In a panic, Cali peers out the front door. "Father," she says quietly, the roar of the crowd drowning her voice. "Father!" she calls again.

Hearing her whispers from behind, Odel looks over his shoulder then back to the crowd before creeping over to his child. "I said, get inside," he scolds.

"The sky man is gone," she says, and Odel's heart skips. Quickly, he motions for her to go in. He follows, taking a few seconds to look around.

"Where could he have gone?" Cali asks, but her father shrugs bewilderedly before checking the back door. With the darkness of night upon them, he takes a lantern, shining it about when his line of sight falls to the odd tracks in the dirt: one shaped like a foot and the other, round and knobby.

"This way—he couldn't have gotten far on his leg," Odel says.

"But why would he leave, Father?" Cali asks as she follows.

"To protect us. The sky man has nothing but good intentions," he assumes.

"Or maybe he's afraid?" Cali says.

Off into the distance behind him, Seldin can hear the indiscriminate vocals and the sounds of steps approaching fast. Picking up the pace, he takes to a labored skip, using his good leg to bounce while applying only what weight is needed to his peg.

Back in the hut, there's a loud banging sound followed by a crash as the front door is knocked from its hinges.

"Where are they? Where did they go?" Gattiel shouts as others fill the space while carrying picks, axes, and torches.

"They went this way!" Pama exclaims, waving them on and out the back door with a pitchfork in hand. The mob moves quickly, leaving the chief and the elder tied up out front.

Not much farther ahead of the crowd, Odel looks back, seeing the glow of torches and lanterns closing the distance.

"Faster, Cali," he says as they start to scamper.

With the sounds of the crowd growing closer, Seldin quickly looks over his shoulder before taking to another skip. His peg catches a rock, twisting awkwardly and slipping the bindings from the stub of his knee.

"Ugh!" he falls forward, tumbling down a shallow incline while trying to stabilize himself with the one arm.

The moment he hits the bottom, he turns, spotting a glowing light rushing toward him. Quickly, he brings a hand up in defense.

"There he is, I found him!" Cali calls out just as she and her father take a knee. Although relieved to see them, Seldin almost wishes he hadn't.

"You have to go, you can't be near me," he says despite their lack of comprehension.

Grabbing his stump, Cali twists the prosthesis back into place when suddenly, shouting can be heard from behind.

"There they are!" Ruso exclaims.

Without hesitation, Odel takes point, holding his arms out defensively. "He's not our enemy; he's just as sick as we are."

"He brought the disease, it's his fault! Now get out of the way!" Gattiel swings his pickaxe.

Using his good leg, Seldin lunges immediately, pushing Odel out of the way.

Shlunk! The pick pierces clean through his back and Seldin gasps, feeling the sudden shock in his heart. He staggers, grasping at the metal protruding from his chest. Finding his breaths meaningless, he soon falls to the ground.

"No!" Cali shouts, dashing to his aid, as does Odel.

"You saved my life," he says tearfully, looking into his glassy eyes as they dilate.

The sounds of their voices grow muffled as Seldin's thoughts recede inward and the image of Cali and Odel's watery faces fade to an ominous black.

Odel turns, sobbing, showing his blood-stained hands to Gattiel, who drops to his knees in realizing what he's done just as the chief and the elder make their way through the crowd.

"We should bury him, Father," Cali suggests before looking to Marta and Keen, who nod as they approach to give a hand.

And the moment they gather around, there's a sudden thud of the pickaxe when Seldin's body transforms to a glowing essence of energy. Everyone gasps, stepping back in shock.

"Thank you," a voice enters them as if being placed directly into their minds, and slowly the ethereal form coalesces into a more tangible shape. Seldin stands there, looking over himself in the moment, contemplating how simple the solution was. It is then that he realizes his error: "I've been thinking like a mortal," he whispers to himself before addressing the crowd.

"I am Sei, the Guardian of Life. A few days ago, I became injured by a dangerous energy; the same energy that was hurting you," he says as they look, finding themselves free of blemishes. "It trapped me in my body, and you..." He looks to Gattiel, who is still crying. "You freed me, thank you," he says before turning.

"Wait!" Cali calls out.

"Where will you go?" Odel asks.

"To study," Seldin replies, while lifting a hand to examine his own matter. "I've been going about this all wrong." He then turns away, seeing for the first time the delicate layers of space and time—superimposed realities separated by the smallest of cosmological events. They weave and bend all around them, moving in sync as one. Seldin gently pokes at them, watching the layers react to his touch.

"So, that's how Dean does it," he whispers to himself, for his eyes have never been so open. He looks around as if staring into a kaleidoscopic menu of dimensions, sub-dimensions—entire universes, until coming to a small pocket of nothingness. There, he reaches out with a hand, letting his fingers slide between the fabric of spacetime like a beaded curtain. He weaves in the next hand. As he moves the layers apart—vvssrroooshh—it tears open with a roiling rim of light, and he stands there staring into the darkened void. Seldin looks back with a gentle nod of farewell to the villagers before stepping through.

. . .

"I don't know how you got in, but rest assured, you will not get out," she says.

"Madeline?" Leon presumes.

"I prefer Mother Earth," she replies, tightening his restraints with a gentle upturn of her wrist.

Gritting his teeth, Leon groans. "I am the Guardian of Earth!" he shouts.

"I am the Guardian of Earth, son," she rebuts in a corrective tone.

"So... am... I!" he grunts, and her expression changes from defensive to indifferent.

"Impossible," she states.

"Welic said—"

"Khyrah dog! Certainly, you don't trust that sniveling Ensantielian," she scoffs.

Leon makes a horrified face. "What? What are you saying?"

"He sided with Khyrah the day she turned," Madeline states, plainly.

Leon's eyes meander in disbelief. "Welic... is a traitor?" he mumbles.

"That would certain fit my definition of the word," she says, watching him work it out.

Leon shakes his head, confused. "Then why would Tillman—" he asks, almost under his breath when suddenly, his face hits the dirt as she lets go.

"So, you've met the Guardian of Death?" Her curiosity piques.

Spitting the dirt from his mouth, he looks up at her. "And Dimension. There's a new Guardian of Life, as well as Time, and the Mind. I'm supposed to be—"

"The new Earth Guardian… you can't ascend?" she asks rhetorically. Leon shakes his head.

"No, you didn't feel it?"

"I can't help you." She turns away, and Leon follows.

"Why not?" he demands.

"Because I'm not ready to give up my position," she answers.

Leon's brow furrows, "Down here in this fantasy while the Earth is in danger?" he shouts.

"I can see what I need to from here," she answers without offering him a glance.

"That's not good enough. What's the point of being a guardian if you're just gonna cower?" he scolds.

"You're too young to understand."

"I understand plenty—like the fact that you're hiding from Khyrah! Well, I've got news for you, lady: I'm down here with my nose in it. We all are. Except you!" he rants.

"If being a guardian is so important to you, then choose another role," she says to him, and Leon stops in place.

"What?"

"Don't tell me the thought never occurred to you," she says, presenting this radical new idea.

'Another role?' he wonders, contemplating the possibility. "You mean, I could be a guardian of whatever I want?" he asks.

Madeline nods. "I guess Tillman's not one to spoon feed. Look, you can either wield aether as a mortal and wait your turn, or you can take a different path. All you need to do is choose," she replies.

Leon stands there, staring at the dirt through his opened fingers. "No." He shakes his head. "No, this is who I am—this is what I'm compelled to be—Guardian of Earth."

"The universe has a funny way of making you feel like that, but you don't have to live by its design," she says.

"If it's that simple, then you change or descend and trade places with me, because the Earth needs one of us, and it's not like you're living up to your purpose," Leon argues.

"I'm sorry," Madeline says softly, "but the answer is no."

"Then I'll fight you for it," he states.

Madeline lets out a hefty bellow. "Please, even if you could power up, these crystals are attuned to my life wave. No one else could set foot in here without being reduced to what you are, or worse."

Taking a stance, Leon readies himself. "Enough talk," he says to her.

Madeline looks at him plainly. "Do you really think you can win?" she asks.

Shaking his head, Leon responds. "No, but if you won't step down, then there's no reason for me to exist." And without warning he attacks, rushing in with a fist to her face, yet there's no satisfying thud. It's like hitting air. Immediately he turns, going for a front sweep and then a roundhouse. Each blow passes through her despite her apparent lack of motion.

"Son, I'm hundreds of thousands of times faster than you. It's not worth it," she claims, but Leon is not finished. Mouthing some words, he gestures a circular motion with his index and middle fingers then thrusts his palm forward, casting a push spell. The effect is minimal, blowing around her like a gust of wind.

Although surprised, Madeline isn't fazed. With hardly a motion, Leon is trapped again.

"I will not have you sully this sanctuary with your sorcery," she scolds.

"Why don't you just kill me?" he huffs.

"Even if I wanted to, I couldn't take that risk. Being this close to ascending, destroying your body might just put you into an energy state—of course, you'd probably just be consumed by my defenses," she says, and Leon's expression changes.

"An energy state?" he asks her.

"You mean, you don't know? Once we ascend, mortal wounds don't kill us. Not even in your condition. I'll admit, knocking the core is a clever way to trap us, but if you can shake the mortal coil…" her eyes shift in thought, "it almost worked against Khyrah," she says, then sighs, and with a quick flick of her hand, she releases him, and Leon meets the ground again.

"Oaf!" He thuds.

"There's a gate to the west." She points. "It'll take you to surface," she says, then turns away.

Leon stands in anger. "You're a coward!"

"I know." Madeline sighs, then glances over her shoulder. "But how brave will you be when a demigod erases your people?"

…

Seldin can't see a thing despite holding a hand to his face, for this place is empty—devoid of even energy, save for his own.

The epiphany of mortal thinking echoes in his mind as he contemplates the battle he'd won, and more importantly, those he'd lost. While each fight pushed him to closer his limits, regardless of the outcome, they relied on martial techniques and beams of aether, but those are human constructs deemed popular by the fantasies of television.

"I need to think bigger." He stares out into the vast emptiness of an uncharted dimension. Bringing his hands together, he takes a breath of nothing—an old habit, he realizes. Then out from the darkness, as he sharpens his focus on the very fabric of space itself, faint wisps of aether begin to emerge.

. . .

There's a look of defeat on Leon's face as he sits on a boulder just outside the cave. He could have had the gate drop him just about anywhere he wanted but nowhere is just the same to him.

"Ugh, back to square one—no guardian, no future," he laments with his chin resting on his knees. A part of him feels he gave up too easily, but the real Guardian of Earth would have torn him a new one. Honestly, what could he have done?

He can't help but sit and stew upon what Ryan and Madeline had said: *'There's always another way,'* and *'choose a different path'.*

"What choice do I really have?" he asks himself when whoop—smack! A small stick pops Leon upside his head.

"Hey!" He jumps into a stance before locking eyes onto Ryan, Theresa, and little Emily.

"Hi," the young one says.

Leon gestures a greeting while rubbing his temple. "What are you guys doing here?" he asks.

"We came to check up on you," Ryan says.

A frown grows on Leon's face. "I failed," he says, "I'm not a guardian."

Ryan sighs with a subtle bob of his head. "We know; we were watching."

"How?" Leon's face contorts.

"Mommy's crystal balls," Emily chimes.

"Those work?" he asks.

Theresa presents a leather-bound book, and he stares at the bizarre rune-like symbols on the cover, etched in a circle around a six-pointed star.

"What's this?" Leon asks.

"You can't read it?" Ryan seems surprised.

"No, why?" He looks at him, confused.

Theresa sits beside him. "I thought you might be able to," she says with a sigh.

"What are you talking about?" he asks.

"The Book of Roe was created by the Guardian of Knowledge, and a copy was given to one keeper on each planet. Every few generations it gets passed on to another. I inherited it a few years ago," Theresa says.

Leon shrugs, "So, what?"

Ryan gestures to it. "It's written in the Language of the Gods, Leon; only people with aether can read it," he says.

"People with aether?" Leon pauses, then opens his duffle bag, pulling out the top of his gi. He hadn't really looked at it since he got back from Peru. His right thumb traces over similar markings of a language he remembers writing but can no longer read. "Wait, that's why you trained with Sei?" He looks to Theresa, and she nods.

"Yes, I needed aether to so that I could become a priestess and learn Roe's secrets, but your connection is so much stronger than mine will ever be. You could—"

"Connection?" Leon scoffs. "My core's misaligned, I have no aether! Those are just meaningless symbols to me now." He gets up, tossing his gi aside. "I might as well be another sorcerer."

Ryan looks between them for a second. "Could... could you realign it?" he asks.

"No," he groans in frustration, "I mean, I could, but why? Madeline would just absorb me," Leon says. "I have to choose to be a guardian of something else, first." He looks down, sadly. "But nothing else feels right."

"What if you chose nothing?" Ryan prompts, and Leon thinks on that.

"Is that an option?" he asks.

Theresa flips through the Book of Roe, running her finger along page after page. Ryan and Leon inch closer.

"Careful." She says as they get too close, and Ryan nods, remembering Joanne, Cory, and Rico, and then pulls Leon back some.

"Right," he says.

"Hmm, here it is," she pauses, "It says... wielders may decline ascension."

Leon steps aside, looking out over the beach and the overcast sky as he thinks. "Then... I choose not to ascend," he says, hearing ominous crack of thunder. He then closes his eyes, peering into himself as he focuses on his core. In his mind's eye, he can see goldish hues of energetic swirls flowing in all directions at his center. Slowly, he moves his mind down from his core through his perineum, then up his lower back. The tendrils of energy start to fill his meridians, and as he works the aether around to his core—whoosh! A surge rushes over him, and his aura ignites in a faint white glow.

"Well?" Theresa asks.

Leon reaches out to a softball-sized rock and concentrates. There's a soft rumble beneath it as it lifts off the ground and floats into his hand.

"Oooh, looks mommy!" Emily points, but Leon doesn't break focus, feeling the weight and the contours of the rock in his hand. Aether flows around his fingers, and he grunts, before dropping it to the ground with a thud. His aura dies down.

"I can't become the rock," he sighs, reaching out, fanning his fingers in the wind as he focuses on the flowing breeze. Again, the aether fills his fingers, but there's no change. "Or the wind." He shakes his head.

Theresa walks over. "You might not be the Guardian of Earth, but…" she reaches out to the Book of Roe, "…kae iit se," she chants in the Language of the Gods, and the book levitates to her.

"What how?" Leon looks surprised by her simple chant as she hands the book to him.

"There are other options," she presents with a smile.

"Sorcery?" he questions as he takes it.

Ryan steps up. "Not just any sorcery, Leon, the most powerful sorcery there is," he says.

Leon shakes his head with a sigh.

"I know what you're thinking, but the Language of the Gods has nothing to do with Khyrah; there's no worship, no sacrifice. It's just your power," she places a hand on his chest, "and the keys to the universe," she taps the book.

Chapter 34

"The Pulsari Have Arrived"

Days pass with Seldin's unrelenting focus as he brings more energy into the system and coalesces it into hydrogen. By the end of the third day, the enormous mass is the size of Jupiter, almost large enough to ignite under its own gravity. He can feel the heat it's already giving off with each second growing closer to critical, and then for the first time in this dark place, there is light.

Seldin rests while marveling at his creation. He's tired, though no worse for the wear, and elated in how impossibly real it is. Although significantly smaller than Earth's sun by comparison, this small star is his own.

"I've never had a sun before," he pants with a smile, then turns his back to the heat. "Now, all I need is a place to stand."

. . .

"Ok, Leon, let's go!" Theresa shouts.

"Yeah, you got him!" Chat yells.

Leon's feet dig into the sand as he charges at Ryan on the beach, just feet away from the roaring shore. He dives for his stepfather's legs, missing by mere inches as Ryan flips back into a handover, splashing sand in Leon's face.

"Oaf!" Leon spits out the grit just as Ryan gets behind, seizing him in a grappling hold.

"Huughh—hmmmgggh!" Ryan heaves to no avail. "All this strength from wielding aether?"

Leon casually stands, lifting his stepdad over his shoulders before throwing him into the rushing waves—splash! "I told you, the flow of aether has honed my body," he says.

"Alright smartass." Ryan sloshes to his feet. "Wind of tsunami, flood of tide..." he begins to chant.

"Lee, counter!" Chad shouts.

Seeing a wave rise behind Ryan, Leon drops into horse stance. "Iba subina su!" he shouts in the Language of the Gods, spreading his arms just as the water crashes into an invisible barrier. He then follows up with a spell to push him back, "Hise poh!"

The force hits Ryan like a wrecking ball to the chest and he is slammed back with a plunging splash.

Chad then rushes in to drag Ryan, coughing and gagging, out of the water. A swift hand takes Leon's shoulder.

"You're catching on, sorcerer," Theresa congratulates.

...

Columns of rock sprout from a molten surface and collide, forming mountains of carbon while the gaseous air condenses into water, which washes over the surface in strategic fashion. He doesn't need an ocean; in fact, Seldin needs very little, but it brings a small touch of home. With four suns in the sky and gravity nearly twenty times that of Earth, this incredibly small world is plenty.

Finally touching down on its barren surface, Seldin, once again, takes a rest and a strong breath of air so fresh it was made today. This place could use a touch of life, he thinks with a smile, but that is a lesson for another time. He's been at it for twenty days and still he has no solution for the pulsari.

"I've tried everything…" Seldin sighs. "Except…"

…

With the go-ahead of the world leaders, Welic and Almir set out to make the array of beljusas, planting them in specific locations all around the globe—and under heavy guard.

"There," Welic says, packing the harsh soil of the Simpson Desert around Lucy's roots as she sinks them down into the Earth. "That's the last one."

"It's not going to die out here?" asks a member of their armed escort, worried about the dry conditions. Lucy simply blooms with petals open, taking in the light of the sun as Almir offers a hand to his kneeling friend.

"I think she'll be fine," Welic replies, dusting his hands off on his pants as he stands when suddenly, the ground beneath the flower begins to sprout new life in an outward radial pattern. The guards and guardians alike look on in amazement as the dusty beige landscape turns lush and green.

"Are you sure this is a good idea?" Almir telepathically asks Welic while taking an anxious gulp.

Welic nods. "I trust Sei's judgment," he replies. Almir's eyes shift to him.

"Yeah, well, if he's wrong, we just gave our planet away."

. . .

In the darkness of space, a faint flicker of bluish-white light comes into Seldin's view as materializes on a lonely planet orbiting a quarter-second pulsar, which casts scintillating beams of gamma-enriched light. Vera, as the planet is called, seems desolate, with life unable to thrive so close to such a star. But Seldin's senses are in tune as he surveys the land with a sweep of his eyes.

"So, this is their world?" He looks about the empty rocky surface. Despite the energy he feels beneath the crust, Seldin isn't sure where their leader is. For all he knows, it could be like Earth, with multiple nations and many leaders.

Another teleport gets him inside a large underground city, alive with all sorts of plants—some of which look like malnar, and various animals of interesting designs. The people are pulsari—disciplined and organized.

'They really are something else,' he thinks, with time catching up to his relativistic presence. The moment they see him, weapons are drawn from all around. But this isn't like the battles he's had before: they are so infinitely slow compared to him.

"I am the Guardian of Life," he says openly, "you may call me, Sei. Where are your leaders?"

Click—tick—tick! Their weapons fail to fire, but none of them answer.

"Very well, then I will address you all. We've been fighting a fruitless war. I came here today hoping to put an end to the bloodshed, and work out a peaceful, more diplomatic solution," he says.

There's a long pause with hundreds of pulsari looking his way. Others gather around. A collection of voices then respond in unison.

"You are not a god. What right do you have to force your authority upon us?"

Seldin sighs, for that's a tough question: what right does he have? "All I am asking, is for you to avoid civilizations far weaker than your own," he says.

"Survival of the fittest, Guardian. We have a right to expand and perpetuate our civilization as we desire," they say.

"You're right, survival of the fittest, but a race that has yet to develop isn't less fit, it's just young; that's like killing children—they deserve a chance at life," he says.

"You guardians are a nuisance; you distort the natural order. We have technology that can destroy you, and we will not tolerate further harassment," they say.

"Is violence all you know?" Seldin asks, looking around to blank stares. "Then maybe you'll understand this." He clenches his fist and the entire planet shakes. Some pulsari stumble and fall while others look to Seldin with weapons trained.

"Do not attack underdeveloped worlds," he commands.

…

Back in the Oval Office, Dean reports. "Just received word: everything's in place, and not a moment too soon," he says to the president, who nods in acknowledgement.

"How much time do we have?" asks the president with eyes to Jasra.

"Hours," she replies before taking a seat on one of the two curved couches.

"I'll be honest with you, Dean, I dread the idea of giving our planet over to those… things. I'd feel a whole lot better if you could give me a guarantee," he says.

"There are no guarantees, John, and while there are some among us who might agree with you, it is the best laid plan by the Guardian of Life."

"And he's dead, along with a world you failed to protect. Why didn't you try this tactic with them?" he questions.

"Because we couldn't locate the plants in time. Why do you think we raided your facility?" Dean quickly excuses the act before continuing. "Our enemies are using these against us, and as you know, we were only able to retrieve five of the six."

The president nods. "Yes, you told me. Some Guardian of Life," he scoffs.

"You must understand, Mr. President, that even if we had all six, it would only prevent a ground assault, and malnar are immune to most energy-based weaponry, which includes many of our abilities. This is going to take everything we have."

Sighing, John nods while rubbing his face before taking up his suit jacket and stepping out from behind his desk. "You'll have our support," he says, slipping the jacket on. "Just as you'll have the support of the entire world. Still, I wish I knew the odds." He lowers his eyes as he leaves the room.

Dean then turns about, looking at Jasra, who is seated comfortably, "You ok?" he asks.

Not breaking from her empty gaze, Jasra replies. "Just watching the future."

"You should get some rest; I can't remember the last time you slept," Dean comments, but she merely shakes her head.

"I couldn't sleep now, even if I wanted to. Besides, I haven't needed sleep since Aphéd. It's like..." she pauses mid-thought, "...what Sei said when he came back—God, I haven't even been hungry."

The news to Dean is slightly unsettling and he averts his eyes to conceal his concern. "You've… ascended. Your body is living off the aether now," he says.

"He's not dead, Dean," Jasra blurts out as she looks to him, and Dean shakes his head.

"I saw the explosion, Jasra," he tries.

"And I see everything, Dean, including the fact that you and Tillman have been lying to us."

…

A surprised jolt of awareness hits Almir, permeating his being as a battalion of powerful minds filter through.

"God, do you feel that?" he asks Welic, who extends his senses to the overwhelming swell of energy approaching, and they both look upward before taking to the sky. Soaring to the edge of the clouds over Australia, they come to a halt, staring out into the vast blueness for any visible signs.

"Augh!" Almir grabs the sides of his head and moans loudly, seeing in his mind's eye the dreadful stares of the pulsari at the heart of each ship—all at once.

…

"Leon!" Theresa calls out to him, while he spars with his younger brother.

Leon stops with a quick turn of his head her way before taking a solid punch to his jaw, which cracks his brother's knuckles.

"Gah!" Chad yelps, rubbing away the sting.

"What's up?" he asks, rubbing his jaw.

Theresa looks southwest. "Remember when you asked if I could sense energy?"

"Yeah." He walks up.

"Something's happening over there. Do you feel it?" She points.

Leon closes his eyes, opening his senses. "Almir?" he gasps, and starts to take off that way, but Theresa grabs his arm.

"Wait!" She waves a hand over the ground, while chanting in the Language of the Gods. "Via sa osu." A small area of sand shimmers, creating a view of his former student, struggling in pain.

"Almir!" he shouts.

...

There's a sudden shift in Dean's pulse as Jasra's words hit home. "You can't tell the others. Not a word," he says sternly.

"Which part? That Khyrah was one of us, or that this whole thing with the pulsari was orchestrated?"

"Jasra—" Dean pleads.

"You could stop this, Dean—you could stop the pulsari right now if you wanted to! Just as Tillman could..." she hesitates with a subtle hand to her lips as she realizes, "Just as I can now." And with that thought, she reaches out a hand toward the pulsari, and Dean immediately grabs her arm.

"Jasra!" He stares into her eyes and shakes his head. "Ascension isn't just a physical transformation, and it's important for everyone to learn that on their own," Dean says.

"Ss-so you set this up—set everything up!" she shouts.

"That's right," Tillman says, appearing from nowhere. "Each of you were given tasks specific for developing your… unique talents." He looks off. "Sei's was the hardest, but I knew once we set his path, the rest of you would fall in line."

Jasra's face grows pale. "You gave him Lucy," she says, scanning through the past.

"You're damn right I gave him Lucy," Tillman says. "The war between the suka and the pulsari made for the perfect training mission. Arius retrieved the flower; we did the rest."

"I'm gonna tell Sei—blow the whistle on this whole thing, and then—"

"You can't," Tillman states.

"And why the hell not?" she yells.

"Because, he has yet to learn life's hardest lesson," he says.

"And that is?" she asks angrily.

"To do what's necessary," Tillman says, and her heart shifts as she realizes. Looking away, Jasra wipes a tear.

"It…" she sniffles, "It'll change him."

...

A pulsari shrills, feeling the encroaching presence of a powerful mind. It writhes and twists in its pod before reaching out to the nearest of its brethren. Almir can see through its eyes, and he works to extend his control, but the other three pods in the command center of the lead ship shift and orient themselves to aid in their comrade's telepathic struggle. Their combined minds force Almir's out.

"Ugh," he grunts, then tries again.

"Almir, you've gotta calm down, man," Welic says, feeling the young guardian's power skyrocket.

Almir starts to tremble. "Uh… I can't stop them all, there's too many of them!" he shouts, focusing as hard as he can. The strain on his mind is unbearable, even for just one ship, but there are dozens. "Ugh!" Almir grits his teeth.

...

Dean swings himself about, facing southwest. "That's Almir!" he exclaims.

"He's about to overload," Tillman comments with concern in his voice.

"We've gotta do something!" Jasra shouts, but then Tillman's hand takes her shoulder.

"Stay here," he demands.

Jasra scoffs. "If we don't act now, he'll die!" she pulls away.

"Better that than the alternative," he remarks.

"Are our lives just a game to you?" Jasra brazenly scolds.

"A game?" Tillman stands tall. "We've waited centuries for the Guardians of Life and Time to reemerge, and I will not have you sacrificed over stupidity! The four of us make up a system of balance. Without us, everything goes to shit!"

…

"Can you make a gate from here to there?" Leon asks Theresa.

She shakes her head. "I'm not that powerful, but you might be able to," she says, flipping through the Book of Roe.

"Never mind that," Leon grunts, pushing his power as high as he can. His aura flares with a furious flow of aether, and he takes off.

…

Passing the moon, the proximity of the pulsari armada closes, showing no signs of slowing, despite Almir's best efforts. Knowing it's not enough, he concentrates harder. Soon, the signs of his intentions are obvious as the moisture in the air around him evaporates.

Welic's eyes widen and his heart races, while he watches dark blue veins streak across Almir's body as his meridians approach their limit.

"Almir stop!" he pleads, and in knowing what's coming, he makes a break for it.

"I... can't... aaarrrgggghhhh!" Almir grunts as he fights against the pulsari's collective control, and out of desperation, he pushes his core well-past three-fold. The immense pressure releases and before Welic can escape, the explosion engulfs them both.

...

Leon's voice resonates across the sky as he feels his apprentice—his friend—sheared apart by the forces of aether coursing through his body.

"Allmiiirr!" He drops from the sky, beating his fists into the ground.

Chapter 35

"The Reckoning"

All around the planet, people are in a panic as they scurry to flee the major cities while the world's military—both on land and in the sea—move into position with air forces standing by, ready to launch at a moment's notice.

Likewise, sorcerers all around the world gather and chant, giving their energies to the Earth's protective field, which shimmers and glows like an emerald grid across the sky. For the first time in history, the Earth is united into a single cause. Broadcasts in all languages alert civilians to the approaching danger.

Many of the world leaders have already taken shelter along with the president of the United States, who sits with his staff, discussing what's coming.

"Our latest satellite scan shows the objects taking strategic formations around the world," says a three-starred general.

"How long before they enter?" the president asks.

"About ten minutes," Jasra answers with glaring looks from the other members of the staff.

"What about this green stuff?" asks the president, while looking at satellite scans.

"Sorcerers," Tillman says, softly.

"Sorcerers?" the general barks, "Where'd they come from?" he questions.

Tillman looks to him. "From Earth. About a third of your population practice it, but these energy levels are insignificant against the pulsari's firepower," he says.

The general then looks to the president. "I just got off the phone with Russia. They have ICBMs standing by."

"John," Dean looks to him. "The pulsari ships are bio-engineered from malnar organisms and interlaced with their technology. Conventional nuclear weapons will have little effect," he says.

The president scoffs at him. "With all due respect, Dean, I was hoping you'd portal some of these babies into their ships. The concussive force should be enough to tear them—"

"That's not advised, Mr. President," says a man in white-silk robes with silver trim. Everyone looks, including Jasra, who turns with a smile before rushing to hug him.

"Sei!" Jasra exclaims.

"Look at you, acting surprised," he whispers to her.

"I missed you," she replies.

"So, you're him. I was told you were dead," the president says.

Seldin shakes his head. "Immobilized, but I've had time to study our enemy. Mr. President, I'm going to ask that you and the rest of the world militaries to stand down," he requests.

"What?" the three-starred general slams a hand to the table.

"It will minimize the casualties," Seldin replies before offering a glance to Tillman. "Glad to see you at a fight for once."

"I'm only here as a consult," Tillman says.

"So, what's your plan?" Dean asks his young friend.

...

Back-to-back, four pulsari sway, suspended centrally within each ship. Their view of the Earth synchronized across all on board, is overlaid with technical data projected directly into their minds combined with the senses of the malnar. Scans throughout the planet reveal an energized grid and several high-level energy signatures, while on the surface, Lucy and the other four beljusas sprout in anticipation of what's coming. From space, a carpet of green engulfs the Earth with floral petals aimed at the sky.

The pulsari take position, enveloping the planet in a formation of ships as they prepare to enter the atmosphere when all of a sudden, images pop and flash into their collective minds.

"Greetings to the pulsari." The face of Seldin appears, projected within their sight. "As you are no doubt aware, I am Sei, the Guardian of Life. This is your final warning. I know what you're about to do, and I will not stand idle as you destroy another defenseless world. If you proceed with your attack on the Earth, I will effectively eradicate your species."

As the vision of their enemy fades, the pulsari begin charging elter cannons. Taking aim, they fire. Within seconds, the blasts shatter through the luminescent energy barrier, showering the sky with shockwaves of green and purple as they penetrate the atmosphere.

The beljusas fire back, growing as tall as trees and drawing energy from every available source; electrical grids fail, structures wither, and even local life is sacrificed—both plant and person alike.

. . .

Alarms go off within the safe room as reports come in from all over the world.

"Mr. President!" A young lieutenant looks to him. "They've taken out our beljusas," he says with a stammer.

The others in the room then look to the Guardian of Life.

"What are you going to do now?" Jasra asks, softly.

Holding back the pressure behind his eyes, Seldin's passive gaze drops from hers. "Make good," he lets out with obvious pain in his voice before looking amongst them. "Make good."

…

The very moment the pulsari breach the atmosphere, spores begin to drop as modified cepella are released into the air, driven by soldiers firing elter rounds. Pulling out all the stops, they take no time in laying waste to everything within their path, for the pulsari are not here for resources. They're here for *them*.

In spite of all his enemies have done—all that they are doing now—Seldin can't help but find himself at odds.

Hovering above the badlands out in front of a large city-sized destroyer, Seldin stares downward. The chaotic howls of people screaming, and the distant echoes of gunfire flood his ears, shaking his heart. It shouldn't matter that it's his planet in shambles down below. After all, it's a sight he's seen many times across several worlds—but it does matter. Especially now that the pulsari have called his bluff.

As the familiar presence of Jasra's hand reaches his shoulder, he closes his eyes in an attempt to compose himself. Despite his stoic appearance, the turbulence of conflict between his convictions and his feelings make it impossible to not shed a tear.

Jasra can feel the force of his unsteady pulse carrying through her hand with each powerful beat as she bears with him in the weight of his decision.

"You don't have to do this, Sei," she says, offering him the choice, but Seldin bobs his head before peering over his shoulder to look at her with his watery eyes.

"A while ago you forgave me for something. I didn't know what at the time. It was for this… moment, wasn't it?"

Lowering her eyes, Jasra fades away, leaving him to his own devices. With that, Seldin takes a deep breath. His eyes closed, he extends his mind, feeling for all those around him.

The pulsari have already detected his presence. Scanning his essence as they approach, they lock on, calibrating their cannons to match the level of his core when unexpectedly there's an incredible upsurge in power.

Molecule by molecule, strand by strand, his mind races, latching onto to the very aether that forms his foes. Opening his eyes, Seldin reaches out with his left hand, taking hold of that precious energy. Instantly, the vessel stops, causing the pulsari on board to immediately slam into the hull. It's the same all over the world. Every ship halted, every enemy soldier frozen—paralyzed by his control.

As their minds fill with panic and fear—the same helpless dread so many of their victims felt— the Guardian of Life returns to them image after image, moment after moment, of the conquests they had once, so brazenly, shared with him.

Slowly closing his fingers into a fist, an overwhelming pressure begins to build. Vibrations can be felt throughout each ship while whining creaks of structural fatigue fill every vessel. Bulkheads fail, bodies rupture, and malnar fibers wither. Screaming, the pulsari cry out, pleading for mercy as they are gradually, mercilessly reduced to nothing.

...

"I thought I'd find you here," Jasra says while approaching Seldin from behind as he kneels down in the crater in the middle of the Simpson Desert. The thought of what he'd done resonates within him as he picks up the dry, withered pieces of Lucy.

"Only one survived; the others are dead," he says with a raspy voice.

Jasra takes a knee beside him, placing an arm over his shoulder, watching as he wipes his tears. "As is Almir," she tells him, and he quickly faces her.

"How?" he asks with a heavy breath.

"You didn't feel it?" she asks, and he shakes his head.

"I was in a different dimension," he replies while looking away.

"Overload. He died trying to stop the pulsari, nearly took Welic with him," she answers.

"Can you go back?" he asks sorrowfully.

"I could, but it would give away our position," she replies.

Seldin's eyes then shift to hers. "Our position for what?" he asks.

Jasra then stares back before answering. "Khyrah is coming."

www.ingramcontent.com/pod-product-compliance
Lightning Source LLC
Chambersburg PA
CBHW051548100726
47898CB00001B/19